THE BILBAO GAMBIT

Huston Michaels

Cover Design by Brandi Doane-McCann

ISBN Number 978-0-9973024-1-7 (paperback)
ISBN Number 978-0-997-3024-0-0 (electronic version)

For my wife, Julie.

Who believed in me, even when I faltered

PROLOGUE

Paris, 1937

There are no street lamps on Rue des Grands Augustins between Quai des Grands Augustins and Rue de Buci. Some light filtered from second floor windows, but at nearly midnight lighted windows were few. An occasional lamp hung above a building entrance or business doorway, casting a fisherman's net of light on the dark, rippling surface of the sidewalk cobbles, but barely enough to cut the gloom.

One such light adorned an elaborate, wrought iron-topped archway that penetrated the ten-foot wall surrounding the Hotel de Savoie. Fifteen feet outside the light, Mikel Lizarraga leaned against the wall, oblivious to the cold and waiting with the patience earned with age. He embraced the darkness and the chill. They would make the night's work easier.

His two younger companions shuffled nervously on the sidewalk nearby, trying to generate heat against the unseasonably cool May night. The ends of their cigarettes glowed brightly in the darkness with each inhalation. They kept their voices low and spoke in Spanish.

Since the three had arrived, pedestrian traffic on the street had dwindled. No one had been in or out through the ornate archway in nearly a half hour.

Headlights created a halo in the fog rising from the River Seine as they approached from the direction of the Quai des Grands Augustins and a sleek Benz 540K came to a stop in front of the archway. Mikel pushed off the wall, revealing the grip of a Trocaola revolver in his waistband, and moved slowly toward the Benz. The smokers pulled long, last drags into their lungs before throwing their cigarettes reluctantly to the ground and stubbing them out with the toes of their boots.

The driver of the Benz scanned the street ahead before turning to Lizarraga.

"I see no transport." He spoke in English, which he knew the Spaniard also spoke, and kept his voice low. He had asked Franco's aide for a German speaker, and been told none was available. He knew it was Franco's way of telling his Fuhrer that he didn't consider this mission important.

"Don't worry, Herr General. It is parked around the corner," Mikel answered. "You would do well to leave your car there as well."

The Benz glided away and disappeared around the corner. Minutes later, the driver returned. Tall and ramrod straight, he kept his hands in the pockets of the black leather trench coat he wore for protection from the chill.

"Have you seen any activity?" he asked, his accent almost undetectable.

"Not that matters," Mikel replied. "Our informant says they are still in Spain."

The German only grunted. He led the way through the archway and across a cobbled courtyard. Originally a 17th century manor house before becoming a hotel, then apartments, the building's beveled leaded-glass doors were unlocked and led to an interior that far outshone the exterior.. Polished marble floors showed off elaborately patterned Aubusson carpets. Crystal fixtures hung from the intricately hammered tin ceiling, and the sweeping, carved stone balustrade carried a gilded railing. There was an elevator, but the German ignored it and led the men up wide marble stairs.

Two apartments occupied one end of the top floor, the doors facing each other across a broad hallway. From there, an ornate spiral staircase led to the landing of an attic apartment. The cadre climbed the stairs and the German tried the door. It was locked. He pounded heavily with his fist and waited. No response. He pounded again, longer and harder.

A door opened below and a man in dark trousers and undershirt, his feet bare and his hair tousled from sleep, stepped halfway into the hallway to protest the hour and the noise.

Mikel drew his revolver, but the German stopped him and looked down at the Frenchman.

"Monsieur, this is not your business," he said. "Go back inside."

The neighbor saw the gun and heard the threat in the German's barely imperfect English. His eyes widened as he hastily retreated into his apartment.

"Break it down," the German said to Mikel.

It took only one young Spanish shoulder to splinter the door off the frame.

The German's eyes narrowed as he scanned the apartment. It was all one large space, with heavy beams between large skylights, and every available square meter was devoted to an artist's work. Easels and tables, arranged to take best advantage of the light, were everywhere. One empty easel was quite large and obviously makeshift. Two stepladders stood before it, a heavy plank between them acting as a scaffold. Bare canvases were stacked against one wall, apparently completed works lined others. The only hints the apartment was a living space were a rumpled double bed, a kitchen, small even by Paris standards, and a water closet tucked into one corner.

His orders focused on a single work, but it was only a rumor. He had no idea exactly what to look for. However, he did recognize an opportunity. The Reich would soon control all of Europe, whose leaders were much more interested in appeasement than fighting, and these works could become significant.

"Search everywhere," he told Mikel and his companions. "Take everything that looks finished."

In less than an hour over forty canvases of varying sizes, some still on stretchers, some large and tightly rolled, had been carried downstairs.

The German wanted to send a message letting the attic apartment's occupant know who was responsible for the theft. Reaching into a pocket, he removed a small piece of silver jewelry; the dreaded Death Mask of the Schutzstaffel. Casually rolling it in his hand, he wandered through the apartment, finally stopping before a work in progress. With a grim smile he dropped the symbol of evil onto the artist's palette.

The transport was a small, nondescript lorry with a canvas-covered cargo area. Fog had beaded on the canvas, and small rivulets had dotted the pavement below. Mikel waited alone in the cab.

"Where are your companions?" the German asked, looking around. "We'll need them at the railway station."

The muzzle of Mikel's revolver appeared above the edge of the window and pointed squarely at the German's face.

"There has been a change of plans."

"How dare you," the German muttered. "We are allies."

"I'm no Carlist. Franco is a maniac, and the work you seek rightfully belongs to The People, not your warmongering, lunatic Fuhrer."

"My orders are to keep the painting from appearing in the Pavilion." He shrugged, but kept his focus on the muzzle of the revolver. "The others are simply an investment."

"You are a thief, not a soldier. Now back away from the door," Mikel ordered.

The German complied. Mikel slid from the seat, keeping the gun trained on the German.

"Walk. Behind the truck."

The German, keeping a wary eye over his shoulder, moved slowly.

"Killing me would be a big mistake," he said.

"One less fascist in the world is not a mistake."

The German moved in close behind the lorry. In the cargo area he saw the bodies of the two young Spaniards, their heads crushed and bloody. He turned back toward the old man just in time to see him reach into his rear waistband and withdraw a short wooden club, the sort transport drivers use to check their tire mounts. Its heavily weighted iron end was already bloodied.

The German was not a young man, but a life in the military had trained and hardened him, and he knew he would prevail if he could just get his hands on the old Spaniard.

"Now," Mikel prodded him in the back, "join my Carlist friends."

When the German felt the push, he knew it was his only chance. He spun hard to his right, throwing his arm violently behind him. He expected the old man to get off a shot. His hope was not to be standing in front of the gun's muzzle when that happened. After that, he'd take his chances.

He was far luckier than he'd ever hoped, catching Mikel clumsily trying to switch hands with his weapons. The gun and tire iron both clattered to the street and the gun slid into the gutter near the lorry's back tire.

It was over in seconds, the Spaniard's windpipe crushed.

"Idiot," the German muttered. He bent and retrieved the gun from beneath the lorry before checking the deserted street. He saw no evidence anyone had been alarmed by the commotion. With considerable effort, he hoisted Mikel's corpse into the rear of lorry, dumping it atop the two already there.

Now the German had a real problem. He couldn't abandon the lorry's cargo, nor could he leave his Benz. He drew the rear canvas closed as tightly as possible while considering his options.

It took him only a moment to formulate a plan. Satisfied that the lorry was secure enough to discourage a casual passer-by, he returned to the Benz.

Thirty minutes later a figure, wrapped in a great coat and with a cap pulled low, walked through the thickening fog and clambered into the lorry's cab. The engine rumbled to life and, lights extinguished, the lorry and its cargo rolled toward the Rue Dauphine and disappeared into the fog.

PART ONE

"Naturally the common people don't want war... But after all, it is the leaders of the country who determine policy, and it is always a simple matter to drag the people along, whether it is a democracy, or a fascist dictatorship, or a parliament, or a communist dictatorship. All you have to do is to tell them they are being attacked, and denounce the pacifists for lack of patriotism and exposing the country to danger. It works the same in any country."

Hermann Goering at Nuremberg, 1946

1

Central Idaho, Present Day

Five miles an hour. A little faster than walking speed, but not really a jog.

It was fast enough.

The faded red pick-up, with paint so thin where countless hands had rubbed edges that bare metal gleamed through, rolled down the once-paved road toward the highway. The truck had been a wedding present. Nearly sixty years later, the old couple still drove together into town for the regular weekly shopping. She always sat in the middle of the big bench seat, close by the husband she still adored.

There was no telling how many miles the truck had on it. The odometer had given up years ago, perpetually displaying 53,716 miles after twice rolling over. Well over a quarter million miles of hay bales and horse trailers, sick calves and full bushel baskets. Two kids carted home from the hospital, after the first three birthed at home. The old truck held many more memories than would ever fit in the well-worn bed.

"Slow down, you old coot," the woman said. It was a long-standing ritual.

"Mama, take a pill," the driver retorted, as always.

The old man did slow some, though. The truck was long past due for brakes. Better to use the three-on-the-tree transmission to bleed off speed before the stop sign came up. It'd be best if there was no traffic. He could coast the sign, maybe not need to use the brakes much.

But there was traffic. A silver sedan, followed closely by a big, dark SUV, was coming down the hill, and a motorcycle was just coming out of the curve that fed the downhill straight. Speed and distances told him he would need to stop. He lifted off the gas, gently nudged the old transmission down into second, and let the engine help slow him some. Back then, transmissions didn't come with first gear synchronizers, making it nearly impossible to shift down again. Thirty feet from the stop sign, still going maybe ten miles an hour, he gauged the slight rise and pushed in the clutch to coast. No reason to use the brakes until it was necessary.

Then the old truck let him down. After millions of uses, the clutch linkage parted. The slack pedal under his foot went instantly to the floor and the clutch disks grabbed. A newer engine would have stalled, but the idle rpm and momentum were enough to keep the truck rolling. The old woman's hand, crooked from arthritis, clutched his thigh in panic and he heard her suck in a surprised breath. Cursing, he went for the brake pedal in hopes of stalling the engine. In his urgency, the edge of his boot sole caught under the lip of the polished metal brake pedal, costing precious time. Reflexively, he spun the steering wheel hard to the right, but it was too late.

The old red truck lurched through the stop sign onto the highway.

Five miles an hour.

It was fast enough.

The driver of the silver sedan had no time to even try braking. If he had, he would have t-boned the old truck and the blue Suburban that was following him too closely would have been in his back seat. Instead, he swerved sharply to the left, almost making it before raking the left side of the old truck with the sedan's right rear, then regaining control before hitting the brakes and beginning to slow.

The old truck careened wildly across the highway before running into the ditch on the far side. Seconds later, thin black smoke began to curl around the edges of its hood.

The driver of the Suburban wasn't as skilled. His reaction was to stand on the brake pedal. The big sport-utility yawed slightly before the ABS brought it to rest in the middle of the road.

From the saddle of his Harley-Davidson, Ben Kaye hit the brakes and began quickly working down through the gears. He activated the Harley's flashers before stopping on the center line about seventy feet uphill from the Suburban.

The silver car was down the hill, stopped on the shoulder. Both front doors were open, and a man was hurrying toward the old red truck. As yet, nobody had gotten out of the Suburban or the truck. Kaye pulled off his helmet and hung it on the right handgrip. He was reaching for his cell phone to call 9-1-1 when he heard the unmistakable sound of a gunshot, followed quickly by another.

Kaye looked down the hill and saw the man from the silver car turn from the driver's side of the red pick-up toward the Suburban. His right hand was extended, the pistol clearly visible. Fifteen feet from the Suburban, he fired twice. Simultaneously, the Suburban's passenger door flew open and a woman dove headlong onto the pavement.

The shooter began to circle the front of the Suburban to get a clear shot at the woman, who had scrambled to her feet and was running hard for the west side of the highway, where the lip of the embankment offered possible escape.

Kaye, still straddling the Road King, reached instinctively for the Kimber .45 ACP in his boot holster. The woman was tall and her long, red hair flailed the air as Kaye watched her run for her life. Her desperation made her cornerback-fast, but he knew she'd never make it.

Then she stumbled, going down hard.

"Hey!" Kaye shouted as loudly as he could, standing up and raising the Kimber. He needed to distract the shooter, or the woman was dead where she'd fallen.

The gunman had almost cleared the front of the Suburban when Kaye yelled. In a heartbeat the man spun toward Kaye and fired twice. The first bullet shattered the Harley's windshield and showered Kaye with droplets from the water bottle stowed in the windshield bag. The second shot hit his dangling helmet, which rocketed backwards off the handgrip and bounced wildly across the pavement. He dove sideways off the bike, rolled quickly and snapped off three shots in the shooter's general direction. Without time to properly acquire his target, his best hope was that return fire would surprise the gunman and drive him back behind the Suburban, giving the woman those few precious seconds.

It worked.

The woman was trying desperately to regain her feet, but panic and the hard fall had momentarily overwhelmed her. She finally stood, wavering like a drunk in the middle of the road, trying to decide what to do and where to go next.

Kaye saw the gunman rise above the Suburban's hood, trying to get high enough to get a firing angle on the woman without exposing himself. He put a round through the SUV's rear glass and drove the man back to cover.

"Come to me!" Kaye shouted, the sound of his own voice dulled by the sharp reports of the shots. "Come to me!"

She turned, frozen on the hot pavement, and stared at him uncomprehendingly.

The shooter rose quickly, snapping off a shot before Kaye could drive him down again. Blood mist erupted from the woman's upper torso, and Kaye saw the look of fear and despair in her eyes before she crumpled to the pavement.

Kaye leapt to his feet and sprinted toward the downed woman, putting two rounds through the Suburban's windshield to keep the gunman down.

Reaching her, he grabbed her belt with his left hand and yanked, lifting her off the ground with enough force that he was able to release his grip and wrap his left arm around her waist. He fired two more quick shots at the Suburban before turning for the edge of the embankment.

Zigzagging, he ran as hard as he could. He felt a bullet snap close by his ear before diving headlong over the edge.

They tumbled down almost twenty feet into the thick, uncut weeds. The woman was semi-conscious, and blood ran from a shoulder wound. Kaye quickly crawled to a position above her, came to a kneeling position and trained the Kimber on the edge of the road above. If the shooter came for them, his head would be visible before he could acquire a target, and Kaye planned to empty the Kimber's magazine into that head.

He waited, scanning and sweeping a widening arc as the shooter had time to cover more distance.

Nothing.

Slowly, he crept toward the top of the embankment, moving obliquely to lessen the slope and avoid reappearing at the same point he'd gone over the edge. It took twenty careful seconds to climb high enough for a view of the road.

The shooter had run. Kaye saw the silver car lurch forward, front wheels spinning wildly in the dirt and gravel of the shoulder as they sought traction. A tire found pavement, grabbed with a loud squeal, and the sudden momentum slammed the passenger door closed as the driver sped away.

2

Kaye's first concern was the woman. She lay motionless, nearly concealed by the thick weeds. Through the long red hair he could see blood staining the left shoulder of her shirt.

He started back down. His boot dislodged a rock and the sound caused her to look up.

"No!" she screamed, scrambling to try and regain her feet.

"It's okay, he's gone," Kaye said, clambering down as he slid the Kimber into his waistband. "He's gone. You're going to be okay."

The panic in the woman's eyes slowly subsided.

"Let me see your shoulder," Kaye said softly.

She looked down at her shoulder.

"Oh, God," she whispered, "I'm shot." Then she fainted.

Kaye scooped her up and carried her to the road. He laid her gently on the cooler pavement in the shade of the Suburban, removed his vest and folded it into a makeshift pillow. A quick check revealed a minor through-and-through flesh wound. She was lucky, she would be fine.

He used his cell phone to call 9-1-1. Someone nearby must have heard the shooting, because the dispatcher told him there were already units en route. He told the dispatcher he also needed an ambulance for a gunshot wound victim, heard her send one while he was still connected, and gave her a quick description of the fleeing silver car before starting to check the damage.

In the Suburban, a young man slumped in the driver's seat, his head between the edge of the driver's seat and the door. Glass from the shattered window glistened in his hair and on his clothes. A small, dark entry wound on the upper left forehead and the stench of emptied bladder and bowels confirmed Kaye's worst fears.

The old truck was next.

The faded red Ford was seriously crunched in the left rear and the trip into the ditch had twisted the left front tire and wheel ninety degrees from where they should have been.

"Damn," breathed Kaye.

The occupants had fared even worse. The driver lay twisted and face down, feet still in the driver's foot well, left arm dangling over the edge of the front seat. His torso rested atop the body of his female passenger. The opposite side of the truck's interior was peppered with high velocity blood spray and tissue fragments. They had probably survived the impact of the collision, but certainly not the close range shots to the head. Kaye reached in carefully and switched off the ignition.

Returning to the Suburban, he dropped the magazine from the Kimber, racked the slide back into lock and laid the empty gun on the hood where it would be clearly visible. Then he moved ten feet down the road and sat down to wait.

He knew what came next.

3

As he rolled up to the scene and checked out with dispatch, Captain Roger Halberstam of the Ada County Sheriff's Office saw a uniformed deputy standing over a man sitting on the road and another walking slowly down the road toward him, hands extended in front with palms out, signaling him to stop.

"Shit, shit and double shit," the Captain muttered aloud. He stopped a few feet from the uniform and rolled his window down. No sense getting out if he might still be able to drive the rest of the way up.

"Sorry to be delayed, Sergeant Carson," Halberstam said. "I'm so tired of all this goddamn road construction I could puke. What've we got?"

"Captain," the sergeant acknowledged his superior. "First things first, I guess. We have a woman with a minor gunshot wound to the shoulder. I let the medics through. Hope that was okay."

Halberstam nodded. "Works for me."

Carson put both hands on the edge of the Crown Vic's roof, winced momentarily at its stored heat, and leaned down.

"Captain, this one's a puzzler," he said slowly before explaining the scene to Halberstam.

"Shit, shit and double shit," Halberstam swore again softly as he slapped the steering wheel with his palms. "Did he have a gun?"

"Well, yes and no," Carson nodded. "There was one unloaded semi-auto on the hood of the Suburban. He told us it was his."

"Wise move by him. Gives you no excuse to shoot him. So, why did you have me stop down here?"

"Sir, bear with me, please." Carson answered. "So, we get here and this guy is just sitting there, waiting. I cuff him – and that's a whole other story. Anyway, he claims to be a cop, and one of the things he tells us is that there was another vehicle, a silver four-door, that left the scene with the shooter driving. Should be damaged on the right rear. Dispatch confirms he relayed that info when he called it in."

"Oh, really, now," Halberstam snorted. "How convenient for him. Does he have ID?"

"No, sir," Carson replied. "Says his wallet's on the bike. But, he was flying biker colors, some bunch I never heard of. Big Boars. He used the vest to make a pillow for the woman. Anyway, he said the other car stopped on the shoulder, just over there."

"Okay, I get it." Halberstam nodded. "So, what's the story on your guy? You said something about him being hard to handcuff. Did he resist?"

"No, and it's a damn good thing. I'd have had to shoot him. When you see him you'll understand. White male, but a biker tan so dark he could be Hispanic, maybe Middle Eastern. But he's got bright blue eyes. Mid-thirties. I'd guess six one. He's got an unusual build, but this guy is at least two-seventy, two-eighty, and not five pounds of it fat. He is seriously large and seriously fit. Cuffs wouldn't fit around his wrists. I had to use a flex."

Halberstam whistled softly. "Big man. You think he's the shooter?"

"No, I think he rode up on it, just like he says. Bike's flashers are on. Wrong place, wrong time. In fact, I think if he hadn't had a gun, he and the woman would both be dead, too."

"Okay," Halberstam said as he got out of the car. "You go on back up there and see how the medics are doing and I'll mosey over here and take a look at the side of the road, just in case." He didn't wait for an answer before angling off to the west shoulder.

Outside the fog line there was about five feet of pavement, then more than enough flat ground for a car to get off the road in case of an emergency. Beyond that was a fairly steep slope that trailed down toward flatter ground. Halberstam guessed the elevation change at twenty-five, maybe thirty, feet. The slope was steep enough that the Transportation Department didn't bother trying to mow the weeds.

Halberstam stopped in the road and looked west. The uncut weeds extended about twenty feet beyond the bottom of the embankment before reaching the right-of-way fence line, and, from the looks of them, there was water down there somewhere. Might be a small creek, or it might just be runoff, but there was water. A dozen or so horses were scattered in the pasture beyond, and several more had moved to the fence line to see what all the commotion was about. Halberstam knew plenty about horses, and right now he was wishing that at least one of them could talk.

One more month, he told himself. *No more beatings or stabbings, or lies and thieving, or pissed off husbands and crying wives and constant conniving. And now, crap, a homicide in my last month.*

Halberstam's reverie broke when he noticed that there did, indeed, look to be a spot ahead where a car had left in a hurry. He moved closer, his attention now focused on the ground. There was an obvious acceleration mark in the dirt where a tire had tried to bury itself before gaining traction and moving forward. The depth of the scar decreased as it headed for the pavement, and where it crossed onto asphalt there was just over a foot of fresh rubber scuff before it faded. The dirt and gravel plume behind the tire mark was considerable, and reached all the way into the weeds.

"I'll be damned," he said aloud.

Halberstam scanned the ground very closely now that it appeared his suspect might be telling the truth about another car. He noticed a footprint in the dirt just off the pavement edge, too fuzzy to photograph or cast, but it looked like whoever left it had been running and then tried to stop, because his – or her, he reminded himself – foot had obviously slid when it came down on the loose dirt. There was no vehicle debris or other litter anywhere, though, that suggested a car that had been in an accident. That caused Halberstam to consider the possibility that maybe these marks weren't connected to this case after all, and to continue looking around.

He widened his field of search toward the edge of the embankment. Adjacent to the weeds there was a tangle of footprints, and there looked to be a spot on the edge of the embankment where the weeds were slightly askew from those around them.

"Now, what caused that?"

He knew a lot of deer crossed this road, and this would be a good spot, with water within easy reach. Being careful not to walk too closely to where a car would have been parked based on the tire marks, Halberstam circled around to the edge of the embankment and peered down.

"Shit, shit and double shit," he swore under his breath, and then, as loudly as he could, he bellowed, "Carson!"

Carson hustled down the road. As he got close, Halberstam raised a hand.

"Slow down, Sergeant," he said. "It appears your man up there was telling the truth. Walk around here, and watch where you step."

Carson walked to the edge of the embankment and stood next to the Captain, who pointed down.

About ten feet below the edge of the embankment, partly obscured by the weeds, was a corpse. White male. Obvious gunshot wound to the head and obviously not there for long.

"Think this might be our shooter, Captain?"

"Not unless his ghost drove that car away." Halberstam's voice was low. Now he was interested. "Okay, Sergeant, let's go talk to your man," he said as he carefully backtracked away from the embankment and started up the hill.

Damn, it was hot today.

4

Kaye sat quietly, his hands caught behind his back by a plastic riot cuff – a large zip tie to the civilian population. He'd expected it. Over the years he'd become accustomed to being treated more like a biker than a cop because of his size and preferred means of transport. But a closer look tended to sort out the confusion. He had no tattoos, and kept his dense black hair cropped short enough to almost be a crew cut. His moustache was strictly regulation.

He'd seen the unmarked unit coming, and a rueful half-smile had crossed his face when the occupant got out and put on a white cowboy hat. Country cops.

At least the senior uniform had taken his account seriously enough to stop the cowboy beyond where the silver four-door had parked. And they'd obviously found something on the embankment. Now, as the detective walked up the road toward him, he could also see the boots. Snake, or lizard maybe? Kaye didn't know and didn't care. At this point he just wanted off the hot pavement.

Kaye and Halberstam locked eyes.

"Good afternoon, sir," Halberstam said casually. "Or, at least it was for these good folks until just a little while ago." He waved his arm to take in the general surroundings. "I'm Captain Roger Halberstam. I have the unfortunate task of determining just exactly what happened here, and, more importantly, apprehending who is responsible. For that, sir, I am going to need your help."

Halberstam stopped, as if expecting Kaye to speak.

Kaye kept quiet, causing Halberstam's eyes to narrow.

"What is your name, sir?" Halberstam asked pleasantly.

"Ben Kaye. I'm a…"

Halberstam cut him off.

"Mr. Kaye, I'm going to advise you of your --"

It was Kaye's turn to cut the Captain off. "Save it. You don't need to read me my rights. I'm a cop. I'm passing through on vacation. That's my Harley in the road up there with a bullet through the windshield. I'm not the bad guy here. I'm a witness, and I'd appreciate it if you'd let me get off this hot pavement."

"Well, well," Halberstam said softly. "Mister Kaye, if that is indeed your name, I appreciate your position, but I ask you to appreciate mine, as well. You were observed by these deputies here in close proximity to the victims and you were in what we call constructive possession of a firearm."

"Yes, I was," Kaye said. "I used it to shoot back at the man who shot these people and tried to shoot me."

"And," Halberstam continued as though Kaye had not spoken, "you have no identification on your person."

"My wallet is in the windshield bag on my motorcycle. If you'd get enough people here to handle this scene, maybe you could start putting two and two together."

"Help is on the way." Halberstam glanced at Carson, who nodded back.

"Look, Captain," Kaye said. "If you feel the need, go ahead and advise me. Either way, I waive my right to counsel and agree to stand for a field identification. The woman will tell you I'm not the man who shot her."

The Captain pondered his options, then walked to where the paramedics were still tending to the wounded woman. He conferred with them briefly before returning. He carried Kaye's black leather vest.

"Okay," he said. "The medics are about to transport her, but they said her injuries aren't life threatening and she agreed to take a look at you."

"Thank you."

"In the meantime," Halberstam continued, holding up the vest, "care to explain this?"

The back of the vest was emblazoned with a v-twin engine, superimposed over an American flag. The outer edges of the cylinder jugs morphed into twin visages of fierce wild boar, their tusks curling away into exhaust pipes. The words Big Boar rode a crimson and gold banner across the top, and a matching scroll across the bottom carried the letters M.C.

"It's not a gang," Kaye said, knowing that's exactly what Halberstam was thinking. "Just a club I used to belong to." He still belonged, but he was the only remaining member.

"Okay," Halberstam said skeptically, "easy enough to check out." He turned to the younger deputy. "McMurray, get me whatever wallet or identification you can find in the windshield bag of that motorcycle." He turned back to Kaye. "Mister Kaye, do you give us your informed consent to search the containers on your motorcycle?"

"Consent given. Wallet's in the windshield bag."

McMurray took off up the hill.

"Carson," Halberstam went on, "stand Mr. Kaye up and take that flex cuff off. I don't want some judge deciding five years from now that our field identification was tainted because the witness thought we had Mr. Kaye already under arrest."

"Yes, sir."

Halberstam glared at Kaye. "If you try to run or fight, I'll shoot you myself. No jury would look at you and look at me and blame me one single bit. You got that?"

"Got it," Kaye said. Without moving his feet, Kaye pushed himself straight up to a standing position. He turned and extended his arms so Carson could cut off the plastic cuff.

While he waited, Kaye worked on the puzzle surrounding him. Why would anyone go to such lengths and take such risks to erase a traffic accident? Drunks would sometimes drive away, thinking it might help them beat a DUI rap later on. But drunks can't shoot straight, and the killer had been an expert. Eliminate things like suspended driver's license and no insurance. Even an ex-con or parolee wouldn't shoot somebody over a paper violation like that. Stolen car? That might be motivation enough to leave the scene, but to try and kill everybody there first? Nobody trades one to two in medium security for death row.

Nothing had been said about why Halberstam had called Carson back down the hill or what was over the embankment, but his instincts told him it was another body.

The pieces in Kaye's mind suddenly fell into place. A traffic accident means cops. For some reason, the shooter wanted nothing to do with the police.

Kaye saw Halberstam lean over and speak to the woman on the gurney. He couldn't hear the words, but the glances in his direction told him the detective was giving her instructions on how to get through the field identification.

The medics wheeled the gurney toward Kaye. Halberstam walked beside it, holding the woman's hand.

Kaye saw the red hair and nearly translucent complexion, and his stomach clenched in a tight knot as memories of another redhead and another accident scene flooded in. He stared, momentarily taken aback by the strong resemblance.

"Now, Cynthia," Halberstam began, "I want you to look closely at the man standing beside my deputy over there, and tell me if that's the man who shot you. And remember what I told you, okay? Take your time. You're safe now. We'll have you on your way to the hospital in just a minute."

The woman turned her head to look at Kaye. Their eyes met and he struggled to contain the sudden burst of emotion.

She looked away, then back again to look him up and down before she turned to Halberstam and said, "No, that's not the man. The other man wasn't nearly that big, that strong looking." She paused for a moment and her eyes squinted in pain before she spoke again. "That's the man from the motorcycle. The man who saved me."

She turned her head back towards Kaye and said weakly, "Thank you, mister, thank you."

"Thank you, Cynthia," Halberstam spoke up. "You'll be okay and I'll be by the hospital to see you soon. I'll have some more questions then, if you're up to it, okay?"

The woman nodded at Halberstam and then, as the medics wheeled her away, she turned again to look at Kaye and he saw her mouth the words, "Thank you."

McMurray returned with the wallet from the windshield bag. It was wet, but the first bullet had missed it.

"Just where he said it was, Captain," the deputy said, holding the wallet out to Halberstam, who took it and snapped it open. The sun glinted off the LAPD detective shield inside. Opposite the shield was Kaye's ID card.

"Appears you are who you say you are," Halberstam said, looking closely at the identification.

"Thirteen years with the LAPD. Last seven as a detective, if it's any of your business."

Halberstam stared at Kaye for a moment before saying, "Mr. Kaye, I don't have enough to hold you, and I no longer have the time to spend giving you a hard time. It's easy enough to call Los Angeles and verify your identity. Believe it or not, I actually know a few folks down there. Now, if you'll excuse me, I have a mess to sort out here and it's going to be getting dark way too soon." Halberstam turned to McMurray. "Escort Mr. Kaye back to his motorcycle and help him get re-situated. And get his contact info, including," he nodded his head and glanced down at Kaye's side, "the number of that cell phone. Then get yourself up the road. When Boise County clears that truck wreck, this road will get busy again. Divert southbound traffic over to Dry Creek on the old Forest Service road."

Then he turned back to Kaye, "I believe you saved that young woman's life. Thank you for that. I would appreciate it, though, if you would enjoy our local sights and attractions for a couple days, and make yourself available when I have the time to take a formal statement. You get my drift?"

Kaye smiled. "Don't leave town, cowboy."

It was Halberstam's turn to smile. "Exactly. And," he held up Kaye's Kimber, "I'll be keeping this until I can run ballistics on it and confirm you are who you say."

***

Kaye walked around the Road King. He flipped the quick release levers and pulled the remains of the windshield from the mounts, emptying the bag of what he needed before setting it aside. He retrieved his helmet, which was worse the wear from the glancing bullet.

"See you around, deputy," Kaye said as he messed with the helmet, trying to get it snug. "I'd say it's been a pleasure, but I've had better days. I'm going to ride through your crime scene."

"Go ahead," McMurray said. "I don't see any other way out of here."

"And, hey," Kaye added, "tell your Captain to call me. I'll hang around for a day or two, but I'm not cooling my heels here indefinitely."

McMurray nodded his understanding and gave a thumbs-up as Kaye slipped the bike's clutch and headed slowly down the hill. The deputy leaned over and picked up the shattered windshield before heading to his patrol car.

Kaye again surveyed the scene as he slowly made his way down the highway, lightly feathering the rear brake and keeping the clutch in the friction zone to keep his speed to a minimum. While he had been busy becoming mobile again, the activity level had gone up exponentially. There were several more marked and unmarked police vehicles, an SUV with Coroner emblems on the doors and another ambulance all parked behind Halberstam's unit.

The Captain had organized his resources. As Kaye rolled slowly toward the Suburban search teams were fanning out. Several small orange evidence markers, each numbered distinctly, already rested at various points on the highway and a forensic specialist was busy photographing and collecting shell casings.

Halberstam stood next to the old Ford pickup, talking to a woman in a blue jumpsuit with 'Coroner' across the back in large yellow letters. As Kaye rolled by Halberstam looked his way, and although Kaye couldn't hear the words over the deep rumble of the Road King, he had no trouble reading the cop's lips.

Stick around.

Farther down, Kaye saw another Coroner jumpsuit start down over the edge of the embankment, about twenty feet from where the silver sedan had stopped. Must be another body, just as he'd suspected.

Kaye carefully threaded the big Harley through the knot of vehicles parked on the highway, then leaned the bike into the right hand traffic lane and accelerated. As the bike reached highway speed Kaye began to miss the windshield. Getting old, he thought ruefully. Fifteen years ago he wouldn't have been caught dead riding a bagger with a windshield, and he still refused to surrender totally to one of the models with a fairing. Maybe in thirty or forty years, he mused.

About a half mile down the road he passed a mobile TV news van headed toward today's big story. Kaye, glad it wasn't his crime scene, knew that Halberstam's life had just gotten a lot more complicated. His next thought was that he really, really needed to get a new windshield.

5

Darkness was beginning to trickle over the mountains to the east, pooling in the valley floor while the last rays of the sun stubbornly held the high ground, gracing the peaks with the peculiar pinkish light of alpenglow. At this latitude and this far west in the time zone it stayed light, and hot, considerably later than Kaye was accustomed to. He knew he'd never make it to the Harley dealer today and decided to find some dinner and a hotel. He could deal with parts and pieces tomorrow.

A mile down he passed another marked Sheriff's unit parked in the highway. The deputy was diverting northbound traffic onto a side road. He caught a break at the construction zone he'd heard about and snuck through, the last vehicle in line. The flagger, a cute little blonde in orange vest and yellow hard hat, flashed a big smile and the peace sign before stepping out behind him and flipping her sign from 'Slow' to 'Stop'.

Kaye followed the signs for Highway 55. McMurray had given him directions to the dealer and a couple different hotels that were on the way.

He'd known he'd be treated as a suspect. It was his size and unusual build, with long legs and arms, and an unnaturally short torso. He'd endured the taunting all through high school until graduation day, when he'd finally beaten one of his tormenters to a bloody pulp. They gave him his diploma, but barred him from the ceremony. A fair trade. His size and strength had been a definite asset in the Corps.

Kaye saw the Hilton sign and turned into the parking lot. He rolled the big Road King under the portico with its 'Check In' sign, shut down and hung the battered helmet on the handgrip. After locking up the bike, he grabbed his wallet out of the saddlebag and headed inside.

The registration desk across the nicely appointed lobby. was unattended. He waited a bit before tapping the service bell on the counter.

A stunningly attractive young woman emerged from the adjoining office. In heels she was nearly as tall as Kaye, and her smile was dazzling against her olive complexion and raven black hair.

"Good evening, sir. May I help you?" She looked Kaye up and down as if deciding whether he was a potential customer or potential robber, then coolly met his gaze. The public relations smile never left her lips, and her nametag proclaimed to the world that she was Maria.

"I need a room, please," Kaye said politely. "One person, one bed, one night for sure, but maybe longer. And I do not have a reservation." He reached out and placed his driver's license and AMEX Black card on the counter.

Maria's smile turned genuine. "Let me see what I have." She stepped to a computer terminal and Kaye could hear the muffled staccato sound of the keyboard as she searched the database.

Maria busied herself for a few moments doing the paperwork. She handed the license and credit card back to Kaye before sliding the registration form across the counter.

"Thanks. Where can a tired, hungry biker get some dinner?"

Maria gave Kaye directions to several nearby eateries, adding comments about quality and prices.

"Thanks, Maria. I appreciate it."

"Hey, no problem," she came back, bright and cheerful.

The room was typical corporate traveler pre-fab. King-sized bed with the headboard bolted to the wall, small table with two chairs, a dresser, and a TV cabinet thinly disguised as an armoire. Since he hoped to leave town tomorrow, Kaye decided to live out of his grip instead of unpacking.

He showered, lingering a bit to let the steam soak the road grit from his pores. He'd never admit it to anyone else, but he knew he wasn't the iron butt he'd been ten years ago.

Relaxed, he dressed quickly, throwing on the Big Boar vest. The empty boot holster felt odd. He'd considered arguing with Halberstam over the decision to keep the gun, but it was exactly what he'd have done if their positions were reversed.

Maria had mentioned there was a sports bar nearby, and when he saw her standing at the desk he veered that way to get specific directions.

"Excuse me."

"Oh, hi," she replied, her dazzling smile widening when she saw him.

"Where exactly is that sports bar you mentioned?"

"Just head out the front door, cross the parking lot and take a right on the sidewalk. That'll take you across the creek." She was pointing as she spoke. "Then, double back between the first two buildings on the right. It's called The Goalkeeper. It's closer than it sounds, but you have to walk around the creek. You can't miss it."

"Thanks."

"No problem. You know," she looked at Kaye hopefully, "I get off in about an hour…."

"Maria, I really appreciate the offer, and I'm flattered, but to tell you the truth I've had a really crappy day and I don't think I'd make very good company. Maybe I could I buy you a drink if I'm still here tomorrow?"

He saw the disappointment flash across her eyes, but her smile never dimmed. A woman that beautiful probably wasn't used to being turned down, Kaye thought.

"That would be great. And, hey, no problem."

Kaye returned her smile and raised a hand in acknowledgement as he turned to leave.

Like most sports bars, The Goalkeeper was replete with televisions, including several big screens. Every seat in the house had a view of at least two simultaneous sporting events. The televisions behind the bar were all tuned to different baseball games. As Kaye waited for his meal, his ear picked up a change in the drone of noise emanating from the closest TV. He glanced up to see an erstwhile young woman sitting behind a news desk. A 'Special Report' graphic scrolled across the bottom of the screen and Kaye could just hear the reporter's voice.

"…more details," the reporter continued, "on this afternoon's apparent multiple homicide on Highway 55 north of Eagle. The Ada County Sheriff's Office has confirmed that four people died at the scene, although they have not released the official causes of death for any of the victims, or their identities. A young woman was also wounded by the unknown assailant. She was transported to a local hospital with unknown injuries." The reporter paused briefly and looked down at the sheaf of papers bundled on the desk in front of her.

Yeah, that's it, thought Kaye. Always keep them hanging on what comes next. He didn't care much for the media, although she had just confirmed another body.

"Channel Five Accu-News has learned exclusively," the reporter went on, "from a Sheriff's office source, who spoke on condition of anonymity, that a member of a Los Angeles-based motorcycle gang was apprehended and detained at the scene. The man, whom the source declined to identify, was later released and has not been officially named as a suspect in this horrible crime. However, a firearm was confiscated and he is being called a person of interest. Investigators say they will be questioning the man."

There was another pause before video footage came up on the screen next to the anchorwoman. Clearly taken from inside a moving vehicle, it showed a man on a motorcycle approaching from the opposite direction, and then passing the vehicle with the camera inside. The video expanded to full screen, and the anchorwoman's voiceover continued.

"Channel Five obtained this exclusive video of the possible suspect leaving the scene shortly after the incident." The video looped and started again. This time it slowed down to near stop action speed as the motorcycle came abreast of the news van.

"The possible suspect was described as a white male, just over six feet tall, with a heavy, muscular build, and was reported to be riding a black Harley-Davidson motorcycle." Her tone made it clear she thought that alone would be proof of guilt.

"Again, the Sheriff's Office is calling this man," the grainy video froze as the motorcycle passed the van's front bumper, "a person of interest in today's terrible multiple homicide north of Eagle. Stay tuned to Channel Five Accu-News for more breaking details, and we will bring you the full story on our ten o'clock newscast. I'm Shea Winslow and this has been a special report from Channel Five Accu-News. We now return you to our regularly scheduled program."

The bartender brought Kaye's meal while the news was playing and stayed to watch. When the report ended he looked at Kaye.

"Hey, that guy kind of looked like you. Weird, huh?"

"You think so?" Kaye asked nonchalantly. "I didn't see the resemblance." He stared at the bartender, who continued studying him, for a second and then began to eat.

Kaye had to grudgingly admit that the news crew had been pretty sharp to think of rolling video on the way to the scene of the shooting, but who the hell did Halberstam think he was, feeding them with that kind of information? As an investigator, Kaye knew that sometimes you had to give the media something. It got them off your back so you could work the case. In fact, more than once he had used the media to help break tough cases without them even being aware of it. They were usually so hungry to get something their competitors might not have that it was easy to lead them by the nose or feed them misinformation. But this was crossing the line. Halberstam would get an ear full from him the next time they met.

The bartender had gone about his business, but kept casting wary glances at Kaye, who was glad when the check finally came and he could settle up. After paying he got some perverse joy out of standing up and turning around so the kid could see the Big Boar colors.

When he entered the lobby, Maria was at the front desk, busy briefing her night shift replacement.

She looked up, saw Kaye, and called out to him.

Kaye changed course and walked to the desk. He noticed the smile had disappeared.

"Yes?"

"You had a visitor come by looking for you."

"I did?" It had to have been Halberstam. "Older guy, cowboy hat and big belt buckle?"

"No. Younger, a little taller than you, dark curly hair. Dressed quite nicely, in fact."

Kaye went through the possibilities in his mind. Maybe McMurray? No, too tall. "Did he ask for me by name?"

"No. He just said he was looking for the man riding the black Harley parked out front."

"Maria, did you give him my name?"

"No, I did not." Her reply was indignant. "Our policy is to protect our guests' privacy. We only release names to the police if they have proper paperwork."

Maria was silent for a moment and stared down at the desk. She glanced toward her co-worker, who was busy organizing the paperwork Maria had given her, before meeting Kaye's gaze.

"I saw you on TV. I mean, it was you, right?"

Kaye put his hands flat on the counter and leaned forward. "Don't believe everything you see on TV. Yes, I was there, but I didn't shoot anybody. I was a witness, that's all. Some news guy got lucky and got some footage of me riding away after the Sheriff's people let me leave, and turned it into their big story. I promise you, I am not the bad guy here."

She looked up and tried to smile, but it just wouldn't light off. He could tell from her eyes she was still skeptical, and inwardly cursed the fact that people are so conditioned to believe everything they see on television.

"So why are the police looking for you?"

"Well, first of all, we don't know that they are looking for me. I don't think the guy was a cop. He would have shown you his ID if he was. He's probably a reporter trying to get a scoop by driving around looking for motorcycles parked at hotels, hoping to find me. Makes sense, right? Thanks again for not giving him my name."

"No problem," she said, then blushed darkly. They both laughed, and then she continued. "But I don't think he was a reporter, at least not a TV guy. I've lived here for a pretty long time, and I didn't recognize him."

Kaye was relieved to see her smiling again, but in the back of his mind he wasn't at all comfortable that somebody was actively looking for him.

Kaye returned to his room after a promise to Maria that he would buy her a drink tomorrow evening if he was still in town.

He decided not to watch the news. Instead, he sat on the floor and folded his legs into the lotus position. His back went straight as he imagined a thread attached to the top of his head, pulling up gently. He placed his hands in his lap, left hand resting gently in his right, and brought the ends of his thumbs together until they touched lightly. His chin dropped slightly and his eyes half-closed.

Before he'd left home his teacher, his *Roshi*, had posed a new, particularly perplexing question for him to ponder and he decided to focus on finding an answer.

Kaye's mind cleared instantly as he focused on his breathing. A moment later, his mind fully leashed, his heart and respiration rate slowing steadily, he entered a deep meditative state.

6

Kaye woke early, as was his habit, to the sun streaming through the open draperies.

He lay quietly for a few moments, planning his day. He needed to find the Harley-Davidson dealer and replace the windshield and helmet, and he was interested in exploring the area. Everything, of course, hinged on when Halberstam called and wanted him to come in and make a formal witness statement.

And he wanted his gun back.

He hoped that would be today, or tomorrow at the latest. He wasn't one to sit around and waste time waiting on somebody else.

First, though, he would practice. After a bit of furniture rearrangement to get the floor space he needed, he began. He'd been blessed with great strength since adolescence, but had to work hard at staying flexible. Rehabbing after a military injury, he'd discovered yoga.

Focusing his mind into synchronization with his body, he began. For a man of his muscularity, Kaye had attained remarkable flexibility. He knew there were some very advanced positions he would never achieve no matter how hard he worked, but those were few, and most had suitable alternatives.

Kaye worked through an increasingly difficult series of strength and balance positions. Finally, he spent time on basic stretches to cool and lengthen his muscles. Then he began a brief, focused meditation on the proposed answer to his teacher's most recent question.

Fifteen minutes later, he was satisfied he could present the answer, which he knew would simply lead to another, more complex question.

The hotel restaurant was busy, with suits in groups of two or three talking about the challenges of commerce to be conquered during the day ahead. Every other table held an open laptop computer, their acolyte's shoulders hunched as they worshipped at their altars of pixels.

Among the suits, Kaye felt a bit conspicuous in jeans, riding boots and a t-shirt under an unadorned vest. After yesterday, he'd made a conscious effort to avoid a black t-shirt or anything that said 'Harley-Davidson' on it. His size drew the usual stares.

Since the odds were slim he would conclude his business with Halberstam this morning, he decided to check with the desk on staying another night. He had also decided last night to go to the hospital and visit the woman from the Suburban.

A young man held down the desk this morning.

"Yes, sir," he said, looking Kaye up and down carefully.

"Good morning. My last name is Kaye. I checked in last evening and only booked one night, but it looks like I'll be staying at least one more night. The desk clerk last night – Maria – said she didn't think that would be a problem, but I just wanted to make sure."

"Let me check." The young man quickly checked the computer. "It looks like we can accommodate you, Mr. Kaye, but I'm afraid I will have to ask you to change rooms. I hope you don't mind."

"That's okay. I didn't have a reservation. I assume I'll need to check out of my current room. Do you have a place I can stow my gear until I can check back in?"

"Absolutely." The clerk was obviously relieved Kaye wasn't going to make a fuss about the room change. "In fact, if you'd like to bring your bags to me, I'll personally deliver them to your new room later."

"That'll work. What about a key?"

The clerk explained that he couldn't issue another key until the current guest checked out, and Kaye agreed to come back later.

Kaye returned to his room and assembled his gear. He dropped the bags at the front desk and saw them safely secured in a locked room before heading out to the Road King.

His first impression was the heat. It was barely eight-thirty and it was already pushing eighty-five degrees. That kind of heat didn't fit into his preconceptions of Idaho, always portrayed as craggy, snow-capped peaks and lush green meadows teeming with wildlife. The marketing department had clearly decided to ignore the southwestern part of the state.

He went through his start-up ritual and let the v-twin warm up while he got organized. He mentally went through the directions McMurray had given him for the Harley dealership. Should be easy enough to find.

After a couple minutes, Kaye reached down and held his hand next to the front cylinder barrel. He could feel the heat, a good indicator the oil temperature was coming up. He slipped on his half-gloves, kicked the transmission into first and eased out of the parking lot.

His second impression was the traffic. It didn't take him long to conclude that Idaho at this time of morning on a weekday was every bit as bad as the 101 through Cahuenga Pass, which surprised him. He also reached the rapid conclusion that the local traffic gurus didn't like bikers, because he sat at the red light for several minutes waiting for it to trip and turn green, but the sensor didn't detect the big bike.

Screw this, he thought, and ran it.

It was about ten miles to the Harley shop. From his years driving a patrol car, he was adept at gauging traffic, picking his spots, knowing which cars to get behind and which to avoid. Even then, it took almost twenty minutes to spot the dealership from about a half-mile away as he crossed the Interstate.

The building was giant, easily an acre under one roof. It was certainly a far cry from the old days, when he'd discovered that riding was in his blood.

For Kaye, the epiphany had come the first time he had ridden a Marine buddy's FXR. After the first five miles he was mentally committed to buying a Harley. After twenty miles he vowed he would never again in his life be without one.

He'd gone to the closest dealership and told them he was there to buy a Harley.

In those days Harley-Davidson stores were motorcycle shops, and the guys who worked there, worked there because the job and place were natural extensions of who they were.

The memory of his first visit to a Harley store still lingered – something about his inadequate Marine pay and a huge biker named Harley Charlie teasing him about a monkey having carnal relations with a football -- and he smiled broadly as he passed the new Sportsters on display outside the front doors.

There were at least a hundred new bikes displayed on the ground floor, and more parked on a mezzanine that ringed the interior on three sides. *Times have sure changed*, he mused. When he bought his first new bike he'd paid cash up front and waited months for it.

Thirty minutes later, new windshield and new helmet in place, Kaye was ready to go. They'd even helped him mount his new windshield bag, on the house. The more things change, Kaye realized, the more they stayed the same. The brotherhood hangs together.

Kaye asked about the area and Jeff, the Harley guy, asked whether he'd ever made the ride up to Idaho City. Kaye confessed he'd never heard of it.

"It's a great ride, brother," Jeff assured him. "Especially on a weekday. No old fuckers in RVs."

After being reassured he'd be in cell phone range, Kaye headed out, following the kid's directions. After the initial fifteen miles or so of Interstate, Kaye took the Idaho City exit onto Idaho 21 and started climbing almost immediately.

7

Jeff had been right. It was a great ride to Idaho City. The road was good and traffic was light.

Kaye stopped occasionally to enjoy the sights and check his cell phone for a message from Halberstam. Nothing. He decided to call the ACSO detective when he got back to town -- if Halberstam hadn't called him first.

It was just shy of four o'clock when Kaye made the turn onto Eagle Road about a quarter mile from the hotel. Even from that distance he could see the flashing emergency lights of the fire engine. As he got closer he picked out an ambulance and several squad cars parked near the entrance portico. He carefully navigated into the parking lot and parked east of the front door. He locked up the big bike and headed for the front door.

There was no visible smoke, but close to a hundred people were milling around outside the hotel's main entrance. A Sheriff's deputy stood guard, keeping everyone outside.

Kaye glanced up just in time to see Captain Halberstam walk outside and engage the uniform in conversation. Then the Captain turned and faced the small crowd.

"Ladies and gentlemen," he said loudly, holding his hands up to get everyone's attention. "The fire department says it's now safe to go back inside. If you are staying anywhere other than the third floor of the west wing, you can go back to your rooms. If you are on the third floor of the west wing, we would appreciate your continued patience and cooperation and ask that you check with the front desk to see whether you might need to be relocated."

Halberstam paused to let the crowd digest the information. The general anxiety level had dropped significantly while he was speaking and it was now easy to pick out the people who'd been directly affected.

"The damage is minimal, but until we determine exactly what happened we need to treat the area as a crime scene." Halberstam switched to folksy mode. "Now, I'm sure you've all watched enough C.S.I. to know we have to keep you out of the crime scene, right?" He nodded to the crowd to emphasize his point and then continued. "So, please be patient and we'll be out of your way as soon as possible. Believe it or not, this is even less fun for us than it is for you. Thank you."

The guy's good, Kaye thought. Some of the crowd, very tense just moments before, laughed when he finished.

Halberstam turned and gave instructions to the uniform to move to the third floor elevator lobby, and not let any unauthorized people onto the west end of the floor. He made sure the deputy knew that 'unauthorized' meant anybody not personally approved by him. When he finished, he started walking toward the unmarked car near the fire engine.

Kaye headed to intercept him. "Captain Halberstam!" he called out.

Halberstam stopped and turned at the sound of his name. His eyes locked with Kaye's and he waited.

"Kaye," Halberstam said. "How are you today? To what do I owe the pleasure?"

"I just came back from a ride to Idaho City. I'm staying here."

"Really, now," Halberstam said. "And would you be staying on the third floor, west wing?"

"Well, yes and no."

Halberstam stared at Kaye. "Let's assume the answer is yes. What room were you in last night?"

"Three twenty-seven. What happened here?"

Halberstam didn't answer right away. He gazed into nothingness while he added Kaye's latest piece of information to the puzzle.

"We're not exactly sure yet. The fire department guys are still looking, but it appears there was an explosion of some sort."

"Where?"

"Room three twenty-seven." The Captain looked hard at Kaye, trying to read any reaction that might help him. "If you know anything about this you'd better tell me right now, or, cop or no cop,

I will bury you so deep in our penitentiary you'll never see daylight again."

"I told you. I've been riding all day and, by the way, waiting for you to call me. I'm at a complete loss here."

Before Halberstam could go on, his radio crackled.

"Halberstam, come in. Batt Chief Mendes on tac two."

"Go ahead, Ralph."

"Roger, you'd better call Rudy. I don't think this was an accident. I think you've got another homicide on your hands."

"Ten-four," Halberstam said into the radio. Then he muttered, "Shit, shit and double shit." He reached into his suit pocket and extracted a cell phone. "Excuse me."

"Sure." Kaye understood and stepped away a few paces. He watched as the fire engine crew came out of the hotel and began securing their gear. With no fire, their job was done.

Halberstam called headquarters and requested an arson and explosives investigator at the scene. He snapped the cell phone closed and turned back to Kaye.

"So, you have no idea what might have happened here?"

"Absolutely none. I heard a reference to homicide. Was someone killed?"

Halberstam hesitated momentarily. What the hell, he reasoned. His phone calls this morning confirmed that Kaye was a cop, and in all likelihood the bomb had been meant for him. Halberstam had to conclude that there was a connection and had the very uneasy feeling that things were quickly getting beyond his ability to sort them out and make a quick arrest. He hated the thought of ending a thirty-year plus career on a case he couldn't clear.

"Yes," he finally answered. "A hotel employee. One Maria de la Rosa, Assistant Manager. She had apparently just entered the room when the blast occurred. We'll know more when the AE investigator gets here."

Halberstam sensed Kaye's reaction to the victim's name.

"Did you know her?"

"Sort of. Not really, I mean. She checked me in last night. Seemed very nice."

"So, why would she be going into your room today?"

"I have no idea. Besides, like I said, it wasn't my room. The kid this morning told me they needed to move me to a different room. I checked out and left my gear at the desk."

"The manager is pretty broken up by the woman's death. I guess they were close. The medics are working on him now, trying to get him calmed down enough to answer some questions. I'll talk to him after my bomb guy gets here."

"Captain, can I sit in when you talk to the manager?"

"Don't see why not. Two heads are better than one, right? Just remember, this is my case, not yours. I appreciate your ideas and input, but you have no jurisdiction here."

"I'm not trying to steal your case. Occupational hazard, I guess."

"Understood. Rest assured, though, that if I could give you this case, I most certainly would. But I can't and it's my neck on the block, so I'll run it my way."

"Sounds like a plan." Kaye looked away to hide his smile.

An unmarked white Chevy Trail Blazer pulled into the hotel parking lot and stopped near the portico area. A small, slight man of about sixty climbed down from the front seat, reached back inside to grab a black salesman's sample case, kicked the door shut, and walked toward Halberstam and Kaye.

"Howdy, Roger. What'cha got?"

"Hey, Rudy," Halberstam responded. "Explosion of unknown origin. No obvious source. One dead. Ralph Mendes said I should call you."

"Well, Ralph knows his business," Rudy said matter-of-factly. Then he looked at Kaye and added, "This has to be the guy from yesterday. Is this a coincidence?"

"Oh, yeah, sorry. Rudy, this is Ben Kaye, LAPD and, yes, he's my witness from yesterday. And no, I do not think this is a coincidence. Kaye, this is Captain Rudy Moore, our chief arson and explosives investigator."

"Nice to meet you, Kaye," the bomb man said. "You're a big son-of-a-gun, aren't you?" He turned back to Halberstam. "I'll go check with Ralph and take a look at the scene. They move the body yet?"

"Not yet. I told them not to, figuring she might be able to tell you something."

"Good man. Makes me almost believe some of you guys are actually paying attention during my training sessions. Almost." Moore smiled again, then turned and headed for the front door of the hotel. "I'll be in touch."

"Competent?" Kaye asked as he watched Moore disappear into the building.

"Very. We're damn lucky to have him. Rudy retired here from the Bureau. Two months later his wife dies. Go figure. He either needed to work or he was going to eat his gun. My boss snapped at the chance to put him back to work. Made him a Captain, both as a show of respect and so we could pay him closer to what he's worth. But he's outside the usual rank structure and he knows it. Doesn't try to boss anybody around. Just does what he does better than anybody else I ever met."

"So," Kaye changed the subject, "shall we go talk to the manager?"

"Yep." As they walked into the hotel, Halberstam mused aloud, "You know, I'd be willing to bet, the world being the kind of screwed up mess it is, that this hotel has video surveillance cameras everywhere but the ladies room stalls, and I might not bet against that. Maybe we got lucky and got some footage of our guy."

"Worth a check."

Halberstam sucked in a deep breath and let it out slowly. "Thank you for the vote of confidence. You must be one hell of a good detective, too."

They found the paramedics in the office. The distraught manager still sobbed quietly, but the medics were packing up.

"How's he doin'?" Halberstam asked the nearest medic.

"He'll be okay. You need us to hang around?"

"No, don't think so. Go ahead and clear. Thanks, gentlemen. Appreciate it."

The medics finished snapping everything up and headed back to their unit.

Halberstam stepped across the office and put his hand on the man's shoulder. "Mister...Chambers, is it?" He asked, glancing at the nameplate on the desk. "I'm Captain Halberstam of the Sheriff's Office and this," he nodded in Kaye's direction, "is Detective Kaye. We'd like to ask you some questions, if that's okay. But first let me tell you how sorry we are about Ms. de la Rosa. You two were good friends?"

The question brought Chambers' attention back. He looked up. "Yes, we had grown very close. She was a beautiful, wonderful woman." He sniffed and dabbed at his eyes with a tissue, then seemed to notice Kaye for the first time. "You're a policeman? Maria said you were a guest."

"Actually, I'm both." Kaye glanced at Halberstam, who gave a quick nod. "But I'm not local. I'm just passing through. Captain Halberstam is extending some professional courtesy."

"But I don't understand," Chambers said between quick breaths. "Why?"

"Because we think that whoever killed Maria was really trying to kill me."

"Killed Maria?" Chambers' voice rose plaintively and he again broke out into loud sobs.

The two detectives let him cry for a moment.

"We don't think it was an accident," Kaye said after the manager regained some composure. "We think it was a bomb meant for me, and we need your help."

"Anything you need. Anything at all for Maria."

"Thank you," Halberstam said. "First, can you tell us why Ms. de la Rosa might have been going into that room in particular?"

The question focused Chambers' mind and he calmed noticeably before answering. "She was taking Mr. Kaye's things back to his room. We thought we might have to move him to another room, but it turned out we didn't. She ended up doing it because my afternoon clerk called in sick. Oh, my God! It could have been me!"

"You can't think of it that way," Halberstam said. "There was no way to know this was going to happen." The Captain changed tacks. "Mr. Chambers, does the hotel have a video surveillance system?"

"Yes. It covers pretty much the entire premises, with the exception of the guest rooms, of course. We keep the recordings for thirty days. Will that help? Please tell me that will help."

"Let's hope so," Halberstam said, glancing at Kaye. "Mr. Chambers, can we get copies of the video files from a particular time frame today? I can get a warrant if we need one."

"I'll have to ask our computer people about that. I really don't know. I'm sorry."

"That's not a problem." Halberstam reached over and grasped Chambers' shoulder in a gesture of reassurance. "At my age I don't even pretend to understand all this computer stuff. I'll have one of our digital forensics techs come out and get what we need from your people, okay?"

Chambers managed a weak smile as he nodded.

"In the meantime," Kaye spoke up, "nobody gets near that system. Okay?"

"I'll make a call right now and wait here personally."

"Good man," Halberstam said. "Now, let's go see what Rudy's got for us, shall we?"

As the two walked to the elevator, Halberstam called in requesting the tech.

"So," Kaye mused out loud once they were on the elevator. "She was taking my stuff back to the room and she somehow tripped a device. Have your AE guy start looking for a trigger device wired to the door."

"Don't worry about Rudy. He's probably already figured that out." Halberstam paused, deep in thought, and then asked, "Answer this for me. How did the bomber know they would put you back in the same room? He would have had to wait for you to leave the hotel this morning before rigging the bomb."

"I don't think the bomber knew about the room change. I think he – and it's almost surely a he, since women don't seem to do bombs – just figured I'd still be in that room."

"Makes sense. But it also means the bomber, and may I remind you we don't yet have a formal investigative finding it was a bomb, knew what room you were in."

"I think he was here last night. When I got back from dinner Maria told me that a man came in looking for me. At first I thought it was you, or somebody from your office, but the guy didn't show a badge. The basic description matches the guy on the highway, but it's pretty generic. Could be anybody."

"Did he ask for you by name?"

"No. He asked for the guy riding the black Harley, which made me think he might be a reporter. But Maria said she didn't recognize him from the TV and thought she would have. Have your computer guy pull those video files, too. It might be our guy." Kaye paused for a half-beat before continuing. "And about the reporters..." He let the statement hang in the air.

"Yeah. About that. I don't know who fed the information to those parasites, but I promise you that when I find out, and I will find out, whoever it was will spend the rest of his career copying accident reports in the jail basement. That pissed me off, and it obviously put you in jeopardy."

"It irritated me more than a little bit, too. So, it wasn't from you and it wasn't an authorized release?"

"Hell, no! You are not a person of interest in this case. In fact, so far you're the damn hero. I figure I got just plain dumbass lucky that you rolled up on that scene when you did and saved that young woman's life at the risk of your own. And how in the hell could I have possibly ended up with as a better witness than an experienced investigator?"

"Thanks. And you've got a leak."

"No kidding," Halberstam said. "No other explanation, but I'll be damned if I can guess who. Besides, right now, that's the least of my – our – worries."

"True enough."

The localization of the damage surprised Kaye. A short stretch of the hallway centered on the door to room 327 was practically obliterated, but outside of that there was almost no damage. He caught a glimpse of Maria's right foot under the rubble just inside the door.

Moore, removing a pair of latex gloves, stepped out of the room just as the two men approached.

"Roger. Kaye." He greeted them brusquely.

"What've we got?" Halberstam got right to the point. He'd seen the foot, too.

"Well, this is preliminary, so don't quote me yet, please. Whoever did this – and it was definitely a bomb, by the way – was very good. He defeated the keycard lock to get in, which means he either had a key or access to pretty sophisticated electronics. The device itself, which appears to be concussion only and non-fragmentary, was placed just above the door. I also got lucky and already found a two-piece contact switch, typically used in security applications, that I think was the trigger, but I don't know yet how the detonator was powered. Probably a small battery. I'll find it. It's just a guess, but it's my professional one, that it took him about fifteen seconds, max, to place the device. The first person to open the door, in this case the unfortunate young woman just inside, triggered it. I'll know more after I do a better analysis of the body's position relative to the blast damage pattern. Questions?"

"Can you identify the explosive?" Kaye was the first to speak.

"Not yet," replied Moore. "I do know from the low amount of residue that it was most likely a synthetic compound. I'll know exactly after I get some of the residue to the lab. With any kind of luck there will be tags present and I'll not only be able to tell you what it was, but who made it, when and where it was sold, and to whom. But, again, it suggests a sophisticated bomber."

"You said it wasn't a frag," Halberstam said. "So, what exactly killed her?"

"Easy," Moore replied. "The concussion alone was more than enough to do the job. The device exploded only about two, maybe three, feet above and behind her head. It killed her just as surely and just as quickly as if the bomber had clubbed her with a sledgehammer when she walked through the door. She never knew what hit her."

"Did it dismember her?" Kaye tried to keep his voice dispassionate and professional. Somehow, even though dead was dead, being in one piece seemed to matter.

"Amazingly enough, it did not. That, to me, again suggests a sophisticated bomber. He used just enough to kill whoever came through the door. In fact, I think the only reason there is as much damage to the structure and as little damage to our victim as there is, is because the door was still open when the device detonated. The location and position of the body also supports that. Had the door been closed it would have better contained and channeled the blast. In that case, yes, I think she might have been in pieces, but I can't be sure. After all, unless I miss my guess, he wasn't trying to kill a one hundred and twenty pound woman. He was trying to kill a, what, nearly three hundred pound mass of muscle." Moore directed his gaze directly at Kaye.

"Close enough." Kaye said.

Moore shrugged. "My point is that an expert hunter doesn't use the same caliber weapon to hunt whitetail deer that he uses to hunt Cape buffalo. Only an amateur does that, and this guy is no amateur."

Kaye glanced quickly around the scene, searching for his gear. That had to be why Maria was entering the room. He spied it several feet from what was left of the door opening, almost covered by dust and shattered pieces of the wall that had once stood between the room and hallway.

"Captain, there's my gear."

"Yeah, fits the fact pattern. Shit, shit and double shit."

Kaye stepped gingerly through the debris in the hallway. He needed to see Maria's body.

She was face down just inside the doorway. Her red suit was covered with dust. Except for the fact that she had bled from her ears, she might have been sleeping.

"Okay to step in, Captain Moore?"

"Sure, go ahead."

Kaye stepped carefully into the room. The lamp from the dressing table was shattered, the pieces strewn away from the source of the blast. He could see small pieces of structural debris against the far wall. The windows were blown out and the bottoms of the draperies still hung outside.

Kaye turned and knelt beside the body. He gently pulled the long black hair away from her face. He could tell her neck was broken and her skull was misshapen from the force of the concussion, but even in death she was beautiful.

"This makes five," he muttered softly to himself. "That's all you get. Next one's you."

"Did you know this woman?" It was Moore, who had stepped into the room and now looked over Kaye's shoulder.

"I met her yesterday when I checked in."

"Well, if it's any consolation, she died instantly and probably never even heard the sound of the explosion. I know it probably doesn't help much, but she didn't suffer."

Kaye stood up and wiped his hands together, as if to expunge the dust of death and sense of loss. He gazed down at Maria while he spoke.

"That's where you're wrong, Captain. She suffered. We all suffer, one way or another. It's the human condition."

8

Kaye and Halberstam left Moore to his work and headed back down to the office. They needed to talk again with Chambers about Maria.

Halberstam's digital forensics tech had arrived and was working on a rack of equipment in a closet down the hallway from the manager's office. Halberstam stopped briefly to issue instructions.

"Not to worry, Captain" the tech assured. "This is a first-rate system, both hardware and software. I've already plugged in and found the video files store, all neatly saved by camera number and date. I shouldn't have any trouble finding the files you asked for and dumping them to my computer via the USB port and a jump..."

Halberstam raised his hand and cut off the tech's speech. "Whoa, cowboy. I don't need to know how it works. Just get me what I need and let me know when you've got it, okay?"

The tech laughed again. "You got it. I'll let you know." He turned back to the console and its mystifying array of cables and blinking green lights.

Kaye had listened to the exchange and smiled.

"So, Captain, not a real technology fan?"

"Not really. Are you?"

"Well, yes, and no, I guess. It helps me a lot, but it scares me, too."

Halberstam bristled. "I'm not scared of computers," he snorted. "It's just a tool, like a snaffle bit or a pair of sharp rowel spurs. Me? I usually got no problem getting my horse to go where I point him without using those kinds of tools. No computer is ever going to replace good old-fashioned police work."

"I wasn't implying you were afraid of computers. What bothers me is that we're all being watched, all the time, or at least it seems like it. I think the cameras change people's basic behavior. Makes us all behave the same, because nobody wants to be the one who stands out when guys like us start looking at the video."

"So, what's wrong with that? If the morons know they're being watched, they behave themselves."

"Maybe so. But think about the other side of it. Doesn't it follow that the good behavior is subconsciously suppressed, too, and that the control we learn to practice because we feel we have no privacy carries over to those times when we really are in private?"

"You're over my head," mumbled Halberstam uncomfortably. "Let's just go talk to Chambers about the de la Rosa woman, shall we? You know...police work?"

Chambers had regained a modicum of composure and was just ending a telephone conversation when the two cops entered the office. His eyes were red-rimmed and still spilled the occasional tear.

"Okay, tell your mother I'm sorry," Chambers said into the phone and then listened before speaking again. "No, really, Louis, I mean it. It's all just so surreal. I'll be home as soon as I can." He hung up the phone and turned to look at the two cops. The look on his face was apprehensive. "How did she look? Oh, God, it didn't blow her to pieces, did it? I couldn't bear to go look. She's – was – much too beautiful to end up like that." His voice trailed off and he looked down, embarrassed.

"She's still beautiful." Kaye spoke as soothingly as he could. "If it's any consolation, she died instantly and never knew what happened. Her family will be able to have a nice service."

"Yeah," Halberstam spoke up. "About her family. I'll need to contact them."

"I don't think she had family around here," Chambers said. "She said something about moving here from California as a teen-ager. Family problems, or something like that. She was pretty private about her personal life, even with me, and I was probably her closest friend."

"You think she was running? Maybe hiding from somebody or something?" Halberstam asked the detective question automatically, though it led in an entirely different direction.

Chambers stared into nothingness for a second, mulling the possibility. "No, I don't think so. I know she lived by herself. Nice apartment not too far from here. I have the address if you need it."

"She was just low-key, right," Kaye said. "Did her job, paid her bills on time, stuff like that?"

"Exactly," Chambers replied. "And, please, I'll handle all the arrangements. I know she was Catholic. I'll take care of everything."

"Thank you for that," Halberstam said sincerely. "You're a good friend. And I hate to ask now, but could we get a copy of Maria's personnel file? If you don't mind, that is. I can get a subpoena if it'll make you feel more comfortable."

"No, no, that won't be necessary. I'll have it for you in a few minutes." Chambers turned in his chair and rolled to a nearby filing cabinet.

"Captain, can we talk outside?" Kaye asked quietly.

Halberstam looked at him questioningly, then shrugged his shoulders and stepped to the front desk area. Kaye followed.

"You know what you're going to find, right?" Kaye asked.

"Uh...no. What will I find?"

"Think about it. She said she was from California. She kept pretty much to herself outside of work. She worked hard at staying under the radar. Maria de la Rosa was illegal."

Kaye saw the light go on in Halberstam's eyes.

"Shit, shit and double shit. I can't believe I didn't pick that up."

"You would have. Remember, I work in Los Angeles, the second-largest city in Mexico." Kaye hoped the joke would make Halberstam feel better.

"Now," snorted Halberstam, "that's funny. But it's not, either, if you know what I mean. Mind if I use that one?"

"Permission granted. But it means you won't find any next of kin, or anybody else. Let it rest. Just let Chambers take care of everything."

"Makes sense, I guess. Nothing to be gained by stirring up that hive, anyway. Poor woman was just in the wrong place at the wrong time. We both know that bomb was meant for you. Damned unlucky for the bomber, too."

"Not necessarily. Sometimes bad luck is good luck in disguise."

"How so?"

"Our shooter is obviously, for reasons we don't know yet, trying to eliminate anybody who saw and might be able to identify him. Agreed?"

"That's my theory at this point, too. Go on."

"He missed me, but did he fail?"

"Yes," Halberstam said firmly, "or it'd be you up there in three twenty-seven."

"I disagree. Let's assume for the moment that it was our boy who came in last night looking for me. Maria saw him, too. In fact, she got a much better look at him than I did. He didn't get me, but he didn't fail. The key is that he doesn't know yet, although this guy's got enough balls that he might have been in the crowd outside awhile ago, checking his work."

"I thought of that. The tech's pulling that video, too."

"So I have two suggestions for you. Suggestions only, mind you, since this is your case."

Halberstam stared at Kaye. He couldn't tell if the big man was playing him or not. "Go ahead, I'm listening."

"Don't release Maria's name to the media. Just tell them it was a female employee of the hotel and you cannot release the name until next of kin are notified. That may take awhile."

"What does that get us?"

"It makes him wonder. It tells him he missed me and now he has to deal with not one, but possibly two, people who have seen him. It might make him careless."

The Captain nodded slowly, seeing the wisdom in Kaye's suggestion. "Okay, I get it, and I like it. But you know that makes you the bull's eye, right? That guy wants you dead."

"Seems like it. I'd much rather be on my way and leave this mess for you, but if we can flush him out, it'll be worth it."

The tone of Kaye's voice gave Halberstam pause.

"Just be damn careful, Kaye. This guy's a professional."

"So am I."

"What's your second suggestion?"

"If I were you, I'd put a guard on the woman from the Suburban. If you haven't already, that is. She saw him, too."

"Shit, shit and double shit! Goddamn it!" Halberstam reached into his jacket pocket and snatched his cell phone. He hit a speed dial number and then spoke rapidly into the phone. Within thirty seconds deputies had been dispatched to provide security.

"Thank you," Halberstam said wearily as he dropped the phone back into his pocket. "Maybe I should just pull the plug today. I missed that completely. I don't think he can get to her, but, then again, this morning I'd have said the same thing about you."

"Have you interviewed her?"

"Yeah, talked to her this mornin'. Didn't get much. She's blocked a lot of it out, which is understandable, I guess."

"What's her name?".

"Cynthia. Cynthia Graham. Local woman."

"Where is she? If you don't mind, I'd like to go visit her, just to see how she's doing." Kaye also wanted to ask her some questions.

"She's at St. Mark's downtown. I think she'd like to see you. She kept telling me to remember to thank you for saving her life."

"Gee, you forgot to mention that." Kaye smiled at Halberstam.

"Bullshit. Just told you, didn't I?"

"One more thing?"

"What else?" Halberstam said with exaggerated weariness. He was actually starting to like Kaye.

"I want my pistol back. I don't know what Idaho law is, but I assume there is reciprocal professional courtesy. And will you vouch for me if the need arises?"

Halberstam laughed. "I'd think you were crazy if you didn't carry. Now, I've got a lot of work to do and I'd appreciate it if you'd let me go do it. I've got a ride scheduled for this evening and my horse gets real cranky if he doesn't get the pleasure of carrying me around once in awhile. Oh, and one more thing for you, too."

"Sir?"

"My office, tomorrow morning at ten. No excuses and don't be late. Your expensive gun will be waiting for you."

"I'll be there."

Halberstam sighed deeply as he watched Kaye head for the black Harley, wondering why a man would choose a motorcycle when God had graced the earth with horses. He reached up, pulled off the straw Resistol and mopped his brow. Even after living his entire life within thirty miles of where he stood, he'd never gotten used to the God-awful hot spells that settled in for a week or so once or twice a summer. In his professional opinion, heat made people do even more stupid things than they did when the moon was full. It put them on edge and made his life more difficult. Four, maybe five, months until it snowed, he thought, and by then it wouldn't be his problem anymore. He sighed again, settled his hat back on his head, and headed back to talk to Chambers and his digital forensics tech again. He didn't worry about Rudy Moore. He knew the report would be on his desk by morning.

9

Since there was still plenty of daylight left Kaye decided to visit Cynthia Graham. He walked slowly toward the Road King, evaluating the situation.

Kaye hated bombers. To him, they were gutless bastards, too cowardly to face their victims. But the fact they could kill you without being close made them doubly dangerous. It was time to start being careful, avoiding patterns, keeping a sharp eye in the rearview mirror for tails and making a conscious effort to remember faces in case they showed up again.

He didn't mind. He'd done it so much it was second nature. As the years went by, he found that vigilance had become the norm and he had to force himself to relax. It was who he was, or at least who he'd become, which was another reason he was thinking about quitting.

The Road King hadn't been tampered with, which meant that the bomber probably hadn't been in the crowd outside. Kaye swung over and went through the start-up ritual. The sound and feel of the big v-twin rumbling to life immediately calmed him and he sat for a minute, listening to the unmistakable arrhythmic bump of the single-pin crankshaft.

As he listened, he plotted his course of action. Visit the Graham woman and talk to her. Change hotels. Sit down with Halberstam tomorrow. That should be the end of it, assuming the Idaho cop told him to butt out and go home. He knew that if their positions were reversed, that's what he would do.

Kaye eased the big Harley into late afternoon traffic and rolled for the hospital.

St. Mark's is an imposing brick edifice, as tall as the surrounding hotels and government buildings, occupying several city blocks. Kaye turned into the entrance driveway. A uniformed rent-a-cop stood outside the main doors, directing traffic and making sure nobody parked there. An inquiry was met with a nod and a thumbs-up, and the Road King ended up on the broad sidewalk just outside the front doors.

"Thanks," Kaye said as he hung up his helmet. "Appreciate it."

"That's cool," the man answered. "As soon as I can save the down payment, I'm getting a Harley. I'll watch yours for you."

Halberstam had given him Cynthia Graham's room number and he headed directly to the fifth floor. The nurse's station was just off the elevator lobby. A prim young woman in scrubs adorned with Disney characters interrupted her electronic charting when Kaye approached.

"Can I help you?"

"I'd like to see Cynthia Graham, please. Admitted yesterday with a gunshot wound."

The nurse went through her chart pile quickly. "I'm sorry, sir, but I don't have a Cynthia Graham on this floor, and I'm not allowed to divulge whether she's a patient here."

"I'm sure she's a patient. I have her room number. I just stopped to check in."

"Let me check downstairs." She picked up the phone and punched in a number. "This is fifth floor one. I have a visitor asking to see a Cynthia Graham. He's sure she's a patient, and I don't have a chart." She listened for a moment before hanging up. "One moment, sir," she said to Kaye.

Kaye could tell she was nervous and trying not to show it. Five seconds later a uniformed deputy turned the corner ten yards down the corridor. He had his hand on the butt of his holstered pistol, but relaxed when he saw Kaye.

"Detective Kaye?" the deputy inquired as he drew closer.

"That would be me," Kaye confirmed. He saw the nurse's shoulders relax as she turned back to her pile of charts.

"Figured it had to be," the deputy said. "Captain Halberstam called and gave us a description. You're a pretty easy guy to recognize."

"A blessing and a curse."

"I imagine it might be, sir. Follow me. Ms. Graham is back this way."

The deputy led him down the corridor, took one left turn, one right turn and pointed to an open door. "She's right through there."

The light in the room was on. Kaye stepped in and saw the telltale red hair. The bed covers were pulled up, and she had an IV drip in one hand and a monitor connected to the fingers of the other. Her eyes were closed. Kaye thought she looked much better than yesterday. He stood quietly, again soaking up the resemblance. She was younger. It was like looking at a ten-year old photograph, almost sure it might be someone you knew now, but hadn't known then. He decided to let her sleep and turned back toward the hallway.

"Wait. Please don't go."

He turned back. Her eyes were open and she was struggling to lift herself into a more upright position.

"You're the man from the motorcycle."

"Ben Kaye," he said and walked to the side of the bed. "How are you?"

"Nice to meet you, Ben Kaye. Cynthia Graham. And I'll live, thanks to you."

"Nice to meet you, too, Ms. Graham, although I wish the circumstances were different."

She smiled weakly and he saw tears start to build.

"I'm sorry about your husband," Kaye added sincerely.

"He wasn't my husband." A tear spilled from the corner of one eye and rolled down her cheek. "He was my brother. Aiden. I was bringing him home from grad school for the summer and… It was my car. I should have been driving." Her voice broke and tears rolled freely down her cheeks.

Kaye moved closer to the side of the bed and gently picked up her hand. He let her cry for a minute before speaking. "Cynthia, listen to me. Look at me. C'mon, look at me," he coaxed, waiting for her to look up. He fixed her green eyes with a stare. "You didn't do anything wrong. It didn't matter who was driving. Be mad at the man who shot your brother, not yourself. There's nothing, not one thing, you could have done differently that would have prevented this."

She squeezed the huge hand that held hers and tried to smile. The look in Kaye's eyes told her he believed what he was saying.

"Thank you for that, Mr. Kaye…"

"Please, call me Ben."

"Ben. I like that. Thank you for saving my life, Ben."

"Believe me, it was pure self-preservation. I'm just glad I had a gun. Otherwise, well, things would have probably turned out differently for both of us."

She looked at him, her brow furrowed, then said, "Oh, that's right. You're a policeman, too. I forgot for a second, but Captain Halberstam told me that this morning."

"Cynthia, would you mind if I asked you a couple questions? Are you up to it?"

She sucked in a deep breath. "Sure, go ahead, but I have to tell you; I don't remember very much."

"That's okay," Kaye reassured her. "It's not a test."

She laughed weakly. A good try, he thought, and a good sign.

"But please, call me Cindy. Only my Dad calls me Cynthia, and that's usually when he's mad."

"Cindy it is. To start, just tell me what you saw, what happened. Give me your version as best you can, okay?"

She sighed and her gaze went to the ceiling, her eyes losing focus.

"We were coming down the hill from Horseshoe Bend. The silver car was in front of us. Aiden was impatient to get home and he was pretty close to the guy. The guys," she stopped and corrected. "There were two guys in the car.

"Anyway, we were just driving along when that old red truck just pulled out onto the highway right in front of us."

She paused and looked at Kaye, tearing up again at the memory.

"It was so stupid!" she continued. "How could he not have seen us? The silver car was too close to even try to put his brakes on, and swerved hard to try and miss the truck. He didn't make it, and the side of his car hit the back of the truck and spun it around. It scared the shit... Oh, sorry."

"That's okay. Believe it or not, I've heard it before. Go ahead."

"It scared us both. Aiden got on the brakes as hard as he could. It felt like we skidded a long way before we stopped. If the silver car had hit the truck squarely, I think we'd have hit them both, we were that close."

"But you didn't hit them, and that's what counts. Your brother did a good job keeping you from being involved in the accident."

"I had a soda in the car. I had it in one hand and my book in the other, and when he slammed on the brakes I spilled my soda all over the place. After we stopped, for some stupid reason that was all I cared about. I was trying to clean up my drink mess and yelling at Aiden for almost killing us and I wasn't even paying attention to anything else. When Aiden stopped, I could tell it scared him, too. My yelling must have made him mad, because he shut the car off and took the keys out and tried to give them to me. He said something like 'okay, Sis, then you drive', or something like that."

That explained one thing. The kid couldn't drive away when the gunman headed his way.

"Go on."

"I don't remember seeing or hearing anything else until I heard loud bangs. It must've been when the guy shot the people in the truck. I looked up just in time to see him coming toward us."

She stopped as the memory hit her head-on and she broke into great wracking sobs of grief.

Kaye reached up with his free hand and rested it on her forehead. Memories of darkness and flashing lights flooded in. Cool pavement, with a crowd gathering. Other red hair, other green eyes looking up at him, full of questions and fear while he held her hand and stroked her forehead and could do nothing but wait for the ambulance while her life ran out onto the pavement.

It took Cindy about two minutes to slow down to an occasional hiccupped breath.

"I'm sorry, Ben. I'm sorry. It's just that…."

"It's okay to cry."

The tone of the big man's voice calmed and reassured the wounded woman. She caught her breath and wiped the tears from her face.

"Okay, so where was I?"

"The man with the gun. What did you do?"

"I ran. It was the only thing I could think of. I thought if I could just make it to the edge of the road, I might have a chance. Then I heard more shooting. That's all I remember until you found me. Then I fainted." She blushed and her gaze dropped.

"Don't forget you had been shot. I've seen hardened Marines do amazing things, then faint when they realize they're wounded."

He saw the blush in her neck again before she spoke.

"You were in the Marines?"

"Yes."

"My brother and father were both in the Corps. Aiden served in Iraq. My dad served in Vietnam, but that was probably way before

57

your time, unless I've been seriously affected by the drugs they're giving me."

Kaye laughed again. "Yeah, I was in after that, but I had a very close friend who pulled several tours there."

That opened the floodgates and the two spent twenty minutes playing 'did you know so-and-so' and 'were you ever stationed at such-and-such'.

"I have an uncle that was in, too," Cindy said. "Did you ever run across a Sergeant Major Dinsmore?"

Kaye was taken aback. Sergeant Major of the Corps Calvin Dinsmore was a legend, having won the Congressional Medal of Honor as a young Marine in Vietnam, and many thought that Clint Eastwood's character in Heartbreak Ridge was based on Dinsmore's exploits. And this young woman was his niece?

"You don't run across the Sergeant Major, Cindy. If you're lucky, he lets you go around. And, yes, I know the Sergeant Major."

"You know Uncle Calvin? Oh, my God!" Cindy gasped with delight. "Wait till I tell Dad!"

"Well, I can't say I know him well. We weren't friends. After all, I was just a grunt and he was a Sergeant Major, but our paths have crossed. Dinsmore was one hell of a Marine."

"That's what my dad says, too. Uncle Calvin saved Dad's life in Vietnam."

There was a long pause, each lost in private memories and thoughts.

"Tell you what," Kaye said to break the silence. "Let's make a deal, okay?"

"Okay. What did you have in mind? "

"For what happened on the road yesterday, how about we file it under Semper Fi and call it even?"

"Okay, we can do that. But I want something else from you, Ben. Or, should I say Officer Kaye?"

"It's just Ben."

"Well, then, Ben, I want your help." She paused. "But not for me. For my dad and my brother."

"What can I do for you?"

Cindy hesitated, looking down momentarily.

"Find the man who did this, who killed my brother, who shot me and tried to kill you. Please. Please. My brother's death will kill my dad. Aiden was his only son."

"Cindy, I…" Kaye started to protest.

"I know what you're going to say. The local police have jurisdiction. Let them investigate. You're passing through on vacation, not official here. Am I right?"

Kaye hesitated. She was right.

"They won't catch him. You know that and I know that. That man wasn't from around here and he's not staying around here for long. He might even be gone already. Right?"

"Probably so," Kaye admitted grudgingly. He saw no reason to tell her about the bomb and Maria de la Rosa.

"It's not that I don't trust the Sheriff's office. They do a good job around here. But this is over their heads. I saw it in that Captain's eyes when he was here. Please, Ben. Please?"

Kaye was silent. Everything the woman said was true, and his first instinct was to excuse himself from the case as politely as possible and let Halberstam handle it, for better or worse.

This wasn't his fight. But it wasn't just another case, either. A report dropped on his desk, the expectation being that he'd somehow repair an unknown victim's mistakes and find that elusive justice for all, then typically have it bargained away by an Assistant DA. He'd been there this time, unable to stop a gunman from murdering four people. Didn't that make him somehow culpable? He also had no doubt Maria de la Rosa would still be alive were it not for him, and that gnawed at him.

"I'll look into it," he said at last. "But I make no promises. I can't stay in Boise indefinitely. What I find I share with Halberstam, and if I find the guy, I cuff him, turn him in and go home. That's the best I can do. Deal?"

Cindy Graham smiled the smile of a woman who has gotten what she wants from a man, even if she has a gunshot wound to the shoulder.

"Deal! Now, what else can I tell you about what happened? What will help?"

They spent the next hour going over and over the events of that day, from the time Cindy and Aiden had started driving that morning up until the shooting. How long had they been driving? When and where had they stopped for food or drinks? When did they first see the silver car? How long did they follow it before the accident? Did they catch up to it, or did it pass them? Was there anything distinctive about the car or the occupants? Any little detail, no matter how insignificant it seemed, might be important, he told her. Don't hold back. Impressions are sometimes as important as facts.

It was a careful interview and Kaye took his time, not pushing. Cindy responded well to his questions and guidance, remembering and filling in enough details to give him a couple of places to start. He'd do some preliminary checking before dumping anything on Halberstam's desk.

They were still talking when the nurse came in and shooed Kaye out. Cindy gave him two numbers to call if he needed to reach her.

As he rode the elevator down, Kaye pondered his next move. In the back of his mind he thought Cindy was probably right. Halberstam had impressed him as a competent detective, but unless the Ada County cop got lucky, or their suspect made a mistake, he wasn't likely to solve this case. Plus, Halberstam had said something about being close to retirement, which meant the case would go right to the bottom of his successor's already full inbox. More than likely, that would be the end of it.

The man on the highway had tried to kill him twice in two days, and that pissed him off. Thinking the guy would probably get away with it angered him even more.

After leaving the hospital, Kaye stopped for a bite to eat. While he ate he went over his interview with Cindy, making notes and formulating a plan. She had remembered enough about the shooter's car to convince him it was a Toyota, probably a Camry or Avalon. She also remembered the car pulling out of a gas station in Horseshoe Bend and being behind them until they started the climb south of town. The road widened to four lanes there and the Toyota had passed them near the top of the hill, cutting them off to get by before the road narrowed again. Angered, Aiden had followed them too closely on the downhill side. It would at least be worth a trip back to the gas station to see if anybody there remembered the two men.

He tried to call Halberstam with the possible suspect vehicle information, but the call went straight to voice mail. It would wait until tomorrow. Only a fool would still be driving that car, and Kaye already knew that he wasn't chasing a fool.

After dinner Kaye swung back by the Hilton. Chambers was still behind the registration desk, his eyes red-rimmed and bloodshot.

"Oh, hello, Mr. Kaye. I didn't expect to see you again."

"I'm not staying, Mr. Chambers. No knock on your hotel, I just think it would be safer for your other guests if I stayed elsewhere. I hope you understand."

"Sadly, I agree. Nothing personal."

"No offense taken. I was wondering if, in all the excitement, my bags might have turned up? They were in the hallway outside the room where" Kaye paused briefly, "the explosion occurred."

Chambers turned and stepped over to the closet near the desk. He opened it to reveal Kaye's bags.

"Here you are. That other policeman, the bomb man, brought them down. I tried to clean them up as best I could. I hope you don't mind." Chambers managed a wan smile.

"I appreciate the kindness. Say, would you mind if I asked you a couple questions about Maria? Off the record, I mean, without the local cops standing around?"

Chambers was silent for a moment, wondering if he might somehow violate Maria's privacy by talking to Kaye. He decided to trust the big man.

"I'll tell you whatever I can."

"Thank you. Tell me about her. What was she like?"

Chambers started slowly, describing to Kaye a good employee and how she had come to work for him. As he went on he began to recount more personal details of his friendship with Maria. It was obvious to Kaye he'd unintentionally given Chambers what the man needed most right now; a cathartic opportunity to remember Maria fondly. He told Kaye about Maria's drive, her ambitions and the posters on the walls of her apartment of exotic resorts she'd hoped to one day manage.

At one point, Chambers recounted how Maria had put herself through college after her husband left her.

"She was married?"

"Was married," Chambers emphasized. "In fact, I forgot something! I'll be right back."

The manager went into his office and opened a desk drawer, pulled something out and returned.

"These are Maria's sons." Saying it almost made him cry again.

The picture was of a younger Maria, dressed in Sunday best, with two young boys in suits and ties posed carefully in front of her. Like their mother, their smiles were a mile wide.

"I thought you said she didn't have a family."

"She didn't, really. I mean, those are her boys, but her ex took them when he left. She hadn't seen them in several years. From what she said, her husband turned out to be a real jerk."

"Why didn't she take him to court and fight for custody?"

The manager hesitated for just a second, then stammered, "I... I guess... I mean, if I had to guess, that is..."

"It's okay, Mr. Chambers. I know she was illegal."

"You knew?" Chamber's eyes opened wide in surprise. "How?"

"Intuition, I guess. But it doesn't matter to me. Good people are good people. May I keep this photograph?"

"Sure, I guess so. I have another just like it on my dressing table at home." Chambers' voice was subdued. "She was like my little sister."

"You obviously cared very deeply for her," Kaye said as he removed the back from the frame and slid the photo out from behind the glass. He flipped it over. On the back was the name of the photography studio and, under that, a handwritten date. "Thank you, Mr. Chambers. Thank you very much."

"That's okay. Just one more thing..."

"What's that?"

Kaye saw raw anger flood the man's eyes. "Catch the bastard. Catch him for Maria, and for me. And when you do, make him pay. Please."

"Oh, I'm going to catch him. And when I do, I'll see what I can do for you."

Kaye turned and headed for the Road King. As he left the lobby, he could again hear Chambers sobbing softly.

It took an hour to find another suitable hotel. He rode aimlessly for the first twenty minutes, making sure he wasn't being followed.

The hotel was closer to the Interstate this time. One of the big franchise places that look the same in Boise as they do in Seattle or Miami or OKC. He circled the building first, looking for a good place to put the bike. Priorities had changed. He had a place to start now, and wanted invisibility and time to formulate a strategy before putting himself back out there. Satisfied he'd found the right place, he went inside and registered. Then he rode around back and eased the big bike into the six-foot gap between the main building and the small structure housing the hotel's swimming pool mechanicals. Hidden from the view of casual passers-by, it would take a specific effort to look into the space.

He requested, and was given, a top floor room away from the elevators and stairs, with a view of the back parking lot. The room's location provided the best tactical advantage possible under the circumstances.

He tried to meditate, but just couldn't focus. The image of Maria's dazzling smile kept intruding, and he decided to turn in for the night.

His teacher had often pointed out to him the obvious conflict between a meditation practice and his chosen profession. Was the violence and death often associated with police work consistent with a serious search for enlightenment? If he could not reconcile the two, Roshi had told him, he would have to choose between abandoning one, or losing both. Kaye had chosen. But it kept dragging him back in.

10

Kaye slept fitfully, with confused dreams of rescuing a redheaded Maria from inside a circle of inebriated gorillas, all with his face, only to have her explode once they reached safety.

He woke with a start just as his mother's voice floated to him from the dust of the explosion. "Oh, Ben, I told you not to join the Marines."

It was full daylight outside, the sun an hour above the horizon. Kaye took time to exercise before showering and packing his gear.

He had his day planned. After going to see Halberstam he'd ride up to Horseshoe Bend and talk to the employees at the truck stop where the silver car might have stopped. With any luck, the place had video cameras and the shooter had gotten gas. Kaye didn't expect the luck of a credit card transaction, or at least not an honest one. On the way back to town he'd stop and do his own search of the shooting scene. He knew Halberstam's troops had gone over it, but he wanted to satisfy himself and thought it would be worth the time.

It was another hot day, but the high, thin clouds riding a soft breeze in from the northwest whispered that it might not be as hot as yesterday.

Kaye checked the Harley closely as he approached and saw no signs of tampering. He warmed up the bike while he stowed his gear.

There was over an hour to kill before he was due at Halberstam's office, so he decided to ride over and check the side roads off Highway 55 between the scene of the shooting and the construction zone. Something bothered him about the chain of events, but it was another of those things he couldn't quite put a finger on. Riding it again, he might see something he'd missed yesterday that would coalesce his thoughts.

Construction was in full swing and this time he had to wait, first in line this time, to get through northbound. Kaye used the time to strike up a conversation with the flagger, a middle-aged woman obviously bored with standing on the hot pavement day after day.

Yeah, she'd been on this job day before yesterday.

Yeah, she remembered all the commotion of the sirens, with ambulances and police cars trying to get through.

She didn't really understand why they all came through here, though, when they could've taken the old road about a half-mile east, back beyond the Home Depot, and gone around the whole mess.

She thought the cops liked being the center of attention and making everybody get out of their way.

Kaye told her he was a cop.

She smiled and told him he could handcuff her any time, but, no, she didn't remember seeing a silver car with body damage come down the hill anytime before the cop car started up. She'd been working northbound that day, too, so it wouldn't have gone past her.

She joked about there being two seasons in Idaho – winter and road construction.

No, they didn't count cars or time intervals. They just played it by ear, but she did enjoy making the impatient assholes driving what she called 'compensation for small penises' wait maybe a little longer than they should.

She flipped the sign from 'Stop' to 'Slow' and waved Kaye through with a playful reminder about the standing handcuff offer.

Kaye cruised the main highway and intersecting roads, not quite sure what he was looking for, but hoping it would click when he saw it. It didn't take him long to figure out that most of the main roads were laid out on section lines, and as long as he stayed consistent in compass and turn directions it would be hard to get lost.

He idled the Road King through the old section of town, the low rumble of the exhaust turning heads as it always did.

Nice little town, he thought idly, *about to be obliterated by the bulldozers in the name of progress.*

He checked the time, decided to head for Halberstam's office, and accelerated onto the highway toward Boise.

***

It was nine fifty-five when he leaned the big Harley onto the kickstand in the County criminal justice complex parking lot. The lot and entrance walkway were the only real estate on the premises not ringed with concertina wire.

The desk deputy assumed the big biker was there to visit an inmate and decided to reinforce the universal pecking order by studiously ignoring him for ten minutes. When Kaye finally got a chance to tell the deputy he was there to see Halberstam, he waited again until the deputy finally deigned to call back and let the Captain know he was there.

"You're late," Halberstam said bluntly when he pushed the security door open.

"No, I'm not," rejoined Kaye, nodding in the direction of the desk. "Talk to him. If he worked for me he'd be writing parking tickets tomorrow."

The desk deputy heard the comment and looked at Kaye with a flat 'screw you' stare.

Halberstam just shook his head and held the door.

The two men walked through the building, with Kaye drawing curious stares all the way. When they reached his office, Halberstam waved Kaye to a chair and closed the door.

The office was lined with bookcases and the desk was cluttered with case files. Bright sunshine, sliced into manageable pieces by the half-open mini-blinds, streamed through the window.

"So," the Captain asked tersely as he sat down, "anybody tried to blow you up since yesterday?"

Kaye smiled tightly and studied the other man. Something about Halberstam's demeanor was different.

"What's wrong, Captain?"

"I spoke to some folks I know in Los Angeles. Seems your vacation, as you call it, is more like a leave of absence. Around here we call that a suspension. Is that right?"

Kaye stared at the Ada County detective before answering.

"I wasn't suspended. I requested the leave first."

"But you would have been suspended, right? Care to enlighten me?"

"Possibly. I broke a suspect's arm."

"That matches what your Captain told me. Go on."

"You talked to Thompson?"

"Yep."

"Did he tell you that the arm I broke was attached to a hand that was holding an automatic weapon that was pointed at two other cops?"

"No, he did not. I got the impression the man doesn't care much for you."

"Very perceptive of you."

Halberstam leaned forward. "But he also told me it was your second incident in less than six months. What happened the first time?"

"I went after the man who killed my wife."

"Your wife was murdered?"

"A drunk driver killed her. I made it my business to find him."

"And how do you know it was a drunk?"

"She was ten feet behind me. The guy missed me, got her, and left the scene. I got him, and my Captain was unhappy about it. Can we move on, please?"

"Can I ask you one more question?"

"Go ahead."

"Are you planning on going back?"

"I don't know," Kaye replied honestly. "The job just doesn't seem worth the trouble anymore, if you know what I mean."

"Never had that feeling myself. And I pull the plug next month after thirty years."

"What are you going to do?"

"Play with my grandkids and ride my horses." Halberstam smiled. "In that order. How 'bout you? I don't really know you, but I get the feeling you're a natural at this. What would you do if you quit?"

"Not sure. I've got an ex-Lieutenant that's a Chief in Colorado. He said they could use my help, sort of like a consultant."

"Really? I know some folks in Colorado. Whereabouts?"

"Near Aspen."

Halberstam whistled. "Hope it pays well. Aspen ain't a cheap place to live."

"My wife did well for herself."

Halberstam hesitated before saying, "Okay, I think we're now in none-of-my-business territory, so I'll keep my mouth shut."

Halberstam reached into the top drawer of his desk and pulled out Kaye's Kimber, a baggie containing the magazine and several loose rounds, a pad of forms and a couple pens. There was a tag tied to the pistol's trigger guard. He slid everything across the desk toward Kaye.

"First things first. The card there authorizes you to carry concealed in Idaho. But don't shoot anybody unless you have to, because that card's got my name on it. What I need from you is a written statement of the events of the day before yesterday. Nothing fancy, just... Well, hell, I can skip the lecture. You know the drill."

"That I do," Kaye said, scooping up his pistol and sliding it into the boot holster after removing the card. "You want me to do the statement here?"

"Sure." Halberstam stood. "I've got to go check in on a polygraph on another case, so if you'll excuse me, I'll be back." He left the office and pulled the door closed behind him.

He's not going far, Kaye mused before turning his attention to the form on the desk. The white cowboy hat still hung on the back of the door.

Kaye finished his statement and turned his attention to the framed items on the wall behind the desk. The qualifications and commendations were impressive.

The door swung open and Halberstam stepped in, this time leaving the door open.

"Get it done?" he asked, settling into his chair.

"Yes. I tried to be brief, but include things I thought were important." Kaye slid the completed form back across the desk. "You know the drill, too."

"Appreciate that. Okay, that'll do it. Thanks for the help, and you're free to go. Have a safe ride home."

"Wait a minute," Kaye said quickly. "I've got some questions for you, too. Can't you fill me in on the investigation?"

Halberstam leaned back in his chair and studied Kaye closely.

Here it comes, thought Kaye. He recognized the look. Hell, he used it.

"Kaye, need I remind you that you have no jurisdiction here? You're a witness to a crime. A good one, but still just a witness. That's all, and...."

"I'm also a victim, and I'm a well-trained investigator, who happens to be pretty good at it. Use me."

Halberstam spun his chair so he could stare out the window. Without turning back to face Kaye, he spoke. "I can't. I've been instructed by my superiors not to permit your participation in the investigation. In fact, as the Sheriff considers it highly unlikely that an arrest will ever be made, the decision has been made that we won't actively work this case and will devote our resources elsewhere." Halberstam spun in his chair and looked at Kaye. "His words, not mine."

"What! That's ludicrous! Doesn't he understand that the best way to guarantee you won't solve the case is not to work it? It's a self-fulfilling prophecy, and moronic police work. Five people are dead and you're just going to turn around and walk away from it?"

"Keep your mouth shut for just a minute, will you, and let me say my piece?" Halberstam studied his hands intently for a moment before looking up at Kaye. "We're turning everything we have, which isn't much, over to the State Police and letting them run the case."

"You mean the State Patrol? Wonderful. Triple A with guns. This wasn't a traffic accident, Captain, it was a multiple homicide."

"Well, actually, it was a traffic accident, or at least it started out that way. And, it happened on a State highway, so, technically, DLE has jurisdiction. They're taking the case."

"And you're going to hand it over, just like that?"

"I just work here, remember? Well, at least for about another month. Truthfully, as an investigator I'm pissed about having this case taken away from me. This isn't how I figured I'd go out. But I'm also a practical man."

"And that means...?"

"Look, we both know the odds of this agency, or, for that matter, anybody, making an arrest in this case are just about zero. The Sheriff knows it, too, and he's up for re-election this November. He's happier than a pig in slop to dump this case on the state boys."

"So, it's politics."

"Well, yeah, I guess it is. But in this instance, I think politics works for the best."

Kaye snorted.

"I know, I know," Halberstam said. "But in this case it does. The state has a lot of very good investigators, including the one this is going to. Name's Unger. He's good. The state also has a lot better internal forensic capabilities and, if nothing else, a broader geographic reach. We both know our shooter could be in Timbuktu by now. I still think this case will go cold, and that gripes the hell out of me, but at least I won't retire and go to my grave blaming myself for that. And if you think that's selfish of me, well, screw you." Halberstam smiled as he said it.

There was an uneasy silence that lasted a full fifteen seconds.

"Okay," Kaye finally said, standing up. "I can't control it, so I'm not going to worry about it. But I'm not dropping this and going away. I promised some people I'd look into it."

"Oh, really? Who?"

"Cindy Graham. Turns out her father and I served with some of the same people in the Marine Corps." Kaye saw the skeptical look on the ACSO detective's face and added. "Hey, I was honest with her and made no promises. In fact, I pretty much told her everything about jurisdiction and capabilities that you just told me. But I said I'd look into it."

A slow smile crept onto Halberstam's face.

"What's so amusing, Captain?"

"Detective Kaye, you don't sound to me like a guy who's retiring to the ski slopes. And I must admonish you again, officially, that you are not to participate in this investigation. Now, again, please sit down."

Kaye looked at the Captain closely before he sat down.

"I would add, though," Halberstam said slowly, "that my superiors did not specifically prohibit me from sharing information regarding this case with duly sworn officers from authorized jurisdictions, when said officers might have reason to conduct their own investigations into aspects of the case that may be of interest to them."

Kaye smiled broadly and completed Halberstam's logic. "And, because there have already been two attempts on my life in connection with this case, it is reasonable to assume that those attempts may continue when I return to my jurisdiction, giving me reasonable need to know. Correct?"

"Abso-fuckin'-lutely, if you'll pardon my French. Besides, what're they gonna do, fire me? This county couldn't process the paperwork in time."

They had recovered the silver car. The owner of a body shop found it parked in his lot the previous morning. It was damaged, and the keys were lying in the seat, so he assumed a tow truck had dropped it off overnight. He thought nothing of it and waited all day for a call from the owner or an insurance company about making repairs. When he saw the evening news, it made him suspicious and he called in about it. It had red paint smear on it, too.

"Toyota Camry, right?"

The Captain shot him a look. "Okay, how'd you know that?"

"I used some meditation techniques to reconstruct my memories," Kaye lied. At this point, with the case going to the State, he didn't feel the need to make the information share mutual and tell Halberstam about his talk with Cindy Graham.

There were several interesting facts about the car. It carried Idaho plates that belonged to a silver Camry, but the computer said those plates should have been on a Camry with a different VIN. The plates had not yet been reported stolen or missing, but when they ran the Camry's actual VIN through the system, it came back as stolen in Spokane five days ago.

"Pretty sophisticated, if you think about it," Kaye mused. "Assuming he had a phony registration, which he took with him when he dumped the car in a place where it was least likely anybody would notice it, he probably could have bluffed his way through a regular traffic stop. If the make, model and color are right, not many guys take the time to cross check the VIN or validation numbers between the plates, the car and the registration on a regular contact."

"Right." Halberstam nodded in agreement. "If the registration looks right, they take it for granted."

Halberstam also told Kaye they hadn't recovered a single piece of usable forensic or physical evidence from the car. The entire interior, including the trunk, had been sprayed with chlorine bleach, contaminating or obliterating anything that might identify the vehicle's occupants.

"Any stolen cars in the area?" Kaye asked. "Cabs dispatched? Hitchhikers?"

"Nothing yet."

The dead man on the embankment was still unidentified. The two detectives agreed there was little likelihood the man was a random victim. He was almost surely an accomplice in whatever the driver was running from, or to. The dead man carried no identification and his clothing was nondescript and commonplace.

"So," Kaye asked rhetorically, "why would the driver shoot his own man?"

"Check this out." Halberstam slid some papers across the desk.

It was a preliminary autopsy report. The coroner had listed COD as a close range gunshot wound to the back of the head. Closer examination had revealed that the man, identified only as a Caucasian between twenty-five and thirty years of age, also had a broken wrist, dislocated shoulder and two broken ribs on his right side. The coroner concluded that the injuries were fresh, sustained in the accident.

"What do you make of that?" Halberstam asked.

"I think the guy wasn't wearing his seat belt. I think he got tossed around inside the car during the accident, and that's how he got hurt. These are injuries you don't just tough out. You need a doctor." Kaye paused, putting it together. "I think this guy went from being an asset to a liability because of those injuries and the driver shot and dumped him because of it."

"I agree. This guy's going to an awful lot of trouble to cover his tracks."

"Anything on the dead guy's prints?"

"Not yet. And I don't expect to get a hit. Plus, the bullet took a good part of his face with it when it exited, and he didn't even have dental work we could work with. I was trying to line up a forensic sketch artist, but with the case going to the state…"

Halberstam continued reviewing the preliminary report. They had recovered 9MM casings at the scene that matched the slugs recovered from the bodies, and the ejector markings indicated a Beretta. The spent brass was checked for fingerprints, but was clean. They had recovered nothing else at the scene attributable to either the suspect or the suspect vehicle.

"This is just too damn clean, Kaye. We've got four dead people at that scene and nothing to go on."

"What about Rudy Moore's report? Bomber's signatures are usually pretty unique."

Halberstam handed the L.A. detective Moore's preliminary report. Small device, concussion only and probably shaped for maximum effect. Residue samples sent to the FBI lab for analysis, results return time unknown, but likely to be extended because national security and suspected terrorism cases got priority. COD was blunt force trauma to the head as a result of the blast. That was confirmed by the coroner's preliminary report. Unless one was requested, there would be no autopsy on Maria de la Rosa.

Somehow, Kaye felt better knowing that Maria would be spared the further indignity of being sliced and diced.

The two spent some time discussing different theories of the case, using each other as sounding boards. In the end, all they could agree on was that there was very little to go on.

"Your people have moved fast on this one, Captain. I'm impressed."

"Well, it doesn't take long to find nothing."

"Maybe not, but it takes time to look, and we both know that the best way to find the needle in the haystack is to get rid of all the hay."

Halberstam smiled. "Our job in a nutshell."

"What about the video from the hotel? Anything on there that might help us identify this guy? Assuming, of course, it was the same guy."

"We're still going through it. We did get a decent picture of the guy who came in looking for you the night before. Based on the description he could be our boy, but we have no clue who he might be. Anything else?"

"I don't think so. Thanks."

"No, Kaye, thank you. Bottom line, you saved the Graham woman's life out there. Too bad we'll probably never catch the bastard. He's long gone by now."

"Maybe," Kaye said as he stood to leave. "Maybe not. Oh, there is one more thing."

"What's that?"

"Go ahead and release my name to the media. Tell them you think I was the target of the bomb that killed Maria de la Rosa and make sure you connect it to the shootings."

"You sure you want to do that?" Halberstam's look told Kaye he thought it was a bad idea.

"I'm sure. Easiest way to find the guy if he's still around is to make him come to me. Make sure you tell them I'm a cop on vacation, too. Just leave out where I work. For now, anyway."

"If that's what you want."

"Thanks, Captain." Kaye extended his hand. "I'll be in touch if I come up with anything."

Halberstam reached out and took the hand. "Damn," he muttered. "Tell me something, if you don't mind. How much you weigh? And where'd you play ball? Surely you must've played ball."

Kaye smiled. "Just enough, and I played a little college ball, but an injury ended that." He didn't add that he'd caused the injury, not suffered it, and that the guilt ended his career.

"Well, you carry it well." Halberstam smiled and added, "Tonight, I'm gonna tell my horse how lucky he is he doesn't have to carry you around. Maybe he'll appreciate me more. You be careful. I've got your number if I need to reach you."

As Kaye left the building he flashed a smile at the desk deputy, who regarded him with all the interest he'd show a piece of furniture.

11

Kaye wasn't happy that the investigation was being turned over to the state cops, but he understood why. Everybody wants a chance to get their picture in the paper. Except him. Been there, done that, and it never seemed to turn out well.

He wanted to time his trip to Horseshoe Bend so he got there about the same time of day he'd rolled through day before yesterday. That would improve the odds that the same people would be working at the gas station, increasing his chances of finding someone who remembered the silver Camry and its occupants. He realized the odds were slim, since the place was probably buzzing with summertime tourist traffic. His real hope was for some video surveillance footage. If he got very lucky the two had used a credit card. Even a stolen or fraudulent card might turn something.

He checked his watch and decided to head that way, stopping to search the scene on the way up instead of doing it on the way back.

It was sunny, but had turned slightly cooler than the last couple of days and the ride was pleasant. Traffic was light. He took the cut-off that the flagger had told him about earlier, taking the old road and avoiding the construction zone.

Kaye slowed as he approached the scene of the shooting. The orange spray paint marks on the road made it easy to find. He pulled onto the right shoulder at the spot where the old red truck's tire tracks had left the pavement and gone into the ditch.

Scanning the scene, he saw there was enough hardpan on the side road the old timer had pulled out of to provide a solid parking surface for the Harley. After waiting for a northbound SUV to go by, he swung the big bike in a tight half circle, rolled a ways down the side road and shut down.

Kaye had seen Halberstam's team start their search of the area, and wondered where he should start. He saw no need to revisit the spot where he'd stopped, figuring there was nothing up there that would help him.

A screech overhead was followed instantly by sounds of alarm from the hillside. Kaye looked up to see two red-tailed hawks circling lazily overhead, their presence noticed by the whistle pigs. As he watched, the pair slid down the wind toward the valley below. A dog barked in the distance. Looking down, he spied the depressions of deer tracks in the dust, headed down the embankment to the green weeds that promised water. Movement up the road caught his eye, and he saw a snake slither quickly across the hot pavement and disappear over the lip of the roadway into the cheat grass.

He decided to make his way down the embankment and follow the fence line down to the point opposite where the silver Camry had stopped. That would put him below where the second suspect's body had been found, looking across and up at the road instead of down from it. He knew the locals had come down from above and wondered just how far beyond the body, out toward the pastures, they had searched.

He'd find out.

The graded fill that formed the last twenty or thirty yards of the side road offered enough purchase that Kaye had no trouble sidestepping through the weeds to the bottom.

The side road passed over a five-foot diameter concrete pipe lined with corrugated steel that allowed drainage from the uphill side. In the spring it ran almost full with snow melt from the high country, and even now a slight trickle of water seeped out the end of the pipe and disappeared into the thick, waist-high vegetation. Deer tracks were everywhere.

He calculated he could cover the area more than adequately with three or four passes, working his way closer to the road with each one.

Kaye worked his way slowly downhill, looking carefully for anything out of place. Close to the fence there wasn't even a hint of the typical roadside litter people casually toss and the vegetation was closely grazed as far as a horse could reach beyond the fence. It was evident that the landowner cleaned up any litter so his livestock didn't end up swallowing something they shouldn't.

He continued downhill. The perspective from down here was markedly different and he chastised himself for not thinking to mark the spot up by the road. He'd just have to guess, and kept going until he was about twenty yards beyond where he thought the Toyota had stopped.

At the end of his first sweep, Kaye took five paces away from the fence toward the highway and started back north. Traffic was light, with only the occasional rush of a car going by on the highway.

He scanned slowly left and right as he went. He saw no other footprints, leading him to conclude the sheriff's people hadn't searched out this far.

About twenty feet from where he had reversed direction Kaye saw a small hint of white, dead center in a thick clump of grass, off to his right. Thinking it was probably nothing more than a piece of discarded Styrofoam, he went over and knelt down to get a closer look. It was plastic, but it wasn't Styrofoam. Buried edge up in the clump of grass, he first thought it was a credit card. It had the right size and proportions, and there was a magnetic strip visible on one side. One end, though, had a small, rectangular perforation. He leaned over to look at the other side, but it was too obscured to see.

Delicately pushing the blades of grass apart, Kaye used his thumb and forefinger to carefully grab the piece of plastic by opposite edges. He slowly lifted it from the grass, then swiveled his hand around to take a closer look at the opposite side.

It wasn't a credit card. A dozen small color chips in various shades of blue, progressing from light to dark, were arrayed down the length of the object. Each color chip had a number adjacent to it, ranging from five on the light end to two hundred on the dark end. The chips adjoined a center strip and at one end there was a larger chip with a black dot in its center. It was labeled 'control'.

"Oh, shit", muttered Kaye under his breath, instantly recognizing the card.

It was a radiation dosimeter, used by someone working with, or around, radioactive material. The chips were reference points for the center strip, which darkened with exposure and warned the wearer when a dangerous dose was being absorbed.

Kaye examined the card closely. He was no expert, but he knew that continued exposure to sunlight degraded the cards, making it impossible for him to tell how long the card had been there.

He held the card carefully. He hadn't really expected to find anything worth collecting, so hadn't brought anything to collect with. But he wanted this card, and he wanted it as uncontaminated as he could keep it. Holding the card by the edges, he continued walking his search pattern, hoping that human nature would help him out. Sure enough, closer to the road there was more litter, and within five minutes he'd found what he needed; two paper cups and a plastic bag. Good enough, he reasoned. It wasn't something that would ever get to court.

Kaye carefully lodged the edges of the plastic card inside one cup, keeping the flat surfaces from touching the cup's sides. Once he was satisfied, he stuck the second cup over the open end of the first one, creating a makeshift closed container. Then he put everything inside the plastic bag.

He finished his search, finding nothing else worthy of attention.

He climbed up the embankment to the Road King and put the makeshift evidence container into a saddlebag. He pondered his options while he snugged down his helmet. He knew an expert with the resources to evaluate the dosimeter, but if he continued to Horseshoe Bend today he wouldn't get back to Boise early enough to make today's outgoing FedEx to Los Angeles.

It didn't take him long to make his decision.

The card might be, in fact probably was, nothing. It could wait a day. He was almost halfway to Horseshoe Bend, and that would be his next stop. Besides, he wanted to call and brief his contact first.

Kaye kicked the Harley into first gear and eased out the clutch. He checked for traffic, saw several vehicles approaching from the north and decided to wait for them to pass.

The last vehicle was a small, yellow four-by-four SUV. As it passed, the male passenger looked at Kaye and then quickly looked away. It seemed unnatural to Kaye and he suddenly realized that the vehicle was the same one that had passed going the other direction as he'd waited on the shoulder to make his u-turn. His cop reflexes took over and he zeroed in on the back of the SUV to read the license plate.

As he watched, the gap between the yellow SUV and the car ahead of it started to widen perceptibly. The SUV was slowing down.

Okay, Kaye thought as a smile crossed his lips, *let's play*.

He pulled onto the highway and turned north. As soon as the back tire was clear of the loose gravel that peppered the edge of the pavement he twisted the throttle wide open. The twin exhausts erupted with a thunderous roar and the bike responded instantly, leaping forward. Accelerating hard, Kaye quickly shifted to second and stayed on the throttle. A quick glimpse in the rearview mirror caught the yellow SUV before it disappeared around the shoulder of the hill. Kaye saw the brake lights come on and the front end dip sharply. The driver was turning around.

Kaye blasted through the gears until the speedometer was touching the one hundred mark. A quick shift to sixth lowered the RPM but kept his speed constant. He blew past two cars and a gravel truck, their horns blaring displeasure.

The Harley came out of a curve and entered a long uphill straightaway. Kaye scanned ahead and saw what he wanted, quickly getting off the throttle and onto the brakes. Using the transmission, engine compression and a deft touch on the brakes, Kaye slowed much faster than possible in almost any car, but he was still going faster than he wanted when the spot came up. He timed it and pushed hard on the right hand grip. The Road King instantly leaned hard over in a tight right turn. The right side footboard scraped the pavement, and when he heard it he pushed hard on the left grip to bring the bike back upright into a straight and true course.

He thanked the motorcycle gods that there had been no gravel and roared down the road toward the cluster of houses at the end.

He'd gotten lucky. First with the near-suicide turn and now with a large RV parked in the turnaround area at the end of the road. He guided the Harley behind the RV, shut down, rested it onto the kickstand and swung off.

Screened from view from the road, Kaye moved toward the front of the RV and peered around it. About a minute later he saw the gravel truck lumbering up the hill, trailed by the same two cars he had passed. The yellow SUV was now last in line, trapped behind the slow-moving truck.

Three minutes later he saw the yellow SUV pass by again, headed down the hill toward Boise at highway speed.

***

Kaye rolled through Horseshoe Bend at a sedate twenty-five mph, looking for the place Cindy had described to him. He found it on the north side of town, where the Payette River looped west toward the Snake in the feature that gave the town its name.

Built as a big log cabin in an effort to capture the mountain lodge look, the Store at the Bend was betrayed by the flat gunmetal gray steel awning providing shelter for the dozen gas pumps out front.

The parking lot was crushed gravel, not asphalt, and Kaye carefully navigated his way to the concrete pad around the pumps. He could use fuel, and buying something was always a better way to strike up a conversation with the employees.

He parked at an open pump, shut down the Harley, and looked around. Plastered on the pumps were signs that read 'Cash Customers Pay Inside First, Then Pump', and the support columns bore signs informing customers to smile, they were being videotaped.

Kaye sighed. Civilization had definitely reached Horseshoe Bend, Idaho.

He walked slowly across the seventy-five feet of parking lot separating the pump island from the store, checking the area. The non-gas customer parking was along the front of the building. A small sign on a post asked customers to please not park in front of the wide steps that climbed to a large porch and the front door. Posters in the windows advertised that night crawlers, cold beer, hunting and fishing licenses, propane and firewood could all be found inside. He took the steps two at a time.

"Nice motorcycle," a faltering voice said from his left. "Harley-Davidson?"

Kaye stopped and peered into the deep shadows of the porch. An old-timer, his bony hands wrapped tightly around a pony can of Keystone Light, reclined in an Adirondack chair.

"Thanks. And, yes, it's a Harley."

"Thought so," the old timer said, his rheumy eyes looking at Kaye. "Can't see too good from here, but once you hear that sound you never forget it. Like a wolf. No other sound just like it. Used to ride an old panhead, many years back." He lifted the can to his lips and retreated once again into his memories.

Kaye entered the store and stopped in amazement. He'd been in lots of places that laid claim to having anything and everything a shopper might need, but this was the first place he'd ever seen that might live up to it. From just inside the door he could see motor oil and windshield wipers, guns and fishing poles, a sign pointing to lumber and hardware, life vests, sandwiches, cold beer and drinks, even plumbing supplies. To his right, a large brass cash register squatted just in front of the grill.

"Pump five, please." He handed a twenty to the young blonde behind the counter.

"Twenty on five, sir," she said cheerfully. "You're all set."

Kaye walked back to pump his gas, glancing as he passed at the old timer dozing contentedly in the deep shade of the porch.

He put almost sixteen bucks of premium in the tank before heading back inside to get, hopefully, some information

Must be slipping, he thought, unable to see the advertised cameras anywhere.

Inside, Kaye settled the gas charges, added a soda, a candy bar and another five bucks, and told the delighted young lady to keep the change. He wandered around for a minute, hoping to see someone who appeared to be in charge. He was standing in the sporting goods section when he saw a woman emerge from behind a door marked 'Employees Only'. Middle-aged, her black hair was gathered in a long braid that snaked from beneath her Boston Red Sox cap and down the front of her t-shirt, almost reaching the waistband of her camouflage pants.

"Excuse me," he said pleasantly as she passed. "Are you by chance the owner or manager?"

"You selling something?"

Kaye laughed. "No, I'm not a salesman. My name is Ben Kaye, and I'd appreciate a couple minutes of your time, if you can spare it. I have no complaints, I promise."

"That'd be a first," the woman responded with a laugh, taking Kaye's hand in a firm grip. "Maggie Hennigan. I own the place. What can I do for you?"

"Is there someplace we can talk?"

"Sure. Follow me."

Maggie turned and led Kaye back into her office. She offered him a seat and settled herself behind the desk.

"I suppose you heard," Kaye started off, "about the nasty business over the hill the other day."

"How could I not? It's been all over the news every..." She stopped in mid-sentence and leaned forward, fixing Kaye with a hard stare. "Hey, you're the guy on the motorcycle they showed on the news. The guy who turned out to be a cop, right?"

"That would be me." Her question also told him that Halberstam had been talking to the media.

"Are you investigating the case?"

"Not officially, but Captain Halberstam at the Sheriff's Office can vouch for me. It turns out that the father of the young woman who was wounded and I have mutual friends from my military days. I told her I'd look into things as a courtesy."

Maggie nodded her head. She got it. "So, how did that bring you to my place?"

Kaye explained about Cindy remembering the silver car.

Maggie sat silent for a minute, figuring it out for herself. "So," she said, "you're hoping they bought something, maybe even used a credit card, right? Or that one of my people might remember something about them?"

Kaye smiled. "Maggie, you should have been a detective."

She smiled back. "Doesn't pay enough."

"Roger that. I was also hoping you might have some surveillance video that would give me a better look at the guys. I can give you a pretty narrow time frame."

Maggie groaned.

"What's wrong?"

"I don't have any cameras."

"But the signs, are they...?" He asked as he figured it out.

"Decoys," she confirmed. "Signs are a lot cheaper than cameras and they don't break. I gave up and pulled the cameras two winters ago. Ninety-nine point nine percent of the customers see the signs and behave. The rest, well, we only got three ways in and out of this town, and this time of year, between the sheriff's office, the state bulls and the fish cops, there's a lot of badges per square inch in this county. During the winter nobody gets in or out of here at all about half the time. Even the dumb thieves can figure those odds. Sorry."

"So much for that idea. Could I ask your employees some questions?"

"Sure." Maggie spun in her chair and looked at the schedule posted on the wall behind her. "Same people working today that were here then. That'd be Caleb, Tiffany, George, and me. I can tell you right up front I don't remember seeing anybody like they've been talking about on the news. You have any more information?" She leaned forward.

"Only that I believe the car was a silver Toyota Camry with Idaho plates. Two men, early thirties, plus or minus, dark hair, clean cut. Could've been brothers, even. Sorry I can't be more specific, but that's all I've got."

"That's okay," Maggie shot back with a grin as she stood up. "If you already knew who they were, you wouldn't be here in the first place. Let's go talk to Tiff."

Maggie led Ben back to the front cash register and introduced Kaye to the young blonde, telling her it was okay to answer his questions.

Kaye went through the brief background and why he was there before asking if she remembered anybody or anything that might help him narrow down his search for the two men.

Tiffany thought for a bit and then said, "We were really busy right then. If they came in, I don't remember them. Sorry."

"That's okay," Kaye reassured her. Then, to Maggie, "Who's next?"

"Let's try George," Maggie said, reaching into her pocket and coming out with a small walkie-talkie.

Before she could key the button, Tiffany spoke up.

"Oh, Maggie, I forgot to tell you. George left about fifteen minutes ago on a tow call up Ola way. Said he'd be gone at least an hour. I'm sorry, I forgot."

"Well, so much for George. Ola's a radio dead spot," Maggie sighed and then keyed the walkie-talkie. "Caleb, come in Caleb. Where are you, son?"

She got an answer almost instantly.

"I'm out front at the pumps. There's a black Harley out here at pump five and it's been sitting here for awhile with nobody around. Should I move it?"

Kaye heard Caleb's question and reached to touch Maggie's arm before she could answer. She looked at him questioningly.

"Tell him not to touch it unless he can afford to write me a check for a new one."

Maggie smiled as she clicked the mike open. "Leave it, Caleb. Belongs to a customer I'm talking to right now. Meet us on the porch. Maggie out." She slid the walkie-talkie back into her pocket.

Kaye and Maggie stepped out onto the porch and saw Caleb walk away from the bike, headed for the store. When he saw his mother and Kaye waiting, he broke into a jog and took the steps three at a time. A tall, raw-boned nineteen, Caleb sized up Kaye closely.

"What's up, Mom?" Caleb asked, glancing back and forth from his mother to Kaye.

"Caleb, this is Ben. He's a policeman and was involved in that fracas over the hill the other day. He'd like to ask you a few questions."

"Nice to meet you, Caleb." Kaye said.

"Likewise, sir. You've got a cool bike."

Kaye gave Caleb the same rundown he'd given Maggie and Tiffany. Caleb listened closely, and then nodded when Kaye was finished.

"Yeah, I do remember them. Drove in on a flat tire. Two guys, very unfriendly."

"Flat tire?"

"Yeah, they came in real slow on account of the flat. Parked over there." Caleb pointed to a spot toward the north end of the building. "George went over to ask them if they needed help, seeing as how the gravel can make it tough to set a jack. One of them saw him and met him halfway, real quick, and told him pretty rude like that they didn't need his help. So we watched them for a few minutes, you know, kind of hoping the car would slide off the jack or something, just to show them."

"Did it?" Maggie asked. "Lord, I hope not. They'd probably sue me."

"Nope, not while I was watching, anyway. But I do remember they had a heck of a time getting to the spare and the jack."

"Really?" asked Kaye. "Why?"

"Well," Caleb thought out loud. "They had a big box in the trunk and it looked like they argued about taking it out. I couldn't hear them from where I was, but that's what it looked like. They ended up having to take it out to get to the spare, which was kinda weird because it was full-size and not one of those donut tires Toyotas usually come with, and it took both of them to lift the box. It looked pretty heavy and they were real careful. I thought about going over to offer to help, but after they were rude to George, I figured screw it."

"How long were they here?" asked Kaye.

"I don't know for sure. Sorry. We got busy with the local after-work rush and the next time I looked they were gone."

"Did they go inside? Buy anything?"

"Don't think so, but I'm not a hundred percent sure." Caleb looked at his mother and asked, "Does Tiff remember them?"

"No," Maggie told him.

Kaye knew there was no way to know for sure whether or not Caleb was talking about the same two men or the same car and, even if he was, the boy hadn't given him anything that would help identify or find the shooter.

"What time was this, Caleb?" he asked, trying to narrow it down.

Caleb thought for a second. "The rush usually starts about five thirty, so it was around then. I know they came in before the logging truck wreck up the road and traffic got messed up."

"I saw that," Kaye told him. "Looked like the driver stacked it into the rocks after he hit a deer. If I'd been in a car, I'd have been stuck. Made it around on the bike." At least the boy had confirmed the timing, putting everybody at the same place around the same time. "Thanks, Caleb. You've been a big help. Say, is there another route from here back to Boise?"

"You bet, and it's a great ride!" He gave Kaye directions.

Kaye stood on the porch and planned his next move. He'd certainly take the alternate route back to Boise, then call Halberstam and suggest to the Captain that he check the inventory list for the Toyota. If it said anything about a flat tire, he'd mention to Halberstam what Caleb had said about a heavy box in the trunk.

No sense mentioning the dosimeter yet. He had his own plans for that. Besides, he expected to find it had been there for months, even years.

"Hey, motorcycle man." The voice broke Kaye's reverie. The old timer was still in his chair, now working on filling the Keystone Light can with saliva and tobacco juice.

"Yes?" Kaye answered politely.

"I saw those two men with the flat tire. Heard 'em, too. Ain't heard talkin' like that in a long, long time."

"Talking like what?" Kaye asked, heading toward the man.

"Euskara."

"I'm sorry. Say that again."

"Euskara," the old man repeated with a touch of annoyance.

Kaye sat down on the edge of the chair next to the man.

"I'm sorry, I still didn't understand. Start at the beginning. I'm Ben. You are....?"

"I am Javier Itzal Aguirre," the old man said, his voice dignified as he held out his gnarled, bony hand to Kaye. "Everyone calls me Itzy."

Kaye guessed the old timer had to be at least ninety and gently took the offered hand. "My pleasure, Itzy. How are you today?"

"About the same as yesterday, Mr. Ben, and about the same as the day before that, the day the Euskalduna were here."

"Please forgive me, but I don't understand. What exactly is Euskara and what are Euskalduna?"

While he waited for Itzy, who was busy adding to the contents of the can, to answer, Kaye twisted the top off the drink he'd bought and opened the candy bar. He'd skipped lunch and was famished.

"Euskara," Itzy said wistfully, "is my native language, which I learned as a child."

"Start from the beginning, Itzy. Tell me about the two men you saw."

Itzy looked at Ben closely and then shifted his gaze to the distant hills.

"Are you a sheep man, Mr. Ben with the Harley-Davidson motorcycle?"

Kaye assumed the old man was asking if he was a sheep rancher. "No, I'm not."

"Too bad. With those hands you would have been a great sheep man, a champion shearer. Too bad." He sighed deeply.

"Tell me about the two men, Itzy."

"My father was a great sheep man, Mr. Ben. Maybe the greatest in Euskal Herria. But when he knew the Carlists would win and the Republic was lost, he brought us all to America, to Idaho. I was a young boy then, Mr. Ben, and there were many, many sheep in Idaho."

The old man's eyes drifted off into memories of the past before he spoke again.

"Not like today, Mr. Ben. Not like today."

"The two men," Kaye prompted him again.

"I'm coming to them, Mr. Ben. Drink your drink and eat your candy bar. In the time you would spend sitting here by yourself doing that, I will tell you about the Euskalduna."

Kaye smiled. "Okay, I'm listening."

"Thank you," Itzy said matter-of-factly before continuing. "I, too, was a great sheep man. I tended large herds of the finest sheep and my dogs – ah, my dogs, they were the champions of the West. They could climb any hill, keep the wolves and coyotes from the herds and find a single lost lamb in a thousand acres of tall grass."

Itzy paused to spit into his can.

"But for twenty years I haven't been able to keep up with the dogs. It's a young man's world now, Mr. Ben, and most of the sheep have gone to New Zealand and Australia and Texas.

"So each day I come to Miss Maggie's store. In the winter I sit inside by the stove where it's warm. In the summer, when it's hot like now, I sit in the shade. Each day, Miss Maggie allows me one can of beer, and each week one pouch of tobacco."

Itzy spit into the can again.

"I was sitting here in the shade when the two men in the silver car with the flat tire came in and parked over there." He waved his hand toward the same spot Caleb had pointed out. "They were not happy, Mr. Ben, and argued about fixing the tire. They should have let George help them.

"I watched them. Just about the time they were finished, Manuel came out of the store."

"Who's Manuel?" asked Kaye.

"Manuel is a sheep man," Itzy said patiently. "Please try to keep up, Mr. Ben. We were talking about sheep men and the Euskalduna, were we not?"

Kaye hid his grin by taking a bite of the candy bar and following it with a swig of his drink.

"As I was saying," Itzy continued, "Manuel came out of the store with a load of provisions. His dogs, of course, cannot go into Miss Maggie's store with him. When Manuel came out, he saw that one of his dogs had jumped out of the truck and gone over to investigate another dog near the gas pumps."

He spit into the can again and then looked at Kaye with a little smile.

"My dogs would never have wandered from where I told them to stay. Unless, of course, the other dog was a bitch in heat. Then, well, maybe." His old eyes crinkled.

"When Manuel saw his dog had wandered off, he called the dog back. And, as all true sheep men do, he taught his dogs to obey commands in Euskara. One of the two men from the car with the flat tire, I believe it was the younger one, but I am not sure, heard

Manuel and called out to him. In Euskara." Itzy nodded sagely and looked at Kaye.

"Then what, Itzy?"

"The other man became very angry. Manuel was as surprised as me to hear the first man speak in Euskara, so he walked over and talked to the first man for a minute. I heard them converse politely and then Manuel left. The other man was very angry at the first man, but I don't know why."

"Itzy, where can I find Manuel?"

Itzy shrugged his bony shoulders and waved at the mountains to the west. "Where the grass is high and there are no wolves or coyotes."

"I'm still confused here. You keep saying 'Euskara', but I don't recognize the word. What does it mean?"

Javier Itzal Aguirre slowly set his spit can down and put his hands over his heart. Kaye could see the pride well up in the old man's eyes.

"Euskara is the oldest spoken language on earth. It is the language of The People, unconquered warriors and vanquishers of the Romans, the Moors and the Gauls. To the rest of the world, we are the Basque."

"Basque?" Kaye asked. "You mean Spanish?"

"Please, Mr. Ben, do not insult me. Spanish, indeed." He snorted in derision and looked away from Kaye.

"I did not mean to insult you, Itzy. Forgive my ignorance."

Itzy shifted in his chair and cast a sideways glance at Kaye as he retrieved his spit can. For a moment Kaye thought the old man would remain silent, but Itzy spoke again.

"Euskal Herria, The Country, lies in what is now Spain and France, straddling the Pyrenees." Itzy's voice was patient. His eyes looked westward, looking beyond Idaho's mountains to the rocky, mountainous countryside of his homeland. "My people, the Basque, have lived there for as long as man has walked the earth. Long, long before there was a Spain or a France, Mr. Ben. We may roam, but we are always Basque, and all true Basque children are raised to speak the mother tongue. Euskara, Mr. Ben. The two men in the silver car with the flat tire were Basque. Of that, I am certain. Did they come here from Euskal Herria? That I cannot know, but there is no doubt that if they did not, their ancestors did."

Itzy lapsed into silence and raised the can to his lips yet again. Kaye sensed the old man was done talking.

"Thank you, Itzy. I understand."

"*Arratsalde on*, Mr. Ben with the Harley-Davidson motorcycle." Good evening.

Itzy was right. In the time it had taken him to tell the story, Kaye had finished his drink and candy bar.

As he walked to the Road King, Kaye mulled over what he had learned. If the two men were foreign nationals it put a new, darker spin on things. If the dosimeter turned out to be connected, well, he tried not to dwell on that possibility. But it was definitely time to make some calls.

Kaye fired up the big bike, looked toward the porch and saw Itzy's chin tilt up in acknowledgement as a smile flitted across his wrinkled countenance. The old man had been right about something else, too. Once that sound gets in your blood, it never goes away.

12

The thirty minute ride along the banks of the Payette through Black Canyon was one of the best Kaye could remember. *This is what Mulholland or Topanga Canyon must have been like once,* he mused. *Maybe a hundred years ago.*

It was too late to send an overnight package to Los Angeles, but with the time difference he might still be able to reach his contact there. But it wasn't a conversation he wanted to have on a cell phone. Too many ears out there these days.

He decided to overnight in Emmett and found a nice local motel not far off the main drag.

The big Harley fit nicely on the sidewalk outside the room's door. There was no reason to be coy now that he knew he was being watched. He mentally kicked himself for not catching on sooner to the yellow four-by-four SUV. He'd like to turn the tables, and vowed next time would be different.

His first call was to Halberstam, but again the call went straight to voice mail. Kaye left a message asking the Captain to check the spare on the impounded Toyota to see if it was flat and asked for a return call with the information. Before he got too focused on Itzy's assertion the two suspects were Basque, he thought he should confirm it was the right car.

Next, he punched the long distance access code followed by a Los Angeles number. He knew the number was answered twenty-four-seven and hoped the man he wanted was still at his desk.

The phone was answered on the second ring.

"Department of Homeland Security." The voice always reminded Kaye of the late night, female FM deejays of his youth; low, sultry and strangely sexy.

"May I speak with Khalid, please?"

"We have several people here by that name, sir. Do you happen to have a last name?"

"Bergman. Khalid Bergman." The name always struck him as an odd combination and he wondered if it was genuine or just a cover. He'd never met the man, only heard the voice.

"May I tell Mr. Bergman who's calling." It wasn't a request

"Ben Kaye."

"One moment, please."

While he waited, Kaye knew the operator was checking his credentials before connecting him.

"Detective Kaye," Khalid's voice came onto the line. "To what do I owe the pleasure?"

The voice was, in every way Kaye had ever tried to dissect it, absolutely average, with a moderate tone range and no discernible accent or regional idiom. It was as though a computer had constructed the voice to make it forgettable and unidentifiable.

"I'm on vacation in Idaho and I got sucked into something. Wrong place, wrong time kind of thing."

"I'm hearing your vacation might be permanent."

"I haven't heard from the Department, and I haven't made a decision yet. But that's not why I called. I ran into something you need to know about."

"Go ahead," Khalid said reluctantly.

Kaye ran through the events of the shooting.

"What makes this Homeland Security's problem? Sounds like a matter for the local police."

"That was my first take, too. But this afternoon I uncovered information I think might interest you. I need your help."

"What's your information?"

"First, I have a witness, whom I consider reliable, that overheard the two suspects – one of whom is now deceased – speaking a foreign language."

"Could he identify the language?"

Kaye decided he would test the Homeland Security officer. "Euskara."

There was a short silence before Khalid responded. "Idaho has a large Basque population. It used to be the largest sheep and wool production center in the world. The Basque are world-class sheep ranchers."

"So I found out today. But these two sheepherders were driving a stolen car, heavy crate in the trunk, headed south not too far from the Canadian border."

"Duly noted. Do you have anything else?"

"Yes, I do. A piece of physical evidence I recovered near the scene of the shootings."

"I recommend that you surrender it to the local police."

"I don't want to do that. I'd rather send it to you so your lab people could take a look at it."

"Why?"

Kaye took a deep breath before answering.

"It's a radiation dosimeter. One of those badges that measures cumulative exposure. I recovered it at the scene of the shooting. You're a smart guy. Connect the dots."

The silence on the other end of the line was telling. That got his attention, thought Kaye.

"How did you originate this call?"

"I'm on a land line."

"Excellent. Please hold."

The line clicked and Kaye waited. Almost three minutes passed before Khalid came back on the line.

"Still there, detective?"

"Yep."

"Good. Thank you for waiting. Where are you now?"

"Emmett, Idaho. Not far from Boise."

"Okay, please listen carefully. The Boise airport, Gowen Field, is also a National Guard airbase. Tomorrow morning at zero nine hundred there will be a Mister Jones waiting for you at the front gate. Please take the item you found to him. Do you understand?"

Kaye was dumbfounded.

"I understand the instructions, but I don't understand why. I was going to FedEx it to you. You think a plane is necessary?"

"I absolutely hope not." Khalid's reply was the most sincere thing Kaye had ever heard the man say.

"Okay, then I'll be there. One more thing?"

"What's that?"

"Would you run a plate for me?"

"Go ahead."

Kaye gave the DHS officer the license number from the yellow SUV.

"That plate is registered on a current model year Jeep Liberty four-by-four, yellow and black," Khalid read back. "Registered owner is Biscay Basin Group, LLC, post office box in Boise."

"Thank you."

"You're welcome. Please be on time tomorrow morning."

Before he could answer, the phone went dead in Kaye's hand.

"Same to you, amigo," he muttered at the handset.

13

In Los Angeles, Agent Donald Straithwaite leaned back in his chair and slowly pulled off his headset.

He'd worked with Kaye before. In fact, the Bergman alias was a contact name reserved exclusively for the LAPD detective.

Straithwaite was also privy to Kaye's LAPD personnel file and USMC service records.

It was the service record that had originally pointed Straithwaite to Kaye. Now in his early thirties, the DHS agent had also served in the Corps before being recruited away by DHS. The money was not only a lot better, he'd been swayed by the pitch that America's largest security threats were no longer foreign, but domestic, and DHS was now the front line.

His first case working with Kaye had involved a burglary that had turned into a national economic security issue. After the case he'd been instructed to develop Kaye as a DHS asset. Straithwaite quickly learned that Kaye was a very talented investigator, solving the most complex and politically charged cases thrown at him. As a consequence, Straithwaite had learned to trust Kaye's investigative instincts.

The call he'd just taken had seriously jangled his nerves.

He punched the intercom button.

"Becky," he said when the operator answered, "Don Straithwaite. Show me off-line for today."

"Will do."

"Oh, hey," he added, wanting it to sound like an afterthought. "Is the skipper still aboard?"

"Still in his office."

He had to go up one floor to the Regional Director's office.

The desk in the reception area was unmanned, so Straithwaite went to the inner office door and knocked.

"Enter," a strong, clear voice called out.

The office was spacious, with two large windows overlooking the Los Angeles skyline. Several impressive pieces of art and an array of awards and photographs of the office's occupant with noted world leaders decorated the space.

Behind the polished walnut desk General Carl Holdorf, Western Regional Director of Homeland Security, finished signing some papers and slid them into a file folder.

Holdorf was a big man, tall and ramrod straight. A retired four-star, Holdorf had taken his current job in response to a direct request from the President.

The General looked up, acknowledging Straithwaite's presence.

"You're here late, Don. Sit, please. What can I do for you?"

"You're still here, too, General," Straithwaite pointed out with a smile as he sat down. Everybody in the office respected Holdorf, who worked at least as hard as they did.

"So I am," Holdorf said ruefully, dropping his pen and leaning back in his chair. "Who'd have thought there'd be all this paper?" He smiled. "So, what's up?"

"I just got a very strange call from one of my – our – assets, an LAPD detective."

"Continue."

Straithwaite summarized Kaye's call and the events of the last two days. He was careful to include only the facts as he knew them, knowing the General preferred to draw his own conclusions. He waited until the end to divulge the existence of the probable dosimeter card and was careful to stress that there was not yet a firm link between the card and the two men in the car.

"But, General," he concluded, deciding to stick his neck out, "I don't think we can afford to discount a possible connection. The ramifications are too dire."

Holdorf had listened carefully and patiently to Straithwaite's summary. He'd shown far less interest or concern than Straithwaite had expected, especially with the possible presence of radioactive material.

"We need that dosimeter, General, if that's what it is, and I trust Kaye's conclusion."

"Yes, of course," Holdorf finally said, rousing himself from his thoughts. "Make arrangements to retrieve it immediately."

"Already done, sir. I'm going myself, early tomorrow in Gulf Two, to meet Kaye and pick it up. We can do preliminary analysis in the lab on the plane."

"Has he ever met you?" The General's tone was concerned.

"No, sir. To him, I'm Khalid Bergman, a voice on the phone."

"Let's keep it that way."

"Absolutely, sir. Tomorrow I am the one and only, inimitable Mr. Jones." Straithwaite smiled. "Of course, Kaye is way too smart to buy it, but also way too smart to ask questions."

***

Holdorf waited five minutes after Straithwaite left before unlocking the bottom desk drawer and removing a satellite phone. Specially modified, it used complex encryption algorithms to scramble the signal, and its GPS feature was disabled. The signal routed through communications and surveillance satellites dedicated to DHS, whose orbits provided total global coverage at all times.

The General hit a pre-programmed button and waited patiently.

"Carl, how the hell are you?" a booming voice asked.

"Fine, Mr. Vice President. Thank you." Holdorf paused for a moment. "Sir, we have a probable hit on Bilbao."

The Vice President's voice immediately turned serious. "Where?"

"Boise, Idaho."

"Boise? Holy shit, Carl, that's not a port of entry. How'd they get in?"

"Unknown at this point, sir. We do know that one suspect, identity unknown, is dead. One is still at large."

"Do we know which one is dead?"

"No sir, not for sure. The physical description would fit the Basque, but so does the description of the one that escaped."

"Shit," muttered the Vice President. "You're sure?"

"Of the descriptions? Yes sir. And, as I'm sure you've already figured out, that means we probably have additional players."

There was an extended silence. Holdorf could barely detect the sound of the Vice President breathing. Finally, the V.P. spoke.

"Carl, this is very important. My ass, and need I remind you yours, are hanging out a mile here. Do not let this operation get out of hand."

"I'll have the team en route immediately."

"Okay, okay. Carl, we need to know who is where. If this doesn't work, we'll both go to the gallows. And you'll be first. Understand?"

"I understand, sir. I'll keep you informed."

Holdorf secured the satellite phone back in his desk drawer, then picked up the desk phone handset and quickly punched in a number.

"Rhoades," a voice answered on the second ring.

"Mr. Rhoades," Holdorf said without identifying himself, knowing the man would recognize his voice.

"Sir?"

"Assemble your team, please, as soon as possible."

"Destination, sir?"

"Boise, Idaho."

"Authorization, sir?"

"Bilbao," Holdorf said slowly. "We don't have an absolute indicator yet, but I need your team up there, just in case."

"I understand, General," Rhoades affirmed.

"Good man. Don Straithwaite is flying up in the morning on Gulf Two. Your team can hitch a ride with him, but this is to remain strictly classified. Understood?"

"I read you loud and clear, General."

"Excellent. Check in with me when you arrive. You may have to cool your heels for a couple days, but if this develops, we'll be in the right place at the right time."

"Let's hope so, sir."

As he hung up the phone Holdorf wondered if this was, finally, what they'd been waiting for. He chuckled aloud at the timing. It was perfect.

14

Kaye found a local drive-in and satisfied his appetite. The one thing he didn't like about touring was that it played hell with his regular diet. Although he tried his best to avoid the national fast food chains, he ended up eating way too much junk food. From experience, he knew he could expect to gain about three pounds a week while he was on the road, which wasn't so bad; except that as he got older it got harder and harder to get rid of it after he got home. He often ended a trip feeling overweight and out of shape, a notion that evoked laughter from his friends. Even with fifteen pounds extra he still looked like a Frank Frazetta painting, but it pushed him to stay lean and fit.

When he returned to the motel he asked the clerk how long it would take him to get to the Boise airport and learned that he'd better give it at least ninety minutes. It would make for an early day, so he decided to call it a night.

As he thanked the clerk for the directions, his cell phone rang. He headed back outside to take the call.

"Kaye," he said into the phone.

"Kaye? Halberstam, ACSO. You called?"

"I did."

"Kind of a strange question about the spare tire. But I'll be damned if it wasn't flat. Wasn't in the inventory report, so I had to go to the impound lot to check, which is why I'm calling back so late. Now, enlighten me. What does a flat tire have to do with the price of tea in China?"

"Nothing, Captain, but it might have something to do with the price of wool in Spain."

"Come again?" Halberstam was clearly mystified.

Kaye gave the Captain a quick overview of what he'd turned up in Horseshoe Bend and how the flat tire went a long way in connecting the two Basque-speaking men to the car involved in the shooting.

Halberstam whistled softly. "Good catch. It'll take the state boys weeks to put that together, if they ever do."

"Pass it along. No secrets now."

"I'll try." Halberstam's voice betrayed his weariness. "But the state boys have a way of forgetting that the good Lord gave them two ears and one mouth for a reason. They tend to talk a lot more than they listen."

"Did you get anything off the hotel video?"

"Nothing worthwhile." Halberstam sighed and Kaye could almost see the Captain lean back in his chair. "We got a look at the guy, dressed like a repairman and carrying a toolbox, coming through the back door of the hotel about the right time. Cameras got him again getting off the elevator on the third floor, but there's no coverage of the hall outside the room. It had to be him, though."

"Could you see his face?"

"No. Had a hat on, and kept it pulled down real low, but he was built the same as the guy from the night before."

"Figures. He's too good to make that kind of mistake. One more question and I'll let you go."

"Shoot."

"You ever heard of a company named Biscay Basin Group? Supposed to be in Boise."

There was silence on the other end.

"Captain? Hello? You still there?"

"Yeah," Halberstam's cautious voice came back on. "I'm still here. How'd you come across Biscay Basin Group?"

"Actually, they came across me. Why? You know the name?"

"Hold on a minute."

Kaye heard Halberstam put the phone down and a moment later heard what sounded like a door closing.

"I'm back," Halberstam said, his voice much more subdued than before. "Hell, yes, I've heard of Biscay Basin Group. Any Idahoan with a pulse has heard of it."

"Tell me about it."

"Not really an it. More of a him. Biscay Basin Group is a privately held conglomerate owned by one Robert Urrestegui, probably the wealthiest and most connected man in the state since J.R. passed. Way up on the Forbes list every year. Real estate, construction, timber, livestock, mining; you name it and Urrestegui's got a finger in it."

"Is he legitimate?" asked Kaye, his curiosity aroused.

"Depends on who you ask."

"I'm asking you."

"I really don't know. Not for sure, anyway," qualified Halberstam. "On the surface, yeah, I'd say he's legit. His family has been here for a long time and they've been players almost forever. But you know the old saying 'what good is power if you can't abuse it', right? Plus, I guess I'm a natural born cynic. Nobody makes that kind of money by being nice and playing fair."

Kaye laughed. "Captain, I think it's a good thing you're about to retire. You've been looking at the dark side for too long."

"You laugh, smart guy. You've got the same view I do. Comes with the territory."

"Too true." Kaye got serious again. "So, is there anything about Urrestegui that sets off your alarms?"

"Not really. Mover and shaker politically, he and his wife are big on the charity circuit, stuff like that." There was a pause and then Halberstam continued. "You know, I do remember a few years back there was something about a suspicious fire that burned down a building on a piece of property Urrestegui was trying to buy, but the owner didn't want to sell. It was part of some big development Biscay Basin was pushing downtown. The owner died in the fire."

"And Urrestegui ended up with the property, right?"

"See, I told you. Cynic. But, yeah, he did. The victim's heirs were more than happy to sell to him after the fire."

"Anything come of it?"

"Not that I recall. City PD and fire did the investigation. I honestly don't even recall if there was even an official finding of arson. I do remember that there was never an arrest in connection with the fire. It just sort of dried up and went away."

"Imagine that. So, Urrestegui is no public sinner, but he's probably no saint, either?"

"I'd say that pretty much sums it up. Oh, and there's one other dot to connect here."

"What's that, Captain?"

"Urrestegui is a fairly uncommon name around these parts," he paused, then, "even for a Basque family."

"He's Basque?"

"Yes, sir. Born in this country, but as Basque as they come. But I'm sure it's just a coincidence and doesn't bear looking into, if you get my drift. You do get my drift, don't you?"

"I get your drift, and I'm sure you're right. Probably just a coincidence." Kaye wasn't convincing himself, so he had no doubt he wasn't convincing Halberstam. "Could I call you? I mean, if I happen to run into any more coincidences like that?"

"Absolutely. But call my cell number. I'll be out of town starting tomorrow for about ten days. Terrible timing, I know, but since this isn't my case anymore I'm not going to cancel. In fact, let me give you my personal cell number, just in case of any more, uh, coincidences. Got a pencil handy?"

The ACSO Captain gave Kaye his cell number.

"Must be nice. Taking a week's vacation a month before you retire."

"It's not a vacation. I'm going up to Sun Valley to help coordinate security for the Billionaire's Ball. Been doing it for years."

"The what?"

"Well, that's not what it's called officially. It's got some kind of fancy name that ends with 'conference'. Big shindig, though. Every summer, a couple hundred or so of the richest guys in the country get together with a bunch of government honchos and try to figure out where things are headed. They play a lot of golf, ride rafts and try to catch some fish. Even though the whole thing is very low key, security is a nightmare. There's so much money up there already that the whole thing doesn't impress the locals much, and most of the tourists don't notice anything but the zillion bucks worth of private jets parked at the airport."

"I've never even heard of it."

"Not unusual. All the big media owners are participants and they keep the lid on. The whole thing takes place in a virtual news blackout. All these powerful people just sort of disappear off the radar for a week or so and get together to talk things over."

"Geez, it sounds like a bad chapter from an Aldous Huxley book."

Halberstam chuckled. "You know, I always wondered about that myself, now that you mention it."

"Just out of curiosity, does Urrestegui go to this conference?"

"Yes," answered Halberstam, and Kaye could almost hear the Captain sorting and cataloging over the phone. "As an Idahoan he's an unofficial host. Has a house up there, too."

"So exactly what's your role in all this?"

"I help coordinate security for the sessions. I act as liaison between the various agencies. Unofficially, that is, just because I've been around so long. My actual job, if you want to call it that, is dignitary protection."

"Sounds like a nice gig."

"It was, until you spoiled it with your Huxley crack. All of a sudden I feel like a co-conspirator."

Kaye's mind was racing. Despite his detective's instincts, he rationally knew that sometimes coincidences were exactly that, and even Khalid had remarked how many Basques there were in Idaho.

It was still all too random and disjointed to make sense.

He shrugged it off. Clearly he didn't have all the pieces. But he would.

***

He had one more call to make.

He was about to hang up before a sleepy voice finally answered, "Hello."

"Hi. Sorry if I woke you."

"Hello, Benjamin," the voice perked up noticeably. "Sorry, I must've dropped off watching TV. How are you, son? Everything okay?"

Kaye smiled. Don't let anybody tell you there's no such thing as mother's intuition.

"Everything's fine, Mom. Just thought I'd call and say hello. I'm in Idaho. On vacation."

There was a slight pause. 'Vacation' had almost become a code word between them since Amy's death.

"You're in trouble again."

"No, Mom. I'm just on a ride."

"You sure?"

"I'm sure." He hesitated again. "But I'm not sure I'm going back. And thanks to Amy, I sure don't need the money."

"I understand. You know, son, it hasn't been very long. Give it time. I know you love her and you miss her. It'll never go away, but it will get better."

"How's Dad?" he asked, wanting to change the subject.

"About the same. Maybe a little worse. Alzheimer's doesn't get better, Ben."

Kaye knew. He'd watched for several years as his father, always robust, had slowly withered physically and retreated mentally. Looking back, everyone now understood that the first sign had been when he'd written the mortgage check for seven hundred thousand dollars instead of seven hundred and hadn't understood what he'd done wrong.

"How's he adjusting to the home?" he asked softly. He knew it had nearly killed his mother to put his father in the assisted living facility, but the last time he'd fallen she hadn't been able to pick him up. It took a call to the medics, so Kaye and his sister had insisted it was time for her to let somebody else help take care of their father.

"He doesn't know the difference, son. Most days he doesn't even know who I am."

"It's okay, Mom. You did the right thing." He tried to lighten the mood. "Does he still tell those gorilla jokes?"

"Oh, Ben, you know it like to have killed him when he figured out that those jokes hurt you. He was so proud of you, you know. Your strength and how well you did in school. He only teased you because he loved you." She hesitated, then added. "I put all your football trophies, your Marine ribbons, and that French medal in his room. Most of his lucid moments now are when he tells people about you. He might not recognize you when you come to visit, but he can still tell anybody who'll listen about you. You're his hero, Ben, whether you ever understood that or not."

There was awkward silence. Kaye's father had teased him almost as mercilessly as some of the kids at school. He understood now, but hadn't as a teenager. The taunts had eventually driven a wedge between them, leading to his leaving school to join the Corps.

"So," it was her turn to change the subject, "how do you like Idaho? Your father always wanted to go there. Ever since he saw that movie with Robert Mitchum and Marilyn Monroe. Something about a river, or some such."

"I remember. It's nice. Dad would've liked it. So, Mom, how are you?"

"Oh, I'm okay. When I'm not with your dad your sister keeps me busy. And she can use the help," her voice brightened. "Those twins are a handful, and, Ben, that boy is just like you when you were ten. He's going to be a handful!"

"I wasn't a handful. Was I?"

"Oh, yes, you were," she retorted, laughing.

"Gee, thanks, Mom."

"Just telling the truth." She laughed again. "So, exactly why did you call?"

"Just to say hello, I guess, and see how you're doing."

"I'm fine, son. Better than can be expected, I guess. You sure you're okay?" Always the mom.

"Finer than frog's hair."

They both laughed. It was an old joke between them from his 'handful' days.

"Okay, then. Sorry to cut this short, son, but I've got to be up early to go sit those kids for your sister before I take lunch to your dad. And, truth be told, I was sound asleep in front of the TV when you called."

"I know, Mom. Go to bed. I love you."

"I love you, too, Benjamin. Call me if you need anything."

"Will do. Tell Dad I love him."

"I will, son. He loves you, too. Good night."

"Good night, Mom."

15

ulf Two, one of several Department of Homeland Security Gulfstream G550 jets, sat inside a large hangar at one end of Los Angeles International Airport being prepped for its early morning flight to Boise. The ground crew was topping off the forty-one thousand pounds of fuel that fed the twin Rolls Royce BR710 engines, capable of pushing the sleek craft to fifty-one thousand feet at a cruising speed of 575 knots.

Most G550s were outfitted to carry between fourteen and eighteen passengers in luxury. Gulf Two, though, was a different breed. Her fifty-foot fuselage contained an impressive forensic laboratory. Instruments and computers filled the cabin from stem to stern, with only small work and seating spaces for technicians and passengers. The only nod to comfort was the communications center behind the soundproof glass partitions at the very rear of the cabin. Gulf Two's computer and communications capabilities were so extensive that she could function as an airborne command center should the need arise.

Only the large, heavy instruments used for the most esoteric kinds of testing and evaluation of evidence were missing.

The jet carried a pilot and co-pilot, with room aft for two forensics techs and up to four passengers, as long as they didn't mind cramped quarters.

***

At the same time, in a hangar-like building near Twin Falls, Idaho, a team of skilled technicians worked feverishly late into the night on the custom motor coach parked in the center of the building.

It was, in a word, exquisite, costing upwards of $1.5 million when new. The interior was fabulously appointed with marble floors, 18-carat gold bath fixtures and exotic hardwood cabinetry. Crystal light fixtures dazzled all who stepped aboard. The driver's position resembled what must face a space shuttle commander. All was titanium, polished walnut burl and the finest leather. Precious stones served as markers on the considerable array of gauges and sensors.

The massive, twin-turbocharged diesel mounted in the rear would push the dazzling monster down the highway all day at whatever speed the driver desired. If one had to inquire about fuel efficiency, one needed to look elsewhere for luxury transport.

It was simultaneously a masterpiece of opulence and engineering, which made the crew's job that much more difficult. Accomplished technicians all, they had struggled mightily with this job and were pleased to be almost done.

The coach had two main storage compartments, one on each side, intended to carry luggage, spares and whatever extraneous items the very rich choose to carry when they travel. The compartments were accessed from outside. The owner, however, was displeased with their capacity, ostensibly because one toy or another would not fit inside, and wanted their capacity increased. He also told Tom Whitworth, the owner of the company employing the technicians, that he wanted the interior reconfigured to add additional storage throughout. All this, of course, the coach's owner wanted done without compromising the visual appeal or functionality of the existing interior.

At first, Whitworth balked at taking the job. Premium coaches, he explained to the owner, are like expensive yachts on wheels. Everything was so co-dependent on everything else that what he was asking was practically impossible. It was like trying to give an eighty-foot yacht the same amenities as a one hundred-foot yacht. If that could be done, Whitworth told the owner, there would be no need for the larger size.

Whitworth politely suggested to the owner, Mr. Markunyian, a used-car mogul from New Jersey with a vacation home in Sun Valley, that he sell the coach and buy another, larger model, better configured to suit his requirements. It was the obvious solution, especially since money was clearly not a limitation, given what Markunyian had offered to pay him, in cash, for making the modifications.

But Markunyian was adamant. He wanted to keep this coach for sentimental reasons. Finally, when it seemed he wouldn't get Whitworth to tackle the job, he admitted with much embarrassment that he and his current wife, thirty years his junior, had had sex for the first time in the captain's chair. Apparently, she still loved to climb over and kneel between his knees to satisfy him during the long days on the highway. Cruise control was such a wonderful invention, was it not?

He told Whitworth that his wife had threatened to eliminate the sexual favors from their trips if he sold this particular coach, and her apparent talents had Markunyian determined not to sell, cost be damned.

Sympathetic and more than a bit envious, Whitworth agreed to take on the job. All he ever got from his wife of thirty-five years on their infrequent long drives was a litany of complaints.

When Whitworth called the original manufacturer, they had cited liability concerns and refused to provide plans and schematics, so he was on his own. Even though he was a wizard at what he did – word of mouth, after all, had brought him this job – Whitworth spent many long days and nights sweating over his design drawings trying to accommodate his client's wishes. This job would make his dream of retirement a reality, so he stuck to it with the tenacity of a pit bull.

He finally came up with the solutions, including ten cubic feet of storage above and beyond the requirement. This received Markunyian's grateful design approval and a significant deposit, and he began work in earnest.

The big concern was the deadline, which accounted for the late night hours. The Armenian had insisted the coach be completed by June first and the contract had included performance penalties for every day beyond that.

A month into the job Whitworth had concluded that Markunyian suffered from a severe case of obsessive-compulsive disorder. On the many occasions the man visited the shop to check on the job, always with a retinue of assistants, he had all but ignored what Whitworth had considered the aesthetic and engineering triumphs of the redesign, spending all his time measuring and re-measuring the reconfigured storage. An assistant took endless, copious notes.

Final delivery was scheduled for this weekend.

Though he'd missed the deadline by several days, Tom Whitworth didn't care. He just wanted to get paid and get this coach, and this client, out of his shop and out of his life forever.

One of the techs on the job, Randy, never wanted to see the client again, either. The guy had been rude to him on the very first inspection visit, all because Randy had made a stupid half-inch measurement error. Randy figured the guy was lucky it was only a measly half-inch. He'd been really hung over that day, and it could easily have been a damn half-foot.

Randy wasn't one to forgive and forget. As he frequently boasted to his drinking buddies down at Rowdies, he didn't get mad, he got even.

So, unbeknownst to Tom Whitworth or the other techs on the job, Randy had added several washers under the captain's chair mounting hardware, effectively reducing the clearance between the seat cushion and the varnished steering wheel. Now, Randy reasoned, the asshole's dumb slut wife was going to bump her head every time she tried to go down on the dude while he was driving.

Randy wished he could be there to watch the first time it happened, but had to console himself with the smug satisfaction that nobody, no matter how good they thought they were because they were rich, screwed with him and got away with it.

16

Kaye's natural alarm clock went off at the usual six o'clock. He rose and spent thirty minutes exercising, holding several difficult strength positions longer than usual to compensate for the road diet.

Meditation would have to wait. He needed to be at the Guard base by nine.

The day had dawned clear and crisp, but was warming quickly. Kaye had realized that the saving grace of Idaho's heat was the near total absence of humidity, and it cooled off nicely at night because of the altitude and dry air.

The black Harley waited for him in front of the motel. A quick pre-ride check confirmed all was well and the v-twin rumbled to life with the first flick of the starter switch. While he waited for the bike to warm up Kaye decided today would be a good day to fly the Big Boar colors. He knew it would mark him for anyone trying to follow him, and that was okay. If someone tried to tail him again, they would quickly discover they had hooked the wrong fish. Kaye had every intention of turning the tables at the next opportunity.

He had a place to start, and it was time to start shaking the trees and see what fell out.

It was nearly eight thirty when he took the exit for the airbase and swung southeast around the west end of the runway looking for the main gate. As the Harley rumbled down Gowen Road, Kaye saw two dark gray A-10 Warthog tank killers climb out above the hangar tops and bank easily into a southwest turn.

If nothing else, they confirmed he was in the right place.

Kaye rolled past the main gate on the first pass. He'd been early on purpose. The Warthogs told him that incoming traffic would approach from the east, so he continued in that direction until he guessed his position was approximately even with the touchdown area of the main runway and he had a good view of the approach pattern. He swung the Road King onto the shoulder, made sure the ground was solid under the kickstand, shut down the bike, took off the new helmet and waited. It was only about two minutes back to the main gate from where he sat and he'd wait until closer to nine to get there.

It wasn't his intention to just sit and waste time, watching the frequent incoming commercial flights or the A-10 pilots logging hours with touch-and-goes. Kaye wanted to identify the DHS aircraft when it came in, because after he handed the plastic dosimeter card over to the surely fictitious 'Mr. Jones', he planned to move to the other end of the runway and wait an hour or so to see if the aircraft stayed on the ground or departed immediately. If it departed he wanted to get some indication of its departure heading.

Of course, the DHS plane could already be on the ground. It was only two hours by jet from L.A. to Boise and it had been last evening when he'd spoken to Khalid. But on the way down Gowen Road he'd kept a sharp eye on the south apron, most of which was visible between the hangars at one time or another. He'd spotted a couple of C-130 Hercules and the rest of the A-10 squadron. There had also been a quartet of F-15s and two C-17s with regular Air Force markings, but Kaye discounted those as likely visitors from nearby Mountain Home AFB. He felt certain he was looking for a corporate class jet, possibly unmarked, but more than likely with the DHS logo somewhere.

His hunch and patience paid off at eight forty-five. A dazzling white aircraft had entered the traffic pattern and was now on final approach some two miles out. The gear came down and Kaye watched as the sleek jet's pilot skillfully rotated the plane into landing attitude as it crossed the outer boundary of the airport. He identified it as a Gulfstream, but couldn't peg the exact model. Before the plane disappeared behind a hangar, Kaye made out red and blue stripes running the length of the fuselage before flaring onto the vertical stabilizer to surround the DHS seal. He heard the plane's tires squeal in protest as they touched the runway.

It was a quick blast back down to the gate. Not wanting to raise a ruckus, Kaye swung the Road King into a parking area outside the gate, shut down, hung his helmet on the grip and waited.

The two A.P. officers manning the gate shack duly noted his presence, but seemed otherwise unconcerned. Why should they be? Kaye thought. He had zero chance of running the gate, with its concrete bollards and heavy steel anti-tank traps.

At precisely nine o'clock, Kaye saw a camouflage-painted Humvee swing around the end of the closest hangar. He extracted the plastic bag containing the dosimeter from his saddlebag and sauntered toward the gate.

As he approached, one of the guards, right hand on the butt of his holstered pistol and his eyes on the bag in Kaye's hand, advanced and challenged him.

"Halt, sir," the guard ordered with authority, extending his left hand, palm out, toward Kaye. "State your business."

Kaye saw chevrons on the man's tunic. "I think that's for me, Sergeant," he replied, tilting his head up and shifting his gaze beyond the guard to the Humvee.

"Remain where you are and I'll check."

The second guard now stood just outside the guard shack, M-4 at port arms.

As the guard headed for the Humvee, the vehicle's passenger door opened and a man stepped out. Just under six feet and fit-looking, he wore a polo shirt, chinos and dress shoes. As he climbed out he donned a pair of dark wraparound sunglasses, the lenses contrasting with his sandy hair and deepwater sailor's tan.

Beach bum, Kaye thought as the two walked toward each other.

"Detective Kaye," the man said in greeting, offering his hand.

"That'd be me." Kaye confirmed and shook the man's hand. "You must be Mr. Jones."

"That I would. You have something for me?"

"Yep," Kaye nodded slightly and held out the plastic bag, which Jones took and examined skeptically.

"Rather unorthodox evidence collection technique," Jones said as he opened the bag. Then he extracted the mated cups and pulled them apart.

Kaye thought he saw the DHS agent, whose name was surely not Jones, blanch beneath the dark tan when he saw the small plastic rectangle.

"Adapt and improvise, Mr. Jones. It's what I had available at the time. Besides, I don't think chain of custody will be an issue."

"True," Jones said, a slight hint of annoyance crossing his face. He carefully put the cups back together and returned them to the plastic bag.

"So, what now?" asked Kaye.

"I have no idea," Jones replied. "I was sent to meet you and retrieve this item" he brandished the bag "with orders to notify the Los Angeles office when it was in my possession."

"Great." Kaye wasn't about to leave it at that, and the sarcasm was plain in his tone. "When you talk to L.A., tell Khalid Bergman I want to know what you get off that card. Someone has tried to kill me twice this week, and if that card is connected, I want to know. Comprende?"

"I can only promise that I will communicate your interest to my superiors."

"Then that's all I can ask," Kaye said, staring into the dark sunglasses. His look communicated much more than his words.

It was the first time Don Straithwaite had met Kaye up close and personal, and he had no doubt the big man's reputation was well deserved.

"Someone will call you. I give you my word."

"Will you give me your name? So I have a reference point later, if I need it?"

"Jones. That's all you need to know. Now, if you will excuse me." The DHS agent turned, walked back to the waiting Humvee and climbed in.

The ungainly looking vehicle whipped a quick u-turn and disappeared around the corner of the hangar, gaining speed as it went.

Kaye watched it go and listened closely. The time he estimated it would take the Humvee to reach the parked Gulfstream passed without the telltale sound of the twin turbofans winding up to taxi speed. The pilot was in no hurry to leave.

It was a short ride to the west end of the runway and a good spot to park the Harley. He settled in to watch and wait.

A shaken Don Straithwaite climbed the steps and boarded Gulf Two. Until Kaye had handed him the bag and he'd looked inside, he'd had his doubts about Kaye's version of events. The whole thing had sounded like a bad case of road rage to him. The bomb that had killed the hotel employee may, or may not, be related.

Kaye's discovery of the dosimeter had gotten his attention. He knew the former LAPD cop was smart and shrewd, and he'd had to take Kaye at his word. Still, until he'd seen the dosimeter himself, he'd held out hope that it might have been something else altogether.

But it wasn't. Now, the question was origin. It would be up to the techs and the equipment aboard Gulf Two to provide the answer.

Straithwaite had at least told Kaye the truth about his priorities. His first task was to contact the General and let his superior know he had the item in his possession.

As he entered Gulf Two's cabin he saw Dennis Rhoades and his team members gathering their gear. When the three had shown up at LAX that morning to hitch a ride, Straithwaite was at first nonplussed, thinking the logistics of the operation had been taken out of his hands. He and Rhoades had worked together before, though, and when Rhoades told him that General Holdorf had cleared them to ride along all Straithwaite could do was smile and welcome them aboard.

He took the bag and its contents directly to the secure, glass-enclosed communications station at the aft end of Gulf Two's cabin. Once seated, he picked up the phone and punched a single button. The elaborate communications system took over from there, and it was several seconds before he heard the intermittent buzz telling him a link had been established and was waiting for a session host on the other end.

It was nearly fifteen seconds before Straithwaite heard the voice come on.

"Holdorf."

"General, Don Straithwaite here."

"So, what have we got? Is it what your man thought it was?"

Straithwaite detected an uncharacteristic note of anxiety in the General's voice. Was the Old Man genuinely worried?

"Yes, sir, unfortunately it is. I don't have an analysis for you yet, but should shortly."

"Damn. Let's hope for the best."

"Yes sir. I'll let you know the instant the techs have something and check in with you as soon as I get back."

There was a moment of silence before the General spoke again.

"Sorry, Don, but I have to change your plans. I need you and Gulf Two to proceed to Friedman Field in Hailey and stand by there for further instructions."

"Do you want Rhoades and his team to continue on to Hailey as well, sir?"

"Rhoades? Oh, shit, I forgot all about giving them the okay to piggy back your flight. No, Dennis and his team will stick to their original plan and remain in Boise. They're on something else, but I thought we might try to save the taxpayers a few bucks in plane tickets. Gotta watch that budget, you know." Holdorf laughed easily.

"Right, sir."

"You're not discussing this in front of him and his team, are you?"

"No sir!" Straithwaite said quickly. "I'm in the booth."

"Good man. They are not – repeat, not – briefed on your operation. You report to me and only me. Understood?"

"Yes, sir. I'll let you know as soon as I have something."

As General Holdorf hung up the phone, he looked at the man sitting across the desk. "We have the item."

"Excellent, Carl. Nice work," the man answered with a tight smile. "If it proves out it will be an unusual stroke of luck, given the unforeseen events of the last few days."

Holdorf leaned back in his chair and clasped his hands together before raising them and tenting his index fingers in front of his pursed lips. This could still work, he realized.

"Luck has nothing to do with it, Harry."

"I hope you're right, Carl," Senator Harrison Chapman, R-ID said pointedly. "When this was first floated to certain ranking members of the committee, I'll admit I was skeptical, but I trusted you to put it together. That things have worked out the way they have was beyond our wildest hopes. It's a huge risk, still, but the Vice President's ambitions are well known, and we share the same goals. Don't let us down. There is too much at stake."

***

Straithwaite hung up the phone and exited the booth.

Rhoades greeted him. "Thanks for the lift. We appreciate it."

"No problem. It's not like I'm buying the fuel."

"You headed back?"

"We're taking off right away." Straithwaite replied, leaving out the destination.

Rhoades gave him a knowing look and said, "Have a smooth flight." Then, to his team members, "Saddle up. We're out of here."

The team left Gulf Two and went to locate the car Rhoades had arranged. Straithwaite waited until the three went out of sight around the corner of the hangar before pulling up the steps and closing the door.

Next stop was the flight deck, where he informed the pilot of the General's orders. The pilot just nodded. He was accustomed to sudden changes and was on the radio with air traffic control informing them of his flight plan change by the time Straithwaite closed the cabin door.

Hal and Kevin, the two forensic techs assigned to Gulf Two, had busied themselves playing Texas Hold 'Em while their passenger completed his ground business.

"Time to go to work, gentlemen," Straithwaite said to them as he passed. The plane lurched slightly and began to taxi.

The two followed him to a counter and took up positions on either side as Straithwaite opened the plastic bag and extracted the Styrofoam cups.

"Oh, God," muttered Hal.

"I know, I know," Straithwaite chuckled. "It's what he had to work with. At least he did it right."

Using a pair of long-handled surgical tweezers, Straithwaite carefully reached into the cup and extracted the plastic card, holding it up for the techs to see.

Both instantly recognized what it was and exchanged nervous looks.

"Guys," Straithwaite said soberly, "I need to know anything and everything you can possibly tell me about this item. It is, obviously, a cumulative radiation dosage exposure badge. It was recovered outdoors and we have no idea how long it had been there.

"I need to know where this came from, who manufactured it and when, who has handled it, how long it has been outside in the sun and any exposure data you can recover. And," Straithwaite paused and looked back and forth at the techs. "I'd like to know all of that as quickly as possible. Yesterday would be fine. Have I made myself clear?"

"Yes, sir", Kevin responded, looking at Hal nervously.

"In the cabin, seats please," the pilots voice came over the intercom. "We've been cleared for take-off."

The men took their seats and strapped in. Gulf Two's engines wound to take-off power and the sleek jet sped down the runway, lifting into the morning sky.

Two minutes later, Hal and Kevin attacked the dosimeter, determined to pry every possible iota of information from the innocuous looking piece of plastic.

Straithwaite put on his iPod earphones, cranked up Tony Bennett and settled back to enjoy the short hop to Hailey.

***

Kaye watched departing traffic from his vantage point near the west end of the runway. The straining engines of outbound traffic could be heard before he could actually see the aircraft, which made it easy to narrow the possibilities.

About thirty minutes after leaving the gate he heard the higher-pitched whine of a mid-sized jet streaking down the runway and saw the DHS Gulfstream lift off well before the typical commercial jet take-off point. The pilot put the gear up as soon as it left the ground and almost immediately the plane swung into a shallow banking turn to the southwest.

Los Angeles would be south by southwest, Kaye reasoned. He watched intently as the Gulfstream continued to climb out and bank before settling onto a due east heading.

Most of the country was east of where he sat, and he knew there was restricted airspace southeast of Boise over Mountain Home AFB, so Kaye concluded the jet could be headed almost anywhere. But one thing was clear. It wasn't returning directly to Los Angeles.

Kaye began the start-up ritual for the Harley, then noticed a dark blue Ford Crown Victoria pull from the main gate and head his way. When it passed, he saw the three occupants stare at him briefly before resuming their conversation. The car and its occupants screamed 'feds' and he had to assume they had arrived on the DHS jet.

"Son of a gun," Kaye muttered to himself. "Somebody's interested."

Kaye considered following the car, but decided against it. They'd probably just go to the local field office and check in, so what would be the point? He also had to admit that their arrival could have absolutely nothing to do with his case.

There were two things on the day's agenda and he decided to stick with the plan.

He fired up the big Harley and headed for town.

17

It took Kaye longer than expected to locate the address. Confusing one-way streets, multiple 'must turn' lanes and construction closures had him going in the wrong direction several times before he finally determined which block he wanted and how to get to it.

The building was only a few blocks from the State Capitol. A restored, ornate brick structure in the middle of the block, its five stories were now dwarfed by the bank tower that anchored the block on the west end.

On the first pass Kaye thought he had the wrong address. The first floor of the building was a restaurant, the front glass panels of which were opened completely, allowing patrons to choose between tables inside or out.

Kaye circled the block and slowed on his second pass. On the east end of the building, facing an alley that appeared to lead to parking, he saw a small, arched opening. There was no way to see inside the alcove from the street, so he turned in.

He slowed as he crossed the sidewalk, relieved to see that the alley went all the way through to the street beyond. He also saw convex polished metal disks mounted on the buildings flanking the alley, allowing pedestrians on the sidewalk and cars exiting the alley to see each other in advance. The alley was narrow and the closeness of the walls echoed the low rumble of the Harley's exhaust.

The arched opening was clearly another building entrance. At the back of the opening, about ten feet from the alley, a double set of glass doors opened into a small interior vestibule, and to the right Kaye could just glimpse the bottom of a flight of stairs.

Far more than the layout, though, the simple gold leaf lettering on the doors caught Kaye's interest.

Biscay Basin Group, LLC.

A horn sounded behind him and Kaye slipped the bike's clutch and rolled ahead into the parking lot. It wasn't large, and signs made it clear the spaces were reserved for patron parking. There was also a ramp that went down to gated underground parking beneath the building. He continued on through the alley and returned to the street on the next block.

Heading back around, he backed the black Road King into the first available on-street spot he found. Though he knew most people couldn't tell one motorcycle from another, he didn't want the bike visible from the sidewalk in front of the Biscay Basin building.

Kaye took off the Big Boar vest and locked it in a saddlebag. He felt the comforting pressure of the Kimber in the boot holster as he walked around the corner.

He scanned the cars on the street as he strolled casually toward the restaurant. No yellow Jeep. He hadn't seen one in the back lot, either, but it could well be parked in the underground garage. Plus, from Halberstam's description Kaye figured Biscay Basin Group probably owned dozens of vehicles.

Kaye decided to sit and watch for a while and stepped through the opening in the wrought iron fence surrounding the restaurant's sidewalk tables. Within seconds he caught the attention of one of the servers.

"Sit wherever you like," she half-shouted to him from where she helped a group at an inside table. "You want a menu?"

"Please. And an iced tea, thanks," Kaye replied. He looked around. The restaurant was on the sunny side of the street and the morning had turned warm. Luckily, several of the tables featured large umbrellas, and a nice row of street trees provided some shade. Kaye walked around casually until he found a table that afforded good views of the street and the mirror mounted above the alley. It gave him a clear view of anyone approaching the east side entry.

The waitress materialized and placed a menu and a glass of tea on the table.

Kaye turned his attention to the entrance to the Biscay Basin building. Vehicle traffic was light, but pedestrian traffic was picking up.

Kaye sipped his tea, taking his time and keeping his eye on the door to Biscay Basin Group.

Twenty minutes, an omelet and a second glass of tea later he saw a yellow SUV about a block away, headed down the street in his direction. The vehicle moved to the far right lane and signaled, turning into the alley headed for the parking lot. The driver was alone in the little Jeep, and Kaye recognized him as the same man he'd seen in the passenger's seat yesterday.

A minute later he saw the reflection as the man, who was quite tall, walked into the Biscay Basin Group entry.

Okay, he told himself, time to shake the first tree and see how many monkeys complain.

Kaye dropped a twenty on the table and headed around the east end of the building. As he passed beneath the arch a quick check confirmed the ever-present surveillance camera. He pushed the glass doors open and stepped inside. The walls were bare, with no building directory.

The stairs went up to a landing and turned out of view. Kaye would have preferred the stairs, but without knowing which floor he wanted he opted for the elevator. The last thing he wanted to do was tug open a door that might be alarmed as an emergency exit or, even worse, discover all the access doors were locked from the stairwell side.

He stepped into the elevator and found a rudimentary description for each floor posted next to the buttons. The fourth floor was labeled 'Executive and Conference' and he decided to start there.

The elevator went straight to the fourth floor without stopping. Kaye stepped out and found himself in a large, well-appointed lobby that reminded him of an English country estate. The floors were polished oak under heavy Persian rugs. The walls were paneled and covered with large landscape paintings, most of which depicted herds of sheep and cattle being driven through mountainous terrain. Luxurious leather furniture was tastefully arranged throughout the space and several large bronzes of what Kaye concluded were native Idaho big game species accented the décor. On one wall, between two paintings, hung the head of a huge bull elk, its giant antlers almost touching the high ceiling. Kaye was no hunter, but it impressed him nonetheless. Three closed doors were visible.

The overall impression was of carefully understated wealth. Had it not been for the well-dressed young woman sitting behind the desk angled in the far corner to his right, Kaye wouldn't have believed he was in an office building. Even an L.A. lawyer would have been impressed.

The receptionist watched Kaye step from the elevator and greeted him with a cautious smile. She noted the flashing red light above the elevator door and her left hand slid casually under the desk to push the concealed security alert button.

Kaye headed across the lobby and stopped in front of the desk, smiling easily.

"Good morning. I'd like to see Mr. Urrestegui, please."

"Do you have an appointment? Mister ..." she left the question hanging, waiting for him to fill in the blank.

"Kaye. Ben Kaye. I do not have an appointment, but if you'd tell your boss I'm here I believe he'll make time to see me." His smile never wavered.

"Are you a business associate?" Her eyebrow cocked skeptically.

"No, I'm a detective with the LAPD."

"Do you have some identification?"

Kaye had had enough of this. "Are you his mother?" His voice took on a hard tone. "Call your boss and tell him I'm here. If he doesn't want to speak to me, that's fine, but tell him my next stop is the Sheriff's Office."

The smile disappeared from her face, replaced by a cold stare.

"Have a seat," she said abruptly, pointing to a nearby leather sofa. She picked up a phone, punched a single button, and swung around to face away. She cast an occasional frosty glance over her shoulder at Kaye, who could not make out the conversation from where he sat.

"Mr. Urrestegui will be out momentarily," she said icily after hanging up.

Kaye waited almost fifteen minutes before the door on the back wall opened and a man stepped through, barely making it through the doorway without ducking. Kaye guessed that would make the guy about six-foot eight, and even with his lanky build he was at least two-fifty.

Kaye recognized him instantly as the man in the yellow SUV.

"Mr. Kaye," the big man said, "I'm Robert Urrestegui. What can I do for the LAPD?"

In his peripheral vision Kaye caught the flicker of uncertainty that flashed on the receptionist's face, hesitated momentarily, and decided to call the bluff.

"No, you're not," he said. "Nice try, junior, but go tell your boss I either get to see him or he can plan on talking to me down at the Sheriff's office. Oh, and I'm pretty sure somebody would tip the press if that were to become necessary."

The man reddened and returned Kaye's stare, obviously trying to decide whether to try and ride out the charade. Then he turned abruptly and went back through the door, leaving it open.

Less than a minute later, he returned. "Follow me," was all he said.

Kaye smiled at the receptionist as he walked by. She answered with a backhanded wave of her hand, middle finger extended.

He'd taken only a couple steps through the door when it swung closed forcefully behind him. As the tall man turned around to face him, his right hand remaining behind his hip, Kaye became aware of someone else behind him to his left. He turned and looked, and saw a bowling ball of a man in his mid-twenties. The man's head was shaved, and, while he was a half-foot shorter than Kaye, he seemed almost as wide as he was tall. The edges of numerous tattoos were visible above the starched white collar of his dress shirt.

He held a security wand in one hand.

"Let's have it," the tall man said flatly.

"Have what?" Kaye feigned ignorance.

"The piece, asshole. The detector in the elevator picked it up."

"I don't know what you're talking about."

The bald man quickly ran the wand down from Kaye's head to his boots and back again. "Right ankle," he said, his voice surprisingly girlish for a man of his size.

"Oh, that piece. Forgot all about it." Kaye reached for the boot holster.

"Hold it, wise guy," the tall man cut in. "My associate will do that for you. Needless to say, don't do anything stupid, okay?" A smile that reminded Kaye of a shark crossed the man's face.

The bald man reached down and pulled Kaye's pant leg up. "Wow, cool holster," he said. "Sewn right into the boot. Very trick." He unsnapped the retainer strap, pulled the pistol from the holster and stood up.

"Hey, a Kimber! I've been thinking about getting one of these. Must be my lucky day, huh?" He turned to his tall partner and laughed shrilly. Then, to Kaye, he said. "March."

The tall man led the way. The bald man trailed far enough behind Kaye to stay out of reach. Kaye tried to stay oriented, and thought they were walking west toward the end of the building opposite the elevator. They passed two elegantly furnished conference rooms before reaching an oversized set of ornately carved doors at the end of the hallway.

The tall man didn't hesitate and pushed open the right side door, then stepped inside and held it open. Kaye and the bald man followed him through.

The office was larger, and even more stunning, than the reception area. The entire north wall was glass, affording a panoramic view of the nearby mountains. Four huge elk antler chandeliers lit the space and, like the lobby, the walls were virtually covered with paintings and big game trophies. One wall held only wild sheep, one of which had horns easily surpassing seven feet from tip to tip. Another wall displayed Africa's Big Five.

The desk was a large slab of exotic hardwood supported by four giant, crossed elephant tusks intricately carved to depict herds of African antelope.

The chair behind the desk was vacant.

The tall man led Kaye to a chair in front of the desk.

"Sit," he commanded brusquely. "Mr. Urrestegui will be right with you."

The two henchmen settled unobtrusively into chairs positioned just behind and to both sides of Kaye.

Several minutes passed before the door on the south wall, nearly invisible from inside the office, opened. A man stepped through and walked across the room, taking the chair behind the desk.

"Sorry to keep you waiting. I'm Robert Urrestegui. I understand you wanted to see me."

Kaye appraised the man across the desk. About his height, but with a tough, slender triathlete's physique that belied his age, which Kaye guessed to be mid-fifties. Urrestegui was deeply tanned, with salt and pepper hair cut in a classic flattop, and the dark, penetrating eyes accentuated the man's decidedly aquiline features.

"I was under the impression that you wanted to see me."

"Really?" Urrestegui leaned back in his chair and looked puzzled, shifting his gaze back and forth from Kaye to his two underlings. "Why would I want to see you? I apologize if we've met before, but...."

"You were interested enough to have Laurel and Hardy here follow me around yesterday afternoon."

A flash of irritation crossed Urrestegui's eyes, but his expression never changed. "I'm afraid you're mistaken," he said quietly. "Why on earth would my employees follow you?"

"I'm not mistaken," Kaye said. "Nobody but these two boneheads would try and run a tail in a bright yellow jeep. I mean, c'mon. Yellow? With plates registered to your company, no less. I recognize Lurch over there from the passenger seat yesterday and he drove it to work today. You really should spend a little more time and money training your people."

Kaye turned toward the tall man and smiled humorlessly, causing the man to hang his head and stare at the floor.

Urrestegui was unfazed. "I'm still quite certain you're mistaken. My business interests are extensive and you may have simply seen Timothy and Sean here while they were out and about on that business. As you said, the vehicle is quite conspicuous and I'm sure an astute observer such as yourself would notice it."

"Possible. At any rate, while we're chatting, I would like to ask you a question."

"What's that, detective?"

"I was wondering if your Basque friends arrived safely the other day." Kaye fixed Urrestegui with a hard stare. "Too bad about the accident. Terrible tragedy."

Even through the deep tan Kaye could see Urrestegui redden slightly and the man's eyes glistened with hatred for an instant before he regained his composure.

"I have no idea what you're talking about," Urrestegui countered, his voice once again calm and controlled. "And I believe we're done here. Timothy, Sean, show Detective Kaye the door."

"With pleasure, boss," Sean, the bald man, said as the two stood up.

"I'll need my pistol." Kaye looked at Urrestegui.

"What pistol?" Urrestegui feigned surprise. "Are you telling me that you came into my place of business armed?"

"I'm always armed, which is something your boys here would do well to remember." He turned to Sean and held out his hand. "My pistol."

"Come and get it, pig."

Kaye started toward him, moving quickly.

"Stop! Stop!" Urrestegui shouted, jumping to his feet. "Not in here. Kaye, the rug you're standing on probably cost more than you make in a year. I don't want your blood ruining it."

"If I were you, I'd worry more about the blood of your boy here. Tell him to return my pistol, or the rug isn't going to be the only damage in here."

"Oh, really?" Urrestegui's tone was mocking. "You think you could take Sean?"

Kaye just stared at the Basque businessman.

"I'll admit," Urrestegui continued, "you're a formidable looking man, but I've seen Sean in action."

"He's the strongest guy in Idaho," Timothy blurted.

"Quiet, Timothy," Urrestegui said.

Kaye stared into Sean's eyes. "Barbells don't fight back, convict. You really want to get hurt for, what, a twelve hundred dollar gun?"

"I'll kick your ass," blustered Sean, working himself up for a fight. "You'll be the one hurting."

"Gentlemen," Urrestegui spoke up. "I have a proposition. Let's make it a contest, shall we? For obvious reasons I do not want two men of your considerable sizes engaging in a brawl in my office."

"What did you have in mind?" Kaye asked.

"I propose that you and Sean arm wrestle for the gun. A contest of strength, the true way two dominant males of any species settle disputes. What do you say, Mr. Kaye?" The man's eyes glittered with anticipation.

"What do I win?"

"Win?" Timothy laughed. "You don't have a chance, cop."

"Timothy," Urrestegui addressed the tall man, the edge in his voice betraying his irritation. "If you would please hold your tongue and let me finish, I would appreciate it."

Stung by his boss's rebuke, Timothy blinked hard, but held his tongue.

"If you win," Urrestegui resumed, "you get your gun back. If you lose, Sean keeps it. Fair enough?"

"Not quite. It's already my gun. I win nothing."

"Well, then, how about I make it worth your while?" A cunning smile grew on Urrestegui's face. "If you win, you get the pistol, and I'll give you double what you said it was worth. Twenty-four hundred dollars."

It was clear to Kaye that he would either deal with Sean or leave without his pistol, and the latter was not an option. A small, confident smile crossed his lips as he turned and looked Sean in the eye.

"Works for me."

"Excellent!" Urrestegui beamed. He quickly instructed Timothy to pull two nearby chairs to positions opposite each other at one corner of the expansive desk.

"You will start on my signal," Urrestegui said enthusiastically, now totally caught up in the impending duel. "One contest, with the loser being the man whose hand is pushed to the table first. The stakes are the pistol against twenty four hundred dollars." He reached into his pocket, extracted a roll of cash and peeled off the money.

"Sean, the pistol, please." Urrestegui held out his hand.

Sean stopped rolling his bull neck and shoulders and flexing his arms long enough to reach into his rear waistband and retrieve the Kimber. He handed it to his boss, who placed it on the table atop the cash.

Kaye took a seat and waited patiently. Sean sat down across from him and glared across the table.

"Gentlemen, elbows on the table," ordered Urrestegui.

Both men put their elbows on the table, forearms extended upwards. The tips of Sean's outstretched fingers fell short of Kaye's wrist.

"Holy crap," the bald man muttered.

Kaye looked across at his opponent and said calmly, "Size really does matter, Sean." Then, with a wry smile, he added, "But I bet you found that out in prison, didn't you? I bet the big boys really liked you before you started pumping yourself up."

"Fuck you!" Sean exploded in rage, his face turning bright red.

"I don't think so." Kaye knew he'd hit the right nerve. Sean was clearly enraged, just like Kaye wanted him.

While the combatants exchanged pleasantries, Urrestegui reached for a nearby bookcase and took down two thick volumes. He grabbed Sean's arm and raised it, placing the books under the elbow. Sean's hand was now roughly the same distance above the table as Kaye's.

"Sean, if he pushes you down parallel to the tabletop, you lose."

"I won't lose, Mr. Urrestegui."

"Good man. If you win, you keep the money, too."

The bald man nodded at his boss. He had thick, powerful hands from lifting heavy weights, but when the two men locked hands he watched in disbelief as Kaye's hand engulfed his, the fingers wrapping all the way around to the base of his thumb and the huge thumb reaching completely across his knuckles.

"Are you both ready?" Urrestegui asked.

Sean merely grunted and nodded. All his attention was focused on Kaye.

"Ready," Kaye said calmly.

"Wrestle!" Urrestegui said sharply as he removed his hands.

Kaye hadn't known what to expect. The kid was a mass of muscle and it was obvious he did this a lot. Sean's reaction was quick and his power took Kaye by surprise. He pushed Kaye's hand down nearly halfway to the table before Kaye measured the kid's strength and slowly pushed back up to center.

Surprised, Sean grunted and shifted in his seat looking for additional leverage. Kaye simply sat still, needing more strength than he'd anticipated to keep Sean at bay, but confident he had more than enough reserve to end this at his leisure.

"You're pretty strong, kid. For a convict."

The jab infuriated Sean.

"Up yours!" he screamed. "I'm gonna kill you!" Sean redoubled his efforts, straining with every ounce of his strength.

Kaye knew there was no way he was going to simply pick up his gun and walk out of Urrestegui's office by winning an arm wrestling match. Urrestegui had obviously suggested it because he expected Sean to win handily. If his man lost, he would likely turn his goons loose.

Kaye needed to win and he needed to do it in a way that would reduce the three to one odds. Goading Sean was part of the plan.

When Sean screamed at him, Kaye knew it was time.

He relaxed to let Sean think he was gaining the advantage. The ex-con felt Kaye yield and mistook it for weakness. He grunted mightily and pushed against Kaye's hand with all his might.

Kaye felt Sean's last-ditch push and acted. He exerted his strength, the muscles in his arm and shoulder knotting with tremendous force.

Sean's eyes widened in shock and pain as he succumbed. Stunned, he heard bones snap as Kaye crushed his hand like putty.

Urrestegui and Timothy heard it to, but before either of them could move, they saw Kaye's jaw clench as he applied one last, terrible push against his opponent.

The sickening sound of Sean's upper arm snapping like a dry branch filled the office.

Kaye immediately released his grip. He wanted to teach the kid a thing or two, not cripple him for life. All in all, it had taken him less than a minute to impart the lesson.

Sean heard the sound of his arm breaking and felt Kaye let go. For a split second he exulted, thinking he had injured Kaye, but then the pain hit him. With a scream of agony his right shoulder crumpled and he grabbed his right arm. His crushed hand lay still on the table.

"You son of a bitch," Timothy growled, bolting from his seat and lunging at Kaye.

Kaye had anticipated Timothy's reaction and quickly spun up from his chair. Although Kaye was overmatched in height, the two men had nearly the same reach. Kaye let the big man come.

Timothy came sliding in with the stance and footwork of a practiced martial artist. When he got within range, he feinted with his left and followed quickly with a right hand strike to where he calculated Kaye would duck to evade the faked left.

Kaye didn't take the bait. Instead, he moved slightly to his right and took a quick half-step forward, getting inside the tall man's guard. Timothy's right hand flashed harmlessly past Kaye's ear. Kaye countered by blocking outward with his left arm, then looping his arm over Timothy's.

Before Timothy could pull back his right hand, his forearm was pinned against Kaye's body with the pressure of a bear trap.

Kaye slammed his right hand up and across as hard as he could, landing the blow directly under Timothy's extended elbow.

The tall man gasped in pain as his elbow dislocated, then he threw a hard left cross at the side of Kaye's neck.

Anticipating the punch, Kaye swung his right arm, forearm extended upward, out to his right in a classic block. He felt Timothy's left arm slam into his forearm and deflected the blow downward, his arm sliding down the length of Timothy's until he gripped the man's wrist like a vise.

Timothy struggled as Kaye exerted enough upward pressure to raise the tall man onto his tiptoes.

"Stop," Kaye said forcefully. "The fight's over."

"Up yours, cop." Timothy grunted as he tried to launch a knee at Kaye's groin.

Kaye was too close for the knee to be effective and deflected it with his leg. He clamped his right hand closed and, with a quick twist, snapped Timothy's wrist.

The tall man's mouth opened, but no sound escaped. His eyes glazed, then rolled back into his head as the pain overwhelmed him. He slowly crumbled. Kaye grabbed the now unconscious man under the arms, lowering him gently to the floor.

Kaye heard the sound of slow clapping behind him and turned to face Urrestegui. Sean still sat in the chair, clasping his broken arm, his eyes glazing with the first signs of shock.

"Very impressive," Urrestegui said slowly. "Very impressive, indeed."

"You need bigger dogs, Urrestegui."

"It would appear so. I'll at least need some new ones."

Kaye walked over and picked up the Kimber from the table. He left the pile of cash.

"Aren't you taking the money? You certainly earned it."

"Give it to your boys. They're the ones who earned it." As he spoke, he put his right foot up on the edge of Urrestegui's desk and snapped the Kimber into the boot holster.

"I'll owe you, detective. How's that?"

"If I find out you had anything to do with the deaths of that old couple, Aiden Graham or Maria de la Rosa, you'll owe me, all right, and you won't be able to pay anyone enough to keep me from collecting. I'll find my own way out."

Urrestegui watched Kaye go. As soon as the door closed he collapsed into his desk chair and broke out into a cold sweat. His eyes fell on the lion's head affixed to the far wall. That lion had killed Urrestegui's tracker and seriously mauled his guide before it had come for him. The look in the wounded lion's eyes as it charged was the look of implacable death. Urrestegui had known he was about to die, overcome by a force of nature he simply lacked the power to resist. In a last act of futile desperation he'd pulled the trigger of his heavy rifle as the lion rose to take him. The slug had somehow found the roof of the lion's mouth, going through to the brain. The huge cat died instantly, but the momentum of the charge had carried it onto Urrestegui, its ponderous weight crushing him to the ground. Expecting to be torn asunder by the lion's fangs and claws, he'd lain there for what seemed like an eternity before realizing the big cat was dead.

When Kaye had risen from his chair to dispatch Timothy, Urrestegui had seen in the big cop's eyes the same look that had shone in the lion's that day. Until this moment those interminable seconds in Africa had been the most frightening of his life.

He composed himself as best he could before shakily pushing the desk phone's intercom button.

"Melissa," he asked, forcing his voice to stay calm, "is he gone?"

"Yes sir. He just took the elevator down."

"Good. Would you call an ambulance, please?"

"Are you all right, sir?"

"I'm fine. Just make the call, please."

"Yes, sir, right away."

Urrestegui punched a different intercom button.

"Get in here. Both of you."

While he waited, Urrestegui checked his two injured men. Sean was clearly in shock, but his pulse was steady and he seemed to be breathing steadily. Urrestegui could tell by looking that Timothy would be okay, although both arms in casts was going to make the kid's life miserable for a couple months.

"Damn," Urrestegui muttered. Now was not the time to be without his two bodyguards and personal assistants.

The same door Urrestegui had used to enter the office opened and two men stepped through.

"Holy hell!" the first exclaimed. "Uncle Robert, what happened?"

"Detective Kaye's handiwork." Urrestegui gestured with both hands.

"The man on the motorcycle?" the second man asked.

"Yes," Urrestegui nodded. "The man on the motorcycle. The man you" he stabbed his finger at the man in anger "should have killed already!"

"Would you have preferred that I blow the entire operation?" The second man's voice was low and threatening. Clearly, Urrestegui did not intimidate him. "There was no way I could have known someone else would enter that room first."

"Maybe, but this was not supposed to include people coming to my office asking questions. We have an agreement."

"Yes, we do." The man stared coldly at Urrestegui. "But our agreement concerns the end result, not the method. Nor does it absolve you of all risk in exchange for the considerable rewards you will obtain. The stupid old man in the red truck changed things. I cannot help that."

"I agree," the first man interceded, wanting to stop the impending argument before it started. "What I'd like to know is how Kaye connected any of this to you. How'd he know to come here?"

"He saw these two numbskulls," Urrestegui gestured at Timothy and Sean, "following him yesterday and got their license number. That's all."

"Did you send them to tail him?" The first man demanded.

"Yes, I did. I had them watch the Sheriff's office, knowing he'd show up there eventually." Urrestegui bristled back, wanting to make it clear who was in charge. "Do you object?"

His tone gave the first man pause and he saw a smirk of contempt cross the second man's face.

"No, I guess not, not if you thought it was necessary. I just wish you'd talked to me first, since these two obviously blew it."

"Still," the second man said, "we cannot be certain that's all this man has. I thought I overheard him asking about your Basque friends. I still worry about Ramon's lapse in judgment, and the accident was a terrible stroke of bad luck. We need to proceed with caution and remain on schedule. Our window of opportunity is very short and almost upon us."

"Agreed," Urrestegui nodded. "The timing is crucial. We've waited a long time for this. I can't afford to miss it."

"So," the first man asked, "what do we do about Kaye?"

"Nothing," the second man answered. "If he had any real evidence he would have brought the local authorities with him. He was fishing, that's all."

"Hunting," mumbled Urrestegui.

"Excuse me?"

"Hunting," Urrestegui said loudly. "He's not a fisherman. Kaye is a hunter if I ever met one, and when he finds what he's hunting for, he kills it."

The second man snorted in derision. "If he comes hunting for me again, I promise you I will not be the one to die."

"Bold words, my friend," Urrestegui smiled thinly.

The sound of a siren outside brought the conversation to a halt.

"Okay," Urrestegui said. "We're agreed. We stay on schedule. Now, you two get out of here. I don't want you in here when the paramedics come up. They'll believe me when I tell them this was a friendly contest between Sean and Timothy that got way out of hand.

"And you," Urrestegui addressed the first man. "Stay in the building for the rest of the day and use the garage exit after dark. If Kaye sees you and connects us, we'll have a real problem."

"But I've got to go to work!"

"Call in sick," Urrestegui said. "If this all works like we planned, you'll never have to work again. Now, get out of here, both of you."

Urrestegui leaned back in his chair and composed himself. He wasn't going to let Kaye, or anybody else, deter him now. It had taken him years to set this up, and if it failed he would be ruined.

***

Kaye walked off the elevator and went outside. Inflicting bodily harm on Urrestegui's two goons didn't bother him at all, but it certainly wasn't the outcome he'd hoped for. He did feel like he'd shaken the businessman, though, and was satisfied with what he'd found out. Urrestegui's reaction to his comment about Basque friends convinced Kaye that the man was somehow connected to what was going on.

The sixty-four dollar question, though, remained unanswered. What was going on?

He turned away from the street, intending to cut through the block and take the most direct route to where he'd parked the Harley, and then stopped short. Something didn't fit, and he suddenly realized what it was.

He reversed direction and headed back to the street fronting the building. Hustling across, he turned and looked back at the Biscay Basin Group building. The ground floor was the restaurant. Above that, between the eatery and the ornate terra cotta pediment topping the structure, were four layers of windows. So, Kaye wondered, why had the elevator call buttons only gone to four if there were five floors? The ceiling height on the fourth floor had been generous, but it certainly hadn't been two floors. Besides, older buildings were often built with twelve, even fourteen, foot ceilings and that matched his estimate based on window size and placement. The top row of windows were slightly smaller and closer together than those below, but Kaye knew that could simply be a design choice made when the building was erected.

Was there a fifth floor? The obvious conclusion had to be that there was one, but it didn't share common access with the first four floors. Why? The second, third and fourth floors had clearly been occupied by Biscay Basin Group interests. Either the fifth floor was un-restored and unoccupied, it was occupied by some entity not connected to Biscay Basin Group, or it belonged to Urrestegui and was used for something else.

Kaye suddenly got it. The fifth floor wasn't business, it was personal space. Urrestegui might live on the fifth floor. What could be more convenient than living one floor above your office? That had to be it. Unfortunately, it also meant the man had a virtually perfect place to conceal anyone and anything he chose to.

Kaye recounted what he'd seen in the building and concluded there was no way to get to the fifth floor to check it out.

Was there?

Kaye dismissed the problem as he walked back to the Harley. He'd worry about it later if the need to get up there became pressing. Right now, he had a more important place to go.

18

He checked the number and dialed from the saddle of the parked Road King.

"Hello," a male voice answered.

"Michael Graham?"

"Who wants to know?" the voice shot back with a hint of irritation.

"My name is Ben Kaye. I'm calling to check on Cindy. She gave me this number."

"This is Cindy's father...Mike. I thought you were another one of those damn telemarketers. Hey, Cindy told me all about you, Marine! Said you even served with that nasty s.o.b. Dinsmore."

"Yes sir, I knew the Sergeant Major. Great Marine. The best."

"I wouldn't be talking to you if he wasn't."

"Could I speak with Cindy?"

"Cindy's not here. In fact, you're lucky you caught me at home. I tried to get that dang girl to come here when they let her out, but she insisted on going home. I was just about to roll out the door in that direction when the phone rang, Hey, I got an idea! Why don't you meet me there in, say, about a half hour?"

"That'll work for me, I think. I'm in downtown Boise right now."

"That's just about right. You know how to get there?"

"Haven't a clue."

Mike gave him directions and had Kaye go back over them with him.

"See you in about thirty, then?" Mike asked.

"I'll be there."

Mike Graham's directions were spot on and, after killing a few minutes cruising the neighborhood, Kaye rolled the Road King into the driveway of a modest, well kept home on a quiet, tree-lined street.

Before he could even get off the bike the front door opened and a razor-thin man, his medium height capped with a steel gray buzz cut, stepped out and closed the door behind him before making a beeline toward Kaye.

"You must be Ben," Mike Graham said, extending his hand. "First off, let me thank you for saving my girl's life. I can never repay you." There were tears in the old man's eyes as he spoke.

"It's a pleasure to meet you, Mike. I'm glad I was in the right place at the right time to help. I'm just sorry I couldn't save your son."

"I'm sure you did everything you could. I'm thankful for what you did, and I don't blame you at all for what you couldn't do." Mike's voice broke.

"Thank you."

"Hey," Mike said with forced cheerfulness. "Nice bike. Tell me about it."

Kaye gave Mike the fifty-cent tour of the Road King, pointing out all the custom features. He was a little surprised when Mike asked if he could sit on the bike, since most people were hesitant – or too intimidated – to ask.

"You bet. Be my guest."

With the grin of a five-year old on Christmas morning, Mike walked to the left side of the bike, grabbed a handful of the left side grip, and stopped.

"You're sure? I always heard most hog riders'd let a fella climb onto their woman before they'd let 'em climb onto their bike." He finished with a lecherous wink.

Kaye laughed heartily. "In this case, I'll make an exception."

Mike planted his left foot and with an exaggerated motion threw his right leg over and settled into the saddle.

"Boy, howdy," he whistled appreciatively. "This is one big hog."

"It's not that big. You'd have no trouble at all handling this bike."

"Well, thanks for the compliment, but I'm afraid it'd be beyond me, for a couple reasons." As he spoke, Mike reached down and grabbed the left pant leg of his Levis and pulled it up several inches.

With a look up at Kaye he rapped his knuckles against the plastic of the prosthetic leg.

"Donated the bottom half of both my legs to the Republic of South Vietnam back in sixty-nine. I can drive a car if it's an automatic, but I'm afraid a motorbike is beyond me."

"I'm sorry," Kaye said, embarrassed. "I didn't... I couldn't tell." Mike cut him off.

"Hey, it's okay. Really. I get around pretty good, and only use my chair on bad days. That you couldn't tell is a compliment.

"My daddy rode a Harley," Mike went on, turning the conversation back to motorcycles. "Got it right after W-W-Two. He gave it to me, but, as you can see – or can't, in your case," he smiled at Kaye, "when I got back from the Nam, well, no motorbikes for me. You know, that old bike's still in my garage covered up with a tarp. It ain't been run in years. I always planned on giving it to Aiden." Mike's voice choked off as he said his son's name and he looked away. "Guess I'll have to find something else to do with that old piece of crap now, eh?" Mike cleared his throat. "C'mon, let's go inside. In case you couldn't tell, I came out to run a little harass and delay action on you. Cindy wasn't quite together yet when you rolled in, but she should be by now."

The two men went inside and found Cindy in the kitchen. Her left arm was in a sling, but she was still able to use her hand as she brewed a pot of coffee.

"Hey, Cindy," Mike announced as they entered. "There's a biker gang member here to see you."

"Ben!" Cindy came over to hug him. "How are you? Thanks for coming. Coffee?"

"Coffee would be fine, thanks. You look much better today."

She was taller than he'd expected, and Kaye realized this was the first time he'd seen her standing still.

"Black for me," Kaye said, anticipating the question.

"I would've guessed that," Cindy said, then wisecracked. "Too bad I'm a redhead."

"Cynthia Elizabeth Graham!" Mike said in astonishment. "Remember, your father is present."

"Dad, it's okay." Then, to Ben, "I hope I didn't offend you."

"Didn't offend me. In fact, after a comment your dad made outside, I was just thinking that you're certainly a chip off the old block."

"Dad?" Cindy looked at him quizzically.

"Hey, that was different," protested Mike, blushing. "It was made in unmixed company. Now, where's my coffee?"

Cindy brought two cups and slid them in front of the men.

"Be careful with that arm, young lady," her father cautioned.

"It's okay, Dad." She came back with a cup of her own and sat down across the table from Kaye. "The doctor said I'd be as good as new in no time. Apparently, I was very lucky. The bullet somehow managed to miss everything important. He said that if I got shot in this shoulder ninety-nine more times, every one of them would cause more damage than this one did. I'll be out of this sling in a couple days."

"I'm glad to hear that," Kaye told her.

"I'm going back to work on Monday."

"Whoa, young lady!" Mike bolted upright in his chair and stopped the cup halfway to his lips. "I thought we agreed you'd take next week off."

"I know, Dad. But I feel so much stronger today, and, besides, I'm so busy right now."

"What do you do?" Kaye inquired.

"She's a computer programmer," Mike piped up. "And a damn good one. Put herself through college on a volleyball scholarship, then paid her own way through grad school. Ever since, I've been watching her boss get rich off her work while he pays her peanuts. I keep telling her she needs to go out on her own."

Mike's tone was reproving and he got a glare from Cindy.

"It's not that easy, Dad."

"I never said it was easy," Mike shot back. "I'm just telling you that the only real way to get ahead is to work for yourself. You gotta own the hammer you swing every day, that's all. Otherwise, all those rocks you break are just somebody else's gravel to sell at a profit."

"Oh, right," retorted Cindy, sarcasm creeping into her voice. "Advice from the man who never swung a big hammer in his life."

As soon as it escaped her lips Cindy knew it was the wrong thing to say, especially in front of Kaye. But before she could say another word, Mike pushed his chair back from the table and stood.

"You're right, Cynthia. You should probably get your career advice from somebody who made something of himself."

Mike then turned to Kaye and nodded. "Pleasure to meet you, Kaye. Sorry it had to be under these circumstances."

"Oh, Daddy," Cindy said, her voice cracking. "I'm sorry. I didn't mean it. Please don't go."

Mike held his hand out toward her. "It's okay, Stretch. When you're right, you're right. I'll be at the funeral home. Keep me posted, please."

With a nod to Kaye, Mike turned and left, the sound of the front door closing punctuating his departure.

"Oh, God," Cindy sighed. "I am so sorry that you got in the middle of that. Me and my big mouth. Obviously, that wasn't the first time we've had that conversation."

Kaye didn't know what to say, so Cindy kept talking to fill the awkward silence.

"It's just that he's my father, you know? I mean, I don't think of him as the man who gave his legs for his country." Her voice broke.

"To me," she continued, wanting Kaye to understand, "he was always like that. He was my dad and he worked hard his whole life taking care of us."

"He worked?"

"Oh, yeah, always. He's not the kind of man to sit home and wait for the disability checks to come in. He worked for the school district. Retired a few years ago."

"Good for him. Sounds like a Marine to me."

"Yeah, that's my dad. And then life kicked him in the teeth again."

"What happened?"

"The month he retired," Cindy went on slowly, staring down into her coffee "my mom was diagnosed with breast cancer. She died within months. They'd been inseparable, except for his time in the war, for over forty-five years and had all these great plans for retirement. Now Aiden. His only son."

"He seems to be doing okay, considering."

"It's a façade, I think. He worked his entire life and now, when he's old, he sees the fruits of his labor disappearing right before his eyes. I don't know how he does it." She sighed softly and added. "I wish Uncle Calvin was here."

"Is Dinsmore really your uncle? Not to be rude, but I don't see much of a family resemblance."

"Honorary. He saved Dad's life during the war, and they became close. I can't remember a time when Uncle Calvin didn't visit. He has no family of his own, you know, so we made him part of ours." Her eyes teared and her breath started to hitch.

"It's okay. Take a deep breath."

"I'm sorry. Aiden's middle name was Calvin."

"Has your dad called Dinsmore and told him about Aiden?"

"It was his first call."

"When is Aiden's funeral?"

She looked at him and he saw more tears well up in her eyes.

"Tomorrow."

"Was there a notice in the paper?"

"It's been all over the press. Disabled Iraq vet murdered on the highway. They're eating it up." Anxiety seized Cindy. "Why? Is something wrong?"

"No, probably not. I would like to attend and pay my respects, if that's okay."

Cindy smiled. "Of course."

Kaye began to tell Cindy what he'd found thus far.

19

It's a short hop from Gowen Field east over the mountains to Friedman Memorial Field in the small town of Hailey, nestled in the Wood River Valley south of Ketchum and Sun Valley. The airport doesn't handle large commercial jets, but the runway was well within Gulf Two's specifications.

Kevin and Hal worked feverishly on the dosimeter during the short flight.

It took them only a few minutes to determine that the magnetic data strip was totally scrambled. Normally it would have yielded the manufacturer's name, date of manufacture, purchaser and dates of exposure control readings. They hadn't really expected it to be that easy, but instead of being disappointed the two techs relished the challenge of using every trick in their considerable scientific bag to pry information from the piece of plastic.

What made them most suspicious about the badge was that it displayed none of the information typically present. There was no brand name. No telephone numbers. No instructions for interpreting exposure. Nothing. Preliminary examination told them that the badge hadn't been manufactured as a blank. It had been cleaned somehow, either chemically or with a very fine abrasive.

Of course, it was also entirely possible that the badge had been out in the sun for years, which could account for its condition. Plastic may last forever, but extended UV exposure could have wiped out any other compounds or inks present on the surface. If not, someone had gone to a lot of trouble to make this particular badge untraceable.

The techs spent ten minutes debating which treatment would give them the best chance of recovering information. Both knew that just because nothing was visible to the naked eye didn't mean nothing was there.

To help them decide, they put the badge under their most powerful onboard microscope and subjected it to a variety of wavelengths from the entire spectrum, hoping to determine how it had been scrubbed. Kevin wanted to find abrasion. Hal wanted to find pitting. They wagered fifty bucks on the outcome.

The badge went into the scope and they hit it with the first wavelength. Nothing. Kevin altered the scope setting. Then again, and again.

"Holy crap," he muttered. "Take a look at that."

On the very upper right corner of the badge was a bright pink splotch. At current magnification, that's all it was, but it excited Kevin.

"I see it," Hal said, "but I don't know what it means."

"Amino acid," Kevin said excitedly. "If I remember correctly, under this wavelength the amino acids in human skin oil glow pink."

"So you think there might be a print on here?"

"Worth checking. Probably should have done that in the first place."

"I glassed it. I didn't see anything."

"Let's fume it."

Hal took a small glass box, sold commercially as an aquarium, from storage and placed it on the counter. A small light bulb had been rigged in the bottom as a heat source. The perforation in the end of the dosimeter, intended to hold a lanyard that went around the wearer's neck, made it easy to hang inside the box. He then dripped several drops of Super Glue onto a small piece of aluminum foil, set the foil inside the box over the light bulb, added a small cup of water and turned the whole thing into a closed system by putting a piece of hard plastic over the top. He then plugged in the light to provide heat.

Cyanoacrylate fuming is a remarkably quick and simple process. About ten minutes passed before the two techs leaned down and looked inside the glass box.

"You've got to be kidding me," Kevin said in a low voice, glancing at Hal.

"Bingo!" Hal smiled broadly.

Barely visible against the stark white plastic of the badge, on the front surface opposite the lanyard slot, were the telltale off-white lines where the fumes had adhered to the oils of a latent fingerprint pattern. It was nowhere near being a full print, but it was something. And it was readable.

"Whoever picked this up was damn lucky," Hal said as he unplugged the light and took the top off the fuming chamber. "Pretty clever with the cups, anyway."

Kevin reached in with a surgical clamp and extracted the badge. He checked the back surface and confirmed there was no additional visible ridge detail before carefully putting the badge face up on the counter.

Hal swung a magnifier into place over the badge and both techs peered through it to examine the print.

"Tented arch?" offered Hal.

"Agreed," Kevin nodded. "It's not much, but we might have enough for a comparison."

"I'll scan it."

"Okay. I'll go tell Straithwaite that today's his lucky day."

Straithwaite was dozing. A legal pad, its front page covered with doodles and question marks, rested on his lap. Kevin's voice startled him awake.

"Sorry to disturb you." Kevin tried to sound apologetic, but couldn't keep the excitement out of his voice.

"What is it? Did you get something?"

"You might say we hit the jackpot. We got a readable print."

"You're kidding." Straithwaite rose quickly from his seat. "Show me."

The two walked to where Hal still peered through the magnifier. He stepped aside when he saw Straithwaite coming and the DHS agent leaned in to take a look.

Straithwaite whistled when he saw the print. "Son of a bitch. Did you scan it in yet?"

"Yes, sir," Hal answered. "I don't think we have enough to stand up in court, but it's a tented arch, and I think we can get enough points for a probable match."

"What's the significance of a tented arch?" Straithwaite, though familiar with basic forensics, had always found the subject boring compared to fieldwork.

"A tented arch," Kevin explained, "is one of two arch classifications for fingerprint patterns. There are only eight classifications, total. The cool thing for us is that only about five percent of people have arches -- plain or tented."

"So," Straithwaite said, "it makes it possible for us to eliminate ninety-five percent of possible suspects right off the bat."

"Exactly," Hal confirmed, nodding.

"Did you start the comparison yet?"

"No, sir," Kevin answered immediately. "We need your authorization."

Straithwaite pondered his options for a moment.

"Okay. Start with the domestic AFIS and – no, check that. Your first comparator will be Benjamin Kaye, detective with the LAPD and formerly of the Marine Corps. His prints can be called up from our files. First, let's make sure our source didn't contaminate his own evidence. Then work your way through the usual databases."

"Yes, sir," the two techs answered in unison.

"And all results come to my eyes only. Direct to the booth. And I still want whatever else you can get off that card." He paused, then added, "Excellent work on the fingerprint, guys. Thank you."

The captain's voice came over the intercom telling them they were on final approach to Friedman Field.

The sleek jet landed and taxied to the apron near the executive terminal. As soon as they parked, Straithwaite went to the booth to wait for possible print matches. He left the door ajar so Hal and Kevin would know he could be interrupted.

Kevin went immediately back to work on the card while Hal pulled up the fingerprint records of one Benjamin A. Kaye from DHS files. It took only a cursory glance at the digitized prints to rule out the LAPD cop. None of his ridge detail resembled anything close to a tented arch.

Hal next entered his search parameters into the terminal and let the computers do their thing. There was no telling when, or even if, they would find a match, but Gulf Two's impressive capabilities would speed the process along.

There wasn't much for Straithwaite to do now but wait for the computers to try and match the print. He put a call through to his home and left a message for his wife not to look for him until she saw him. He marveled that she had stuck with him over the years, but reasoned that him being late getting home from the office was a lot easier for her than wondering if he'd come home from

Afghanistan. At least she had some permanence in her life now, even if he didn't.

The techs were busy giving the badge the full once over. After finding the print some of the pressure was off and after a brief, heated argument they decided to try another fuming technique to try and raise any ink residue still present on the badge.

Straithwaite was debating whether to call the General with an update when the computer console chirped to alert him to incoming traffic. A message on the screen told him that a probable match to his fingerprint submission had been found and asked if he was ready to receive the information.

"Okay" Straithwaite muttered to himself as he clicked the 'Proceed' button. "Let's see who you are." He hoped it would be a radiology tech with an arrest for DUI.

The monitor suddenly filled with data, including the submitted partial print, the full matching print with the points of comparison marked on each and a data sheet on the individual matched. A photograph was also displayed.

Straithwaite bolted upright in his chair, his heart racing.

"Oh, shit," he muttered, then reached over and secured the comm booth door. He shakily grabbed the handset and punched in the connection code for General Holdorf. "Come on, come on. Pick up. Be there." He fidgeted nervously while the system established a link and waited for a session.

Twenty seconds felt like a lifetime to Don Straithwaite before the DHS agent heard the General's voice.

"Holdorf. What've we got, Don?" No wasted preamble or false camaraderie this time.

"It's not good, sir. We were lucky enough to recover a partial print our guys found on the badge. We got a match, sir, although I must caution you there are not enough...."

"Cut the bullshit. I'm not a lawyer. Just tell me who it is."

Straithwaite took a deep breath.

"Doroteo Arango Janicot."

"Pancho? You're sure?"

"Yes, sir. Doroteo Arango Janicot. AKA Pancho. Exact date of birth uncertain, but believed to be around nineteen eighty-four or five. Spanish national of Basque descent." Straithwaite paused momentarily before continuing. "And, sir, as you know, Janicot is a member and suspected leader of Euskadi Ta Askatasuna, which is classified as a terrorist organization by the United States."

"ETA here? That doesn't make sense. You sure about the match?"

"The computer says ninety-nine point four percent probability, sir. The techs said the print type is relatively rare."

"Who matched it?"

"Uh," Straithwaite scanned the data on the monitor. "Interpol. Janicot has been in and out of Spanish prison several times. His last release was in the most recent cease fire amnesty granted by the Spanish government to placate the Basque separatists."

"It just doesn't make sense. ETA has never operated internationally. Not that we know of, at least."

"No, sir. Other than France, that is, but France also has territory the Basques consider theirs, so to them it's still home turf. Historically, ETA has focused on Spanish government officials, judges, civil guardsmen, people like that. And, sir, they prefer bombs and it says here that Janicot is a demolitions expert."

"Is that pertinent here?"

"Yes, sir, I believe it is. Remember, sir, a bomb killed that woman in Boise."

"That's right, that's right. I'd forgotten about that." Then, switching tracks, the General added, "Do you have anything else from the badge?"

"No sir. Not yet. They're working on it now. It was pretty cleaned up. The fingerprint was a real stroke of luck. I think Janicot made a mistake because of the accident."

"Didn't you tell me there were two men in the car? That one was killed at the scene?"

"Yes, sir."

"Can we be sure the dead man isn't Pancho? In fact, without an ID from Kaye we can't confirm either man was Pancho. He could have handled the dosimeter God knows where."

Straithwaite hadn't considered that and felt momentarily foolish. "No sir, we can't."

"Hmmm," Holdorf sighed into the phone before going silent, thinking.

Straithwaite waited patiently. He knew this was one of those times not to offer his own conclusions, all of them bad, to his boss.

"Okay, here's what we do next." Holdorf's voice was forceful. "I want you in Sun Valley. Go ahead and send Gulf Two back to Los Angeles. I'll have Rhoades get a copy of the dead man's prints from the coroner in Boise, and I'll take command of the testing on the badge. I hate to strand you there, but I have a feeling we may need an asset on the ground."

"Not a problem, sir. I always pack a duffel, just in case, and I can think of worse places to be stranded. And, sir, how much can I tell Kaye?"

"Well, I think it's safe to tell him what we know, which is only that we think that either the man who tried to kill him or the man who was killed at the scene is Doroteo Arango Janicot, a member of ETA. Show him Janicot's picture for a possible ID. However, since this is now a matter of national security, tell him not to give information to the local police. We'd have a public relations nightmare on our hands."

"I'll tell him, and thank you, sir."

"Excellent work Don. Pass that along to Kaye for me, too."

"Will do, sir. Thank you. Ending session."

The link went dead. Straithwaite leaned back in the chair and went over the situation. In his mind, they now had physical evidence linking a known terrorist to possible radioactive material inside the country. It certainly wasn't the first time, and it was tenuous, but the apparent involvement of ETA was mystifying. It just wasn't their style. Assuming one of the men was Janicot, where was he going? And why had the General parked him in Sun Valley? He had confidence in the Old Man, but to him it would have made more sense to return to Boise and hook up with Dennis Rhoades.

Straithwaite checked his watch. If he stretched it, Gulf Two could spend about another hour on the ground here and still get back to LAX in time for the crew to miss the worst of the evening traffic. He'd give Kevin and Hal that much longer to work on the badge before relinquishing it to Holdorf. With any kind of luck he'd get more information and fill in some blanks before they left.

***

Holdorf returned the handset to the cradle and leaned back in his chair, the fingertips of his hands together and flexing just below his mouth, which pursed in deep thought.

He sat quietly for a moment, then spun around and retrieved the secure satellite phone from the desk drawer.

"Yes, sir," Rhoades answered on the second ring.

"Dennis, how are you? How was the flight?"

"Fine sir, as usual."

"Good, good," Holdorf said, and then became serious. "I have a confirmed mission authorization for you."

"Go ahead, sir."

Holdorf took a deep breath before speaking. "It's Bilbao. Straithwaite just matched a print. It was Pancho's. But we don't know the source, if he survived the accident, or if he was the KIA at the scene. We need the dead man's prints, and I'll let you know as soon as I find out."

"Do we know if the other...?"

"Not likely. Physical doesn't match at all."

"Understood, sir." Rhoades's pulse had gone up twenty points while the General spoke. "We'll get on it, sir."

"Dennis, do you trust your team?" Holdorf's voice betrayed his concern. It was the one aspect of the operation he hadn't overseen personally.

"Absolutely, sir. They've performed perfectly up until now. Trust them, sir, as you would me."

"Good. Keep me apprised."

Holdorf clicked off before Rhoades could reply. Then, the General counted slowly to thirty and punched another destination code.

"Yes, Carl," The Vice President answered on the first ring.

"We have confirmation, Mr. Vice President. They're in." He filled in the details.

The Vice President was quiet for a moment. "Then I guess we're committed," he said finally. "I don't have to remind you that Pancho alone does not attain our objective."

"I'm aware of that, Mr. Vice President. The team is in Boise already."

"Let's not blow this, Carl. We're close. Real close."

"Understood, sir. I'll keep you informed." Holdorf terminated the call. He leaned back in his chair and used a tissue to wipe the beads of sweat off his forehead. God help me, he thought, if I've thrown in with the wrong side.

20

Kaye had barely finished telling Cindy what he'd learned from Itzy, the old Basque sheepherder, when his cell phone rang. Kaye glanced at the caller ID screen. It said only 'secure', a message he'd never seen before.

"Hello," he answered cautiously.

"Kaye." It was the toneless voice of Khalid Bergman.

"That was fast, Khalid."

"I'll take that as a compliment. Are you near a land line?"

"Yes."

"Call me, please."

The call went dead before Kaye could answer.

"Who was that?" Cindy asked. "Was it about Aiden?"

"Might be. Mind if I use your phone?"

"Go right ahead."

Kaye punched in the number. The operator answered and they went through the confirmation procedure before she told him to hold.

Kaye waited patiently before hearing a series of clicks, followed by Khalid's voice on the line.

"How's the weather in Boise?" Khalid asked in the way of greetings.

"Sunny and hot. Is that why you wanted to talk to me?"

"No. I have some information for you, courtesy of a mutual acquaintance. Are you by chance near a computer?"

"Hold on," Kaye said to Khalid, then asked Cindy.

She laughed. "I'm a programmer."

"I heard," Khalid spoke up. "Give me an address."

Kaye relayed the necessary information before Cindy rose and headed for the back bedroom she used for a home office.

"Who's the woman, Detective?"

"Cindy Graham. She's a victim of our shooter. Her brother was killed. I assume that's okay with you."

There was a pause before Khalid answered. "I believe that's an acceptable exposure. Please make sure that Ms. Graham understands that this is a matter of national security and treats the information accordingly."

"National security?"

"That is correct. We were able to retrieve a partial fingerprint from the item you turned over to Mr. Jones this morning and have made a probable identification. The fingerprint belongs to Doroteo Arango Janicot, a known member of the Basque terrorist group ETA. Since he is prohibited by the Spanish government from leaving their country, there is little doubt he is here clandestinely."

"So, he is Basque." Kaye silently thanked Itzy.

"Your suspicion was correct. However, it's possible, based on the physical description, that Janicot is the man who was executed at the scene. It's also possible that Janicot wasn't even there and handled the dosimeter elsewhere. I'll need you to make that determination when you see the photo."

"I can do that. Were they transporting radioactive material?"

Khalid hesitated before answering. "We cannot confirm that at this time, but neither have we ruled it out. We're still analyzing the item."

"Right. It's routine for a known terrorist to carry a radiation exposure badge, you know, just in case."

"Detective, personally I agree with your reasoning. But I cannot officially confirm it. File it in the 'theory' category for now."

"What else can you tell me?"

"You'll get everything I have." Khalid's tone was actually sincere.

"Okay, great. What do you want me to do?"

"I should tell you that this is no longer your concern, but I'm not."

"Thank you. I can't just walk away from this now."

"I guessed as much. There is, however, one restriction."

"What's that?"

"Do not share this information with the local authorities. We must be very careful. Dissemination to the general public could cause widespread panic."

"I'm not sure I agree. Seems to me that the more people we have looking the better off we are."

"It may change, but let's keep it quiet for now. We'll catch Janicot, or whoever his accomplice is. We already have assets on the ground in Idaho."

"Yeah, I saw the team leaving Gowen Field this morning."

"You did?"

"Yep. Two men, white, and an African-American woman. Left the gate in a Crown Vic just after the Gulfstream took off. When are you guys going to stop using transportation that screams 'hey, look at us, we're feds'?"

"I'll pass your concerns along to my superiors."

"You might want to hire some new pilots, too. If Mr. Jones, or whoever he really is, wanted to surf this afternoon the departure heading was off by about a hundred degrees. Unless," Kaye thought he might as well cast all his bait at this point, "he wanted to go skiing. But even he should know there's no snow there this time of year."

The silence from the other end didn't last long, but it was long enough for Kaye to know he'd hit a nerve.

"I wouldn't know about that," Khalid said at last.

"I didn't expect you would. Is there anything else?"

"One thing. Our lead Boise agent's name is Dennis Rhoades. He may want to talk to you. Is that all right with you?"

"Works for me." Out of the corner of his eye he saw Cindy lean around the office door into the hallway and wave to get his attention. When he looked at her she nodded to let him know the information had been received.

"We got your file. Thanks."

"No thanks necessary. Just help us catch these people before they have a chance to do whatever they came here to do. And please let me know if Janicot's photo matches either of the men at the scene of the shooting."

"The locals ran the dead man's prints. No match in AFIS."

"Our hit came from Interpol."

"Got it. I'll let you know."

Kaye hung up and walked down the hallway to the converted home office.

He could tell immediately that this was what Cindy did for a living. Several top-of-the-line systems rested on the built-in desk that spanned two walls. All of them were linked by the kind of networking gear typically found in high speed, ultra-low fault tolerant environments.

Cindy sat in front of one system. "I thought I'd wait until you were here to open it."

"Go ahead. Let's see who this guy is."

Cindy clicked on an icon and the system opened the file in the blink of an eye. There was no cover page and the left half of the monitor was filled with a full-face photo, obviously a mug shot.

"Oh, God!" Cindy stifled a cry as her hand flew to cover her mouth. "It's him!"

Even without a close look at the man on the highway, Kaye knew Cindy was right. The shape and coloring of the face, the hair, the eyes; they were all right. There was no doubt this was the man. Doroteo Arango Janicot.

"It's okay, Cindy." Kaye squeezed Cindy's good shoulder in reassurance. "It's okay. Now we have the advantage."

"We do?"

"We do. We know who he is, and he doesn't know that. We're going to find this guy, no matter what."

As he spoke, Kaye's eyes scanned the data included with the photo. Janicot had an alias of 'Pancho'. Six feet one, about a hundred and ninety pounds, black hair and brown eyes. Arrest record in Spain for political crimes against the government, including suspected involvement in the Madrid subway bombing. Skilled with small arms and a known explosives expert. Last known whereabouts of Bilbao, Spain, with no current record of his passport at any U.S. border checkpoint.

"How will we find him? He could be anywhere by now." Cindy's voice was plaintive.

"I don't think so. I think he's still around. In fact, I think I know where he's going."

"What? Where? How could you know that? Tell me."

"Well, I don't know for sure, but I have a theory."

"Okay, so tell me your theory."

"I think he's here to set off a bomb in Sun Valley. Either a nuke, or a dirty bomb."

It took Cindy a second to digest what Kaye had said. Then her eyes went wide and she gasped involuntarily.

"Oh my God."

"It all fits. This Pancho is a known terrorist. He's here illegally and is willing to kill his allies to keep his presence and identity a secret. He's supposedly a demolitions expert. And we have reason to believe he is in possession of something radioactive."

Cindy's programmer's mind kicked in and she started dissecting Kaye's arguments.

"Yeah, but the guy's Spanish, right? Spain doesn't have an axe to grind with America. Do they?"

"Basque, not Spanish. To us it might be a small distinction, but not to the Basques. But, yes, I admit it's a stretch. It doesn't fit ETA's known pattern, or, at least what little I know about them."

"Okay. What about what he was driving? How big a bomb could he carry in a Toyota? Wouldn't he need a truck or something for an atom bomb? And some protection from radiation? Aren't those things really, really heavy?"

"I don't know that, either. But the old sheepherder I talked to said they had a crate in the trunk that was heavy enough to take both of them to lift. Plus, a terrorist doesn't need a very big nuclear device to make a point."

"How much would they need to make a bomb?" The worry in her voice was now obvious.

"Depends on the material, I guess. I'm no expert, but I think you have to have enough mass for it to stay critical. Then you need some kind of trigger explosion to take it super-critical. Nuclear weapons are simple in theory, but very, very difficult to construct so they work. And mistakes are fatal. That's why the club is so small. If I had to bet, I'd put my money on an RDD. Much easier to make."

"RDD? What's that?"

"Radiological dispersion device. They're called dirty bombs on the news. You make a regular bomb and include some radioactive junk in it. When the bomb goes off, it's not a nuclear explosion, but it spreads the radiation. Instead of killing everybody fast, it kills them slowly. The terror factor is astronomical."

"Okay, but he'd still need conventional explosives, right? He must have some, because he blew up that woman at the hotel, but wouldn't he need more than that? So, I come back to the little car again. He couldn't have been carrying much dynamite or fertilizer in that thing."

"If his goal is to make a statement and get on CNN, then, yeah, the car is probably too small. If it's a targeted assassination, maybe he could carry enough."

"But if it's a targeted deal, he wouldn't need the radioactive stuff, would he?"

Kaye smiled. She asked all the right questions. "Okay, detective, put it together for me. What's the logical conclusion?"

Cindy's eyes narrowed while she sifted the information. It took her less time than Kaye thought it would.

"He's not working alone?"

"That's what I come up with, too."

"But who, and how?"

"Well, I think I know part of the 'who', but the 'how' is still a mystery."

Kaye told her about being followed by the yellow Jeep and where it had led him. When he told her about his visit to Biscay Basin Group and his encounter with Robert Urrestegui's two associates, she blanched.

"Ben, you could've been hurt! Promise me you'll call the police next time."

Kaye laughed. "I am the police. Plus, I can take pretty good care of myself. If you don't believe me, just ask Urrestegui's boys. Besides, I didn't, and still don't, have enough to support a search warrant, even if I could get one in Idaho."

"But couldn't you press charges for assault, or something?"

Kaye laughed again. "Right. The local cops would take one look at the end result and put me in jail. No thanks."

"I guess you're right. So, what do we do now, Mister Detective?"

"To tell you the truth, I'm not sure."

"Couldn't we do, you know, like a stakeout, or whatever you guys call it, and see if Pancho comes out or goes in?"

"You're really starting to think like a detective. I thought of that, but we don't have the resources. There are lots of ways in and out of that building and you can't see all of them from a common vantage point. Plus, Pancho may not even be in there, but I'll suggest that to Khalid. DHS already has resources here."

Kaye saw the questioning look in Cindy's eyes and explained to her about seeing the three agents leaving Gowen Field.

"Holy cow, they didn't waste any time!"

"No, they didn't, but under the circumstances you can't blame them."

The statement, with all its implications, hung in the air as they thought about what could happen.

Kaye finally broke the silence.

"I wish we could dig into Urrestegui a little bit. I'd like to know more about what makes him tick, which might help us figure out why he's involved in something like this – if he is."

"Can't you just do your police thing? You know, like they do on TV, with all those computers and stuff."

Kaye wasn't sure if she was teasing or not. "If only it really worked like that."

Cindy suddenly sat upright and slapped the arm of her chair.

"God, I can't believe I didn't think of this sooner!" She leaned over and reached for the phone.

"What?" Kaye asked. In response he got an upraised index finger while Cindy punched in a number, then waited patiently for someone to answer. When they did, she leaned forward and put her elbow on the desk.

"Special Assistant Calvin Dinsmore, please," she said. "Cynthia Graham calling."

She waited. While she did, he called Khalid Bergman and told the DHS agent that Pancho Janicot was, indeed, their quarry.

"I see," Cindy said just as Kaye ended his call. "It's imperative that I speak with the Sergeant Major. Please have him call me as soon as possible. It's important. No, he has my number."

"He's out of the country," Cindy said as she hung up.

"Why'd you call him?"

"Because he can help us, silly. You obviously don't know what he's been doing since he retired from the Corps."

***

The operator in Langley who took Cindy's call was, if nothing else, an absolute stickler about her job's duties and protocols. So, she made note of the name Cynthia Graham in the log and, though she didn't recognize it, made the required check of The List.

The List was exactly that: A roster of people, who, if they called looking for certain employees of the Agency, were deemed important enough to track that employee down and deliver the message.

The first name on Special Assistant Dinsmore's list was the President. Then several people in line for that job, plus several Generals and Admirals. The operator was stunned to see the bottom three names. Michael Graham. Aiden Graham. Cynthia Graham.

"Holy crap", she muttered. She had no idea who Cynthia Graham was, nor did she care. It was enough that the name was on The List. She picked up a handset on her desk that required no dialing.

A voice answered, "Yes".

"Priority One for Special Assistant Dinsmore. Cynthia Graham."

The operator slowly relaxed. She was new and had done her job. The Sergeant Major wouldn't come looking for her, which, she concluded after further reflection, might or might not be a good thing.

PART TWO

"America will never be destroyed from the outside. If we falter and lose our freedoms, it will be because we destroyed ourselves."

Abraham Lincoln

21

Just before Christmas, Pancho Janicot sat at a window table in his favorite café. The owner was sympathetic to The Cause and frequently allowed her establishment to be used as a rendezvous and meeting place.

Pancho had long since finished his lunch, but he lingered, pondering the future and his place in it; something he lately found himself doing more and more.

He was increasingly frustrated with ETA and its leadership; the triumvirate known as The Cupola; whom he considered timid old men. He was seriously considering renouncing his association and forming his own, more militant independence movement. He knew he was not the only disaffected member of ETA, but he was also a pragmatist. Where would he get the money to build the infrastructure needed to support such a move?

Lost in his thoughts, the light drizzle outside mirrored his mood. The sudden scrape across the stone floor of the empty chair opposite him broke his reverie.

"May I join you?" a voice asked in English.

Pancho looked up. A man in his fifties, tall, gray hair in a crew cut, regarded him closely. The smile belied the piercing look in the man's eyes.

"Do I know you?"

"No," the man admitted, looking around cautiously. "The Cupola told me where I might find you."

Pancho examined the man closely. Clearly, he was an American, and his mention of The Cupola intrigued Pancho.

"*Eseri mesedez,*" he said. A test.

"*Mila Esker*," the man responded with a nod as he sat down. He extended his hand across the table. "Robert Urrestegui."

"You are Basque?"

"My ancestry. I was born in the United States. My family escaped just before the Republic fell to Franco. But I assure you, I am loyal to The Cause, as was my father, and my grandfather before him."

"Many Basques left Euskal Herria then."

"And many died defending it." Urrestegui paused a beat. "Including Mikel Lizarraga, your great-grandfather."

Pancho froze. His great-grandfather had disappeared during the Civil War. No word of his fate had ever reached his family.

"What do you know of my great-grandfather?"

"A good deal, as it turns out. I believe Mikel Lizarraga was killed by a German military officer after they committed a burglary in Paris on May 27th or 28th, 1937."

"You're lying. My great-grandfather was no thief."

"He wasn't a thief. He was a spy. He was there to stop Hitler from stealing something that rightfully belonged to us, the Euskalduna."

"What?"

Urrestegui leaned forward, his elbows on the table, and said conspiratorially, "A painting. A painting that today will be worth hundreds upon hundreds of millions of dollars."

Pancho eyed the American suspiciously.

"I know, I know." Urrestegui leaned back and spread his hands. "Sounds crazy. But it's true. What do you know about Guernica?"

Pancho laughed. Every three year-old Basque child knew about Guernica. On April 26th, 1937 the Basque village was bombed by Hitler's Condor Legion and Mussolini's Aviazione Legionaria as a show of support for Francisco Franco. The attack was history's first aerial bombardment of a civilian population.

"I know that many Basques died that day and the world did nothing."

"What do you know about Guernica, the painting?"

"That Pablo Picasso, even though he was Catalonian, painted it for the Spanish Pavilion at the 1937 World's Fair. I've been to Madrid to see it."

Urrestegui leaned forward again. "What would you say if I told you that the painting hanging in the Sofia Reina wasn't the painting Picasso first intended for the Pavilion?"

"I'd say you really are crazy."

"Not as crazy as you think. It's taken me years to unravel this. Listen to the story, and then tell me I'm crazy."

Urrestegui told Pancho how, nearly ten years ago, three previously unknown Picasso's had appeared on the world market. None had made it to auction, each instead selling ahead of time for huge sums. For security reasons, the identities of sellers and buyers were protected in such transactions.

Hoping to finally acquire a Picasso, Urrestegui had set about confirming the paintings' provenance and determine their source.

He hired experts to evaluate the printed images of the questionable paintings against Picasso's body of work. They determined that the paintings, if genuine, were likely painted during the time Picasso lived in Paris before World War Two.

"By then, Picasso was already famous," Urrestegui continued. "How could paintings simply disappear when he had agents and galleries clamoring for everything he did? So I went to Paris and started digging. You'll never guess what I found."

"Let me guess. My great-grandfather stole them."

"Not exactly, but you're close. What do you know about the 1937 World's Fair?"

"Nothing. Look, this is…."

Urrestegui raised his hand toward Pancho, palm out. "Please, hear me out. I know it sounds nuts, but let me finish. There's something in this for you."

Pancho nodded. Self-interest was always worth exploring.

"I won't bore you with the politics of the time, except to say that the Exposition turned into a huge contest between the Fascists and the Bolsheviks. Germany and the Soviets spent fortunes building their pavilions, which were directly across Trocadero Plaza from each other. Ironically, the Spanish pavilion was right next to Germany's. There were rumors, and I believe Hitler sent a high-ranking officer to Paris to retrieve whatever Picasso was painting for the Spanish Pavilion. He didn't want to risk being embarrassed in front of the world, especially Josef Stalin.

"And I think Franco sent men to help. I think your great-grandfather went along to try and stop the whole thing, and got himself killed in the process."

Pancho shook his head in disbelief. "I assume you have some sort of proof."

"It's mostly circumstantial, but it's pretty solid. Thankfully, the French never seem to throw anything away. My investigators were able to find an old record of a report to the Paris police of a disturbance early on May 28th. The caller lived at the same address as Picasso.

"I also tracked down one of the caller's descendants, who told me her father often told a story about the Germans invading the apartment above them, and how the police refused to respond until the next day when they put two and two together after finding three bodies in an alley not far away. The report also said that the woman who later answered the door at the address of the original disturbance call refused to cooperate, but that the officers noted fresh damage to the front door." Urrestegui reached into his pocket and removed a well-worn piece of paper, holding it up for Pancho to see. "It's a note to Mr. Marchand, the neighbor, dated May 31st, 1937. It mentions a painting intended for the Pavilion, thanks Marchand for his concern, but says they decided to keep the matter private. It's signed Dora M." Urrestegui smiled. "Dora Maar was Pablo Picasso's mistress in Paris in 1937. I think the Germans missed Guernica, but got something else."

"So, you have a note." Pancho said dismissively, looking out the window. It was spitting sleet. It would be snowing by dinner time. "If you had the painting, I might be interested, but...."

"I don't have it." The American's smile broadened, "but I think I know exactly where it is."

22

"And you intend to steal it back?" Pancho asked.

"I intend to recover it for Euskal Herria. If there are more paintings, and I believe there will be, I will keep those."

Pancho shifted slightly in his chair. "Why me? So far, I fail to see how I benefit from this."

"I asked The Cupola for help. Aside from the fact I believe your ancestor died trying to keep the painting from Hitler, you have a very useful skill set. You'll be a hero to our people."

A sneer curled Pancho's lip. "I am already a hero to our people. If you knew my role within ETA, you would be embarrassed for offering me fame as an incentive."

"I know your role," Urrestegui said stonily. "I may live in America, but I support The Cause. I've been giving generously, just as my father did, for many years. If you knew how much, you, my young friend, are the one who would be embarrassed. I also happen to know that your standing with The Cupola has been, shall we say, shaky since your release. They believe you defied them. Do this and you will be forgiven."

Pancho squirmed under the American's gaze. Urrestegui was right. He chafed at his estrangement from The Cause, and wanted back in.

Urrestegui noticed Pancho's discomfort and decided to sweeten the pot.

"The painting is in America. Ironically, after all these years, not far from where I live. The man who has it is a direct descendant of General Heinrich Maximillian von Hacke. The Nazi who murdered your great-grandfather, and who was executed after Guernica was hung in the Spanish Pavilion in late June, 1937."

Pancho's eyes lit up. Revenge was something he could understand, something he could taste, savoring it as he rolled it around his tongue and the sweet aroma filled his nostrils. He was silent for two full minutes, the American staring at him steadily.

"I will require a percentage of any money made from the sale of any paintings we recover," Pancho said at last. "The Pavilion painting, if it does exist, returns here to Bilbao as a joint gift to the Guggenheim, from your family and mine. And the offspring of the man who murdered my great-grandfather belongs to me."

"Done."

An idea was slowly taking shape in Pancho's mind. He told the American he needed twenty-four hours to decide.

Urrestegui was fine with that. He knew he had his man.

***

Pancho returned home, stopping on the way to buy a prepaid cell phone. He emptied the bottom drawer of a guest bedroom dresser and then pulled it out completely. Flipping it over, he peeled off a small piece of paper that looked like a manufacturer's inventory tag, but was anything but. Pancho had made it. The SKU number actually contained an embedded telephone number.

He used the disposable phone to call the number.

"Exotic Travel Agency," a male voice answered.

"Yes," Pancho said, hoping he remembered the pre-arranged code correctly, "I'd like to inquire about reservation availability for a once-in-a-lifetime vacation."

There was a brief pause before the voice inquired, "And where would you like to visit, sir?"

"I was thinking of New York, or possibly Madrid."

The silence was a bit longer this time. "And your name?"

"Pancho Villa." His namesake, Doroteo Arango de Arambula, a Mexican of Basque descent, became known by that name as a revolutionary and bandit. It was his agreed-upon moniker.

"We will call you." The call ended.

He waited many minutes before his phone rang.

"Doroteo Arango!" a voice boomed. "It is good to hear from you, my brother! Are you well?"

"I am, indeed, Yousef. I trust Allah is being kind to you as well."

Yousef laughed. "Allah, just as Jehovah does, helps those who help themselves. And he will be kind to those who help his faithful. Had you not found the error on the schematic, our Madrid mission would have been a disaster. So, what can I do for you?"

"I have been presented with a unique opportunity, and was wondering if you would like to invest."

"And where is this investment opportunity?" The jocularity disappeared from Yousef's voice.

Pancho held his breath. "The United States of America," he said in a rush.

Silence.

"Yousef?"

"I am here, Doroteo Arango." Yousef paused. "Your timing is impeccable, my brother. Give me time to make some preparations and I believe I can arrange for our investment to yield spectacular results. I will be in touch."

23

Two months later Pancho boarded a Malev Air flight at Charles de Gaulle airport. He carried a fictitious passport, but no one bothered to ask him for it. The old days of borders in Europe were gone and the flight to Budapest was uneventful.

Well over half the passengers deplaned in Budapest and, after a brief wait, the relatively few Budapest to Beirut passengers boarded. Pancho, absorbed in a magazine article, paid little attention until a polite voice interrupted his concentration.

"Pardon me, please. I am seated in this row."

Pancho looked up to see a tall, silver-haired man, nattily attired in a western business suit and carrying a briefcase, looking down at him.

"Of course," Pancho responded politely. He stood to make room.

The man settled into the seat next to Pancho and quickly fastened his seat belt.

"Peace be upon you, Doroteo Arango Janicot," the man said to Pancho.

"And upon you, Yousef bin Ali Mahmoud. This is a surprise."

"Indeed," the smiling Mahmoud replied. "But even the Americans cannot eavesdrop on conversations at high altitude and five hundred knots."

"An airplane is hardly private."

"It is if you also purchase the surrounding seats."

The second leg of the flight was much less crowded, with barely half the seats occupied. The cabin crew had changed and all now looked to be Middle Eastern.

The two spent the flight talking politics, the deplorable state of the world and the longed-for homelands of both their peoples. Though remarkably different in appearance and background, they were remarkably similar in attitudes and ideals, and had become fast friends during Mahmoud's Madrid operation.

After clearing customs and immigration at Rafic Hariri airport Mahmoud led Pancho from the terminal to a waiting black Mercedes. The driver hurried around to hold the door open for the tall Arab. With a curt nod, Pancho was consigned to the back seat. A bus blocked them in and the driver waited patiently.

"So," Pancho asked curiously, "where are we going?"

Mahmoud smiled broadly as he replied, "Why, to the airport, of course."

***

Fifteen meters east of the Mercedes, a casually dressed man, a suitcase next to his left leg, watched from behind dark sunglasses as the car pulled away. He pulled a cell phone from his pocket and punched a speed dial code.

"Yes," a voice answered.

"He's here, but not alone. I don't recognize the second man. They're probably headed your way."

"We'll be ready." The call ended.

The Mercedes left the terminal grounds and went north on the airport access road. Instead of continuing north to the expressway and into the city, it went around the roundabout just beyond the control tower and turned west into an area of warehouses and hangars.

The car rounded the corner of a large hangar and drove a short distance on the runway apron before coming to a stop near a single-engine Cessna 208B Caravan.

"Our next conveyance," Mahmoud announced as he climbed out of the car.

Pancho grabbed his bag and climbed into the Cessna. The rear portion of the cabin was crammed with cargo and quarters were cramped.

"Where are we going?"

"In good time, Doroteo Arango. In good time."

After take-off the Cessna turned west over the Mediterranean Sea and held that heading for about ten minutes before turning north. Despite the noise, Pancho dozed.

The pilot turned east just before the golden orange disk of the sun touched the sea. Moments later he could make out the Syrian coastline ahead.

"You are certain we are safe?" the pilot asked nervously.

"Yes," Mahmoud replied. "My allies control the sector. Assad has no effective forces within fifty miles. We are guaranteed safe passage."

"I hope you are right," the pilot mumbled under his breath, but maintained his course.

A sizable city and very busy seaport, al-Lathqiyah crowds the Mediterranean in northwest Syria. It lacks one amenity: an airport.

Approaching the pre-arranged coordinates, the pilot descended to five hundred feet and started searching for anything that looked like a landing strip. A minute later he was able to make out a dirt runway ahead. As he passed overhead he saw what looked like a set of vehicle headlights at the west end of the strip flash on and off several times before staying on.

Half turning back into the cabin, the pilot said loudly, "We have arrived."

The pilot continued east for several miles before banking into a lazy one-eighty and coming back to line up with the headlights that cut the growing darkness.

The Cessna settled gently to the ground, its propeller spinning to a stop. The pilot was pleased to find fuel for the trip back to Beirut, and that he would not have to wait for his passengers to return.

The car that had flashed its lights was there to meet Mahmoud and Pancho. Mahmoud thanked the pilot and then addressed Pancho.

"Come, we must hurry. Our meeting will not wait if we are late."

Al-Lathqiyah has no natural harbor. It could be generously described as bordering a shallow bay, now sheltered from the sea by the construction of a massive breakwater. From shore the necklace of giant boulders juts into the Mediterranean in a northwesterly direction for well over two miles before turning due north and continuing for several more miles, where its terminus and the headlands opposite bracket the harbor's entrance.

The black Mercedes cruised slowly along the roadway atop the breakwater. Pancho was astounded by the number of large ships at anchor in the harbor, awaiting their turns at the container docks or pumping snorkels. Their numbers dwarfed anything he'd seen in Barcelona or Marseille.

At the bend in the breakwater there was a small parking lot, built to service an adjacent picnic area and small park. The driver turned the car into the lot and waited, engine idling.

Pancho and Mahmoud disembarked and Mahmoud issued orders to the driver, who nodded in understanding before turning the car around and heading back the way they'd come. Mahmoud then motioned Pancho to follow him. The Arab led him to a picnic table on the harbor side of the park and sat down, inviting Pancho to join him.

"Who are we waiting for?"

"I cannot tell you, my friend, because I do not know. Introductions will be made when he arrives."

"We've come all this way to meet a stranger?"

"Be patient, my young friend. I know this man as a referral from a trusted associate, which, if I may remind you, is how I came to know you. I know what he is and the masters he serves, and he will be well worth waiting for."

Before Pancho could reply, the sound of a small motor from the dark surface of the harbor reached their ears. As they stared into the darkness, the noise grew louder until they could just make out the shape of a small inflatable boat approaching slowly. Three crouched silhouettes were visible. As the craft nudged against the boulders of the breakwater, the figure in the bow, a weapon slung over one shoulder, leapt agilely onto the rocks and tied off before moving twenty meters north and climbing to the park level to take a position partially concealed behind a large boulder.

The motor went to slow idle. The figure seated amidships clambered slowly forward and stepped carefully onto the breakwater, climbing up the rocks directly toward the park. The figure in the stern remained aboard.

The second figure reached the park and stopped, looking around momentarily before spying Pancho and Mahmoud and advancing slowly toward them. The shadowy figure, dressed in dark trousers, a seaman's sweater and knit cap, stopped some five meters from Pancho and Mahmoud.

"Good evening." The voice was male, a trace of Russian accent in the English. "Pleasant evening for a picnic."

Mahmoud stood and answered. "Personally, I prefer the Black Sea to the Mediterranean."

"Then you must visit my dacha some time."

"Is it near Odessa?" Mahmoud asked automatically.

"No, mine is nearer Sochi."

Satisfied, Mahmoud walked forward.

"Permit me to introduce myself. I am Sheik Yousef bin Ali Mahmoud. My associate is Doroteo Arango Janicot. Thank you for agreeing to meet with us."

Pancho had never heard Mahmoud use the title Sheik before, nor had he ever heard the Arab address anyone so deferentially.

"Colonel Viktor Yevgeny Crenovich," the man replied courteously. "My associates are inconsequential, so long as I am not betrayed." He grinned.

"Please," Mahmoud gestured to the bench, "sit down."

Pancho and the Russian exchanged greetings.

"You are very young to be a Colonel," Mahmoud said.

The Russian shrugged. "I am a scientist, not a soldier. I have never been anything but a Colonel, and never will be. But, because I am a scientist and not a soldier, I am in possession of a commodity I understand you may be interested in acquiring."

"That depends," Mahmoud replied smoothly, satisfied by the man's explanation, "upon what you have, how much you have and your price."

"How much do you have to spend?"

Mahmoud laughed. "I know a reputation for haggling is a curse my people bear, Colonel, but I was unaware Russians were so inclined."

Crenovich's lips curled into a smile, but even in the dark Pancho could see that the Russian's eyes were cold.

"This is risky business," Crenovich said carefully. "If I am caught, I will be executed. I do not take such risk lightly, or cheaply."

"Nor do we. What have you to offer?"

The Russian leaned forward onto his elbows and looked at the two men carefully before speaking.

"Strontium-90. Sixty kilos."

"Sixty kilos?" Mahmoud looked closely at the Russian. "So much!"

"It has taken quite some time to accumulate. I do this only once."

Mahmoud looked at Pancho and smiled. "I told you, did I not, that the trip would be worthwhile?"

Pancho was stunned. "You're selling nuclear material?"

"Yes. Although in the quantities I can deliver, while it may be very toxic, let us just say that the options are limited. It is, however, relatively easy to deal with, all things considered."

"Where did you obtain the material?" inquired Mahmoud.

"None of your business."

"But it is," Mahmoud shot back. "Is it stolen? Obviously. Is it traceable? Is it tagged? These are things I need to know if we are to do business."

Crenovich again scrutinized his two potential buyers.

"All right," he said finally, spreading his hands on the table. "Strictly speaking, the material is not stolen, because it was never accurately accounted for originally." He glanced at Pancho and Mahmoud. "Are either of you physicists?"

"No," each replied.

"Well, I am. I will not bore you with the technical details of radioisotope thermoelectric generators. Very useful devices if you require only small wattages. The best way to achieve the high temperature needed is with fissionable material. Originally, the technology provided power for deep space satellite missions."

"So," Pancho interrupted. "Did you suddenly come into possession of several fallen spacecraft?"

Crenovich laughed, genuinely this time. "Hardly! It was much simpler than that. The military implications of generating electricity from a self-contained, self-sustaining and long lasting reaction requiring no outside interaction should be obvious. During the last years of the Soviet Union and the first years of the new Russia the military built thousands, if not tens of thousands, of RTGs. Each contains a modicum of Strontium-90, and no accurate inventory or accounting of them has survived. I," he put his hand on his chest, "am charged with finding and safely decommissioning the oldest of them."

"And some of the fuel has managed to rub off on your hands?" Pancho asked.

Crenovich shrugged again. "Thanks to Ronald Reagan and Mikhail Gorbachev, the world – my world, at least – is a very different place than it was when I was young. It is now every man for himself."

"What is the half-life of this material?" asked Pancho.

"Slightly less than thirty years. As I said, it has certain advantages over other materials of equal toxicity."

"But," Pancho pressed the Russian, "it sounds as though most of this material is beyond its half-life and continuing to decay. Is it still viable as bomb material?"

"Yes, and no. As I said, I am a physicist. The reclaimed material has been refined and re-concentrated, but it will never, strictly speaking, be bomb material. It is, however, an intense source of radiation."

Mahmoud spoke up. "Will it explode?"

Crenovich looked at Mahmoud coldly. "Perhaps we should reschedule this meeting when your superiors can send someone who better understands the value of what I have to offer."

"That is not necessary, Colonel," Pancho quickly assured the Russian. "I understand and will explain it to Sheik Mahmoud later. What form is your material?"

Crenovich smiled thinly. "Small pellets, very friable. They will pulverize very effectively. Perfect for maximum dispersion.

"Another beauty of the material," Crenovich continued, "is that it does not require heavy metal shielding. In fact, because of the Bremsstrahlung effect, that is not desirable. I have packaged it in glass-lined aluminum canisters, in five-kilo increments, which makes for ease of transport. That is how it will be delivered. After that, safe handling is your problem."

Pancho looked at Mahmoud and nodded slightly.

"How much?" Mahmoud asked.

Colonel Viktor Yevgeny Crenovich smiled inside. The deal was done. He knew the Arab would haggle over whatever price he named, and that he would make concessions to give the man satisfaction, but the deal was done.

"One hundred thousand per kilo."

An epithet neither Pancho nor Crenovich understood burst from Mahmoud's lips as the Arab bolted to his feet. "One hundred thousand dollars per kilo? Absurd!"

"Euros," Crenovich said quietly.

"Even more absurd," Mahmoud spat.

"Colonel, would you excuse us?" Pancho asked, standing up.

"Certainly." The Russian smiled politely.

Pancho and Mahmoud walked to a point where they could talk privately.

"Buy it," Pancho said bluntly to Mahmoud, thinking of his agreement with Urrestegui. "I have additional money if you need it."

"Oh, I will certainly buy it. But in good time. He expects me to haggle, so he has set an artificially high price as a starting point."

"Do you have any questions about the material?"

Mahmoud smiled at Pancho. "When will you learn, Doroteo Arango? Never expose your strengths to your adversaries. Bait them with weaknesses, even if you have none. Besides, it is easier to judge a man's honesty if he thinks you do not know what he does. Now, come, and let us buy the devil's powder that we may visit it upon our enemies."

It took two hours of spirited negotiations and name-calling for Mahmoud and Crenovich to settle on a price, then another hour to agree upon the terms and logistics of verification, payment and delivery.

The three men finally stood and exchanged handshakes before the Russian headed back to the waiting boat. As Crenovich clambered down the boulders, he turned to wish them a good night.

"And may Allah be with you," rejoined Mahmoud before adding, "Do not betray us, Colonel. There are worse ways to die than from radiation poisoning."

Even in the chill darkness on the breakwater, Pancho could see the Arab's eyes glittering.

PART THREE

"Honor to the Soldier and Sailor everywhere, who bravely bears his country's cause. Honor also to the citizen who cares for his brother in the field, and serves, as he best can, the same cause -- honor to him, only less than to him, who braves, for the common good, the storms of heaven and the storms of battle."

Abraham Lincoln 1863

24

After Cindy had been unable to reach Dinsmore, she and Kaye sat and talked about normal, everyday life, as two people wanting to know more about each other.

Cindy told him about playing volleyball in high school and college, her job, and he told her about his brief football career and life as a police officer. She had just started to talk about her mother when the phone on the desk rang, startling her.

She made a hopeful face and picked it up.

"Hello," she said, then listened briefly. "Oh, hi, Uncle Calvin!" she continued with obvious pleasure. "No, no, everything's okay – as okay as it can be, anyway." She listened again. "No, Dad's still doing okay. Uncle Calvin, I'm going to put you on speaker, okay? There's a friend here who needs your help. Hold on."

Cindy punched a button on the phone and then laid it on the desk.

"You still there?" she asked.

Kaye heard the voice of Sergeant Major Calvin Dinsmore boom across the line. "Yes, Stretch. I'm still here. You sure everything's okay?"

"Yes, we're okay. Dad's holding up and I'm doing better. The doctor says I'll be as good as new in no time." Then she asked tentatively, "Uncle Calvin, are you coming for Aiden's funeral tomorrow?"

"I'm going to try, but I can't promise," Dinsmore replied. "I'm in Seoul and I don't know if I can get away. If I don't make it I'll be in Boise in a couple of days and pay my respects."

"I understand." The disappointment in Cindy's voice was palpable.

"Now, you said something about needing my help. What can I do?"

"Uncle Calvin, you remember when Dad called you about Aiden?"

"I'll never forget it."

"And he told you about the man on the motorcycle? The man who saved my life?"

"I remember."

"Well, it turns out he's an ex-Marine and he knows you, and...."

"Who is it?" Dinsmore interrupted, clearly suspicious.

Cindy looked at Kaye and nodded, pointing at the phone in an obvious 'you talk' gesture.

"It's good to hear your voice, Sergeant Major. I'm not sure you'll remember me. This is Ben Kaye."

There was a pause before Dinsmore spoke.

"Cindy, describe him."

"Well, he's pretty distinctive looking, Uncle Calvin." Cindy spoke slowly as she appraised Kaye. "A little taller than me, dark hair and eyes, very muscular and, as we ladies like to say, well put together. Ruggedly handsome, I guess, if you can get past the huge nose and one eye in the middle of his forehead."

Kaye could see Cindy blushing as she avoided his gaze.

"I remember him. How are you, Kaye?"

"Fine, sir. Except for being in the wrong place at the wrong time, I guess."

"Wrong. Right place, right time. You saved my niece. That's a debt I can never repay."

"No repayment necessary. I'm just sorry I didn't get there in time to help Aiden."

"Me, too." Dinsmore said quietly, pausing for a second before continuing. "Me, too. Cindy, how's the investigation going? Do you know?"

"Well," Cindy piped up, "that's actually why we called. Turns out Ben's a detective and he's helping find the man who killed Aiden."

"A private detective?"

"Not private, Sergeant Major," replied Kaye, "I work for the LAPD. I was riding down the road on vacation when all this started right in front of me."

"Okay, first, stop calling me sir and Sergeant Major. I'm retired. If you're a friend of Cindy's, you're a friend of mine, and my friends call me Calvin. Now, bring me up to speed on the investigation and tell me what you need. I'm a little pressed for time right now, but we'll catch up when I get to Boise. You'll still be there?"

"I wouldn't dream of leaving now," answered Kaye. He looked across at Cindy, who was beaming like she'd just won the lottery. He gave Dinsmore a quick rundown on what had happened and what he'd learned so far. Dinsmore was impressed when Kaye told him he'd already identified a suspect, but skeptical when Kaye told him he'd done it with the help of Homeland Security.

"You trust those guys?" Dinsmore asked.

"I trust them if you work for them."

That elicited a hearty laugh from Dinsmore.

"I'm with, uh, another agency at the moment. Cindy can fill you in."

"Then I only trust DHS about as far as I can throw them."

"Your instincts are good."

When Kaye finished briefing Dinsmore, he told him he'd like whatever deep background information Dinsmore might be able to provide on Doroteo Arango Janicot and Robert Urrestegui.

"Okay. Give me a day or two and I'll see what I can come up with. Going into a weekend in the States might delay me a little. If you don't hear from me by, say, Sunday evening your time, call me back. Got that, Cindy?"

"Got it, Uncle Calvin," Cindy confirmed.

"With any kind of luck," Dinsmore said, "I can wrap it up here today, in which case I should be in Boise soon."

"I can't wait to see you, Uncle Calvin."

"Likewise, Stretch. If there's any way to make it to the funeral tomorrow, I'll be there. If I don't make it, tell your dad I'm sorry. And, hey, Ben?"

"Here, Calvin."

There was no humor in Dinsmore's voice now. "Anything happens to Cindy or Michael, you answer to me personally. You read me?"

"Loud and clear, Sergeant Major."

"Till Sunday, at the latest, then," Dinsmore said. "Love you, Stretch."

"Love you, too, Uncle Calvin. Bye." She hung up the phone and looked at Kaye. "So, what do we do now?"

Kaye checked his watch. "I say we go find some dinner, then pack you over to your dad's place."

"No way," Cindy said matter-of-factly. "I'm fine. I do not need to go to Dad's."

"Look, Cindy, Pancho has killed five people so far, and he's trying to kill me because he thinks I can identify him. You saw him, too. Don't you think he can find you if he wants to?"

"I don't retreat."

"Don't think of it as retreating. Think of it as a strategic withdrawal to a superior tactical position." Kaye tried to keep a straight face. He almost succeeded.

"Bullshit! Spoken like Uncle Calvin dodging questions at a Congressional hearing. You missed your calling, detective."

"So, you'll go?"

"To dinner, yes. To Dad's? Definitely not. But," Cindy looked sideways at Kaye, "I do have a suggestion."

"Go ahead."

"Why don't you stay here? You can protect me and it'll save you the cost of a hotel. I have plenty of room, really."

"And let Pancho get us both with the same bomb?" Kaye feigned incredulity. "Not a chance. Come up with a Plan C, or it's off to your dad's."

Cindy went momentarily silent, thinking.

"Okay, how about this? I go with you to your hotel." She stared directly into Kaye's eyes.

He stared back, tapping his lips with two fingers while he evaluated the options.

"Actually, that'll work. You'll be even safer in a hotel than you would be at your dad's."

"Right! And I'll have you right there to protect me."

"Good, that's settled. We put you in a safe place for a few days and I'll be close by, just in case."

Kaye thought he saw a smile cross Cindy's lips as she swiveled her chair and stood up.

"I'll go pack."

"Pack light. We'll be riding."

Cindy leaned back around the door. "Great! I'll have you know I even have a motorcycle helmet." Then she was gone.

25

D on Straithwaite headed for the Hailey terminal rental car counter.

Hal and Kevin had labored over the plastic badge for nearly two hours before throwing their hands up in defeat. For analysis of possible radiation exposure and a desorption electro-spray ionization test, which might tell them if their suspect had handled explosives before leaving the print on the badge, they needed equipment too sophisticated even for Gulf Two's capabilities.

Straithwaite cut them loose and sent them home. He'd get the test results when they became available.

For Straithwaite, being detailed to remain in Sun Valley was an unexpected bonus. He certainly wouldn't mind killing a couple of summer days here, especially on the taxpayer's dime.

The weather was glorious. Eighty degrees felt like a bit more because of the altitude. The deep blue skies, salted with a few cumulus clouds, had that unusual clarity of light now so uncommon at lower, more polluted elevations.

"I need a car, or an SUV, please, if you have one available," Straithwaite told the young woman behind the counter.

"I think we have something," she said cheerfully, clicking away at the keyboard. "Ford Explorer okay?"

"Perfect."

They chatted while the young woman completed the rental agreement. She then handed Straithwaite a set of keys and directed him to the Explorer.

"Thank you," Straithwaite told her, bending to pick up his bag.

"Thank you, Mr. Straithwaite. Enjoy the conference."

For a second he almost let it go, but his professional curiosity got the better of him.

"Conference?"

"Oh, I'm sorry. I saw the jet, and I guess I just assumed, with your credit card and all, that you were here early for the big shindig. That'll teach me, huh?"

"That's okay...Sandra." Straithwaite read her nametag. Now, he was interested. "I didn't even know about a conference. Tell me about it. Is it a big deal?"

"Oh, gosh, yes. Everybody who is anybody is here. We get tons of private jets, all the Hollywood and Internet people, and all the big business executives. And politicians. Oh, God, they are the worst! Oh, sorry. I forgot you're with the government."

Straithwaite laughed. "I'm no politician. I'm just a guy who works for a living and got lucky enough to hitch a ride on the boss's plane today."

He saw the relief in her eyes.

"So," he went on, "what do all these big shots do while they're here?"

Sandra leaned across the counter and looked around before answering. "That's the thing." She kept her voice low and conspiratorial. "They don't tell anybody. They don't even let the press in."

"Really?"

"Really. Of course, most of the locals think they get together so they can figure out how they're going to screw us regular folks out of more money next year."

"Do you think that?"

"No, not really. I'm not real big on the conspiracy stuff. I think they come here because it's the coolest place on earth. Besides, a conspiracy would mean that people can actually organize something complicated that works, and we both know that doesn't happen these days."

Straithwaite laughed. "You're probably right. I'm not a big conspiracy guy, either."

"I'll tell you one thing, though. Those people show up," she hesitated and looked around again, "and it doesn't take long to figure out that in the good old U. S. of A. these days, money and brains aren't necessarily, um, mutually inclusive, if you know what I mean." Sandra nodded wisely and raised her eyebrows.

"I'll have to remember that. Me, I hope I got some brains, because I sure didn't get any of the money."

It was Sandra's turn to laugh. "Me, either! Hey, thanks a lot. Catch lots of fish, okay?"

"Hope so!"

Straithwaite threw his bag across into the passenger seat and slid behind the wheel. He was reaching for his cell phone when it rang. The caller ID was blank.

"Straithwaite," he answered, expecting it to be the office operator.

"Don? Dennis Rhoades. Are you someplace where you can speak freely?"

"I just sat down in a rental car."

"Okay, listen up. As you know, my team and I are in Boise. I just talked to Holdorf and he briefed me on why you're here. It's good luck we hitched a ride with you. Anyway, the General told me to tell you this is now an authorized operation. Bilbao Gambit. You'll be reporting to me as a member of my team."

Straithwaite knew what that meant, and it made him mad.

"The General said you could fill in the blanks for me," Rhoades said.

Straithwaite told Rhoades everything he knew, starting with the wreck-turned-murder, the parties involved, the bombing that had killed Maria de la Rosa, the recovered dosimeter card and the fingerprint match it had yielded.

"Have you heard of Janicot?" Straithwaite asked.

"Pancho? Yeah, I know who he is. I thought he was in prison. The Spanish government thinks he made the bombs for al-Qaeda in the Madrid train station bombings back in oh-four. But all they could tag him with was conspiracy. Bastard should have been executed. How'd he get out?"

"They released him as an expression of goodwill during the last peace talks with ETA."

"Dumb shits. They never learn. But we'll catch him. What else you got for me?"

Straithwaite relayed the rest of what he knew. Captain Halberstam of the Sheriff's Office had headed the investigation originally, but it had been handed over to the State Police.

"What makes you think that?" Rhoades inquired.

"DNA samples from the unidentified shooting victim were submitted to Quantico this morning under the name of a State Police lieutenant named Unger, which I think means Halberstam's boss either kicked the case or the state took it."

"Okay, I get it. But it doesn't matter."

"Why not? Aren't you going to talk to them?"

"Hell, no. Right now they think they're working a random road rage homicide. You want to be the one to tell them there might be a nuke in Boise?"

"I see your point. I haven't contacted anybody local yet, per the General's instructions."

The alarms went off in Rhoades' head. His investigator's gut told him that Straithwaite was leaving something out. It took a few seconds for it to click.

"So, if you haven't talked to the locals, where are you getting your information?"

Straithwaite cursed to himself. He hadn't wanted to give up Kaye, but neither could he withhold pertinent information. Kaye was his asset, but Rhoades hadn't missed the connection. If he had to give up Kaye to catch Pancho, he could live with that.

It was suddenly hot in the car. Straithwaite turned the key and rolled down the windows to get some air.

"You know the guy on the motorcycle I told you about, the one at the accident scene?" Straithwaite hesitated, wondering if he was doing the right thing. "Well, we got lucky. That guy was Ben Kaye, detective with the LAPD. We've worked together before. He found the radiation badge and called me for help."

"No way! What was he doing here?"

"Pure dumb luck."

"Is he reliable?"

"Absolutely, and he's good. In fact, he's already made you and your team. Told me on the phone a while ago."

Rhoades was stunned. No way in hell. He quickly went over the day in his head.

"Oh, shit. The biker. Really, really big, right?"

"That's Kaye."

"Son of a bitch. He waited outside the airfield this morning. We drove right past him. We need to start driving something different."

Straithwaite laughed. "That's exactly what Kaye said."

There was momentary silence.

"Okay," Rhoades finally said. "It's okay. Kaye is one of the good guys. You think we should use him?"

"We are. Per the General I am authorized to share information with him. After all, he found the dosimeter after the locals missed it. Without it we wouldn't know about Pancho."

"I agree. Since Kaye knows you, you handle him."

"That works for me. Thanks." Straithwaite was relieved. Kaye would remain his asset. "Oh," he added, "I almost forgot. It might be nothing, but you never know. Kaye had me run a license plate. Didn't give me a solid reason. It came back on a vehicle registered to a company named Biscay Basin Group in Boise."

"Think it's relevant?"

"Didn't you take geography in school?"

"Yeah, I took geography. So what?"

"Well, Pancho's ETA, right? ETA is Basque. The Basques are from northern Spain, which is where the Bay of Biscay is...as in Biscay Basin Group."

"Missed that one, but I'll check it out. Got anything on the company yet?"

"Only that it's privately held by the Urrestegui family. Note the Basque name, please. First name of the guy that runs things is Robert. I haven't started digging into him yet, but my guess is we'll find that he's connected."

"Okay. Anything else?"

"I just rented a car here in Sun Valley and I had a very interesting conversation with the counter girl. There's some kind of big conference here next week, and people are starting to arrive. Happens every year, according to this gal, with lots of big names. It's kept pretty hush-hush. No press."

"You think this conference might be Pancho's target?"

"I don't know. I don't want to commit to that operationally yet, but I think it could be. What else in Idaho is worth blowing up?"

Rhoades laughed. "You've got a point. Sounds like this conference puts a large concentration of movers and shakers in one place at one time. Might make a very tempting target."

"So, what do you want me to do on this end?"

"Poke around a little bit. Find out what you can about this conference. Attendees, venues, agenda, stuff like that. Just don't raise any red flags yet. Maybe if we know what everybody's doing at any particular time, we can narrow down the time frame a little bit."

"I can do that. You guys coming up here, or staying there?"

"We'll stay here for now. I want to check out this Urrestegui guy. Besides, for all we know Pancho could be in Dallas or L.A. by now, and...."

"I don't think so. I think he's close."

"Well, for what it's worth, my gut tells me the same thing. Don, we need to find this guy."

"Yeah, I've got a bad feeling about this one. Oh, hey, I was just about to call the General with the conference information. You want me to call him, or do you want to do it?"

"I'll call him. From now on, communicate with me first. Send me a copy of what you sent Kaye on Pancho." Rhoades paused. "Check that. Send it to Alison. And let me know immediately if you get anything more from Kaye."

"Will do. Anything else?"

Rhoades hesitated, thinking. "Don't think so. You have anything else for me?"

"Have a nice weekend? Does that count?"

"Smart ass."

Straithwaite checked his watch. With any kind of luck he could still make it to a decent sporting goods store before they all closed for the day.

Dennis Rhoades closed his cell phone and leaned back against the headboard in his hotel room.

Son of a bitch, he thought ruefully. Pancho Janicot was here and the bastard had made it in without being detected. If it weren't for the accident and the total dumb luck of having an LAPD detective stumble into the whole thing, they still wouldn't know. And the cop knowing Pancho's identity changed the entire picture.

The General must be plenty pissed.

Rhoades pondered his best course of action and decided to talk it over with his team.

"Stan, Alison, you both on?" He spoke into a small hand-held radio.

Both team members, in rooms on the same floor, answered promptly.

"My room, five minutes," Rhoades ordered. "Alison, bring Toto."

Stan Kaminski arrived first. A former SEAL, Kaminski was the perfect undercover agent. He looked like an insurance salesman and had that remarkable ability to disappear in a crowd of three. By almost all appearances totally average, Kaminski had three talents Rhoades found indispensable. First, the man had a nearly eidetic memory. He never forgot anything or anybody. Second, he spoke so many languages that Rhoades, who was himself fluent in Russian and German, had lost count. Third, and most endearing, was that Stan Kaminski loved to fight, and enjoyed killing people with his hands. He was so good at it that Rhoades was constantly reminding Kaminski that he was required to carry a firearm. Kaminski, true to form, chose to irritate his boss by carrying a cut-down Smith and Wesson .44 magnum revolver instead of the agency-issue Glock 9MM. Rhoades didn't like it, but he'd long ago given up arguing about it.

"Hey, boss," Kaminski greeted Rhoades laconically and slumped into a chair to wait for Alison Washington.

"Hey. Alison should be here shortly. You want a drink?"

"No, thanks."

Two sharp knocks on the door announced the arrival of Alison Washington. A scant five foot three and one hundred ten pounds soaking wet, Washington was a former D.C. Metro cop and a computer and electronics expert. Rhoades had recruited her after she'd been fired for hacking the District's computer system and raising her own pay to twenty grand a week. It had only been a demonstration, intended to focus attention on what she considered to be an extremely vulnerable system, but the Chief wasn't amused and canned her.

"What's up?" Washington sat down on one of the queen-sized beds and opened the laptop she carried. Its encrypted wireless capability could access the DHS system from anywhere.

"Just thought we should get together and decide what to do for dinner," Rhoades answered casually.

Kaminski just smiled.

"Sure," Washington said sarcastically. "And you had me bring Toto so we could make on-line reservations, right?"

"Truthfully, I just confirmed that Pancho is in the country, probably within a few miles of us right now. Alison, you should have his most recent sheet in your inbox.

That got Kaminski's attention and he sat up in his chair. "You sure?"

"Fingerprint identification."

Washington and Kaminski exchanged glances.

186

"Fingerprint?" Washington's skepticism showed in her voice. "How? Is he alone?" She looked at Kaminski, worry evident on her face.

Before Kaminski could get his two cents worth in, Rhoades motioned them both to be quiet.

"Okay, here's what we know."

It took him almost twenty minutes to brief his team with the details. They were both good investigators and asked all the right questions, several of which Rhoades had to admit he couldn't answer.

"You know what I know," Rhoades told them when he was done. "Oh, except that we've already been burned. The LAPD, at least the vacationing LAPD, knows we're here."

"What? How?" Both agents asked at once.

Rhoades didn't answer. He wanted to see if either of them would figure it out.

"Oh, shit." Kaminski's memory got him there first. "The big sucker on the Harley parked outside the base was Kaye."

"Bingo," Rhoades said. "So, the first thing we need is at least one car with local plates to use while we're here. And no cop car look-alikes."

"I want a Mustang!" Washington spoke up quickly.

Rhoades looked at her sideways and frowned.

"Sorry, boss." She was smiling.

"Why here, boss?" Kaminski asked. "Seems to me we should be headed for Sun Valley."

"Maybe so. But first I want to check out this Urrestegui guy. If he's involved we need to know."

"I'm already all over the guy." Washington was typing furiously. "Let's see... No arrest record. Five-year passport record shows several trips to Europe, Spain in particular, two trips to African countries, one to India, and one to... Mongolia? Why does a guy go to Mongolia?"

"To hunt," Kaminski said. "Except maybe Europe, those are all places to hunt exotic big game."

Washington nodded. She believed Kaminski. The guy's memory was almost as good as the computer.

"Okay, let's see what else," she continued. "Domestic trips, mostly to L.A. and New York." She glanced at Kaminski, who just shrugged.

"Hey, I'm good, but not that good."

"Oh my God! Mark this day on the calendar, boss. Stan actually admitted he didn't know something."

"Alright, children," Rhoades said calmly. "Back on task, shall we?"

Washington sent a sneer in Kaminski's direction and he responded by sticking out his tongue.

Rhoades saw the exchange and was struck with the sudden certainty that his two subordinates were sleeping together. How had he missed that until now? He tried to talk himself out of it, but the feeling just wouldn't go away. It was a serious breach of security protocols, but he decided just as instantly not to make a big deal out of it until Operation Bilbao Gambit concluded.

"...pillar of the community." Washington's voice brought Rhoades' attention back to the situation. "Active in local charities and the art scene."

"New York and Los Angeles," Kaminski interjected casually.

"What?" Rhoades asked, lost.

"Art," Kaminski elaborated. "That's why he goes to New York and L.A."

"Makes sense, I guess," Rhoades said. "Go on, Alison."

"That's about it, at least on a preliminary search. Nothing out of the ordinary."

"What about his business?" Rhoades asked. "Biscay Basin Group."

Washington's fingers flew over the keyboard.

"Um, no website, which is kind of unusual these days," Washington muttered, more to herself than Rhoades. "Public records show real estate, timber, mining, livestock. Lots of money, but... Uh-oh, hold on one second. Biscay Basin Group is in our system, investigated for customs violations and, I'll bet... Yep, the IRS has a file on the company for questionable overseas investments and there's some kind of application pending with Interior, but it doesn't say here what it is."

"Got an address?"

"Yep."

"Satellite imagery," Rhoades instructed.

The two men took seats flanking Washington as downtown Boise appeared on the screen. Washington zoomed in on the address. The image didn't tell them much, only the parking lot in the rear and shadows hinting at the height of the building compared to its neighbors.

"Get a street view," Kaminski suggested.

Two mouse clicks and the DHS team stood on the street in front of Biscay Basin Group.

"Is not the Internet a wondrous place?" Washington sighed, glancing at the two men.

"Looks like a restaurant to me," Rhoades said. "Urrestegui's offices must be upstairs. What is it, five floors total?"

"Yeah, I think so, boss. His address in our system matches this address, so I'd bet he lives there, too."

"Find out if he owns the restaurant or just leases out the space," instructed Kaminski.

Washington's hands flew over the keyboard, working their magic.

"Owns it," she said after a minute.

"It looks like the west wall of the building is common, or at least right up against the building next door, but there's an alleyway or driveway on the east," observed Rhoades. "Alison, can you move us up the street east just a little bit?"

"You bet."

The image shifted, giving the DHS agents an oblique view down the alley. The east side entry vestibule was clearly visible.

"Okay," Rhoades said thoughtfully. "That's probably the main entrance to the upper floors. I wish we could tell if there was a way upstairs from the restaurant."

The team leader stood up and paced impatiently, deep in thought.

"Alison," Rhoades said at last, "cross reference hotels within a one block radius of that address."

"Surveillance?" Kaminski asked, raising his eyebrows.

"Yep. I want to sit on that building for," he stopped and looked at his watch, "thirty-six to forty-eight hours, depending on what else breaks, and see who comes and goes." He looked at his team members and smiled. "If we can get a room in the right place, only one of you has to sit in a car."

"Hey, we're in luck," Washington exclaimed. "There's a hotel a half-block east on the other side of the street. And," she paused and checked the screen, "they have rooms available."

"Okay," Rhoades clapped his hands several times, "saddle up. We're moving. And we also just decided where we're having dinner."

It took Rhoades and his team twenty minutes to check out.

An hour later they were settling into adjoining rooms, one of which was a third floor corner suite with street views to the west, at the hotel near the Biscay Basin Group building.

An hour after that Kaminski and Washington walked into the restaurant on the ground floor and asked for a table for two.

Dennis Rhoades circled the block twice on foot, snapping pictures and playing tourist. Before his team had finished ordering dinner he sauntered in, took a corner stool at the bar, and ordered a cold beer.

26

It only took Cindy a few minutes to pack and she heeded Kaye's admonition to keep it to a minimum. The only extra items were clothes for the next morning's funeral. The Road King's saddlebags still had some room and Kaye rigged Cindy's small bag onto the rack. Knowing he would be in a hotel, he left the bedroll at Cindy's.

Kaye stood back and looked at the big bike.

"Christ almighty. Looks like you belong to a bunch of gypsies."

"Did you say something?" Cindy asked as she came across the lawn. She wore stout boots and carried a helmet.

"No. I was just thinking out loud. Hey, where's your sling?"

"I don't need it. Honest. I'll be fine without it. Besides, I'm not riding on a Harley with my arm in a sling. What would that do to my tough biker bitch image?"

"I'm not..." Kaye started to answer, then thought better of it and shrugged. "You're a big girl. It's your call."

"Okay. Where are we going?"

"You tell me."

"Head into town and I'll give you directions on the way."

Cindy told Kaye to turn right when they reached the main road. There was an opening in the building Friday evening traffic and he took it, accelerating hard up through the gears to the fifty miles per hour speed limit. The force pushed her back against the backrest and the wind took her breath away. She had ridden dirt bikes and ATVs, but never expected anything like this on a big street bike. She laughed out loud from the sheer joy of it. The bike was loud enough that she had to lean in and half-shout directions into Kaye's ear. She didn't mind at all.

Twenty minutes later they were shown to a table overlooking the river as it coursed through downtown.

"So," Cindy said after they'd ordered a glass of wine, "tell me more about Ben Kaye."

"Such as?"

"Oh, you know. The usual stuff. For instance, you don't wear a ring, but I can see that you have." The telltale blush crept up her throat. "Are you married?"

"Used to be."

"Divorced?"

"No. She was killed in a motorcycle accident. About six months ago."

"Oh God. I'm so sorry. Me and my big mouth."

"That's okay."

"Tell me about her. I mean, if you want to."

Kaye sat still for a moment. How could he tell the young woman sitting across from him that she was a fifteen-year younger, near-replica of his dead wife? He decided he couldn't.

"Her name was Amy. She was a writer. We'd just celebrated our fifteenth anniversary."

"What did she write?"

"She was a novelist."

"Amy Kaye," Cindy said softly. "Sorry, I don't think I ever read any of her books."

"She used a pen name. Shaeffer Kaye. Shaeffer was her maiden name."

Kaye heard Cindy suck in her breath.

"On, my god. Your wife is Shaeffer Kaye?"

"Was."

Cindy got a stricken look on her face, and the blush blossomed up her throat into her cheeks.

"Oh, Ben, I'm so sorry." Cindy barely whispered. "I love your wife's books, her writing. I've read everything she ever published. I didn't know she had died. I'm so sorry."

The waiter came with their wine, interrupting the conversation, and the talk turned to dinner orders.

Just as they finished ordering, a tall black woman hurried toward their table. Cindy smiled broadly and stood up to embrace her.

Cindy turned to Kaye, keeping one arm draped over her friend's shoulder. "Ben, this is my all-time best friend Charlene. She owns the place."

He stood up, smiling. "Nice to meet you, Charlene."

Charlene embraced Kaye.

"Thank you for saving my best friend's life. Your money is no good here, ever. Lifetime freebies." She looked back and forth from Cindy to Kaye. "Look, I've got to get back to work. Hang around. I'll join you later…if that's okay?"

"You'd better!" Cindy exclaimed, looking at Kaye, who nodded.

They ate a leisurely dinner and Kaye steered the conversation away from himself. Just after dessert, Charlene returned.

"How's your dad doing?" she asked Cindy as she sat down.

"He's holding up, on the outside at least," Cindy replied. "I just hope he makes it through the funeral tomorrow. I wish Uncle Calvin was coming."

"Are you staying at your dad's until you're back to a hundred percent?" Charlene was clearly concerned. "I think that would be a good idea."

"No," Cindy said. "Ben's stashing me in a hotel until things calm down. He thinks the guy who shot Aiden might come after me."

"You really think so?" Charlene stared at Kaye.

"I don't think it's worth the risk not to consider it," Kaye replied. "He's already come after me."

Charlene sat quietly for a moment before saying, "Look, Cindy, why don't you come stay with Steve and me for a couple days? You'll be safe at our place, and I can help you if you need it."

Clearly caught off guard, Cindy fidgeted nervously at the suggestion. Kaye sat back and put his hands together in his lap. He liked the idea, but held his tongue.

"I don't know," Cindy said, twisting her hair around her fingers and looking quickly at Kaye. "I don't want to be a bother, and there's the funeral tomorrow."

"Oh, stop," admonished Charlene. "It's no bother. And you can ride with us to the funeral. We're going, you know. Aiden was like my little brother, too. Please, Cindy? Ben, tell her."

"I think that's a splendid idea."

Outvoted, Cindy capitulated. "Okay, okay," she said, a hint of resignation in her voice. "Your place it is. Hey, do you have room for my bodyguard?"

"Oh, no, not a chance," Kaye spoke up emphatically, raising his hands in defense as he saw Cindy's mouth start to open in protest. "Forget it. I'll find a hotel. End of discussion."

"That's settled, then," Charlene said. "Stretch, I still have about a half-hour's work to do, and then we can go. Steve will be so happy to see you."

"I'll be off, then," Kaye announced, standing up.

"I'll come get my bag." Cindy jumped up, wobbling slightly.

"Sit back down, have another cup of coffee, and I'll bring you your bag. Good thing you're not riding. I'd have to tie you on."

Cindy grimaced, but sat back down. "Thank you."

Kaye left Cindy in Charlene's capable hands. The restaurateur had given him directions to a good hotel nearby, and the deep rumble of the Harley's twin exhaust reverberated off the downtown buildings as he set off.

Five minutes after leaving the restaurant, with the hotel in sight, he found himself cruising past Biscay Basin Group. The restaurant was still crowded with the late evening bar crowd. On the spur of the moment, Kaye decided this might be a good time to reconnoiter the building. With any luck, he might get into the underground garage or the upstairs floors. The residence was out of the question.

Kaye leaned the Road King into the left lane, took the next left and swung into the first available parking place. Walking back to the corner, he stood and looked at the building. The middle floors, with the exception of one dimly lit corner window, were dark. The top floor was ablaze with lights and Kaye could see fleeting shadows of movement cross the windows. It looked like Urrestegui was having a party. The extra traffic might make entry into the garage a possibility.

He stood quietly for a while, watching and formulating a plan. He wished he was dressed a little differently, but there was nothing he could do about it now. When he was satisfied he had a plausible cover story, he sauntered across the street toward the restaurant.

"Good evening, sir," the hostess said from behind a perfect, gleaming white smile. "Would you like a table? The kitchen is about to close, but…."

"No table, thank you. I just came in to meet some friends before we go upstairs to Robert's party."

"Oh! You're a friend of the Urresteguis? Welcome."

"I only know Robert casually. Met him on a hunting trip last year. Haven't met the missus yet."

"She's the greatest. But I think she's still out of town. New York, I think, for another art auction."

"I hear they're quite the collectors."

"Gosh, yes." Her voice became conspiratorial. "It's Mr. Urrestegui's only vice."

"So, if I wanted to go on upstairs and have you send my friends up when they get here, how would I get there?" Kaye kept the question casual. "To be honest, I didn't know Robert had this kind of layout. Couldn't even find the front door! Now I'm worried about not getting a little more dressed up, too." He smiled sheepishly.

"Just go around to the east side of the building and push the call button for the elevator. Someone will be down."

"How 'bout the garage? I'd kind of like to get my rental car off the street."

"There's a call button, sir, outside the gate."

Kaye saw the first flicker of doubt flash in the woman's eyes as she answered.

"Hey, what the heck. Maybe I'll just wait down here for everybody else. Sounds easier." Kaye put on his best smile. "Please tell me there's a men's room on this floor I can get to without a top-secret clearance."

It worked. Kaye saw the tension disappear from the hostess's eyes.

"Yes, sir, that we do. Go back through the bar toward the exit sign. Could I get your name, please, in case the other guests come in looking for you?"

"You bet'cha. Pete. Pete Richards, PR Construction. I build big stuff out of concrete."

Kaye scanned the interior as he headed for the bar. The front glass panels were closed against the evening breeze and the only other visible exit sign was over the hallway leading to the men's room.

Confirming no one was close behind, Kaye passed the men's room door and continued to the exit door at the end of the hallway. It was alarmed, but had a small window of laminated glass with mesh sandwiched between. Kaye peered through it, seeing a stairwell with flights leading up and down. There was also another alarmed exit door, doubtlessly opening to the outside rear of the building. From the shape of the space, Kaye guessed there was another elevator shaft at this end of the building to connect the residence with the garage.

One thing was obvious. He wasn't getting to the garage this way, at least not unnoticed.

He decided to concentrate on the exterior. If there was a hole in the garage large enough to drive a car through, he ought to fit through, too.

On the way out, Kaye passed the hostess's desk again.

"Any sign of my friends yet?" he asked.

"No, Mr. Richards. Sorry."

"Well, hey. That's good, because I decided to run back to the hotel and change into something a little more respectable. If they show up, please tell them I was delayed and send 'em on up."

"It would be my pleasure."

Kaye headed for the alley at the east end of the building. He wanted a wider view of the building's rear side and headed to the north end of the parking lot.

The party was more evident from this side of the building. Several people were visible on a large rooftop terrace, and the sounds of conversation and laughter drifted down to the parking lot.

"Well," Kaye muttered to himself. "They all had to get here, and they've all got to go home sometime."

27

The DHS team completed their reconnaissance and returned to the hotel, where Rhoades contacted the concierge and arranged for a rental car. Much to Washington's delight, the car would be a Mustang.

"You know what that means?" Kaminski taunted Washington.

"No. What?"

"You get the first night sitting in the car watching the back door."

"I don't think so," interjected Rhoades, shaking his head. "Stan, you get the first watch. I want Alison here to monitor the electronics, just in case." He saw the look that passed between his two subordinates. "Alison, set up the camera to cover the front of the restaurant and east vestibule entry. You can get them both from here, right?"

"Easy money, boss. But we're going to have an angle problem with facial ID on anybody wearing a hat. We should be at least one floor lower."

"Do the best you can. Oh, and one more thing."

Washington looked up from her computer, where she was establishing a secure link with the DHS mainframe and database.

"Get into Don Straithwaite's files and get the cell phone number for Kaye. I want a GPS fix on his phone at least every thirty minutes. I want to know where he is and where he's going."

"Straithwaite will go to the General if he finds out," Kaminski told his boss.

"Let him. Too much prep has gone into this to worry about hurt feelings."

"Hey, don't piss on me," Kaminski said with a shrug. "I'm just saying..."

"Duly noted," Rhoades said curtly. Then, to Washington, "Do it."

"Yes, sir."

It took Washington only a few minutes to find Kaye's cell phone number. She breathed a sigh of relief when it turned out she didn't have to hack Don Straithwaite's secure files to do it.

Five minutes later, she reported the first location fix to Rhoades. It was five blocks away.

Washington and Kaminski then assembled the surveillance gear Kaminski would need in the car. The key items were a digital video mini-cam and a hand-held night vision scope with recording capability. Both were sophisticated enough to function in near-total darkness, recording identifiable images to run against the DHS facial recognition database.

The concierge called to tell Rhoades the car had arrived.

"Okay, I'm good to go," Kaminski announced. "I just hope I can find a parking place with a decent field of view. It's Friday night, you know."

"Do the best you can," Rhoades told him. "Remember, do not relocate without leaving the lot completely. If somebody is monitoring cameras that's a sure attention grabber."

"I could go, too, boss," Washington volunteered. "It'd be safer."

"No, I need you here." He turned to Kaminski. "Stan, you've done this a million times. Check in every five minutes. Once the bars close we'll give it an hour."

"Hey, I'm cool. Washington is the nervous Nellie."

"Okay." Rhoades clapped his hands together rapidly. "Saddle up. I want you in place before the restaurant closes." He saw Washington and Kaminski exchange a quick glance before Kaminski picked up the duffel and headed out.

Washington went to the window and looked out. She saw Kaminski cross the sidewalk and toss the duffel into the dark blue Mustang parked at the curb below.

"I sure wish you'd have let me go with him," she said, turning to Rhoades.

For a second, Rhoades thought about making a crack that would tip Washington to the fact that he thought she was sleeping with Kaminski, but thought better of it.

"He'll be fine. Listen for his first check-in, will you? I need to call the General." He headed into the suite's bedroom and closed the door.

"Holdorf," the General answered on the first ring. "Hello, Dennis."

"General, I have an update." Rhoades could hear quite a bit of background noise. "Is this a bad time, sir?"

"No, go ahead, Dennis. I'm not in the office, though, so keep it brief. I cannot answer questions."

"Understood, sir." Rhoades then briefed the General on the surveillance setup and his monitoring of Kaye. He also told Holdorf that Kaye knew his team was in Boise and relayed the information he'd gotten from Straithwaite earlier.

"Very interesting," Holdorf said when Rhoades mentioned the conference.

"Sir?"

"I'm attending that conference. That's why I sent Don on up there. I want you and your team there by Monday."

"We'll be there, General."

"You and your people are doing good work. Let's see this through to a favorable outcome."

"Thank you, sir. We..." The line went dead before he could finish.

Rhoades walked back into the sitting room just in time to hear Kaminski's first check-in.

"Found a good vantage point," Kaminski told them. "How's the link from here?"

"Good," Washington told him. "Good visibility, no interference. They're not running any kind of damper."

"Well," Kaminski said resignedly, "time for every agent's favorite unpaid overtime."

"Remember, check in every five minutes."

"I'm fine, Alison, but thanks for worrying."

Washington glanced sideways to see if Rhoades had noticed the tone of Kaminski's voice. Their boss was busy adjusting the camera, positioned in the northwest window, apparently oblivious to the conversation. She decided to run another GPS fix on Kaye's cell phone.

"Hey, boss, come look at this." Washington said.

"What've you got?"

"I just got Kaye's location off his cell phone again. You're not going to believe it."

"What? Where is he?"

"Well, according to my computer, he's somewhere very close to, or inside, Urrestegui's building."

"You're kidding!"

"Nope. He's there."

"Son of a bitch. If nothing else, the guy has brass." Rhoades thought for a moment before picking up the two-way. "Stan, come in," he said into the microphone.

"Go ahead," Kaminski replied.

"Alison's cell phone fix puts Kaye at your location."

"Here? What the hell would he be doing here?"

"Probably looking for Pancho, just like us."

"What do you want me to do, boss? You want me to look for him?"

"No. Don't give up your surveillance position. It's Pancho we want. If you see Kaye nosing around, advise me. I'll have a little chat with him about his role in this investigation. Which, by the way, is officially zero. Got it?"

"Understood."

"And be careful. He's big and has a bad reputation."

A chuckle came back over the link. "I've run into big and bad before, and I'm still here."

Kaminski put the two-way down on the Mustang's passenger seat. He hoped Kaye did show up. Big and bad, huh? He'd see about that.

Stan Kaminski was a pro. He'd chosen his surveillance location well and saw Kaye as soon as the LAPD cop turned the corner from the sidewalk into the alley. Curious, he watched Kaye walk to the back of the parking lot and stand there, studying the building.

Kaminski deduced that the big cop was looking for a way inside.

"You won't find it, asshole," Kaminski said aloud. "I already looked, and if I didn't find a way in, you won't, either."

Kaminski watched Kaye move quickly toward a corner of the building above the underground garage entrance and take up position in a deep shadow.

"Thought of that, too," Kaminski said softly. "You'll break your legs." The DHS agent had considered getting through the gate when a car opened the garage, but the only way to do that without being noticed involved a drop of at least fifteen feet onto concrete, and he wasn't about to attempt that without a rope and some gear. Plus, there was a camera mounted above the gate.

Kaminski considered calling Rhoades to let him know that Kaye had shown up, but he wanted to meet this wise guy and size him up. Kaye was a wildcard in the operation and he needed to go away. If he took the hint and went home, so much the better. If he didn't take the hint, well, there were stronger suggestions Kaminski was prepared to make.

He made the decision to deal with Kaye first, then call his boss.

A car turned into the alley and swung onto the garage ramp. It disappeared from Kaminski's view, but a moment later he heard the heavy metal door rattle as it raised, then begin to close behind the car.

Okay, Kaminski told himself, time to go deal with Kaye. He took a drink of water and double-checked the chopped .44 magnum in the shoulder rig. Satisfied, he got out and quietly locked the door with the key, avoiding the electronic lock button on the key fob that blinked the parking lights.

There was no way to approach Kaye's position without possibly being seen. Kaminski had to be satisfied taking a route that kept him behind the larger vehicles parked in the lot, and he breathed silent thanks that everybody in this redneck burg seemed to drive the biggest pick-up or SUV they could find. He was to the point where he would have to step from behind an F-350 quad cab and reveal himself – if Kaye hadn't already spotted him – when he heard the garage door start to raise.

Kaminski froze and waited. A vehicle started up the ramp and he saw headlights shining on the side of the building next door. The door began to rattle down. Kaminski was watching the car emerge from behind the concrete retaining wall when he caught a flicker of movement in his peripheral vision. He spun his head just in time to see Kaye jump onto the retaining wall and, without hesitation, step off and drop out of sight.

Kaminski reacted immediately, running to the retaining wall and looking down at the concrete below. He fully expected to see Kaye, injured from the fall.

"Son of a bitch!" Kaminski hissed, slapping his hand on the top of the retaining wall.

The driveway below was empty and the door had closed.

***

Kaye waited patiently in the deep shadows close to the back of the building. He saw the surveillance camera and avoided moving through its field of view.

Now all he needed was some traffic.

He was in luck. A few minutes later, a car turned the corner from the alley and descended the ramp. Two-thirds of the way down the car stopped and the driver pushed a button on the wall-mounted call box. Kaye couldn't make out the conversation, but the garage door started to rise. The car pulled forward and turned through the door into the garage. The door rumbled back down.

While the car was on the ramp Kaye watched the surveillance camera closely. When the driver pushed the call button, a red light on the camera came on, flashed until the door was almost down, then went off.

Kaye smiled. It was a small chink in the armor. Building security obviously had enough confidence in the garage door that the camera was active only when the door was raised. He guessed that there would be a door button inside that also activated the camera. There might be an inside camera, but he doubted it. With entrance security so tight there was probably little concern with who left.

Several minutes passed. Kaye's patience was rewarded with the sound of the garage door lurching into motion. He watched from his hiding place. Almost as soon as the door began to open the red light on the camera began to blink. He saw the exiting vehicle's headlights swing against the ramp's outer retaining wall, then flood the ramp itself before lighting up the building next door.

He knew it would be close. With the car approaching the top of the ramp, Kaye stepped forward from the shadows. He knew from the sound that the door had reversed and was closing. His timing was perfect. Just as he stepped onto the retaining wall the exiting car reached the top of the ramp and the camera's red light went off.

The fifteen-foot drop was no problem for Kaye. He absorbed the impact and directed his momentum to put himself into a prone position before rolling quickly toward the lowering door. He got under with only inches to spare.

Rising quickly, he moved left, staying close to the door until his back found solid wall. From outside he heard a voice mutter 'son of a bitch'. Someone knew he was in the garage. He decided not to worry about it and deal with whoever it was, friend or foe, when the time came.

The garage was dimly lit. One floor, it looked to have about forty spaces, mostly filled. At the west end Kaye saw an elevator and the stairwell that undoubtedly connected to the restaurant. Checking for cameras and seeing none, he headed toward the stairs. Immediately outside the elevator was a line of spaces marked 'Reserved'. In the first space was a silver Range Rover. The license plate read 'BBG'. Next to that was a dark blue Escalade, then a silver 500S Benz and, finally, a sleek, red Ferrari. All bore vanity plates easily connected with Biscay Basin Group. Urrestegui's personal vehicles.

It was the vehicle on the end, two empty spaces beyond the Ferrari, that piqued Kaye's curiosity. Backed in, the white Ford F-350 panel van had no front plate, but was in a reserved space. A sunshade was propped up in the van's windshield, looking very out of place on a vehicle parked underground. Unless, thought Kaye, you were trying to keep people from seeing inside.

The van was so close to the walls on the back and passenger side it was impossible to walk around. He tried unsuccessfully to peer through the darkly tinted driver's window. Reaching into his pocket, he withdrew the Road King's key ring. On it, Kaye always carried a small penlight, a habit born years ago when a lost fastener on a dark roadside had stranded him until daylight.

He shined the little light through the tinted window and was satisfied to make out the driver's seat. With some experimentation, Kaye was able to angle the beam and get his palm-shielded eyes close enough to the glass to see into the rear of the van.

A wooden crate, some four feet long and eighteen inches square, was lashed to the floor. A bench seat was visible on the passenger side of the cargo area, but what puzzled Kaye was the dull, unburnished metal appearance of the van's interior behind the front seats.

Suddenly, it struck him. Shielding. The metal was protection against radiation. There was a nuke in the crate.

But that didn't make sense. Why put something dangerous in a wooden crate and then shield the van? Why not just shield the crate? Clearly, the van was set up for people to ride in close proximity to the crate, and a van full of people in containment suits was sure to attract unwanted attention.

As he pondered his next move, the elevator door opened and the sound of laughter filled the garage. He quickly threw himself behind the Ferrari, thankful that nobody risked getting a car that expensive too close to a concrete wall. Four sets of legs walked into his field of vision, headed into the garage. A moment later, over the fading sound of giggling conversation, Kaye heard the double chirp of a car alarm being deactivated, the slamming of doors and an engine starting.

It was time to leave. He needed to contact Khalid and pass along what he'd seen in the van.

The departing vehicle turned toward the door, which began to rise when the car was some ten feet away. When the door was high enough, the driver exited, the glare of brake lights turning the inside of the garage an eerie red.

Again, Kaye had to time it perfectly. Too late and he'd have to wait for the next chance, even risk getting stuck. Too soon and he risked being obviously visible to the departing car's driver and the overhead camera.

The door began descending. At the last possible second Kaye sprinted across the garage and threw himself under the door.

Quickly glancing up, he breathed a sigh of relief. The red light was off. Then, remembering that someone outside had seen him go in, he stood and hugged the inside corner, and watched.

Ideally, he would have liked to go up the same way he'd come down, but fifteen feet of smooth concrete wall was a stretch, even for him. He'd have to go part way up the ramp. He didn't worry about more partygoers coming or going. He could easily deflect their questions.

Illuminated only by the single light over the door and scattered light from the surrounding buildings, most of the ramp was in shadow. Kaye confirmed the camera was inactive and, keeping a keen ear open for approaching vehicles, started up.

Near the bottom of the ramp, its entire width was in shadow. As it rose, however, the shadow crossed obliquely until, about halfway up, the entire ramp was dimly illuminated. Kaye stopped as far up as he could while remaining in the shadow. There was still ten feet of retaining wall to deal with. Gauging the distance, Kaye exploded like a sprinter coming out of the blocks. When the timing was right, he leapt up and toward the wall. His left foot hit halfway up and he used the leverage to redirect his momentum upward. At the same time his foot pushed off, his hands closed over the top of the wall, and with a mighty pull he vaulted neatly over the top, landing softly several feet beyond the wall.

"Very impressive," a quiet voice said from Kaye's right. "If I hadn't seen it, I wouldn't believe you could do that."

Kaye wheeled quickly. Leaning against the front fender of a truck about ten feet away was a man about his height, dressed in denims and a light windbreaker over a t-shirt.

"I'm a cop," Kaye said.

"Bullshit," Stan Kaminski replied, pushing himself away from the fender and walking toward Kaye. "I'm a cop. From what I just saw, you look like a burglar to me."

"I'm a police officer. I'm working a case."

"Cut the crap, Kaye. I know who you are, and you're out of your jurisdiction. As far as I'm concerned you're just another asshole on the street."

"Who are you?"

"Kaminski. Homeland Security. I'd say it's a pleasure to meet you, but it isn't."

Kaye ignored the insult. "Are you following me, or watching the building?"

"Not your business. Like I said, to me you're just another...."

"Yeah, yeah, I know," Kaye cut him off. "Asshole on the street. You looking for Pancho?"

"Who?"

"Pancho Janicot. ETA bomber. Maybe you've heard of him?"

"Sorry, I'm not at liberty to discuss national security issues with civilians."

"You're an idiot. I think Pancho is in Boise. In fact, I think he's in this building right now, waiting to use the nuke in the back of a white van in the garage."

At the mention of a nuclear weapon Kaminski's eyes narrowed slightly.

"Why aren't you sharing with the locals?" Kaye asked sharply. "Pancho's killed five people here in the past week and you guys are playing turf games."

Kaminski stepped in close and stared into the big cop's eyes. The DHS agent was Kaye's height and, while the LAPD cop had at least sixty pounds on him, he wanted Kaye to know he wasn't intimidated.

"You listen to me. Go home. Vamoose. Get out of Dodge. I don't give a shit what you call it, just get off this case, or your favorite Uncle will find a nice, cozy cell where you can spend the next ten to twenty years."

"Really? So far, I haven't seen any identification, Agent Kaminski, or whoever you are. You're a long way from telling me what to do."

"Go home," Kaminski repeated, poking his right index finger into Kaye's chest.

Kaye looked down at Kaminski's finger, then back into the agent's eyes. "Don't do that."

"What?" Kaminski asked with eyebrows raised. "This?" He poked Kaye in the chest again, harder this time.

"Fair warning. Last time."

"Or what, mister tough guy? You going to assault a federal agent? Go right ahead, if you think you're tough enough." The ex-SEAL wasn't worried about Kaye. He'd defeated – even killed – bigger men and had the medals and trophies to prove it.

Kaminski poked Kaye hard in the chest again and taunted, "Come on, big man. Bring it, if you've got it, that is."

Kaye had had enough. He brought his left hand up quickly, grabbing Kaminski's hand and twisting it down and out. It was a move intended to put strain on the agent's elbow and shoulder, bending him sideways.

Kaminski smiled inwardly. Kaye was a street cop, trained not to hurt anybody. Instead of resisting Kaye's move, Kaminski went with it, twisting his torso hard to the right and downward. At the same time, he brought his left hand across and down hard onto Kaye's wrist, breaking Kaye's hold. He expected the blow to break Kaye's wrist, too. As soon as he felt the big man's grip release, he twisted hard back up and around to the left, directing his elbow at the side of Kaye's face.

Kaye was surprised by Kaminski's strength and obvious hand-to-hand combat skills. He saw the elbow coming and ducked, turning his head, but couldn't avoid it completely. Instead of catching him flush on the face the elbow grazed his left ear and glanced off the top of his skull.

Kaminski used the torque of the twist and followed with a lightning strike with the heel of his right hand directly to Kaye's sternum. Against a typical opponent the blow would have broken ribs and ended the fight. But Kaye wasn't a typical opponent. The strike drove him back a step, but he didn't go down.

Kaminski pressed his advantage. Gliding forward, he reversed his body's torque again and used the momentum to launch a vicious left hand at Kaye's head.

Kaye saw it coming and swept his right arm up and out to block, intending to use the same slide and capture technique he'd used on Timothy earlier that day.

Kaminski was too skilled. When Kaye blocked the punch, the DHS agent instantly rotated back, pulling his hand away while he pivoted on the ball of his left foot and launched his right foot at Kaye's head.

Kaye was on the defensive and knew it. He needed an opening, a chance to get his hands on the DHS agent, or the guy was going to use him as a punching bag and, sooner or later, get through his defenses and land a debilitating blow.

Kaminski was a microsecond slow launching his kick. Kaye anticipated it and swept upwards, his immense left hand closing around Kaminski's ankle, stopping the kick just inches from his head. He pushed upward with all his strength, intending to upend the DHS agent and drive him back and down into the ground.

Kaminski was surprised when Kaye caught his ankle, thinking his first strike had broken the big man's wrist. Instead, his ankle felt like it was caught in a crusher. Kaye's strength stunned him momentarily, but his fighter's instincts took over and he did the only thing he could. With Kaye's hand clamped on his right ankle and his balance going rapidly over backwards, he used Kaye as a fulcrum, springing into the air off his left leg and sending a front kick straight into Kaye's face.

The kick caught Kaye flat-footed. He lost his grip on Kaminski's ankle and stepped backwards, trying to clear his head before his opponent could close again. He could taste the blood from his split lip.

Kaminski landed on his back and somersaulted backwards to his feet. Eight feet now separated the two men. The entire exchange had taken less than five seconds.

"That all you got?" Kaminski taunted. "With your reputation, I thought you'd be tougher."

"I'm still standing here," Kaye replied evenly, wiping the trickle of blood from his chin. He knew he had to change his tactics, or the DHS agent would hand him his head on a platter.

"Round two, tough guy?" sneered Kaminski.

"Like I said, I'm still standing here."

The DHS agent came fast in a flurry of moves intended to confuse Kaye. It was time to hurt the cop and end this, and he intended to take out one of the big man's knees.

Kaminski closed, supremely confident.

Kaye stood easily, balanced in a boxer's stance, his relaxed hands up in defense.

As the DHS agent launched his first strike he stared into Kaye's eyes and realized too late that the rules of engagement had changed. The eyes had gone flat and cold, and Kaminski saw no fear, only danger. Committed, he lashed out with his left hand at Kaye's head, preparing to follow with a right to the throat he knew would be exposed as soon as Kaye's head snapped back from the left.

Kaye saw the left coming, but instead of trying to block it and give up his hand position, he simply let it through, tucking his chin and rolling his left shoulder up. Let him hit me, Kaye thought, just not where it'll do damage.

The blow glanced off Kaye's shoulder and arm and grazed his ear, its force expended.

Kaminski had already stepped forward and started the follow-up right hand, but when the left missed, he had no target. Surprised, he hesitated, left arm still out and right arm partially extended, for a split second.

It was the opening Kaye needed.

Kaminski never saw the huge right hand coming. He went down like a bag of rocks, fighting against the darkness trying to swallow him. His mind was stunned and his first thought was that Kaye had shot him. Nobody could hit that hard. He rolled away from his opponent and staggered to one knee as he tried to get the .44 mag out from under the zipped-up windbreaker. Blood flowed freely into his left eye.

"That all you got?" He heard Kaye mock him. "For a guy who hits so hard, I thought you'd take a punch better than that."

"You son of a bitch," Kaminski rasped. "I'm gonna kill you."

"You're not going to kill anybody." The voice came from Kaye's right and he spun toward the sound. A man approached from the alley and Kaye recognized him as the driver of the car he'd seen leaving Gowen Field.

"Dennis Rhoades, Homeland Security," the man said, flashing an ID and badge in Kaye's general direction as he hurried over to Kaminski.

"Pay attention, Kaminski," Kaye said. "That's how it done properly. Present identification and announce who you are before you threaten somebody."

Rhoades cast a dark glance at Kaye before turning his anger on Kaminski.

"Stan, what the hell are you doing? Are you nuts? I told you to call me if you saw him."

"I was gonna call as soon as I finished talking to him."

"You call that talking?"

"He went inside the building, boss. Into the garage," protested Kaminski, his bravado returning as the effects of Kaye's punch wore off. "When he came out, I figured I needed to talk to him before he left."

"Is that why you failed to check in and didn't answer your radio? You could've just blown this entire operation. What if our friends just recorded you getting your ass kicked? Huh?"

"I wasn't..." Kaminski started to protest, but Rhoades cut him off.

"Just shut up and go have Alison take a look at that cut. You might need stitches. Damn it, Stan. Damn it!"

Kaminski stood up and started to walk into the parking lot. "Next time, Kaye," he said back over his shoulder.

Kaye ignored him.

Rhoades turned to Kaye. "Kaye, what the hell are you doing here?"

Kaye stared dispassionately at the DHS man. "Before we continue this conversation, might I suggest that we move to another location?"

"Follow me," Rhoades said curtly.

"Now," Kaye said as they walked, "to answer your question, I'm here for the same reason you are, Agent Rhoades. Pancho Janicot."

"You have no jurisdiction in Idaho, and certainly none on this case."

"I've had the same talk with the locals and I'll tell you the same thing I told them. This is personal. Pancho almost killed me and did kill people who matter to me. I'm acting as a private citizen and there's nothing you can do about it."

"Private citizen, eh? Then you just committed a crime."

"Arguable. The garage isn't posted. Besides, even if I did, you have no authority to make a local trespassing arrest. Try again."

"Just go home. This is a federal matter and we're all over it. I've talked at length to your DHS contact and have all the intel – and then some – that you do. Butt out. We've got this."

"I wish that inspired confidence. But Pancho has killed four locals and one of his own people in the last few days, he may be in possession of a nuke, and DHS isn't sharing with the locals. Something stinks."

"We're trying to avoid a general panic."

"Oh, good strategy. Several hundred thousand potential victims might be vaporized, but at least they'll be calm when it happens." Kaye couldn't keep the contempt out of his voice. "You people are idiots."

"Look, for what it's worth, we don't think Boise is Pancho's target. I think he's long gone already."

"Yet you're watching Urrestegui."

"Orders. One day, maybe two."

"You're wrong. Pancho is still in Boise. In fact, I think he's at that party upstairs right now, and I think whatever he's transporting is in the back of a white van parked in the garage."

"You saw something?" Rhoades was suddenly interested.

"Yep. It's there right now."

Rhoades was silent while they walked slowly.

"Unfortunately," the agent said at last, "no federal magistrate would ever give me a warrant based on information gathered during the commission of a crime. Especially when the perpetrator is a police officer who should know better."

"Since when has the federal government let a little thing like the Constitution get in the way of the war on terror?"

"Some of us try to follow the rules, but it is a war. Don't forget that."

"Good for you. Look, I know we could argue about it all night, and both sides have valid points. But when you abandon the precepts you claim to be protecting as a means of protecting them, you've already lost. It's circular logic."

"Abraham Lincoln would probably disagree, and he saved the Union. Look, Kaye, I'm not here to talk politics. I'm here to find Pancho Janicot, so do me a favor and spare me the lesson."

"Have it your way."

"I intend to. And let me tell you how that's going to be. In fifteen minutes I will have an order from the Regional Director of Homeland Security to arrest you on sight if you interfere in my investigation. Maybe it's legal, maybe it's not, but I guarantee you, you will sit in a cell for the three or four years it takes the lawyers to argue about it and a judge to decide."

Kaye stared coldly at Rhoades. "Try to arrest me and you'd better bring more help than Kaminski. Have a nice evening." He turned and walked back the way they'd come.

Heading back to the Road King, Kaye went over what had just happened. Something bothered him. Kaminski had known he would be there. How?

"Geez!" he exclaimed aloud, causing a couple on the sidewalk to step into the street and give him a wide berth. Shaking his head, he reached to his side, grabbed his cell phone and turned it off.

28

Saturday morning dawned clear, but the air had changed. Even early there were towering clouds building over the mountains and the forecast included the possibility of scattered thunderstorms later in the day. Kaye rose early and devoted an hour to his practice. His encounter with Kaminski had left him sore and tight, but the swelling in his lip had gone down.

Ninety minutes after rising he sat in the hotel coffee shop, lingering over breakfast and the first newspaper he'd read in over a week.

The murders on Highway 55 were still front-page news and the paper made no bones about the fact that the investigation was going nowhere, fast, even with the State Police in charge. The lead investigator, Lieutenant Unger, was quoted admitting the investigation was stalled and laid that blame on the FBI forensics lab, but expressed confidence an arrest would be forthcoming.

Kaye smiled ruefully. It was obvious that Dennis Rhoades hadn't driven straight from Gowen Field to State Police headquarters yesterday morning to share information. If they shared Pancho's identity with the local agencies there would be several hundred additional pairs of eyes out there looking for the ETA bomber. Instead, the feds were worried about turf.

Kaye hadn't packed for a funeral. He did the best he could, making time on the way to the funeral home to stop and purchase a black polo shirt and wearing black chaps over his pants.

Aiden Graham was to be buried at the Idaho Veteran's Cemetery after a graveside service. As a decorated combat veteran he would be accorded full military honors, and all stops had been pulled out for Mike Graham's son. Newspapers across the country had carried the tragic story of a Marine maimed in combat coming home alive, only to be gunned down during a senseless, random street crime, and his countrymen responded.

A cadre of two-dozen motorcycle officers from various agencies had assembled in front of the funeral home to officially escort the procession. There were also no less than two hundred Patriot Guard riders on hand to assure the solemnity of the occasion. There would be no protesters here today.

Inside, uniformed Marines attended the casket. It took Kaye a moment to realize that one of the Marines was Mike Graham.

Cindy saw Kaye arrive and excused herself from the knot of mourners that surrounded her. Dressed in black, she also wore a black sling supporting her arm.

"Thank you for coming, Ben," she half-whispered. "It's an honor to have you here. What happened to your lip?" She reached up and touched it gently.

"Just a little souvenir of your tax dollars at work. And the honor is all mine. How's your dad?"

A tear trickled down her cheek. "He's holding up okay under the circumstances. Between this and what I said the other day, he's just kind of gone into autopilot mode. God, I wish Uncle Calvin was here." She dabbed at her eyes with her handkerchief.

Mike saw Kaye from across the room and detached himself from the well- wishers to walk over.

"Kaye, it's an honor to have you here. Thank you for coming. Aiden would have been proud."

"I'm honored to be here and proud to honor a fallen fellow Marine. I just wish…"

Mike put a hand on Kaye's shoulder. "We've been over that. It's not your fault. Please, let it go."

"Yes, sir."

"Good, good." Mike glanced at his watch. "Well, it's time." He walked away and headed to the commander of the honor guard detail.

"Ladies and gentlemen," Mike raised his voice to be heard. "We'll be leaving for the cemetery in a few moments. The procession will leave from behind the building and form up as we leave the parking lot. Please, if you are driving your own car to the cemetery, fall in behind the cortege. We'll have a police escort, so don't worry about being left behind. Thank you all for coming. I'm deeply grateful."

Everyone began to disperse from the visitation room. Kaye escorted Cindy to the black limousine that would carry the family and saw her safely seated inside. Moments later, Mike and some half-dozen others, including Charlene and a man Kaye assumed was her husband, arrived and joined her.

Kaye went back to the black Road King.

The procession stretched well over a mile as it made its slow way to the cemetery. The motor officers did an admirable job of leapfrogging the major intersections and blocking cross traffic to keep everyone together.

Kaye knew there was little chance Pancho Janicot would make an attempt at foul play in view of this many people, but stayed alert nonetheless.

As the procession turned off Hill Road and began the climb to the cemetery, Kaye caught the sudden glint of sunlight off metal in the sky to the west. An aircraft was coming in their direction, and it was coming low and fast. A flyover, Kaye thought.

Making nearly three hundred knots, the ungainly looking craft roared over the procession at less than three hundred feet. It had the fuselage of a helicopter and the wing of an airplane, but its most unusual features were the two turboprop engines mounted at the far outboard end of each wing, the propellers so large their tips barely cleared the fuselage.

Painted in USMC colors, Kaye recognized it as an MV-22B Osprey. It banked steeply and turned south, roaring out over the valley.

The access road twisted up the hill for nearly a mile before entering the natural bowl of the cemetery. The beauty of the setting struck Kaye, with the high country looming to the north and commanding vistas opening to the other points of the compass. As the lead vehicle entered the cemetery proper and headed for the grave site, Kaye saw the Osprey coming in again.

During the swing over the valley, the pilot had rotated the engine nacelles almost ninety degrees, converting the craft from an airplane to a helicopter, and it was clear to Kaye that the pilot intended to set down on the knoll forming the northern rim of the cemetery.

The Osprey settled gently to the ground just as the procession rounded the last curve before the gravesite, marked by a large white canopy filled with chairs and surrounded by American flags.

Curious, Kaye stopped and focused his attention on the Osprey.

With engines still at only slightly less than liftoff rotation, the pilot lowered the rear ramp. A lone figure emerged and turned to walk down the hill, one white-gloved hand securing his cover against the blast of the Osprey's rotors. Even at this distance Kaye could make out the heavy metal covering the front of the tunic, and the pale blue ribbon of the Congressional Medal of Honor around the man's neck.

Calvin Dinsmore, Sergeant Major of the Marine Corps, Retired, had arrived.

Ahead of Kaye, the limousine carrying the Graham family came to an abrupt halt and one back door flew open.

Cindy erupted from the vehicle like it was on fire. In three strides she had hiked her dress above her knees and left her shoes behind. Three more and she jettisoned the black sling. Her long legs churned, eating up ground at an amazing rate as she sprinted up the hill toward Dinsmore. The Sergeant Major maintained his pace until Cindy was almost upon him, stopping to absorb the impact as she threw herself headlong into his encircling arms. She clung to him as a found child might for a full minute, then turned and tucked herself under his arm as they came together down the hill.

The ramp of the Osprey rose and the pilot lifted off, rotating the engines to forward flight as he climbed rapidly.

Mike exited the limousine and stood waiting for his longtime friend. As Dinsmore and Cindy approached, Cindy disengaged and stood aside. Mike snapped to attention and saluted. Dinsmore said something Kaye couldn't hear. The two men then fell into an embrace. For the first time since the shooting, Mike cried, his grief finally released. Dinsmore held his friend silently and turned to look at Cindy, who stepped into the encircling safety of her uncle's arms and embraced her father.

Everyone stood silently and respectfully as the family grieved. After several minutes Mike stepped back and nodded to Dinsmore. He was ready to proceed. The honor guard formed up at the rear of the hearse, ready to carry the casket to the bier.

Dinsmore saw them and spoke briefly to Mike, who nodded as he looked in Kaye's direction. The Sergeant Major then strode over to the honor guard, all of whom snapped to rigid attention, awed and unnerved by Dinsmore's presence.

Dinsmore spoke quietly to the NCOIC, who saluted smartly and then led his team to the west side of the canopy and formed them up.

Dinsmore then turned and walked directly to Kaye.

"Sergeant Kaye, I see you still can't hide in a crowd."

Dinsmore had aged, but still had overwhelming command presence.

"A blessing and a curse, Sergeant Major, as you also know."

"Indeed. Sergeant, would you do me the honor of assisting me in carrying Lance Corporal Graham to his final resting place? I might still be able do it alone, but I think Mike and Cindy would be grateful if you helped."

"I'd be honored."

The two men walked to the rear of the hearse and waited while the back was opened and the casket slid out. Dinsmore stepped to one side and took up station, and Kaye positioned himself on the opposite side.

As it became clear what was about to happen, whispers and murmurs of doubt ran through the crowd of mourners. Two men advanced uneasily from the crowd and started forward to help.

"Stand down, gentlemen." Dinsmore's voice stopped them in their tracks. "We can manage, thank you." Then, to Kaye, "You ready?"

"Ready, Sergeant Major."

"Okay. One, two, and three."

The flag-draped casket rose into the air as lightly as if it were empty cardboard. Before the gasps died out, the casket rested steadily on two strong arms, and a strong hand on each side grasped the brass rail for extra balance. Neither man showed the slightest sign of exertion.

"Oh my God," a woman's soft whisper broke the awed silence.

"Forward, slow cadence, march," Dinsmore said, just loudly enough for Kaye to hear.

It was fifty feet from the hearse to the bier. After the casket settled gently into place, Dinsmore reached across to shake Kaye's hand, and Kaye saw tears on the man's cheeks.

"Thank you, Sergeant. I'd prayed I'd never have to do that again."

Kaye nodded in acknowledgement and the two took up their places with the family. Dinsmore hugged Cindy and then embraced Mike again. Mike looked at Kaye, the gratitude evident in his eyes. Cindy came over and hugged Kaye.

"Thank you so much. We can never repay your kindness."

The service was nice, Kaye thought, if that word can be used to describe such an occasion. Cindy flinched at the sound of gunfire during the salute and shrunk closer against Dinsmore. The Governor and Attorney General each spoke, lamenting the loss of a young man to senseless violence and promising justice. The squadron of A-10 Warthogs from Gowen Field performed a flyover, executing the missing man maneuver.

Dinsmore presented the folded flag from the casket to Mike, who clutched it to his chest in despair.

At the conclusion of the service, the mourners slowly dispersed.

When the family gathered and loaded into the limousine, seating was crowded because of Dinsmore's unexpected arrival. Cindy volunteered to ride back to her father's with Kaye, but her uncle would have none of that.

"I need to talk to you," he told her firmly. "Family conference."

"Go with them," Kaye agreed. "I have an errand to run. I'll meet you at your dad's later."

"Okay," Cindy relented. "Promise?"

"Promise."

Kaye leaned in and said his goodbyes, then helped Cindy slide in before watching the limousine slowly head back down the hill.

He stood alone by his iron horse, the now-empty cemetery eerily quiet and beautiful. Such occasions always left him melancholy. He wanted to finish his other task for the day and then ride for a while before returning to Mike Graham's. He started to gear up.

"Sergeant Kaye?" a man's voice inquired from behind.

"I'm not a Marine anymore," Kaye said brusquely as he turned around. "Don't call me Sergeant."

In front of him stood a short, lean, man of about forty, dressed in a dark funeral suit. The eyes in the sun-lined face studied Kaye intently.

"I'm sorry, I don't know anything about the Marines. I'm looking for Sergeant Ben Kaye of the LAPD."

"Sorry. I didn't mean to be rude. I'm Kaye. Not sergeant, just detective. You are…?"

"Lieutenant Garth Unger, Idaho State Police. I've been assigned to lead the investigation into the incident that occurred on Highway 55. I was wondering if I could have a few minutes of your time."

"What can I do for you, Lieutenant?"

"I just have a couple questions. Let's go sit down, shall we?"

They walked to a nearby bench. As Unger sat down he stretched his legs and breathed an audible sigh of relief.

"Well," Unger began, "I've spoken at length with Captain Halberstam and the two deputies who were first on scene. I've read Halberstam's interview with Ms. Graham. I still need to do a face-to-face with her, but I figured that could wait until after today. Besides, it's just a formality. I doubt she can give me anything worthwhile. And I've read your statement."

Unger stopped talking and stared at Kaye intently, signaling that it was now Kaye's turn to talk.

"Okay, and...?"

"I was wondering if there was anything else you'd like to add. Anything else you've remembered since then?"

Kaye looked at Unger carefully. Good cops never ask lead off questions they don't already know the answers to. It's the tried and true way of immediately establishing someone's truthfulness. Kaye decided to be absolutely straightforward with Unger. Less than the whole truth is, after all, still truth.

"Lieutenant, I put everything I knew into the statement I gave Halberstam."

Unger's eyes narrowed slightly at the response. He stared silently out at the magnificent view while he rolled it over in his mind.

"Okay, I can accept that. But let me ask you another question."

"Go ahead."

"What do you know now that you didn't know when you wrote the statement?"

"Look, Lieutenant, I've been told not to talk to you and threatened with long term incarceration if I do."

"By whom?"

"Homeland Security."

"Homeland Security. That actually explains a lot."

"I thought it might. They're in Boise working this case, except they're not investigating a local murder, if you know what I mean. I had a little meeting with them last night." Kaye gestured to his split lip.

Unger sat quietly, staring out at the horizon.

"Look, Kaye," he said at last, leaning forward and tapping the ends of his fingers together. "I don't expect you to go to jail to help me solve this case. I'll go to the Governor and get him to rattle some cages back in D.C. if it comes to that." Unger swiveled his head to look at Kaye and squinted against the sun. "But five people have died. They deserve justice, and right now my gut is telling me they won't get it from Homeland Security."

"Unfortunately, I think you're right. And I'm not telling you how to run your case, but I think that conversation with your Governor might be in order."

"Maybe I'll do that. What are you going to do now? Head home?"

"No, I think I'll stick around for awhile. I've become quite interested in the Basque culture recently. I thought I'd keep looking into it."

"Basque? Really? Never thought about it much myself."

"You should. It's fascinating. I had quite an enlightening conversation with an old sheepherder at the truck stop up in Horseshoe Bend just the other day." Kaye glanced sideways to see if Unger was paying attention and saw that the state cop was hanging on every word.

"In fact," Kaye continued casually, "he gave me quite the lesson on Basque history. Told me that the Basques speak the oldest language on earth. He also told me all about the Basque migration to Idaho because it's a great place to raise sheep. Used to be, anyway."

"Sheep? Sorry, I must've missed something."

"But the really fascinating thing the old timer told me was that while a lot of the sheep are gone, the Basques are still coming. Almost weekly, in fact."

Unger was silent, staring at the horizon again. Finally, he said, "Sounds fascinating. Maybe I should brush up on my Basque culture, you know, as a tolerant Idaho citizen interested in a diverse population."

"Finding that old timer would be a good place to start."

"Thanks," Unger said sincerely, standing up and smoothing the front of his suit pants. "Enjoy the rest of your stay and be careful out there."

"I'll do that." As Unger started to walk away, Kaye called after him. "Hey, Unger, I've got a question for you, if you don't mind."

Unger stopped and turned around. "Shoot."

"Is it true that some town in Idaho was the first place to get electricity from a nuclear reactor?"

"Yep. A little place over east called, appropriately enough, Atomic City. Why?"

"With that kind of history, I imagine your troopers started carrying radiation detection gear a long time ago, right?"

"No." Unger shook his head. "We don't see..." He stopped in mid-sentence and stared at Kaye, the color draining from beneath his deep tan.

"That might be something else you could bring up when you talk to the Governor. That is, if you talk to him."

Unger looked stricken. "I think I'll do that. Right away, in fact. Thanks."

"Don't thank me. Like I said, I'm not supposed to tell you anything. It's all in my official statement. I'm just a tourist now."

Unger smiled wanly, then turned and practically ran to his car. As it disappeared down the hill Kaye heard the sound of its siren.

"Screw you, Rhoades," he said aloud before sighing deeply and heading for the Road King.

***

Kaye's second funeral of the day was a much smaller gathering.

He arrived a few minutes late and slid inconspicuously through the huge carved doors of the Our Lady of Mercy chapel, settling into a back row pew. Twenty or so mourners sat near the front, close to the casket carrying Maria de la Rosa to her final reward.

Kaye recognized Chambers, seated in the front pew with another man and an elderly woman.

The scant gathering of mourners alternately stood and sat as they responded to the traditional Latin liturgy of the service.

When the priest finished his recitation Chambers rose and approached the small podium next to the casket, beneath the pulpit. Turning to face the small crowd, he saw Kaye and smiled through his grief. Maria's former boss delivered a nice eulogy, confirming that he and Maria had been close friends.

When the service concluded Kaye went forward to pay his respects and offer condolences.

"Thank you for coming," Chambers greeted him sincerely. "Maria would have been pleased."

"Wouldn't have missed it. I owe her that, and more."

Chambers smiled weakly, then clasped his hands together and exclaimed, "I'm so sorry! Where are my manners?" He introduced

Kaye to Louis, his partner, and to Louis's mother Joann, a sharp-faced woman who looked as though she'd rather be anywhere else.

They exchanged handshakes and condolences, with Louis remembering Maria fondly to Kaye. When the conversation lagged, Chambers steered Kaye a short distance away from the group.

"So," the hotel manager asked, "are you any closer to catching who did this?"

"As a matter of fact, I am. I at least know who I'm looking for."

"Really? Already? Did our surveillance video help? Oh, please tell me it helped."

"It helped," Kaye told him, and left it at that.

"Who is it?"

"I'm sorry, but the authorities have asked me not to release any information about the investigation."

Chambers was crestfallen. "Please, just tell me it wasn't some stupid punk and that Maria died senselessly."

"No, it wasn't just some punk. It was one of the real bad guys. Now, may I ask if you found anything in Maria's apartment that might tell us where she was from?"

Chambers folded his arms and his brow furrowed.

"You know," he said, raising a finger for emphasis, "I might have. I looked specifically for her Bible so I could, you know, put it in with her, and when I found it I noticed it had an unusual bookmark in it. Most people use a prayer card, and some Catholics use their rosaries, but this was, well, odd."

"How so?"

"It looked like an old ticket stub, maybe from a train or a bus. It was torn and so faded I couldn't be sure."

"Did you keep it?"

Chambers' shoulders slumped as a pained look crossed his face. "No, I'm so sorry. I thought it had been important to her, so I left it in the bible."

"That's okay."

"But I do remember that Boise was the destination and it was issued in a place that started with M-A." The man paused, concentrating hard, and then added excitedly. "And I remember that the fare was itemized and it had a line for California sales tax! It was from a California city that starts with M-A. Does that help?"

"Yes, it does. Thank you. Maria was fortunate to have a friend like you."

Louis came over just in time to prevent Chambers from collapsing into tears again.

"Excuse me," Louis said to Kaye. "But I need to drag him away. We're ready to leave for the cemetery."

"Will you be going with us?" Chambers asked hopefully, dabbing at his eyes with a tissue.

"No, I'm sorry,"

He took his leave and left the church. Before he pulled away Kaye watched the funeral procession, this one with no police escort, leave the church parking lot.

29

It was a big day at Tom Whitworth's RV shop. The demanding client from Sun Valley was picking up his refurbished coach. It couldn't be too soon for Whitworth. It had been the job from hell from the very first day.

But Whitworth and his crew were proud of the end result, and the entire bunch had shown up this morning to participate in the delivery. Ed Larson even brought his teen-aged son to show off his work on this one.

Everyone showed, Whitworth grumbled to himself, except that irresponsible drunk Randy, who was probably hung over at some woman's house. If the damn kid wasn't so good with his hands he'd have been gone a long time ago.

Tom Whitworth waited and fretted. He hadn't slept well last night, tossing and turning fitfully between nightmares of things going horribly wrong.

At nine-thirty the black Escalade, followed by a dark blue Suburban, turned off the highway into the parking lot. Whitworth's blood pressure spiked as he went out to meet and greet.

A man from the Suburban ran to the right rear door of the Escalade and opened it. Markunyian stepped out.

"Good morning!" Whitworth greeted cheerfully. "Are you ready to see your new baby?"

"Indeed!" Markunyian smiled broadly, then turned and extended his hand back into the Escalade. A woman took it and gracefully stepped down onto the pavement.

Tom Whitworth stopped in his tracks. If this was the client's wife, he now fully understood the man's insistence on keeping the coach. She was the most beautiful woman Whitworth had ever seen. She was dressed to show it off, too, with no bra under a thin, clingy t-shirt that didn't reach the ends of her long, ebony hair, much less the low waistband of the short shorts that showed exquisite legs.

Whitworth heard a commotion behind him and glanced over his shoulder. Every man in the shop stood in the open overhead door ogling the woman.

"My lovely wife, Serenya. Serenya, this is Mr. Tom Whitworth, the genius responsible for reconfiguring our wonderful home away from home."

"My pleasure, Mrs. Markunyian," Whitworth sputtered, blushing. "But your husband is being too kind."

"I doubt it. He has been raving about the genius of your design and craftsmanship from the beginning. I cannot wait to see my beautiful land yacht. It's very special to us, you know."

"Well, then, let's not wait," Whitworth said effusively. Maybe this would turn out okay after all. "Please, come inside."

The group turned and headed for the shop. Whitworth quickened his pace to get slightly ahead.

"Okay, you guys, break it up and put your eyeballs back in your heads." He turned to Serenya, who had come up beside him, and added, "Sorry, ma'am, but we're not used to being graced with such beauty."

Serenya smiled. "Why, thank you."

Whitworth blushed deeply and glanced at Markunyian. The man's lips were smiling, but his eyes were not. Whitworth's blood pressure spiked again.

Whitworth spent the better part of the next two hours going over the coach with the couple. Each worker answered questions, explained how problems had been solved, and demonstrated how everything worked.

"Well, what do you think?" Whitworth asked when they were done.

"It's too beautiful for words," Serenya gushed.

"Very nice, indeed," Markunyian agreed. "Shall we retire to your office and settle the balance on the account?"

"That would be fine by me. Please, follow me."

"Serenya," Markunyian said. "Would you have the men start loading the coach, please? Oh, and bring me the briefcase. It's on the floor in the back seat."

"Certainly, darling," Serenya replied. Then, seeing the quizzical look on Whitworth's face, she added, "We're leaving from here on a short, um, maiden voyage, I guess you could call it. We can hardly wait."

Whitworth thought she blushed just a bit and he smiled. "Of course, ma'am."

Once settled in the office Whitworth went through the work order and billing invoice item by item. He was an honest man and hadn't padded the bill by a single cent. In the end Markunyian insisted on, and Whitworth granted, a one-year warranty on parts and workmanship.

Serenya brought the briefcase, and when the two men had finished reviewing the paperwork Markunyian lifted it onto Whitworth's desk and unsnapped it. He began removing bound bundles of one hundred dollar bills, stacking them neatly on the desk. Tom Whitworth's eyes were as big as saucers.

Finally, when the stack was quite large, Markunyian stopped.

"Cash, as promised. And now," Markunyian reached into the briefcase again and removed several more bundles of bills, adding them to the pile before closing and snapping the case. "This small token of my appreciation is for you and your workers. I know you missed the deadline, but the work is so wonderful I am not concerned. Please keep half for yourself and distribute the remainder among your workers as you see fit."

"Thank you!" Whitworth was elated. "Thank you very much. I won't lie to you and tell you this was an easy job, because it wasn't, but we're all very pleased with the result. I think you will be, too."

"I'm certain of it, Tom. May I call you Tom?"

"Mr. Markunyian, paying in cash gives you the right to call me whatever you want."

Markunyian laughed easily. "Tom, I believe that when my friends see what you have done, you're going to be a very busy man. How did you put it? Turning eighty-foot yachts into one hundred foot yachts?" The man laughed again as he stood up. "Thank you again. We'll be on our way."

In the shop, Serenya stood near the coach, the crew clustered closely around her. She saw her husband and called out.

"Oh, darling, would you please get the camera bag for me? I want pictures of everyone, and we can send copies to Mr. Whitworth to remember us by."

"Yes, my love," Markunyian replied, signaling to one of his assistants to retrieve the camera bag. Then, he asked Whitworth, "Is everyone here?"

"Yep," Whitworth lied. The hell with Randy.

The group spent the next fifteen minutes posing for pictures in and around the coach.

"Now," Serenya said at last. "I'd like one of the entire crew."

The group posed, but Serenya wasn't pleased when she looked through the viewer.

"There's too much glare," she said loudly. "Everyone move over there," she waved in the direction of the far wall. "Mr. Whitworth, could we lower the big door, please? The sun is too bright."

Whitworth obligingly walked over and pushed the down button.

"Okay, smile everyone," she said cheerfully, then lowered the camera and frowned. "I think the battery just died! Everyone stay there, please. Darling, please get my bag. I packed the spare camera in it."

Markunyian went outside, returning momentarily to place another bag at his wife's feet.

"Thank you darling," she cooed and knelt down to rummage in the bag. "Ah, yes, here it is. Everyone smile!"

Serenya stood up, but there was no camera in her hand. Instead, she held a small automatic weapon. Before anyone could react she raked them with thirty rounds of 9MM fury.

Tom Whitworth died with his crew and, as death grabbed him, his last conscious thought was that this was exactly how his nightmares of the previous night had ended.

"Excellent work," the client said to his wife.

"Thank you, Sayyid, May I please put some clothes on now? I feel like a prostitute."

Yousef bin Ali Mahmoud smiled at his protégé. "Yes, but not too many. We may have further need of your charms."

The tall Arab quickly issued orders to his entourage. The bodies were piled into the coach's newly expanded side compartments and the shop floor was scrubbed before being re-splattered with grease and oil. It took only a few minutes to erase the obvious signs of the carnage.

Mahmoud retrieved the cash from Whitworth's office and secured it in the coach's safe. He also gathered up the pile of paperwork and contracts he and Whitworth had reviewed so meticulously and stuffed them into the briefcase.

"I will drive the coach," Mahmoud told the group. "Mohammed," he addressed one of the men, "remain and clean the office. We must leave no recoverable evidence. If someone comes before you finish, do what you must. Understood?"

Mohammed nodded.

"Everyone follow your assigned routes on the assigned schedules," Mahmoud continued. "We will rendezvous at the barn this evening."

***

Still half-drunk, Randy drove his battered pickup into the lot less than thirty minutes later. He had a blinding headache from too much cheap tequila the night before, but he'd be damned if he was going to miss this payday.

"What the...?" he muttered softly when he saw all the doors down and the 'Closed' sign propped up in Tom's office window. He drove around back. The usual group of pickups was there, including Tom Whitworth's big Dodge Ram dually.

Getting madder by the minute, Randy pulled back around front and got out of his truck. He walked to the big overhead door, pounded on it with his fist, and waited. No response. He went to a window and peered inside. The Sun Valley asshole's coach was gone. Randy stood there perplexed, trying through the tequila-induced haze to make the pieces fit. The shop was closed and locked, and there was obviously nobody inside. But, everybody's rig was parked out back, just like a weekday. What the hell was going on?

"Sumbitch," he shouted at the sky, slapping the big door with the palm of his hand. He needed that money! He'd promised the gang down at Rowdie's that he'd buy the first round of shots tonight

"Damn! They all went for a cruise in the asshole's new coach. Damn!"

Pissed, but satisfied he'd solved the riddle, Randy climbed back into his pickup and fired it up. He'd just have to come back later and get his bonus money. In the meantime, he might as well head on back over to Sheila's. By the time he got there, she'd probably be awake and ready to go some more. Her reservist husband had gotten himself deployed and, well, somebody had to take care of her while the poor turd was gone. Might as well be him.

30

K aye idled the Road King out of the church parking lot, thinking about his conversation with Unger. He'd stretched it, but hadn't really revealed any absolute facts about the case. Besides, he thought again, screw Rhoades. Catching Pancho, not covering DHS's ass, was his priority.

He headed for Mike's house, looking forward to catching up with Dinsmore and hoping the Sergeant Major had come up with something that would help them.

A black Kawasaki Ninja pulled out from a restaurant parking lot and took up position in the right lane, three car lengths behind Kaye. The rider wore full leathers and a full helmet with a darkly smoked face shield.

Saturday traffic was moderate. The road had a center divider and left turn lanes, so Kaye stayed in the left lane to avoid the right turners and traffic pulling out from the side streets. He needed to make one more stop before going to Mike's. If he turned on his cell phone DHS could triangulate his whereabouts. He didn't like being incommunicado, so he kept a lookout for someplace to buy a disposable phone.

The black Ninja moved in and out of traffic, always returning to the right lane. At last, the rider was satisfied with his position behind the big black Harley in the left lane, with no cars between them and the right lane clear some distance ahead.

The Ninja rider downshifted and his right hand cranked hard on the throttle as his left hand reached to unzip his jacket.

Ahead on the right Kaye spied a sign for a wireless company. His right thumb reached reflexively for the right turn signal switch and he checked the right side mirror. He'd noticed the Ninja when it had pulled into traffic, but, other than thinking how hot the rider must be in full leathers, he hadn't paid particular attention to it. The sport bike crowd was out in force today.

Just as he glanced in the mirror the Ninja began to accelerate hard. The whine of the Kawasaki's run-up to high RPM reached Kaye's ears as he watched the bike coming. The rider reached into his open jacket with his left hand. When he pulled it out it held a black pistol.

Kaye was making between thirty-five and forty miles per hour. The Ninja was coming hard, already passing sixty. With that kind of jump, Kaye instantly knew there was no chance the big Harley could stay ahead. A raised concrete center divider hemmed him in on the left. With a split second to make a decision, he took the only available option.

Yanking in the clutch lever, Kaye grabbed the front brake lever and squeezed hard while his right foot feathered the rear brake pedal, avoiding a slide and the inevitable high side flip. He played the big, double-rotor brakes of the Harley like a fine instrument, and the motorcycle decelerated like a Grand Prix car. The drivers behind him slammed on their brakes and horns started blaring. Somewhere, Kaye was aware of the sound of bending sheet metal and breaking glass.

The alarming rate of Kaye's deceleration surprised the Ninja rider, who whipped past at a forty miles per hour speed differential.

Kaye saw the Ninja flash by, the pistol in the rider's hand glinting in the sun. He heard two shots in quick succession and saw the pistol jump from the recoil.

It was an impossible shot, but both slugs snapped by so close that Kaye felt the air crack. Still watching the Ninja, which was braking hard as the rider began to swivel in the saddle, Kaye was vaguely aware of westbound traffic becoming a tangled clot of sliding cars and screaming drivers.

For a millisecond he thought of stopping to render aid, but his anger overwhelmed him. Kaye's left foot mashed down twice on the shift lever. His left hand let go off the clutch as his right hand grabbed a huge handful of throttle. Feeling forward momentum return to the bike under him, he leaned the Road King into a hard right swerve across the back of the Ninja.

The Ninja rider, desperate for another shot, swept his left arm too far backward and lost his equilibrium. His brain automatically compensated by directing energy to his right hand, which grabbed what it held in an effort to maintain balance. The Ninja rider suddenly found himself in a hard lean while decelerating, his weight off-center, and the bike began to wobble. For an unskilled rider it would have been a deadly combination.

But the Ninja rider was no amateur. He twisted hard on the throttle to bring the Ninja back up. Abandoning the possibility of another shot, he tucked the pistol back into his jacket and concentrated on escape. He leaned forward onto the Ninja's tank and applied maximum throttle. The piercing shriek of the Kawasaki became the counterpoint to the pursuing Harley's thundering, primal roar.

The Ninja wove in and out of traffic, its engine screaming. The rider cast occasional glances back under his arm, tracking Kaye and no doubt perplexed about not being able to distance himself from the heavier, unsophisticated Harley.

Kaye caught a break with the traffic flow and swung into an empty left turn lane, passing a line of cars before cutting back into the left through lane, gaining on the Ninja, which had to slow before risking splitting the traffic between lanes.

Ahead, Kaye could see a major intersection. The light facing the two speeding motorcycles was red, with waiting cars stacked several deep in both lanes.

The Ninja rider swerved wildly to the right. Using a Starbuck's driveway to get onto the sidewalk, he hit the intersection at sixty, braking and swerving crazily through cross traffic.

Kaye went left, where a double left turn lane had only one car waiting. Luck was with him and the left turn arrow turned green just before he hit the intersection. Getting back on the throttle hard, he went through at seventy, the stopped drivers honking their horns wildly.

Then the Ninja rider made a mistake. He turned off the main road into the side streets of an industrial area. Kaye thundered through the turn, sparks flying as the footboard scraped asphalt, a scant hundred feet behind his quarry.

The Ninja twisted and turned through the truck-lined streets, but the blocks were short and the unswept streets strewn with scattered gravel. Twice the Ninja lost traction, nearly sliding out. The short blocks limited the run-up time for the Kawasaki, keeping the bike's RPM below its optimum power band.

The Harley kept coming, closing the gap as its prodigious low-end torque and Kaye's uncanny riding ability began to turn the tide.

Coming off each wild, half-sliding turn, the big v-twin roared thunderously as Kaye poured power to the back tire, gaining noticeably during the first half of each block, holding even until the next turn, when the gap was narrowed again.

Kaye suddenly realized that the Ninja rider might simply be baiting him, getting him close enough to stop suddenly and get a good shot. His Kimber was tucked in the boot holster, but the Ninja rider's gun was accessible in his jacket. Still, he wasn't about to give up. In two or three more turns, he'd be right on the Kawasaki, and decided to try and unseat the Ninja rider at speed.

As if reading Kaye's mind the Ninja rider suddenly spun in the seat and snapped off a shot. It missed, but it backed Kaye off and made him more conscious of his line. If he stayed to the Ninja's right, he'd be a tougher target to line up.

Desperate, the Ninja rider hit the next turn, a right, a little too hot. He saw the gravel too late, over-braked, tried to straighten up and then lost the back tire as he tried to power through the turn.

Coming fast, Kaye saw the Ninja hit the gravel and braked early, swinging wide to cut the turn on as straight a line as possible.

Gotcha, Kaye said to himself, seeing the perfect line that would allow him to come up fast to the Ninja's right rear, where he could try to unseat the rider with the least possibility of coming under the muzzle of the gun.

At that exact moment the weatherman's forecast of isolated thunderstorms became a reality, and the skies opened up. The rain fell in torrents, instantly soaking everything. A classic Idaho summer storm, it would last only a few minutes, dumping a lot of water in a small area.

The Ninja rider, already slowed because of the gravel, simply recovered his line into the next straight and sped off, the rain shrouding him almost immediately.

Kaye wasn't as lucky. Traveling at a much higher speed into a hard turn, he felt the big Harley start to skitter sideways as the tires surrendered to the wet pavement. With no other choice, he released the throttle as he pushed the left grip to straighten up, taking a stable straight line and missing the turn completely. Braking as quickly as he could on the wet road, he made a tight u-turn and turned into the street the Ninja had taken. The rain was blinding and the black Kawasaki was nowhere in sight. Even its screaming engine had been swallowed by the hard drumming of the rain.

"Damn it," Kaye muttered as the rain streamed from his visor.

It didn't rain for long, stopping by the time Kaye made his way back to the wireless store. As he backtracked, he saw several police units handling fender benders near the spot the Ninja rider had taken his first shots, but he didn't stop. He'd call Unger later.

The kid in the store tried to be cute when a soaking wet Kaye said he needed a prepaid cell phone.

"Sorry, dude. We don't carry the waterproof model."

The look he got from Kaye snapped him back to all-business mode and five minutes later Kaye left the store, phone in hand.

***

It was mid-afternoon when Kaye rolled into Mike Graham's driveway. The only vehicle there was Mike's pickup and he worried he'd broken his promise to Cindy.

Just then she came out the front door and bounded down the steps and across the yard to greet him.

"Thank God! Are you all right? I was starting to worry, with the rain and all."

"I'm fine," Kaye told her, hanging his helmet on the handlebars. "You ride, you get wet. Got hung up talking to a state cop and," he reached into his pocket and took out the new phone "I had to stop and get this."

"Did yours go dead?"

"No, but Homeland Security was tracking mine. That's how they knew I was Urrestegui's place last night, and…"

"You were at Urrestegui's last night? Without me? Is that where you got that lip?"

"Slow down. I'll tell you all about it, but let's do it inside." He reached out and took the elbow of her good arm and steered her toward the front door.

"Dad! Uncle Calvin!" Cindy shouted as they entered. "Ben's here!"

Mike and Dinsmore rose from kitchen chairs when Cindy and Kaye came in.

"Good to see you, Ben," Dinsmore greeted him. "You look well."

"As do you, Sergeant…" Kaye stopped. "Sorry, but it's going to be tough for me to call you Calvin. I'll worry about going to the brig."

Mike and Dinsmore laughed.

"Call me whatever you like. I'm sure you used to call me lots of things back in the day."

That led to two hours of reminiscing, with Cindy listening raptly, sometimes in total disbelief. Except for the day he'd lost his legs and Calvin Dinsmore had earned the CMH, she'd never heard her father talk about his Vietnam days like this. It dawned on her that her Uncle Calvin, whom she worshipped, obviously held her father in very high esteem and she was proud as Dinsmore related her father's exploits to Kaye.

"Dad, why didn't you ever tell us any of this before?"

"Stretch, there are some things so horrible that you try to keep them from your children, hoping they never experience them. War is tops on that list."

"Amen to that," Dinsmore said softly. He turned to Kaye. "So, tell me about what happened and what you've found out since."

Kaye told Dinsmore the whole story, up to and including the attempt on his life on the way there.

Cindy gasped when she heard, but a stern look from Dinsmore kept her from interrupting.

Throughout, Dinsmore remained absolutely poker-faced, betraying no emotion and asking no questions. The only indication he was even listening was an occasional rapid tapping of his index finger on the table.

"And that's about it," Kaye said seriously. "That brings us to right here, right now."

"So," Dinsmore said, "there is a known terrorist, possibly with a nuclear device or material, here in Boise but destined for Sun Valley. You believe he has help from this Robert Urrestegui. And Homeland Security is working the case, but not sharing with the local police. In your professional judgment as an investigator, you believe that is a mistake."

"Absolutely."

"I disagree."

"Uncle Calvin!" Cindy exclaimed.

"Hear me out," Dinsmore said patiently. "I'm not questioning Ben's professional expertise. He's obviously very good at what he does, but I think Janicot has gone to ground. The odds of a casual observer seeing him shopping at the mall are zero. I think our focus has to be on preventing a general panic, and we all know that as soon as the local police have it, so does the media. As much as it pains me," he looked over at Mike "I think approaching this as finding Aiden's killer is now secondary to preventing a national catastrophe. Besides, to do one includes the other."

"I hope you're right," Kaye said evenly, leaning back in his chair. "But I still disagree."

"I think so, too," Cindy spoke up, showing support for Kaye. "What do you think, Dad?"

Deep in thought, Mike didn't answer immediately. This was the first time he'd heard the entire story.

"I'd give the rest of both legs to get my hands on the man who killed my son, but I think your Uncle Calvin has a point. I think we have a bigger picture to consider."

"In light of Ben's conversation with Lieutenant Unger this morning," Dinsmore continued, "the point is probably moot, anyway. Unless I misunderstood, it sounded like he put two and two together. Ben?"

"I think so. It might take him a day or so to get to Horseshoe Bend and locate Itzy, and there's a large Basque population here for him to winnow through after that. I never mentioned Urrestegui's name, so he may never even connect those dots. But, yeah, he got the nuclear reference."

"Speaking of Urrestegui..." Dinsmore said casually.

"Yeah," Cindy said excitedly. "What did you find out about him?"

"Well," Dinsmore began, looking at Kaye, "It seems that until about a year ago, Urrestegui invested a lot of money outside the United States. Anyone care to guess where?"

"Northern Spain," Kaye said without hesitation.

"Give the man a cigar," Dinsmore nodded. "Without exception the money has gone to projects in Bilbao and the surrounding region."

"Basque country?" Cindy inquired of Kaye.

Kaye nodded.

"He's pretty cagey about it," Dinsmore went on. "Invests or donates to high profile legitimate projects that invariably run into budget problems and cost overruns."

"Let me guess," Kaye spoke up. "Classic money laundering schemes, even if the projects are legitimate, and I'll bet the construction companies are known, or at least suspected to be, fronts for ETA."

Dinsmore nodded.

"So, why isn't he arrested?" Cindy asked. "I thought funding terrorists was a crime."

Dinsmore sighed. "Somebody got to the U.S. Attorney. Because they couldn't show that it was actually Urrestegui's dollars being siphoned off, no indictment came down."

"I still think Urrestegui is the key to finding Pancho," Kaye said. "But for the life of me, I cannot figure out what's in this for him."

"Meaning...?" Dinsmore prompted curiously.

"This can't just be about Basque politics. He has too much to lose by committing treason for a cause that doesn't benefit him directly. Urrestegui is about money and power. I think the link to ETA is solid, but there has to be more to it."

"Okay," Mike Graham spoke up again. He'd been following the conversation closely. "Let me ask a question. Why does a man, any man, risk everything he has by doing something so obviously stupid to an objective outside observer?"

The group exchanged glances.

"I can only think of a few reasons," Mike went on, raising his fingers and counting them off. "First on the list, a woman. Greed, which can include coveting something somebody else has. Desperation. Revenge, which is self-explanatory, or power, also self-explanatory."

"Excellent observation," Dinsmore said. "But you left out the most dangerous and unpredictable reason of all."

"Really?" Mike was doubtful. "What?"

Kaye and Dinsmore spoke in perfect unison. "His God."

Mike nodded. "Yeah, you're right. That probably tops the list nowadays."

"We don't have much time to find out." Cindy stated the obvious. "What'll we do right now?"

"I, for one," Dinsmore said as he stood up, "need to make a phone call and see if we can buy ourselves a couple days before this goes public." He turned to Kaye. "Can you reach your DHS contact on the weekend?"

"Yes."

"Good. Call and see if he's got anything new."

31

D on Straithwaite was hip deep in Silver Creek, the new waders keeping him dry and his new fly rod whipping the size 14 Caddis fly toward the deep eddy just downstream, when his cell phone rang.

"Shit," he muttered. It would have been his best cast of the day.

The familiar voice of the weekend DHS operator came over the line.

"Agent Straithwaite, I have a relay call from a Ben Kaye. He says he works with you."

"Connect us, please." The line clicked rapidly several times. "Khalid Bergman," he said flatly when the clicking stopped.

"Khalid, Ben Kaye here."

"What can I do for you?"

Kaye brought his DHS contact up to date, passing along details of the previous evening's incursion into the Biscay Basin Group garage, the white van and its strange configuration and cargo, the attempt on his life earlier and what he'd found out about Urrestegui. He was careful not to mention Calvin Dinsmore.

"Do you have any more information on the radiation badge?" Kaye asked when he'd finished.

"I'm no longer the supervising agent on this case. That information would go to the new supervising agent."

"Please tell me that's not Dennis Rhoades."

"It is. Did he call you?"

"I had the dubious pleasure of meeting Rhoades and an Agent Kaminski last night. They knew I was there, Khalid. I don't appreciate the surveillance. I've turned my cell phone off for the duration and have no intention of giving you a new number. I'll call you."

"My apologies. I thought he might call you, but I was unaware he was tracking you. Did you tell Rhoades what you observed in the garage?"

"Yes, I did. He didn't seem interested."

"What did you expect?"

"Frankly, I expected a DHS tactical team to storm the building, search for Pancho and seize whatever is in the back of that van. Let the lawyers argue about it later. In my opinion, we're not after a conviction here. If Pancho has a nuke we need to find him, and it, fast."

"That's Agent Rhoades's call, not yours," Straithwaite responded, even though he agreed with Kaye. *What the hell was Rhoades doing?* "But I will pass your information and concerns along. Is there anything else?"

"Can you tell me anything about Sun Valley?"

Straithwaite smiled.

"The weather is absolutely glorious, but the fishing could be better."

"Thank you, Khalid. I'll be in touch."

"I look forward to your calls."

The DHS agent stood in the creek, the cold water swirling around his legs, thinking about what Kaye had told him. He was having a tough time believing that Rhoades had ignored Kaye's information about the van. He flipped his phone open again and hit a speed-dial code. One minute later he had the number Kaye had called from, Mike Graham's address and a call in to the General.

Three minutes later, his cell phone rang again.

"Don," the General's voice boomed in his ear. "What can I do for you?"

"Sir, I just had a call from Kaye. He had some very interesting information about our situation up here, and I was wondering if you'd spoken with Dennis Rhoades yet today."

"Yes, I have. He told me he had a run-in with Kaye last night, and what Kaye told him. Why?"

"We're not moving on that, sir? Kaye is very reliable. I also agree with him that our priority has to be securing any threat. Convicting Pancho Janicot is secondary."

"To answer your first question, no, we are not moving on Kaye's unlawfully obtained information. Second, your opinion is duly noted, Agent Straithwaite, but you are not in charge here. I am. Is that clear?"

"Yes sir," Straithwaite said quickly. "Sorry sir."

"No apology necessary. Just follow the chain of command and you'll be fine. You're doing important work, Don, and doing it well."

"Yes, sir. Thank you, sir."

"I'm arriving there tomorrow afternoon. I'll brief you completely."

"Sounds good, sir. See you soon."

The conversation ended. Straithwaite stood in the water for another five minutes, trying to figure out what had just happened. Finally, with an inward shrug, he went back to fishing. If anything the General had told him had rung true, it was that he was not in charge.

***

"So?" Cindy asked casually as her Uncle Calvin walked back into the kitchen,

"I think I bought us a couple days," Dinsmore said as he twisted off a bottle cap. "But the President didn't know about this situation. I don't understand that. Ben, did you call your guy?

"Yeah. Nothing new. No confirmation either way on the radiation badge. In fact, it was more what he didn't say."

"Huh?" asked Cindy, a skeptical look on her face.

"I got the impression that he agreed that DHS should have gone into Urrestegui's, warrant or no warrant, but he wouldn't come right out and say it."

"But you can't go in without a warrant," Cindy said, looking around the table questioningly. "Can you?"

"Sure you can," Kaye replied. "There are numerous exceptions to the warrant requirement, and I think at least one or two of them would stand up here. If a judge disagrees, you can't use your evidence, but you don't necessarily have to give it back."

"Big deal," Mike said. "We need to find that nuke, if there is one."

"Could Captain Halberstam get a warrant?" Cindy asked.

"Not with what he has now," Kaye told her.

"I know a couple of U.S. Attorneys," Dinsmore said, "but I can't get to them until Monday. And I hate to say it, but I need to saddle up. I'm due back in Seoul."

"Uncle Calvin! You can't leave!"

"I have to, Stretch. I'm officially UA right now, but this is more important. I'll be back."

"Thanks for coming, Calvin." Mike grasped his best friend's shoulder affectionately.

Dinsmore turned to Kaye. "What's your next step?"

"Well," Kaye said thoughtfully. "I think I've seen all of Boise I care to see, and I just heard that the weather in Sun Valley is beautiful."

32

General Holdorf was packing for the Sun Valley conference when the phone rang.

"Carl, we've got a problem." Panic tinged Senator Harrison Chapman's voice.

"Calm down, Harry. What's wrong?"

"I just had a call from the President, and...."

"The President?" Holdorf interrupted. Chapman had his attention now. "Of the United States?"

"Yes, of the United States. Who did you think I meant?"

Holdorf ignored the question. "What did he want?"

"He didn't want anything. He said it was a courtesy call so I wouldn't be blind-sided when the Governor calls me."

"Governor? Harry, take a deep breath and tell me about the call."

"The President told me he was calling Idaho's congressional delegation as a courtesy to let us know he was about to call our Governor regarding a matter of national security."

"National security?" Holdorf cut in. "You're sure the President used the term national security? That's what he said?"

"Yes, I'm sure. I asked him if he could share any details with me so I could be prepared in case the Governor called me."

"And....?"

The General heard Chapman suck in a deep breath before speaking.

"The President told me – and this is exactly what he said, because I wrote it down – that he had just received credible intelligence that the Department of Homeland Security was investigating an imminent threat, possibly involving nuclear material, in Idaho."

"You're sure that's what he said?"

"Don't patronize me, Carl. But that's not all."

"What else?"

"The President said he was going to ask the Governor not to make any information about the threat or the investigation public in order to avoid a general panic. He was also going to reassure the Governor that he had every confidence Homeland Security was on top of things and would be making arrests in the very near future. I thanked him for the courtesy of the call and he hung up." Chapman paused briefly and then asked, "So, what do we do?"

"We do nothing. If the Governor calls you, tell him you've been briefed by the President, express your confidence in Homeland Security, and leave it at that."

"But...."

"But what? The President knows? For Christ's sake, Harry, he's supposed to know. He is the President. If anyone's in trouble here it's the Secretary, because I'm willing to bet the President didn't hear about this from her. I'm also willing to bet that right about now the President is asking the Secretary why that is."

"So, we're covered?"

Holdorf sighed. "Yes, we're covered. I have an operational summary prepared for the Secretary. I'll explain that I thought an alarm before now was premature, and we're working diligently on analyzing our intelligence. It'll look like whoever leaked this to the President was being overzealous and looking for political advantage."

"You're a wizard, Carl."

"Plus, look on the bright side."

"Bright side? How the hell can there be a bright side?"

"The President of the United States just told the Governor of Idaho to butt out."

"I hadn't thought of that," admitted Chapman.

"So, we okay? You okay?"

"Yeah, I'm okay. Thanks for the fresh perspective." Chapman changed the subject. "Are you still coming up to Sun Valley?"

"Wouldn't miss it. I'm packing right now."

"When are you scheduled to arrive?"

"Around three tomorrow afternoon."

"I assume you'll be staying at the house?"

"Yes, of course. Hey, Harry, I've got an idea. Why don't you plan on staying with me instead of at the Lodge? I've got plenty of room."

"Why, I'd love to," replied Chapman, thrilled with the invitation. "Thank you. I'm scheduled to arrive tomorrow morning."

"No problem. Just go on out to the house. Ilsa will get you settled. I'll see you when I get there."

"Great. And I'll get us a tee time for early Monday morning."

"Sounds good, and bring your 'A' game, Senator. I want a chance to get back some of the money you took from me at Pebble Beach."

Chapman laughed into the phone. "In your dreams, Carl. In your dreams."

General Carl Holdorf leaned back in his chair and smiled. Harrison Chapman would make a very compliant asset in the Senate.

Holdorf pondered the situation, half expecting the telephone to ring again and find a very irate Secretary of Homeland Security on the other end. The Secretary had aspirations, and she was going to be very upset that the President had heard about the Idaho situation from someone else first.

Who could that have been? Kaye? No chance. There was no way an LAPD detective had access to the President. Rhoades had checked in earlier and told him about the contact with Kaye, including the information about the van containing the crate. The General had praised Rhoades for his team's work and told his agent to stay on top of things. So, who had gotten to the President? That was the only thing he couldn't figure out, and it nibbled at the edge of his confidence.

The General unlocked the bottom drawer of his desk and retrieved the secure satellite phone.

The Vice President answered on the first ring. "Carl, how are you?"

"Fine, sir. I have an update."

"Go ahead."

"The President is now aware of the situation. Senator Chapman just called and told me the President called him and was going to call the Governor in Idaho." Holdorf filled in the details.

"The President has briefed me, too, Carl. What I want to know is how the hell he found out."

"I'm still trying to determine that, sir."

"Carl, I worry about Chapman. You sure he's up to this?"

Holdorf hesitated before answering. "Don't worry about the Senator, sir. I've got him under control. And remember, he's in this up to his eyeballs."

"I remember. Any more information on the whereabouts of our man?"

"Nothing new sir."

"That is disturbing."

"Yes, it is. I'm working on it. We'll find him."

"We'd better find him in time, Carl, and we'd better hope nobody else finds him first. Too soon is as bad for us as too late."

"It's under control, Mr. Vice-President."

"You'd better be right. If this goes as planned, we'll make history, and the election will be nothing but a formality. If it falls apart, well, I don't need to tell you I won't be alone in the dock."

The connection terminated.

The angry Secretary's call came in five minutes later, and the General handled it exactly as he'd told Chapman he would.

33

Pancho Janicot was bored. Despite his assurances to Urrestegui that his arrival in Boise remained undetected, the American had steadfastly refused to let him leave the Biscay Basin Group building following Kaye's visit.

"We can't risk it," Urrestegui argued. "We're not jeopardizing years of planning because you want some fresh air. Be patient. We leave soon."

Pancho knew Urrestegui was right, but still he longed to get out, and he kept after Urrestegui about it.

"One hour," Pancho cajoled. "One stroll around the city. I need to get outside."

Urrestegui stood firm. "Absolutely not. What if they've identified Ramon? They'll be looking for you."

"Ramon was *legalek*; never arrested, never photographed, never fingerprinted. He lacked even a single filling in his mouth. They will never identify him. That's why I chose him."

So, Pancho stayed inside. To assuage his cabin fever he wandered the building after hours.

It wasn't as satisfying as actually going outside, but for Pancho it was the next best thing, especially with the video monitoring station. He could watch people outside and, more enjoyably, watch the women who came into the restaurant. He also kept an eye on the garage cameras, making sure no one tampered with the van parked downstairs.

The party on Friday evening was a great relief. He'd immensely enjoyed meeting Urrestegui's American friends, whom, he concluded, were all blithely unaware of what was happening in the real world.

There was no party tonight, though, so Pancho found himself on the fourth floor watching the security monitors. Saturday evening traffic was heavy and people thronged the sidewalks. The restaurant was still busy and several women Pancho found exceptionally alluring laughed and enjoyed themselves a mere three floors below.

The crate was also safe.

Pancho's eyes scanned the monitors again. At first glance, the dark colored Ford Mustang struck him as just another patron looking for a parking place and he paid it little attention. His eyes continued scanning, eventually resting again on the stunning brunette seated alone at the bar downstairs.

"Ah, senorita," he muttered to himself. "You are much too beautiful to be so alone." He watched for another second and sighed as he saw the woman smile and stand to kiss the man who'd come to meet her.

He looked again at the parking lot monitor and saw the dark Mustang still circling the lot, despite plenty of available spaces.

Pancho's curiosity was piqued and he watched the car more closely. Why was it not parking? Perhaps it was teenagers, looking for unlocked cars and an easy score. As he watched the Mustang circled slowly around again and pulled into a space. The vehicle's lights went out. But no one got out.

Curious, he kept his attention focused on the Mustang. Minutes passed and still no one got out. He couldn't see into the car well enough to make out details, but could pick out an occasional movement in the driver's seat.

Thirty minutes passed. The brunette left the bar, arm in arm with the man she'd kissed. The Mustang remained parked and Pancho realized he was seeing movement at regular intervals. He timed it. Five minutes, almost exactly, every time. He stood up quickly and went to the nearest desk, picked up a phone and punched the 'residence' button.

"What now?" Urrestegui answered petulantly.

"I think we have a problem. Come to the video monitors immediately."

Urrestegui was there within two minutes.

"What's wrong?" he asked.

"The dark blue car." Pancho pointed at the monitor. "It drove around the parking lot for several minutes before picking that space, which is the most advantageous surveillance position available."

"Coincidence," dismissed Urrestegui.

"It's been there for well over a half hour."

"So?"

"No one has gotten out."

That got Urrestegui's attention. "Nobody? After that long?"

"Correct." Pancho glanced at his watch. "And observe. Any second now you will see a movement, and – there," he said. "Almost exactly five minutes. Someone is reporting in at five minute intervals."

"You think the building is being watched?"

"I do. At the very least, we must investigate. If it is the big policeman from Los Angeles, I want to kill him myself."

"If they're watching the back, won't they be watching the front, too?" This was unfamiliar territory for Urrestegui, but it made sense. "Can you get out without being seen?"

Pancho's lips curled in a cunning smile. "I've already thought of that, in case I simply decided to ignore you about staying inside."

Urrestegui let the remark pass. "I still think you should stay inside. I'll get somebody else to check it out."

"Perhaps Timothy, or Sean? What time does the restaurant close?"

Urrestegui glanced at his watch. "They stop serving in a few minutes. The bar stays open later."

"Good. Get me a busboy jacket and a baseball cap. And bring my pistol."

Pancho stayed and watched the Mustang. "Who are you?" he mused, hoping it was the detective who had visited Urrestegui. He realized the car could be completely innocent; people having sex or doing drugs; but it still needed to be checked.

Urrestegui returned with the busboy uniform and pistol. Pancho kept an eye on the Mustang as he put on the clothes. Finally, he slipped the 9MM into his rear waistband and dropped the short suppressor into his front pants pocket. The two watched and waited, and still no one got out of the Mustang.

"It's time," Urrestegui said. "You're not going to use a bomb, are you?"

"Of course not. That would bring too much attention to our own back yard. Besides," he added with a vicious smile, "if it is your hunter, I want him to see me before he dies. Disable the alarm on the fire door from the stairwell into the restaurant."

Pancho quickly descended the stairs to the first floor. Through the stairwell door's small window he could see into the restaurant.

There were only a few occupied tables in the dining area, but the bar was busy.

After a few minutes Pancho saw what he was waiting for. The manager dismissed all but one waiter and one busboy for the evening. Those two stayed out front while the others headed toward the employee lounge, just beyond the door where he waited.

Minutes later, two busboys exited the lounge. One still wore his uniform jacket and the other had his over his shoulder as they walked together toward the front door. Pulling the baseball cap low over his forehead, Pancho slipped through the stairwell door and hurried across the restaurant behind the two young men. Only two paces behind as they walked outside, Pancho stopped and quickly removed the white busboy jacket, letting the other two widen the gap slightly. He wanted to see which way they turned and hoped they didn't go in opposite directions.

They didn't. Once beyond the wrought iron fence of the sidewalk dining area, they turned east and headed up the sidewalk, conversing animatedly in Spanish as one tried to convince the other he knew a pretty senorita who would gladly entertain them both if they brought tequila, but he had no money.

Pancho stopped at the wrought iron gate and waved after the two departing busboys as if saying goodnight, then turned west, laid the jacket across his left shoulder to conceal the bottom half of his face and, keeping as close to the buildings as he could, walked quickly down the block. Several other staff members came out the front door as he passed the west end of the Biscay Basin Group building.

***

In the hotel up the street, Stan Kaminski saw the three busboys leave, closely followed by the other group.

"Dining room must be closed, boss," he told Rhoades. "Staff is going home."

Rhoades walked over to the window and peered out, seeing eight or ten individuals, all dressed in restaurant attire, dispersing in various directions.

"Okay, let Washington know they're all clear."

***

Pancho turned north at the end of the block, slowing his pace and checking occasionally for any signs of being followed. The crowd had thinned considerably in the past hour and none of the pedestrians within view aroused his suspicions.

After two blocks Pancho turned east and looped back toward Biscay Basin Group. He knew he could cut through the block behind the building and approach the Mustang from behind. He soon had the parking lot in view. Cautious, he stepped into a shadow at the edge of an adjacent building to stand and watch. No one on the sidewalks nearby stopped when he did, or raised a hand to their mouth to talk. Satisfied he wasn't being followed, Pancho turned his attention to the Mustang.

Pancho plotted his approach. The streetlights cast very little light through the space between buildings into the interior of the block. There was only one spot where the occupant of the Mustang might catch a glimpse of him as he approached, and they would need to be watching closely to do that.

As he left the shadows Pancho retrieved the Beretta from his waistband, attached the suppressor, and held it close to his right thigh. He moved swiftly until stopping at the rear corner of a truck parked in the alley. He dropped the busboy jacket into the truck's bed. Now only twenty yards from the Mustang, he had to cross the alley, exposed and visible in the Mustang's rearview mirror.

The human eye is among the best motion detectors in the animal kingdom. Pancho knew that the odds of being seen were actually higher if he tried to cross the open space quickly, because the rapid movement was more likely to register with the Mustang occupant's peripheral vision. He needed a diversion, something to draw and hold his target's attention.

Pancho detected motion inside the Mustang twice before an opportunity presented itself. A man and woman, arm in arm, laughing and weaving slightly, rounded the corner of the Biscay Basin Group building and headed for the parking lot. He gauged their progress closely. A half-second after he calculated they had entered the Mustang occupant's field of vision, Pancho stepped from the shadows and casually crossed the alley. He stood and watched as the couple, after a brief argument over who was drunkest, departed. If their car turned the right way, its headlights would sweep across the interior of the Mustang, giving him perhaps one second to get a look inside.

Luck was with him. The Mustang's occupant was a heartbeat slow in ducking down as the headlights washed over the interior. It was a woman. Pancho felt a pang of disappointment that it wasn't Kaye.

The noise of the departing car covered the sound of Pancho's approach as he neared the Mustang. He took a position crouched behind the car parked on the Mustang's passenger side and waited, listening carefully.

The heat of the day was dissipating, but it was still warm outside. Pancho could see the driver's window was down nearly halfway, and he heard a whispering voice emanate from the opening.

"Washington. Time check, twenty-two fifty-five. Code four."

Pancho was patient. Bomb makers learn the trait early, or not at all. Five minutes passed while he watched and waited.

"Washington. Time check, twenty-three hundred hours. Code four." Pancho again heard the muted voice from inside the Mustang.

Where were they? Surely they could not see the Mustang, or they would have swarmed over him by now. How close were they?

Pancho pondered his options. He wanted to kill the woman, and it would be a simple matter to shoot her from where he was. But was it worth jeopardizing the mission and The Cause? No, it would be better to wait, knowing the building was being watched, and let these people waste their time and resources. He would only be there for one, possibly two, more days and was confident he would leave Boise undetected. The Beretta went back into his waistband.

There was only one more thing he wanted, and that was to get a good look at the woman in the car.

Pancho searched carefully around his hiding place and found a discarded brick behind a nearby dumpster. Now, he just needed to wait and hope the right circumstances developed.

It was a long two hours for both Pancho and Washington before the bar closed at one o'clock.

Pancho focused his attention on who was coming and going. He knew he was in danger of exposure if the owner of the car he hid behind showed up before he had a chance to lure the woman out of her car. But it was his night. A group of three rowdy young men headed for a jacked-up four-wheel drive truck at the far end of the lot. A second group, two couples, made their way to a Volvo station wagon.

The driver of the oversized truck started the engine and revved it wildly. As the Volvo started to pull out the truck spun its tires in the gravel and slewed its way directly into the Volvo's path, which jerked to a stop just in time to avoid a collision. The driver of the truck cursed loudly at the Volvo driver and then continued through the parking lot toward the Mustang, gravel flying.

As the truck slid around the turn toward the parking lot exit it passed directly in front of the Mustang. Pancho watched, and as the driver of the truck gunned it and spun the tires even more wildly, he lobbed the brick he'd picked up in an arc over the top of the Mustang. His aim was perfect. It landed on the windshield, directly in front of the driver, just as the gravel from the truck's spinning tires showered the Mustang.

"Oh, shit!" Pancho heard the woman in the car shout. The windshield now had a sizable ding, from which radiated several long cracks.

"You asshole!" the woman shouted after the truck, which by now had reached the solid asphalt of the alley and was speeding away.

The Volvo drove slowly across the parking lot toward the woman, who had exited the car to inspect the damage. She looked up, and its headlights caught her squarely, lighting her up as effectively as a spotlight.

"You okay?" the Volvo driver called out as he came to a stop in front of the Mustang.

"Yeah, I'm okay. Just mad. The jerk broke my windshield, and it's a rental. My boss is going to kill me."

With a wave, the Volvo driver rolled up his window and drove away.

Washington ran her fingers over the broken windshield one more time.

"Shit," she muttered again. She went around the open car door, sat down sideways on the seat with her feet still on the ground, and pressed the transmit button on the two-way. "Hey, Dennis? Stan? You guys there?"

"Washington, you code four?" the radio crackled in response.

There was a brief pause.

"Yeah. I'm okay, but some drunk just broke the Mustang's windshield. Threw a brick at it."

"What?"

"Yeah, it's really broken, boss," explained Washington. "Right in front of the driver."

"Stand by."

Pancho listened closely. Shortly, the radio crackled again.

"Okay, Alison, bag it. Everybody's gone home, anyway. Is it drivable?"

"Yeah, I can drive it a few blocks. See you in a few." Washington sighed, then reached up and pulled her earpiece off. Turning, she tossed it across the console onto the passenger seat.

Pancho watched and listened intently. What troubled him was the comment about the car being a rental. The local police would not use rental cars. This woman and her companions were more likely agents of the American federal government. If that was true, Pancho knew he might have a real problem, and it changed everything.

He needed to know who this woman was and what she knew. He smiled when he saw Washington remove her earpiece and toss it aside. Pancho pulled the Beretta from his waistband and stuck it into his right front pocket as far as it would go, then pulled out his shirt so it hung to cover the butt of the gun.

After tossing her headset aside, Washington stood up and walked around the open door to the front of the Mustang. It wasn't her car, or her problem, but she wanted to check the damage. She pulled a penlight from her pocket and began a quick scan of the hood and fenders.

"Miss, are you all right? I saw what happened." The voice came from behind, startling her. She hadn't seen anyone approaching a moment before.

"I'm okay, thanks," Washington said as she turned. "Can you believe what...." She stopped in mid-sentence, a slight gasp escaping her lips as her eyes widened slightly.

Pancho saw and heard the woman's reaction. *She knows who I am,* he thought.

"Is there anything I can do to assist?" he asked smoothly, watching the woman's eyes dart to the car's interior, searching for the radio set on the passenger seat.

"I'm fine," Washington bluffed. Her heart was racing and she could feel herself starting to sweat. "Thank you." She dropped her eyes again, unable to meet Pancho's steady stare.

"Good, good. It appears you are in the wrong place at the wrong time."

"You can say that again. You know, I don't really want to drive with a broken windshield. If I could just get my phone's headset, there on the seat, I'll call my boyfriend and he can come get me. I'll be fine." Washington tried to step around the door and get to the front seat, but Pancho took a half step sideways and blocked her path, pinning her against the edge of the door.

"I have just one question for you."

Her heart in her throat, Washington managed a croak. "Yes?"

A thin smile played on Pancho's lips as he spoke, but his eyes were cold. "So, which is your boyfriend, Agent Washington? Dennis, or Stan?" He moved his right hand slightly, exposing the butt of the Beretta, and his smile turned to a sneer.

Washington saw the gun and knew instantly that Pancho had made her. With lightning quickness she launched a knee at the Basque's groin, but Pancho saw the subtle shift of her weight and anticipated, turning slightly sideways to block the blow.

Pancho pushed hard against Washington's shoulder, turning her sideways, and the DHS agent never saw the short chop Pancho delivered behind her left ear with the Beretta.

She collapsed into Pancho's arms. He carried her sideways and lowered her into the driver's seat. He quickly searched her for weapons and any other electronics. He didn't let the fact she was a woman keep him from being thorough.

Pancho checked his watch. It had been just over two minutes since the woman had spoken to her unseen partners, telling them she would return within ten minutes. He went around to the passenger's side of the car and tossed the headset onto the floor in the back, then bent inside and unceremoniously dragged Washington across the center console to the passenger seat, where he propped her up and belted her in.

Once in the driver's seat, Pancho considered his next move. He had to assume that the front of the building, and thus the street, was also under surveillance, which made driving that way a poor choice. He started the engine and headed north, down the alley. As he drove, he pulled the video camera from the dash and tossed it over his shoulder into the back seat.

Once on the street, Pancho pulled the pre-paid cell phone from his pocket and dialed.

"What the hell are you doing?" Urrestegui's angry voice answered. He clearly had been watching from the monitor room.

"Protecting us. This woman recognized me."

"What?"

"Precisely. I need to know who she is and how she came to be watching your building."

"But they'll be all over the place looking for her."

"I don't think so."

"Where are you taking her?"

"To the original safe location. I can put the car in the garage and have the necessary isolation and privacy."

"Oh, God," muttered Urrestegui, knowing exactly what Pancho intended to.

"It cannot be helped. It is a cost of doing business. A business, I must remind you, from which you stand to profit handsomely."

"Okay, do what you have to do."

"Oh, I will, my friend," Pancho cast a glance at his unconscious passenger, "and I will enjoy it immensely." He closed the cell phone and drove carefully through the darkness, watching closely for any signs of the police.

It took Pancho fifteen minutes to reach his destination. The last quarter mile was a driveway leading to the house nestled under the brow of a hill, close enough to downtown that the brightly lit Capitol dome was plainly visible. He stopped the car at a stone pillar next to the driveway. Reaching out, he flipped up the weatherproof cover and keyed in a four-digit code. The garage door rose and Pancho pulled the blue Mustang inside.

Just then, the woman began to stir, slowly regaining consciousness. Her eyes, still glazed, opened and stared at Pancho. As her faculties returned her eyes darted around, taking in the surroundings.

"Where are we?"

"Welcome to my home."

"I'm a federal agent. Federal. Do you understand what that means?" Washington tried to sound as threatening as possible. "You're in enough trouble already, Janicot. Make it easy on yourself and let me go."

Pancho laughed. "I am in trouble? Forgive me, but I have a slightly different appraisal of the situation." With that, he lashed out with his right hand, which held the Beretta. Though she saw it coming, Washington's reactions were still too dulled to avoid the blow. It caught her flush on the forehead and she sank again into unconsciousness.

***

In the hotel downtown, Stan Kaminski paced nervously.

"She should be here by now," he said to Dennis Rhoades, who sat by the window watching the street below. "Something's wrong."

Rhoades sat silently. "Washington!" he barked into the radio for the tenth time in the last two minutes, "Come in! Washington, do you read me?"

"I'm going to check," Kaminski said urgently, grabbing his jacket to cover the .44 magnum under his arm.

"Go."

Kaminski, too impatient to wait for the elevator, went down the stairs in near freefall. He sprinted across the street toward the Biscay Basin Group building. Rhoades watched from above.

"Stan, slow down. If the cameras are monitored, they'll make you."

"Fuck that," Kaminski shot back without breaking stride. "You really think they haven't made us already?"

Kaminski rounded the corner from the sidewalk to the alleyway and disappeared from Rhoades' field of vision. There was nearly thirty seconds of agonizing silence. Finally, Kaminski's voice came over the radio link.

"The car's not here. No sign of her. She's gone."

Rhoades was stunned. What the hell had happened?

"I'm calling the cops," Kaminski's voice came over the radio. "We've got to get a BOLO out on the car while it's still close."

"Negative!" Rhoades hissed into his microphone. "No locals! Those are the orders."

"Fuck the orders!" Kaminski's voice was rising in anger and frustration. "It's Alison, for God's sake! Call it in!"

"Repeat, negative! If you call the locals, I swear to God I'll see your ass in Leavenworth or Gitmo by the end of next week." He meant it, knowing full well he'd likely be in the adjoining cell, courtesy of General Holdorf.

"Okay," replied Kaminski, his voice now controlled and seething with anger. "You're the boss. But hear this, boss. If she dies, it'll be because of you, and I swear to God you will answer for it."

The radio went dead in Rhoades's hand.

34

Pancho sat backward on the chair, his crossed forearms resting atop the wooden back, chin planted on them, waiting and looking across at the woman in an identical chair, so close her knees were under his nose.

It was clearly a bedroom. One door, closed, one window and a closet, also closed. One overhead light fixture, turned off because it was daylight and the sun shone brightly through the half-drawn curtains. Hardwood floors covered with taped down plastic sheeting, as if recently refinished. No furniture except the two chairs occupied by captive and captor.

She was naked. Pancho knew that clothes are much more than fashion to humans, providing a sense of security and protection. He also knew that people, especially women, feel more vulnerable if their genitals are exposed, and he wanted this woman as psychologically weakened as possible before he began. It might not be much of an advantage in Agent Alison Washington's case, however. She was extremely fit, which lent an additional degree of self-confidence, and Pancho found her body quite beautiful.

Her forearms and lower legs were securely duct taped to the chair. He'd also duct taped her mouth before covering her head with the hood, just in case. There were no neighbors close by, but people sometimes walked their dogs in the hills, and he took no chances.

As he watched, he heard her murmur, and her head lifted slightly.

He reached across and lifted the hood from her head.

"Welcome back, Agent Alison Washington, United States Department of Homeland Security."

Washington blinked hard against the sudden light.

"For a moment, I feared I struck you too hard, too soon." The Basque flashed a malevolent smile.

Washington stared at him, defiance in her eyes.

Pancho recognized the look. It didn't worry him in the slightest. He'd learned much from the Americans who had come frequently to interrogate him during his last imprisonment in Spain.

"Where are my manners?" Pancho asked suddenly. He leaned forward and grabbed the edge of the tape covering Washington's mouth. With a quick jerk, he pulled it off. "You may scream all you want, Agent Washington. Believe me when I tell you that there is no one close enough to hear you. Are you thirsty?"

Washington's face stung from having the tape pulled off and she slowly worked her jaw to dissipate the pain and stiffness. The look in Pancho's eyes told her it would, indeed, be pointless to scream.

"Yes," she replied hoarsely. "I am thirsty."

"As soon as you answer my questions, I will let you drink."

"Fuck you."

"Agent Washington, please. Your situation is tenuous. If you answer my questions, you will see your boyfriend again. If not, I will leave the outcome to your assuredly vivid imagination." He leaned back in his chair and stared at the woman, letting his eyes roam over her nakedness.

Washington saw the look. "I have a question for you first."

"Ask me anything."

"Why am I naked? If you'd raped me, I'd know, and you haven't. So, why am I naked?"

Pancho leaned back and smiled at his captive. Her question told him she was an inexperienced interrogator, which would help him.

"You are naked because you bled onto your clothes from the nasty cut on your forehead. I am washing them now. And you are also naked," he went on, truthfully this time, "because you have an exceptionally beautiful body. And, no, I have not, shall we say, imposed myself upon you. That, too, may depend on how cooperative you are. So, will you answer my questions?"

"Drop dead, asshole."

Pancho sighed heavily and shook his head. He had never raped anyone, nor would he. It wasn't in his psychological makeup, but his captive didn't need to know that. The next several hours would be all about leverage and the Basque had the feeling he'd need all he could get to break this woman.

Either way, he knew the outcome was inevitable.

"May I call you Alison? Yes?"

Washington looked at the bright day outside, not hearing what Pancho was asking her. Somewhere out there, Stan was searching for her with help from hundreds of other law enforcement officers. *Dear God,* she prayed silently, *please let them find me in time.*

***

Skillful as he was, it took Pancho nearly the entire day to break Alison Washington.

He had almost given up. The woman was unbelievably tough. He started with small physical pain, simply slapping her face when she refused to answer or supplied information he knew to be false.

He got nothing.

He then started working her body, and knew he'd broken at least two ribs.

Still, he got nothing except gibberish and profanity.

He had no cattle prod. The battery from the Mustang and a set of jumper cables from the garage worked, but elicited only screams, and Pancho could tell Washington was sliding quickly into pain-induced delirium. He could not allow that. He had limited time.

"Alison," he said softly, grabbing her hair and raising her face up to his. Her eyes were swollen slits, but he saw the pupils constrict when he looked into them. "I am most impressed. You've done magnificently. You should be proud. I know your boyfriend and your superiors would be proud of you. But they want you back, Alison. They would want you to talk, because getting you back is much more important to them than anything you might tell me. Tell me what I need to know and I will send you back to them. Back to your lover, Alison."

Pancho felt Washington's neck stiffen under his hand. She looked into his eyes and he saw her focus on him.

"Go fuck yourself," she said almost unintelligibly through split, swollen lips, and then let her head fall to her chest when Pancho released his grip in frustration.

There must be something, he thought. Everyone has a key. He just needed to find hers, and it obviously wasn't fear of physical pain. He had no water in sufficient amounts to use as an interrogation technique, so his next escalation would be permanent injury and disfigurement, starting with the Achilles tendons, but he doubted it would work.

He thought of all the days and months he'd been at the mercy of his captors after the Madrid bombings. In his efforts to stay sane, he'd dubbed his American inquisitors The Marquis and Torquemada. They hadn't broken him, though, even after all that time, even with the water. Pancho knew they hadn't broken him because they'd never found his key. Of course, he understood that he really had no key. His had died with his father, at the hands of the Guardia Civil.

Pancho stiffened as if struck by lightning. Could that be it?

He left his captive sobbing quietly and hurried to the kitchen. The contents of Washington's pockets and her cell phone lay on the table. The small wallet Pancho had found lay open, the bright Homeland Security badge glinting in the sunlight streaming through the French doors that opened to the patio.

Pancho sat down and began going through the wallet more carefully. He knew he had little chance of finding anything significant, but he looked anyway. Aside from her DHS badge and ID card, a Maryland driver's license and a government credit card, the wallet was empty.

Twenty-seven dollars and some change made a small pile. No help here.

That left her cell phone. Pancho picked it up and pushed the button, got a screen, and cursed. The phone had a security code. He leaned back in his chair and pondered his options. He knew he had three tries to enter the correct four-digit code. After the third incorrect entry, the phone would lock and possibly erase all the data on it. If he couldn't get into the phone, he could always bluff, but Washington was so tough she might not fall for it. He needed to crack her phone.

He looked at the driver's license. Picking up the phone, he brought up the security screen and entered the month and day of her birthday. The phone vibrated and returned to the security screen. One try down.

He considered his options again and entered the month and last two numbers of the year she was born. The phone again vibrated and returned to the security screen.

Pancho put the phone down and leaned back, again scanning the items on the table.

There has to be something, he thought. *Nobody uses random numbers because they are afraid they will forget them.*

He sat there for several more minutes, studying the items on the table. Just as he slumped back, ready to admit defeat, his eyes swept over the badge nestled in the wallet's recess. It had a four-digit number.

Might that be it? Pancho wondered. *It was a number she would not forget, and it was certainly important to her.*

With nothing to lose, Pancho swept the phone from the table, brought up the security screen and entered the four numbers from Washington's badge.

It worked. The phone in his hand now showed the typical array of icons.

The first thing Pancho did was disable the security time out and need for a code. Then he spent fifteen minutes going through all of the photographs and videos stored on the phone, and, after that, a quick perusal of her contacts gave him what he needed.

"Alison?" he whispered as he sat back down. He wasn't sure she was still conscious, and repeated, louder, "Alison?"

Slowly, Washington raised her head and looked in his direction.

"Alison, I really wish you would answer my questions. If you don't, well, I'm afraid I'll have to go to an alternate source."

"Alternate source?" Washington croaked, her voice barely audible. "What alternate source? You're bluffing."

"I wish I were, Alison. But if you won't tell me what I need to know," he held the cell phone up for her to see a family photograph on the screen, "I'll have to go to Baltimore and visit your parents." The Basque paused for effect and then added, "Or perhaps your lovely sister. She looks very much like you."

Washington glared across at Pancho, her anger and fear overcoming her pain.

"You son of a bitch!" she tried to scream, struggling against her restraints. "Leave them out of this. They know nothing!"

Pancho gloated inwardly.

"I wish I could believe you, Alison, but people talk to their families about their work. They tell them things to impress them with their success. Especially their parents. Maybe you've told yours things I need to know."

"They don't know anything. I swear. Leave them alone."

Pancho stared at the DHS agent. "Alison, I have a proposition for you, so listen carefully. Are you listening? Alison?"

Washington broke eye contact with Pancho and looked out the window. She was willing to die for her country, and she now fully expected to die in this room. The plastic sheeting on the floor made perfect sense to her now.

But she was not willing to loose this man, this monster, on her family.

"I'm listening." It was an admission of defeat.

"Excellent," Pancho said, the relief in his voice palpable. "Here is my proposition. I have no desire to hurt you any more than I already have. This is not personal. We are soldiers. If you answer my questions truthfully, I will feed you and leave enough water to get you through at least the next several days. Please understand that I must leave you restrained. In two or three days my business here will be concluded and I will be out of your country. I will contact your people and inform them of your whereabouts. You will see your family again, Alison."

"Could I have a drink of water first?"

"Of course."

"And would you cover me up so they don't find me like this?"

"Certainly."

There was a long moment of silence. Pancho held his breath. If she refused to talk now, he was out of time and options.

"Okay. What do you want to know?"

"Let me get you that drink of water first," Pancho said, hiding his exultation.

It took him two more hours of careful questioning to extract and confirm the information he wanted from Alison Washington. The more she told him, the angrier and more surprised he became. He pressed her hard, sometimes starting over with a different line of questioning to see if the answers remained consistent. It always ended with the same information and Pancho was convinced she was telling the truth.

"Thank you, Alison," he said at last. "You made a wise choice, and," he lied easily, "if it makes you feel any better, you told me nothing I did not already know. Now, would you like something to eat?"

Washington could only nod. Her energy was gone, exhausted by the ordeal of betraying her country and her team.

"Very well," Pancho said cheerfully as he stood up and headed for the door. As he passed beyond Washington's line of sight he reached into his waistband and removed the ice pick concealed there. He stepped quickly in behind the slumping Washington. At the same instant his left palm slapped her forehead back sharply his right hand drove the ice pick in and up at the juncture of her spine and skull.

Washington never felt it, dying instantly.

"See," Pancho leaned over and whispered in her ear as he withdrew the ice pick. "I promised it wouldn't hurt."

35

Senator Harrison Chapman stopped in the open doorway of the private jet and surveyed Friedman Field before descending the steps to the tarmac. He loved coming to this conference every year, considering it the top perk of his office. Of course, he chuckled to himself as he walked toward the executive terminal, having friends with private jets ranked right up there, too.

"You're sure moving up in the world, Harry." The Senator heard the familiar voice over his shoulder and turned that way.

"Rodge!" Chapman said cheerfully. "Great to see you, buddy. Thanks for coming to get me."

The two men embraced warmly, slapping each other's backs with affection.

"Are you kidding me?" shot back Captain Roger Halberstam, stepping back to look his life-long friend in the eye. "Thanks for keeping me in this gig all these years."

"I need security. You're the best man for the job."

Halberstam laughed. "Right, security. I think that means I just need to make sure my Smith and Wesson nine iron is in my bag. Seriously, Harry, thanks."

"Rodge, it's all perfectly legit. If the U.S. Senate wasn't paying you, we'd be paying some tight-ass kid in a black suit and sunglasses who'd want to taste my food first."

Both men laughed at the image. They'd been best friends forever, growing up in houses a quarter-mile apart on the same county road. Each had stood as the other's best man, and their friendship had endured through the years despite their different directions in life.

"Where are your bags?" Halberstam asked.

"The steward said he'd bring everything out to the car."

"Oh, yeah, the steward," Halberstam teased. "How could I not know that?"

The two old friends laughed again as they walked outside. Halberstam's thoughts were of how powerful and important his friend had become, flying all over the world making important decisions for millions of people. Chapman basked in his friend's closeness, knowing he didn't have to impress Halberstam and thinking how lucky the man was to have made a successful life, close to family and friends, without leaving this place they both loved so much.

"There's been a slight change in plans, Rodge," Chapman said tentatively as the steward loaded his bags into the rented Lincoln Navigator.

"Oh?"

"Yeah, I'm not staying at the Lodge. I've been invited to stay at a private residence."

"You lucky dog! Whose?"

"General Carl Holdorf. You've no doubt heard of him. He's now the Western Regional Director for Homeland Security."

"He can afford a place here on a civil servant's paycheck?"

"Family money, I think."

"Oh, okay. So, do you want us to...?"

"No, no. You and Leona keep your suite at the Lodge. You did bring Leona, right, not one of those twenty-something hard bodies?" He grinned.

Halberstam looked Chapman in the eye and then looked down at himself before fixing the Senator with a stern look.

"What do you think?"

Chapman stepped back and performed an exaggerated head-to-toe examination of Halberstam before deadpanning. "Yeah, you're right. Leona it is."

The two roared with laughter again.

"Gentlemen," the steward interrupted politely. "You're all set, Senator. The aircraft will be here on Thursday afternoon to take you back to D.C. If your schedule changes, just let us know."

"Very good, young man." Chapman went senatorial. "Thank you very much."

The steward nodded and began walking back to the jet.

"Very good, young man," Halberstam mimicked stuffily when the steward was out of earshot. "Harry, you can shovel it with the best of them!" He laughed yet again.

"Hey," Chapman protested with mock indignation. "It's my job."

"Yeah, well, get in the car, Mr. Senator Muckety-Muck. I'll drive."

36

Dennis Rhoades and Stan Kaminski spent hours canvassing downtown Boise, searching the streets and parking garages for a blue Mustang with a broken windshield.

Nothing.

Rhoades called every hospital and clinic within a hundred miles.

Nothing.

Kaminski called Washington's cell phone every five minutes, getting only the automatic notification that the number was not available. The phone was off, making its GPS feature worthless.

Kaminski pleaded with Rhoades to call it in. "Get some more eyes out there," he begged.

Rhoades refused. His heart and his head told him it was the right thing to do, but the fear of what Holdorf would do if he blew this operation twisted in his gut like a rusty knife, and his gut won out.

"No locals," he told Kaminski over and over. "It's not within operation parameters."

And every time, Stan Kaminski was pushed a little closer to the edge.

Finally, emotionally and physically exhausted, they returned to the hotel and collapsed.

"Are you going to call the General?"

Rhoades checked his watch. "Not yet. It's still too early."

Kaminski stared at him. "You're a real asshole, Dennis. Do you know that? A genuine, certified asshole. You won't call the cops to save Alison's life, and you won't call the General," his voice rose until he practically shouted the last words, "because you're too fucking polite to wake the son of a bitch up!"

"Stan, calm down. I..."

"Go fuck yourself. I'm tired. I'm going to try and get some sleep. Don't wake me up until you decide to do something."

Kaminski went to the bedroom and collapsed onto the bed. Exhausted, his vision of Alison's face faded as he fell into a fitful sleep.

Rhoades sat on the couch, too exhausted to sleep, trying to rationalize his way around the knife in his gut. *I'm a soldier*, he told himself over and over. *I followed orders, just like Stan and Alison. I knew the risks and so did they. Losses are part of the game.* He finally fell into an uneasy sleep, jerking awake every so often to the sound of Alison Washington screaming for him to help her, to save her life, while his gut laughed raucously.

Rhoades waited until noon to wake Kaminski.

"Stan, wake up!" he called from the bedroom door. "Stan!" he called again a little louder and saw his team member stir. "Wake up. I ordered room service. I'll call the General while you shower. You've got fifteen minutes, soldier, so get moving!" He hoped the reference would help his team member get a grip on things.

Rhoades waited until he heard the shower running to call the General.

"Good morning, Dennis," Holdorf answered cordially. "How are you?"

"Not good, sir. We believe Pancho has Washington."

"What happened?"

Rhoades gave his superior the quick and dirty version. Plus, he knew few details except that Washington was missing. He didn't mention Kaminski's reaction or the likely reason behind it.

"Not good," Holdorf said when Rhoades finished. "But we don't know much of anything for sure. So let's not give up on her just yet."

"We're not giving up, sir."

"How's Agent Kaminski taking it? As I recall, they worked together early on."

"Yes, sir, they did." He hesitated and then lied. "But he's okay. He's a soldier. He understands."

"The important thing is the operation. Remember that."

"Yes sir."

"Good." The General sounded pleased. "What's your recommendation?"

"I think Kaminski and I need to go in. In truth, we've seen nothing here. Everything has been predicated on what that L.A. cop told Don Straithwaite. Sir, we could be sitting on a dry hole here, while Janicot is somewhere else entirely."

"We have a positive fingerprint identification and a last known location," Holdorf countered, playing devil's advocate. "And I doubt Washington's disappearance from the same location is a coincidence."

"I agree, sir. And that's another reason to go in. We need to make sure she's not being held in that building."

"We don't have enough probable cause for a warrant. I can't authorize an entry without a warrant issued by a federal magistrate."

"General," Rhoades spoke cautiously, "I'm not exactly talking knock and announce here."

"I can't hear this, Agent Rhoades. I repeat, I cannot authorize a warrantless entry. Do you understand what I'm telling you?"

"Yes sir."

"Good. Now, I want you and Kaminski in Sun Valley by tomorrow. Straithwaite is already there and I arrive later today. Plug Don in as the third member of your team and complete this operation. Understood?"

"Yes, sir," Rhoades answered automatically. "Am I authorized to fully brief Straithwaite?"

"I'd prefer you didn't."

"But, sir, I…"

Holdorf cut him off angrily. "Just manage the damn operation, Agent Rhoades. That's what we're paying you to do. You might want to remember that."

"Yes, sir, I'll handle it."

"I knew I could count on you."

Yeah, you can count on us, Rhoades thought. *You can count on Kaminski to find you and give you the beating of your privileged life when this is over.*

***

The General was unsettled by Rhoades's call. So far, he'd been able to cope with the cracks in the operation and stay on track, but losing an agent would be hard to explain. Of course, he reasoned, there was no confirmation that Washington had met with foul play. Officially, she was simply missing.

He debated whether to make the call now or wait until he arrived in Sun Valley. He pulled out the secure phone, trying to decide how to explain the latest setback to the Vice President.

A knock sounded on the door.

"Come," he barked.

His Exec Admin stepped into the room. "Sir, just a reminder that the car is waiting."

He'd wait to call the Vice President.

It was a forty-five minute drive from the house in Pacific Palisades to the airport, during which Holdorf regained his confidence. He would take charge of the operation personally and deflect the blame for the missteps thus far onto Dennis Rhoades. This would still work.

He still had worries. How had Janicot gotten in? They'd been waiting for the son of a bitch and he'd still gotten past them.

And where the hell was Mahmoud?

Most of all, though, what really worried the General was that nobody knew for certain yet where the material was, or what had happened to it. They needed to know its whereabouts in order to control the operation.

37

A few minutes after Rhoades had awakened him, Stan Kaminski emerged from the bedroom, showered and looking refreshed. At the same time, there was a knock on the door, and room service delivered a late breakfast.

"Did you talk to Holdorf?"

"Yes," Rhoades answered through a mouthful of eggs.

"And...?"

"I asked him if we could go in."

"I can guess his answer to that."

"And you'd be right. He said he would not authorize a warrantless entry, and said we don't have enough probable cause to get one."

"What else?"

"We're to move to Sun Valley by tomorrow, hook up with Straithwaite, and complete the operation."

"So, we just write Alison off?" Kaminski's voice was calm, but his eyes bored into Rhoades'.

"Of course not. We don't give up. We have all day and all night to find her. We double and triple check the hospitals. We keep looking for her phone and credit cards. And then we do it again until we find something."

Kaminski looked flatly at Rhoades. "Whatever you say. You're the boss, right?"

Rhoades looked back at his friend and partner, unable to read him at all. It made him uneasy.

"Look, Stan...."

"Don't sweat it." Kaminski waved his fork, a piece of ham impaled on the tines, dismissively. "We're soldiers, right? Alison's not the first casualty we've had in the unit. You grieve, you honor, you thank God it wasn't you, and do your job. Right?"

"Right," agreed Rhoades, glad to hear Kaminski say it. The man was hurting, but he'd work through it. Rhoades added casually, "And tonight we go into that building and see if she's there."

"That's not authorized."

"So we do it without authorization. Maybe we can keep this all from turning to crap in a hat."

"Better late than never," was all Kaminski said before turning his attention to his food.

The two men circled each other warily for the rest of the day. Rhoades worked the computer and phone ceaselessly, looking for any trace, any electronic footprint that might provide a lead. Kaminski finally couldn't take the waiting anymore and took the Crown Vic to cruise the streets and parking garages one more time, hoping to find the blue Mustang.

Nothing.

***

Dressed in dark gray and black under navy blue windbreakers, with full ski masks rolled up to look like watch caps, Rhoades guided the Crown Vic into the alley north of the Biscay Basin Group building while Kaminski checked their gear yet again.

The lot was nearly empty, the late Sunday evening restaurant and bar crowd thin. They had dined at the restaurant earlier, barely tasting the food as they concentrated on the layout and dimensions of the spaces.

During dinner the two agents had also refined their plan, agreeing there was no need to bother with the first floor. While they had no desire to be caught on-site, this was not a covert op. They didn't care if their entry was detected later, nor about leaving behind any indications they'd been inside. The mission was to find Washington and, if they got really lucky, Pancho.

At the alley end of the parking lot they split up. Rhoades headed for the west end of the garage ramp, above the door. Kaminski continued south down the alley to where the ramp came up to grade.

Rhoades leaned over and reached for the surveillance cam, intending to grab it and pull it from its mounting bracket, but it was just out of reach.

Instead, he pulled the silenced Glock from under his windbreaker. Careful of the ricochet angle, he put the end of the silencer against the camera body and fired. It disintegrated, pieces showering the ramp below. He used the silencer to break the light.

Kaminski heard the soft spit of the shot, followed by Rhoades' low whistle signaling that the camera was disabled. He hustled down the ramp to the keypad. Using a small power screwdriver, he removed the cover plate and pulled the circuitry from the box before using a small pair of pliers to quickly cut and strip two incoming wires. By this time, Rhoades had circled around and joined him.

"Ready?" Kaminski asked.

Rhoades nodded.

Kaminski touched the two bare wires together. They sparked slightly and the garage door immediately began to roll up. They entered quickly and stood against the wall next to the door, scanning the nearly empty garage for possible threats. The sudden sound of the door starting back down jarred them both.

"There's the elevator," Rhoades gestured. Having decided that the stairwell was too visible from the restaurant, the plan was to take the elevator to bypass the first floor. The two DHS agents quickly rolled down the ski masks to cover their faces.

"Hey," Kaminski said, touching Rhoades' arm as they approached the elevator. "There's the white van Kaye told us about."

They peered through the darkly tinted windows, finding it difficult to see the cargo area. Kaminski pulled a small flashlight from his pocket and used the same method Kaye had to get a look inside.

"Son of a bitch," he swore. "It's empty."

"That's okay. We don't know for sure what, if anything, was in there in the first place. Let's do what we came to do."

At the elevator they encountered no extraordinary security. With their faces obscured, they didn't care about the camera.

"That's strange," Rhoades mused aloud. "I expected another key pad or something."

"Well, let's try it and see." Kaminski pushed the 'Up' button.

They heard the elevator start down. It stopped at the garage level and the doors opened. The bell that rang sounded to them like Big Ben.

"What happens if we run into somebody?" Kaminski asked.

"Non-lethal force, if at all possible. If anyone offers resistance, well, this will turn out not to be their best day."

It took them thirty minutes to carefully search the office floors. Each locked door gave them hope, but all opened into empty conference rooms, offices, or closets. On the fourth floor they found the surveillance camera monitoring station.

"Smell that?" Kaminski asked softly. "Bleach."

Rhoades leaned over and sniffed the counter. "Cleaning lady, maybe?"

"Maybe." Kaminski scanned the bank of monitors. "Hey, check this out." He pointed at a monitor.

"Jesus. They have the whole back parking lot covered. That's got to be how they made Washington. Damn it! But there aren't any cameras on the outside of the building. Must be inside."

"I blew it, Dennis. I messed up with Kaye. They didn't make Washington, they made me. It's my fault."

"Stan, don't beat yourself up. We don't know that. No matter what, somebody had to be sitting here watching, and they had to be lucky."

They moved on, but there was no trace of Washington or Pancho.

"Just the residence floor left," Rhoades said quietly. "What's the best way up?"

"Follow me." Kaminski turned back into Urrestegui's office. He lifted one of the bronze sculptures off its pedestal near the window and headed to the keypad-controlled door near Urrestegui's desk.

"This must be it," he said, looking at Rhoades.

Kaminski hefted the heavy chunk of metal over his head and hammered it down onto the knob and locking mechanism on the door. The bronze became a hundred pound sledgehammer and the force of the impact sheared the entire assembly off the door, leaving a gaping, splintered hole.

"Somebody should tell this guy to use metal doors," Kaminski smiled.

"What the hell are you doing? If there's anybody upstairs, they sure heard that."

Kaminski looked at his boss, his face devoid of expression. He reached to his side and pulled the cut down .44 magnum from the holster.

"I sure hope so."

Kaminski was disappointed. The residence floor was unoccupied, but the agents couldn't miss the unmistakable signs that someone had recently gone to a lot of trouble to clean out one bedroom and its en suite bathroom.

There were no linens on the bed, dresser doors were open and vacuum tracks covered the carpet. The bathroom reeked of bleach and smear marks were plainly visible on the mirror and shower enclosure glass.

"This is where they kept her," Kaminski said quietly. "We're too late. We waited too long."

"We don't know that. My bet is that this is where Pancho bunked. I don't think Alison was ever here."

"She was here. She had to be. We're too late. I messed it up and you waited too long."

Something in Kaminski's voice tweaked a nerve ending in Rhoades' brain. He turned from where he'd been double-checking the dresser drawers to face his team member, intending to console and encourage him not to give up.

Kaminski stood six feet away. His right arm was extended, and to Rhoades the muzzle of the .44 looked more like a howitzer than a handgun.

"Stan, what are you doing?" Rhoades held his hands out to his sides in a gesture of supplication. The Glock was tucked into his waistband. "Don't be stupid, soldier. We'll find her."

"Shut up, Dennis. We're not going to find her alive and you know it. I blew it and I'm supposed to fix it. But I know you won't let me. Because you're the boss, right? The one who gives the orders. But the bitch is that it makes you responsible for the results. Boss."

"I was following orders, too. Just like you. We're soldiers, Stan. We're at war. People die in wars. I'm sorry about Alison, I really am, but I can't change my orders, and neither can you."

"I accept your logic. But I cannot accept the fact that Alison was sacrificed because the command structure makes decision based not on tactics, strategy, or achieving victory, but on covering their own asses. That's not what I signed up for, and neither did you."

"You'll have to take that up with General Holdorf." Rhoades watched Kaminski carefully, weighing his chances of avoiding a fatal shot long enough to get to his own weapon. They weren't good. Keep talking, he told himself, keep talking and look for a lapse. "My orders came directly from him."

"Oh, I intend to talk to the General. He dies, too."

Rhoades tensed to jump to his left at the same time he grabbed desperately for the Glock.

Kaminski didn't hesitate. The roar of the heavy caliber revolver filled the room. The jacketed hollow point hit Rhoades on the point of the chin, deforming and deflecting slightly downward to enter his throat, completely destroying his trachea, esophagus and larynx before turning several cervical vertebrae into splinters and leaving a fist-sized hole on the way out. Rhoades fell to the floor in a heap, eyes still open and seeing while his brain struggled with hypoxia before shutting down.

Kaminski's voice intoning, "How's that for orders?" was the last sound he ever heard.

***

Two hours later, a showered and freshly dressed Stan Kaminski stood at the hotel desk, the sleepy night concierge trying to conceal her irritation at having been awakened at such an early hour.

"I'm sorry to bother you, miss," Kaminski said pleasantly. "I know it's very late, or very early, I guess, but I have an emergency and need a rental car."

"Rental car?" she asked, still groggy. "Um, okay, I think we can do that." She checked the clock again. "Yeah – I mean, yes, sir, I can get a car for you. Will you be returning it here?"

"I may need to return it in Sun Valley."

"That will cost extra," the concierge told him as she started to dial.

"Cost isn't important. Oh, and if they have one, I'd like a blue Mustang, with a GPS if possible."

38

It's about three hours by car from Boise to Sun Valley. Alone on the big black Road King, Kaye could have done it in considerably less. Following Mike Graham's vintage motor home, though, was adding considerably to the trip. Going anywhere in The Mayflower, as the old Winnebago had long ago been christened, involved a lot of extra time on the road.

Kaye followed The Mayflower as she chugged up the hills and lumbered through the switchbacks between Mountain Home and Top of the Hill, across the Camas Prairie to Fairfield and on to the Wood River Valley before turning north toward Sun Valley.

Sun Valley lies at 6,000 feet in Idaho's Sawtooth Mountains. The resort didn't just spring up in the middle of nowhere. Step west across the city limits and you're standing in Ketchum, where the large majority of the area's five thousand or so year-round residents live, work and shop.

North of Ketchum, beyond the new championship golf course, just as you start the climb to Galena Summit's nearly 9,000 feet, down off the highway past the pines and into the river bottom cottonwoods, is Merl and Elaine's Resort Cabins and RV Park.

Merl and Elaine's is a family place. A lot of their regulars are second- and third-generation visitors. They'd been there so long, and had so many returning customers, that they just never bothered turning off the old neon 'No Vacancy' sign up by the highway. If you could call ahead, they appreciated it, but even if you just showed up, and they knew you, they found a place for you. If you were a new face and wandered in off the highway despite the sign, well, sorry, they were full up. Always.

The Grahams had been regulars for almost thirty years and Merl, tall, lanky and looking like a lumberjack in plaid shirt and denims held up by suspenders, came running from the little log cabin with the carved wooden 'Manager' sign hanging from the porch when he saw The Mayflower coming down the road from the highway.

"Michael! Michael!" the old man yelled joyously as Mike came to a stop and slid back the driver's side window. "It's so good to see you! Where you been, boy? We miss you."

"Hey, Merl," Mike yelled back, the affection obvious in his voice. "Long time no see. You're looking well." Mike reached across and took the gnarled hand Merl thrust through the open window.

"Where you been?" Merl asked seriously, holding onto Mike's hand. "We do miss you."

"Sorry. It's just been tough to get away, you know, since Madge died."

"I understand Michael. I do," Merl said, and Mike knew he really did. "And we were so, so saddened to hear about Aiden and Cynthia. Mother cried for two days straight. It like to broke her heart, and mine, too. What's the world coming to, Michael, when children are called home before their parents? That ain't part of God's plan. Leastwise, no God I know."

"Thank you."

"Sorry we didn't make it to the funeral. Mother's not doin' too well. We just don't leave this mountain much anymore."

"Don't worry about it. What's wrong with Elaine? Nothing serious, I hope."

"No. Just getting old, I guess. Both of us," he smiled, looking with twinkling eyes past Mike to where Cindy sat next to her father. "Hey, I see you got yourself a new lady friend. She's quite a looker."

Cindy laughed. This was a ritual that had taken place since Cindy had begun to blossom into the beauty she became. "It's me, Grandpa Merl!" There was love in her voice. "Cynthia!"

"Cynthia?" The old man peered through the window with eyes still as sharp as a soaring eagle's. "You're not Cynthia. She's a sawed-off little redhead with pigtails, afraid to put a worm on a hook."

"It's me, Grandpa Merl. I'm all grown up, but I still don't like worms."

"Well, we'll work on that while you're here," Merl glanced to his right and then looked back up at Mike. "Hold tight, Michael. Some fella on a motorbike followed you down from the highway. Must be lost. I'll get rid of him and be right back." He turned to walk away.

"Grandpa Merl," Cindy called him back. "He's with us."

Merl craned his neck to look back across at Cindy. "You sure? I can get rid of him if you want."

"I'm sure, Grandpa Merl. He's… a friend of the family. Dad, I'll get out here."

Merl looked at Mike, who nodded.

"Well, then," Merl said soberly. "I best go tell him where to put that motorbike. Only got one place with hard enough ground to hold up one that big. Michael, you go on down and park in A-2. I believe it's empty. Water's still coming up, so don't get too close. Mother and I will be down to visit after awhile. I know she'll want to pay her condolences in person."

"Thank you, Merl. It's really, really good to see you."

"Likewise, Michael. Been way too long." His eyes twinkled again. "I'm sure Mother will want to talk to you about that, too. Now, you go get settled. I'll help your motorbike fella."

Cindy stepped down from The Mayflower's side door and walked back to stand with Kaye, who waited astride the idling Harley.

"Grandpa Merl, this is Ben Kaye. Ben, this is Merl Bates, my honorary Grandpa and the love of my life."

"Pleased to meet you, sir," Kaye said.

"My pleasure, Ben," Merl nodded graciously. One of the perks of Merl's age was no longer feeling the need to call anyone 'mister'. "You camping out?"

"He's staying in The Mayflower with us." Cindy spoke up first.

"I am?" Kaye inquired.

"Ben, we have plenty of room, and extra bunks. Trust me," she said seriously. "This time of year it beats being out in the bugs."

"She's right about that," Merl confirmed. "Just had a big hatch. Good for the bug spray makers and fishermen, bad for folks sleeping outside. Besides, still gets cold up here at night this early in the season. Inside would be better." He winked at Cindy.

Kaye smiled. "Consider my arm twisted."

The two men began discussing what to do with the big Harley. Merl told Kaye he could park the motorbike, as he called it, up by his cabin where there was a small concrete pad for their truck. When Kaye told Merl that all he really needed was a reasonably flat piece of wood, Merl raised an index finger in the air, winked, and walked away quickly, disappearing behind the cabin. Almost immediately he reappeared, carrying a small piece of flagstone.

"This do?" he asked, holding it up.

"Perfect."

"Okay, then," Merl said with a nod. "You two get on down and help Michael get set up. I got some chores to do, but we'll be down to visit later. Pleasure to meet you, Ben."

"Thank you, Grandpa Merl." Cindy stepped over and gave the old man a long hug. "I love you."

"Careful there, Cynthia," the old man beamed as he eyed Kaye. "Don't make your boyfriend jealous. I'm getting old and he looks pretty stout."

Cindy instantly turned bright crimson, stammering, "He's not... We're just...."

"Whatever you say, Cynthia," he said with a wink and a nod at Kaye.

Still blushing, Cindy looked at the two men and half-croaked, "I'll go start helping Dad." She turned and set off toward the sound of rushing water.

"Quite a gal, ain't she?" Merl looked sideways at Kaye as they watched Cindy walk away.

"That she is."

"One more thing."

"Sir?"

Merl turned to face Kaye squarely. "I don't know what your business is, young fella, but I got folks with young children in the park right now. So you keep that pistol safe, you hear me? Don't leave it around where curious little hands can find it."

Kaye stared at the old man and broke out in a broad grin. "Mr. Bates, how did..."

"Never you mind," admonished Merl, not smiling back. "Old don't mean the same thing as stupid. Just do what I'm telling you, or, big or not, I'll personally toss you out of here on your butt." To emphasize the point, Merl kept an eye on Kaye while he leaned over and spat.

"I'm a police officer. I'll be careful."

"You here to protect Cynthia?"

"In a manner of speaking, yes."

"Good to know. You look like a capable fella. Now, get on down and help Michael get set up. Mother and I'll be down to visit later. And don't eat too much of whatever Cynthia feeds you for dinner. Mother baked today." The old man turned to walk away.

"Excuse me, Merl?"

"Yep?"

"Where did they go?"

Merl laughed, then pointed Kaye to space A-2.

***

Kaye, Cindy and Mike sat outside The Mayflower. The glow of their small campfire fought against the deepening dusk, which came early under the towering pines and thick cottonwoods that grew along the river. Through the trees they could see several other campfires, but the rushing water effectively drowned out any intruding noise.

Merl and Elaine stopped by to visit and Kaye saw the worried look Mike and Cindy exchanged when they saw the old woman. She was clearly ailing, leaning heavily on Merl's left arm, her walk hardly more than a shuffle, while Merl balanced the fresh huckleberry pie in his right hand.

Kaye knew without doubt it was the best pie he'd eaten since leaving home for the Marines, and told Elaine that. She beamed at the compliment and then proceeded to roundly chastise the Grahams for staying away too long. Both adopted the appropriate hangdog look and promised not to wait so long before the next time.

When Elaine started in on Kaye, Mike grinned from ear to ear while his daughter turned bright red and stared at the fire. When she started asking about children, Cindy could take no more.

"Grandma Elaine, please. Ben and I are not, um, we're just friends. We only met a week ago."

"I'm sorry, Cynthia," Elaine said, not sounding one bit like she meant it. Then she leaned against Merl and looked up at him with complete love in her eyes. "I knew Merl was the man for me the first minute I set eyes on him."

Merl's mind had been wandering, but the comment snapped him back to attention. "Uh-oh," he said humorously. "Mother's taking another detour on one of her Memory Lane trips again." He stood up. "Time to get her back to the cabin."

"Oh, Merl," Elaine giggled. "I am not. It's God's truth and you know it." Then she winked at Cindy and added, "Course, it did take me nearly a year to get him to see things my way. But, he's right about one thing. It's time for us to go." She raised her hands to her husband, who lifted her to her feet and steadied her. "I'll have Merl bring you a fresh coffee cake in the morning. Good night, good friends. Oh!" she exclaimed suddenly. "Speaking of memory, Merl, did you remember to tell Michael that Calvin called for him?"

Merl got a stricken look on his face. "Dang it! Michael, he said you needed to call him. I'm real sorry."

"That's okay," Mike said. "I'll give him a call."

"You'll need to come up to the cabin. Cell phones don't work down in this hole."

"Then I'll walk up with you."

The three walked back toward the cabin, the men taking care to match Elaine's pace.

"She doesn't look good," Cindy said softly.

They sat quietly until Mike, Merl and Elaine turned out of sight on the path.

"So," asked Cindy. "What do we do now?"

Kaye stared into the fire in concentration.

"We need to find out what we can about this conference, where it's being held, stuff like that."

"That's easy. It'll be at the Lodge."

"You sure?"

"I'm sure. You've never been here before, but trust me, the Sun Valley Lodge is Sun Valley. It's not just a hotel, it's a tourist destination all by itself, and it has a conference center."

"Okay. One down. I need to call Halberstam. He's here working conference security. He should be able to tell us what's happening. And I think DHS already has people here. I'll call my contact and ask him to set up a meet for us. I hope it's not Rhoades, though." Kaye took the disposable cell phone out and activated it. "Merl was right. No service."

"It'll work in Ketchum."

They heard someone approaching the campsite and Mike Graham hurried out of the darkness into the light of the campfire. He was agitated and breathing hard.

"Dad! What's wrong? Is it Grandma Elaine?"

"I talked to your Uncle Calvin. He's back in Korea. The information was waiting for him when he got there. Turns out Pancho spent time in U.S. custody in Europe. He was only released because ETA demanded it during ceasefire talks."

"Did Calvin say why he was arrested?" Kaye asked.

"They had evidence connecting him to an Islamic terrorist named Yousef bin Ali Mahmoud. A very bad guy, according to

Calvin, and get this. They think this Mahmoud has been trying for several years to get his hands on nuclear material."

"Did he know Mahmoud's current whereabouts?"

"He dropped off the CIA radar six months ago. Last confirmed location was the United Arab Emirates."

"Ben," asked Cindy, "do you think Mahmoud could be here, helping Pancho?"

"I wouldn't bet against it. But I still can't figure out the connection for Urrestegui. We're missing something."

"One more thing," Mike said. "Based on Pancho's connection to Mahmoud, Calvin said he was taking the whole thing to the President and asking him to blow it wide open. If he can't convince the President, he'll call us, and he wants us to go public."

"Let's hope we have time for that," Kaye said.

"So," Mike asked, echoing Cindy's question. "What do we do now?"

"I've got to get in touch with Halberstam and DHS," Kaye said. "We need help and resources here, now. How close to town do I need to be to get cell service?"

Mike looked at Cindy for help, but she just shrugged her shoulders. "I don't know," he answered. "Within a mile, maybe two."

"Were Merl and Elaine still up?" Kaye asked.

"Merl was," Mike nodded. "Let's go."

"Dad," Cindy said, "you stay here. I'll go with Ben." She turned to Kaye and added, "Follow me." With that, she was off at a pace Mike could never have maintained.

At the cabin Cindy knocked solidly on the door. After a brief wait, the door swung open.

"Grandpa Merl," Cindy said quickly. "We need to use your phone. It's an emergency."

"Come in, come in," Merl said. "But please keep your voices down. Mother's gone to bed."

Kaye decided he'd try Unger first, knowing that on a Sunday night the odds of actually getting in touch with the state cop were slim to none. He was right. The number went straight to voice mail. Kaye left a message asking the Lieutenant to call him as soon as possible, leaving both Merl's number and the disposable cell.

Next, he tried Halberstam, who answered on the second ring.

"Captain, Ben Kaye here. I'm sorry to bother you this late on a Sunday, but it's an emergency."

"What is it?"

Kaye spent the next several minutes bringing Halberstam up to date, giving him the basics but leaving out some of the details. When he relayed the information about Yousef bin Ali Mahmoud, the Ada County detective was skeptical.

"Islamic terrorists? Here? Kaye, half the kids in American high schools can't find Idaho on a map. You sure about this?"

"It's speculative, but we can't discount it. You know how this works."

"Yeah, I know. Shit, shit and double shit. Have you tried calling Unger? It's officially his case now. I'm in Sun Valley working security."

"I'm in Sun Valley, too."

"You're here? Where?"

"At an RV campground north of town. No cell service, unfortunately. And I just left a message for Unger to call me."

"Well, you might wait awhile for him to call you back, so keep trying to call him."

"Why?"

"I don't know any details, but I heard through the grapevine the Governor pulled him from your case to help out on a missing persons case."

"You're kidding. Somebody asked for state help on a missing person case?"

"Persons, plural. Eight, I think, but I'm not sure. All males and they all work together, except one. That's about all I know."

"Sounds to me like they decided to go fishing and drink beer for a couple days."

Halberstam chuckled. "That's exactly what I told the guy who told me about it. But there must be more…" The Captain stopped briefly and then continued, "Hey, Kaye, I've got another call coming in. Hold on, okay?"

"Now I'm on hold," he told Cindy, who rolled her eyes. Almost two minutes passed before Halberstam came back on the line. His voice was subdued.

"Kaye, you still there?"

"Still here."

"That was my office. They called to tell me I might be needed back there. Seems they just found another body, and get this. They found it on Highway 55 in exactly the same place your shooting happened."

"What?" Kaye was incredulous and his tone made Cindy sit up straight in her chair, her eyes imploring him for information.

"Yep, about a half-hour ago. Young black woman, naked and wrapped in that translucent plastic stuff contractors use."

"Cause of death?"

"Don't know yet, except they don't think it was a gunshot. They do know one thing, though."

"What's that?"

"Whoever killed her tied her up first. Lots of ligature marks. Then they spent a goodly amount of time beating the holy living shit out of her."

Kaye's brain whirled, digesting what Halberstam had just told him.

"Captain, I think the odds are better than even that your victim is a Department of Homeland Security agent. I think Pancho killed her and then dumped her at that exact spot to send us a message."

"Kaye, where do you get this stuff?"

"Hear me out, please. I told you about the DHS agents I had a run in with. The third member of their team was a young black woman. I saw them leaving Gowen Field. We know that the team was running surveillance on Urrestegui's building. I think Pancho made the surveillance, snatched the woman and killed her. The beating tells me he probably interrogated her first. Believe me, this guy hates America and Americans."

"Why? The man's Basque, for Chrissakes. Basques love Idaho."

"We tortured him."

"And how do you know that?"

"All I can say is that my source is extremely reliable. Pancho was previously in American custody for interrogation related to possible terrorist activities. We both know what that means."

"Shit, shit and double shit," Halberstam muttered. "Okay. I'll call my office back and tell them to get a set of the victim's prints to the FBI right away, with possible law enforcement officer identification. They take that seriously, so we should know something by tomorrow."

"Thanks."

"Also, I might be able to help you out for a change. My so-called security gig this weekend is really more of a vacation."

"Gee, imagine that."

"No, no, nothing improper. I am working security, strictly speaking. I'm the bodyguard for Senator Harrison Chapman during the conference. But it also just so happens that Harry and I have been friends since we were old enough to get in trouble together, so it's a pretty cushy job. I brought the wife, I get to play golf when Harry does, stuff like that."

"I'm convinced. What's your point?"

"My point is that Harry – Senator Chapman – usually brings his wife and we stay in adjoining suites at the Lodge. Been doing it since they started having this wingding. Except this year Harry didn't bring his wife, and at the last minute he told me he wasn't staying at the Lodge."

"Where's he staying?"

"That's what I'm trying to tell you. He's staying with General Carl Holdorf of Homeland Security."

"Holdorf is here?"

"Yep. Dropped Harry off at his place earlier today. Anyway, you want me to talk to him?"

Kaye thought quickly. "I'll leave that to your professional judgment." A thought suddenly occurred to him. "You told me that Urrestegui has a house here. Do you know where it is?"

"Hold on," Halberstam said, and Kaye heard him put the phone down. A few seconds later, the Captain was back. "Lemme see here," he paused, and Kaye could hear the sound of shuffling paper. "As security, I got a binder with the particulars on all the registered participants, complete with pictures, and – oh, yeah, here it is. You got something to write with?"

Halberstam read off the address. As Kaye wrote it down, he saw Cindy looking at him, her brow furrowed questioningly.

'Urrestegui,' he mouthed. She nodded in understanding.

"Kaye, I've got one last question for you," Halberstam said seriously.

"Ask away."

"Well, this is the one week of the year Leona; that's my wife; gets to see what it's like to live the life I could never give her on a cop's salary. She always starts talking about next year before we even get home from this year, if you know what I mean."

"I understand."

"So, I'm asking you, cop to cop, okay, what you think is going on. If you were me, would you send Leona home? Get her out of Sun Valley?"

Kaye hesitated. He'd asked himself the same question, wondering if he should insist that Mike and Cindy stay home and let him do the police work. But he hadn't, mostly because he knew neither of them would have listened. For them, this was about Aiden. For Halberstam, though, it was just a job to do before he started drawing his pension next month.

"Yeah, I would. At least I'd try." He wanted to tell Halberstam to go, too, but knew he'd be wasting his breath.

"Shit, shit and double shit."

"Okay, okay, tell me," Cindy said impatiently after Kaye hung up, then gasped and put her hands over her mouth when Kaye told her about the young woman found dead on the highway.

"It's Pancho," Cindy said "I know it is. The bastard is rubbing our noses in it, just daring us to catch him."

"I agree. I've got one more call to make." He glanced over at Merl, slack-jawed and snoring lightly in the rocker next to the woodstove.

Cindy followed his gaze and smiled, then nodded.

"Department of Homeland Security," the operator answered.

"Could I speak to Khalid, please?" Kaye asked, beginning the ritual.

"We have…"

"Sweetheart," Kaye interrupted, "I don't have time to dance tonight. Just give him a message for me. This is Ben Kaye. Tell him he just lost an agent in Boise and I'll bet he hasn't heard about it from Rhoades. If he wants to meet with me, call me. He has my number. Got it?"

"Sir, I…."

"Just give him the message." Kaye hung up, then dug into his pants pocket and pulled out his personal cell phone. "Well," he said to Cindy, "time to turn on the homing beacon. We have to get to somewhere that has service first thing in the morning."

39

onday morning dawned crisp and beautiful in the Wood River Valley, promising to be a perfect Chamber of Commerce day for the conference attendees. Business didn't officially start until that afternoon's kick-off session, but, as is typical of dealings at this level, a lot of business was already being done unofficially. There wasn't a single tee time left at any of the local golf courses, the fishing outfitters were totally booked and rental bicycles were scarce.

Halberstam woke early after a restless night, still trying to decide what to do about Leona. If she stayed and something happened, he'd never forgive himself. Of course, he realized that if he sent her home and he stayed, and if something did happen it probably wouldn't make much difference to him. He finally decided to consult his best friend, Senator Harrison Chapman.

Halberstam paced. He wasn't due to meet Chapman at the golf course until nine-thirty. He decided to go early and hit a bucket of balls. He knew Chapman usually played for money, and usually won, but Halberstam wasn't about to get sucked into that. Not on a cop's salary and a handicap of about a hundred. He made sure the 9MM Smith&Wesson was tucked into his golf bag and headed out.

When he arrived at the course he was irritated to find Harry and, he assumed, Holdorf, already on the practice tee.

"Damn it, Harry," he tried to be mad, but fell short. "Let me do my job, would you? You're not supposed to be in public venues without me, remember?"

"Sorry." Chapman tried to sound contrite. He, too, fell short.

Chapman introduced Halberstam to Holdorf.

"Pleasure to meet you, General," Halberstam said sincerely. "I've heard good things about you."

"Thanks, but I learned a long time ago not to believe one's own press clippings." Then, seeing Halberstam's bag, he asked, "Are you playing with us today?"

Chapman spoke up. "Carl, Roger and I have been friends since we were kids back in the Stone Age, but he's also my security this week. I play, he plays, and I hope that's not a problem."

"Let me clarify," Halberstam threw in, smiling. "I play, but I do not bet. I don't make a Senator's paycheck."

"Nor do I," Holdorf said with a chuckle. "Rest easy, Roger. Any friend of Harry's is welcome company."

"Thank you," Halberstam nodded, turning to Chapman. "Say, Harry, this is a bit awkward, but I need to talk to you."

"No problem, gentlemen," Holdorf said. "Why don't I run to the clubhouse and see if I can find us some refreshments?"

"Truth be told, sir," Halberstam said, "I wouldn't mind if you stayed. This is right up your alley."

Holdorf frowned and looked at Chapman, who asked, "What is it, Rodge?"

Halberstam hesitated, wondering if he should just keep his mouth shut, but then thought about Leona.

"Well," he cleared his throat, looking around to make sure no one was close enough to overhear. "I have information, which I consider reliable, that something bad could happen during the conference this week, and," he cleared his throat again, "I'm worried about Leona and thinking of sending her home. Sylvia didn't come, Harry, and I was wondering what, if anything, you'd heard about all this and what you'd do if Sylvia was here."

Halberstam saw Holdorf's eyes narrow almost imperceptibly and realized, *he knows.*

"What do you mean, something bad?" Chapman asked, looking back and forth between Halberstam and Holdorf.

"A terrorist attack," Halberstam said bluntly, staring at Holdorf and keeping his voice low. Vacation or not, he was still a detective. "Possibly nuclear."

"Rodge, how…"

"Allow me, Senator," the General interrupted. "Mr. Halberstam, may I ask where you obtained this supposedly reliable information?"

"I'm a Detective Captain with the Ada County Sheriff's Office. That's Boise, in case your Idaho geography's a little rusty." Halberstam was pleasant about it, but direct. "Last week I caught a multiple homicide case. Long story short, since then I've learned that the individual I believe cold-bloodedly murdered six people is a known terrorist and might be transporting nuclear material. This conference is the logical target in Idaho for such an attack, unless," Halberstam smiled thinly, "somebody has an axe to grind against potatoes or cowboys."

Holdorf listened carefully. Halberstam was dead on with some of his information, but the General knew the man was guessing on some of it, too.

"Captain," Holdorf said, "I appreciate your concerns, but, quite honestly, for all we know the person who committed your murders, even if he is a terrorist, could be anywhere in the world by now. It has been nearly a week, right?"

"I don't think so. He killed again in Boise last night. You should know that, General, because she worked for you."

"Carl?" Chapman said, alarm in his voice.

Holdorf eyed the Ada County detective closely. "I'm impressed. Your information is very current and almost accurate. Yes, she is one of mine, but as of now she's still officially considered missing."

"Not any more. We found her body last night. Can I get a name, please? She was so badly beaten my guys haven't been able to identify her. Yet," he clarified, with all its implications.

Halberstam saw a flicker of anger cross Holdorf's eyes.

"Sorry," Holdorf said, "but for reasons of national security I cannot tell you that. Yet."

"General," Halberstam said. "Officially, I'm no longer working the case, but when good people die unnecessarily on my watch, I stay interested."

"Tell him, Harry," Holdorf said, glaring at the Senator.

"You sure I can do that?"

"I can't, but, yes, I believe you, as the ranking member of the Oversight Committee, are empowered to share certain critical public safety information with local law enforcement based on your on-site judgment."

"Well, it sounds good," said Chapman. "I just hope you're right, or I can kiss my career good-bye."

"Harry, I can't believe you just said that." Halberstam couldn't decide between mad and disappointed. "Your career? We're talking about people's lives here."

"Tell him, Senator," Holdorf repeated.

"Rodge, we know. In fact, it was the General's people who identified your suspect. I've spoken to the President directly about this and I know he has called the Governor. Believe me when I tell you that the General's people are all over this. He has, and has had, assets on the ground in Boise and Sun Valley for days now." Chapman looked at Holdorf. "Isn't that right?"

"That is correct."

"What about the nuke? And why didn't you share the suspect's identity with the State Police?" Halberstam stared directly at Holdorf.

"Carl?" Chapman, too, looked to the General.

"I can say unequivocally," said Holdorf, "that at this time we have no hard evidence that Janicot is in possession of nuclear material. As far as sharing Janicot's identity, surely you can understand the sensitive nature of the investigation."

"Besides," Chapman said, "we're here. I'm here. Do you think I'd come up here if I thought it was dangerous? I mean, Rodge, c'mon."

"What about the radiation badge, General?" Halberstam pressed.

Holdorf hesitated, then looked at Chapman. "Senator," he said quietly. "Would you get me a Bloody Mary, please? I need some deniability here. You understand, of course."

"Absolutely. I think I'll have one, too. Rodge, you want a drink?"

"No, thanks, too early for me. And I'm working."

Chapman walked toward the clubhouse. As soon as the Senator was out of earshot, Holdorf stepped closer to Halberstam.

"I see Kaye has been providing you with information."

"You know Kaye?"

"Certainly do. Best detective in Los Angeles, which is why we retained him for this operation. You do know he's on leave of absence, right?"

"Retained him? You mean you hired him?"

"Of course. He frequently works with us on important cases." Holdorf saw the doubt creeping into Halberstam's eyes and continued. "Captain, please, don't tell me that you, an experienced detective, honestly believe it was a one-in-ten-million coincidence that Kaye just happened to be right behind Janicot, nine hundred miles from Los Angeles."

"But, Kaye told me…"

"Of course he did. That traffic accident almost blew this entire operation. He had to tell you something."

"Shit, shit and double shit," Halberstam muttered under his breath.

"Excuse me?"

"Oh, nothing. Just thinking out loud." Halberstam recovered. "But you still haven't answered my question about the radiation badge."

"Captain, I can draw the same inferences from that badge that you can. After all, it had Janicot's fingerprint on it. But," he paused a beat, "believe me when I tell you that all tests on the badge for exposure to radiation were negative. Nothing at all."

"That could just mean they were careful."

"It could, but I cannot operate on supposition. Besides," Holdorf lowered his voice to a conspiratorial whisper, "there is more to this than I am at liberty to tell you, even privately like this."

Halberstam was quiet, thinking, sorting and cataloging.

"Just wait till I get my hands on Kaye."

"I'd rethink that if I were you," Holdorf said. "I don't think those who try to lay hands on Kaye fare very well."

"Yeah, well, you might be right about that. He's one big sumbitch, ain't he?"

The General laughed, sounding pleased. "And to answer your original question, no, I don't think you need to send your lovely wife home. Let her stay and have a good time."

"Thanks."

"Okay, then. Let's say we play some golf, eh?" Holdorf looked around. "Harry should be... oh, here he comes."

Halberstam turned and saw Chapman approaching, cradling a paper drink holder filled with four plastic glasses. He wasn't alone, though. A distinguished, fit looking man in his fifties, golf bag slung over his shoulder, walked beside him.

"Hey!" Chapman called as he approached. "I ran into a friend and asked him to make it a foursome."

Chapman made introductions as he passed out drinks. "This is Robert Urrestegui. Robert, this is Roger Halberstam, my BFF, as my granddaughter would say, and General Carl Holdorf, whose name you no doubt recognize."

Halberstam shook Urrestegui's hand warily. This was the man Kaye thought might be in league with their shooter, yet here he was, smiling and friendly, ready to play golf. In the Captain's mind, it scrambled everything, especially after what Holdorf had just told him about Kaye.

"Harry," Halberstam said quietly to his friend, "I told you…"

"Relax." Chapman smiled as he handed a cup to Halberstam. "Raspberry iced tea, no additives."

The group moved toward the first tee box while they talked. Halberstam sensed the instant tension between Holdorf and Urrestegui. He watched the two study each other surreptitiously, like a mongoose sizes up a cobra, but he couldn't decide who was the bigger snake.

"Robert is the chairman of Biscay Basin Group," Chapman explained as they waited to tee off. "He heads one of Idaho's most prominent and successful enterprises."

"What does Biscay Basin Group do?" Holdorf inquired politely.

"Oh, a little bit of everything," Urrestegui answered off-handedly, lazily swinging his driver in warm up. "Mining, timber, livestock, real estate. You know, this and that, trying to make a buck."

"Robert and I have been working together," Chapman said, "trying to push through approval for a new mining concession on Forest Service land."

"The operative word being trying. No luck so far." Urrestegui shrugged.

"What's the holdup?" Holdorf asked

"Location," Chapman said immediately.

"Where is it?"

"Well," Urrestegui smiled. "As a matter of fact, we're almost standing on it."

Holdorf whistled. "I can see why you've hit some snags. I don't imagine they're going to let you dig up Sun Valley."

"It's not like that," Chapman said.

"He's right, General. According to my engineers, the north end of the vein is just east of here, about a quarter-mile down, and extends southeast, away from town. There would be no surface mining operations."

"Except for trucks and equipment," Halberstam said. He'd been silent, feeling out of his depth, but he'd heard of this proposal.

"That is true," admitted Urrestegui. "And, unfortunately, also according to my engineers, the best place, economically and geographically, to sink a shaft would mean running most of that traffic through Sun Valley and Ketchum. Hence, the resistance."

"So, what's down there that's so valuable?" Holdorf asked, genuinely curious now.

"High grade nickel," Urrestegui replied, "that contains an extraordinarily rich concentration of cobalt."

Holdorf's eyebrows arched at the mention of cobalt. "How'd you get samples without a concession?" The General looked at Chapman, knowing the answer.

"I have certain connections," Urrestegui said. "We drilled at the remote end of the vein, helicoptered in equipment to avoid building roads, put in a closed loop water system, things like that. Very stringent environmental protections were followed."

"That's quite an investment with no guarantee of a return," observed Holdorf.

"You're telling me! Not to mention a permit application screw-up that's been in court forever. But we're hoping that the strategic implications of a reliable, long-lasting domestic supply of cobalt will sway some opinions."

"You sound confident," Holdorf remarked.

Urrestegui put a hand on Chapman's shoulder and smiled. "That's what friends are for, right?"

Chapman blushed and looked at Halberstam. The look his friend gave him reminded him of the time Sister Mary Evangeline caught him committing a very personal sin in the junior high restroom.

Halberstam played miserably. He was both preoccupied with what Holdorf had told him about Kaye and crushed to think that his best friend, the man he respected more than anyone else in the world, was just another politician for sale to the highest bidder. The situation worsened when he ended up sharing a cart with Harry while the General rode with Urrestegui.

By the fifth hole it became obvious to everyone that Urrestegui was a scratch golfer and would win the day. On the sixth hole, thanks to some deft steering of the conversation by Urrestegui, Holdorf discovered that the Boisean shared his passion for art.

Holdorf was a calculating man. If Urrestegui was somehow connected to Pancho Janicot, he reasoned, it likely had something to do with this mining scheme and the best thing he could do was keep the man close. On the ninth hole, Holdorf invited Urrestegui to his home for dinner that evening.

Urrestegui graciously accepted, a careful smile concealing his excitement.

40

Except for Kaye, the Graham campsite was still asleep when Merl came down the path toward The Mayflower, several fresh-from-the-oven coffee cakes in hand. Merl stopped a short distance away and watched as Kaye worked through a series of progressively more difficult strength exercises, shaking his head in wonderment that a man of Kaye's size could perform such contortions.

"Morning, Ben. That's quite an exercise program you got there. Never seen a fella your size could do stuff like that. Figured you for a weightlifter."

"I've been working at it for awhile," Kaye said, lowering himself to his feet. "Came across it while I was recovering from an injury. I come by my strength naturally, but flexibility is a challenge. I could show you the basics, if you like."

Merl guffawed heartily. "Hardly! First twist and I'd snap like a dead stick!"

"Holy cow, Grandpa Merl." Cindy yawned and rubbed her eyes as she stepped out of The Mayflower. "What time do you get up?"

The old man chuckled. "Mother got up at four-thirty to bake, but I slept in till five. Getting lazy in my old age. I know it's a bit early, but someone called for Ben. Said it was important."

Kaye heard. "Did he leave a name?"

"Yep," nodded Merl. "Funny one, too. Cleed, or Clete, or something."

"Thanks, Merl, I know who it was. I'll ride into town and call him from my phone. Do you happen to have showers here?"

They did, and Merl told Kaye how to find them before heading off to deliver the next coffee cake.

"I'm coming," Cindy said matter-of-factly.

"Not this time."

"I can help you find Urrestegui's place," she said, her voice sly.

Kaye thought it over and relented. "Okay, but if anything even halfway hazardous comes along, you become an instant pedestrian."

"Ben!"

"Take it or leave it."

"Okay, I'll take it. But I don't like it."

Thirty minutes later, with Cindy on the back, Kaye pointed the big Harley toward Ketchum.

As they neared town, Cindy yelled into Kaye's ear that they were probably in cell phone range and Kaye pulled into the parking lot of a still-closed hardware store.

"Khalid Bergman," he said into the phone when it was answered.

"Is this Mr. Kaye?"

"Yes, it is."

"Stand by, please."

Several clicks later a familiar voice asked, "Kaye?"

"In person."

"I got your message. Most unorthodox."

"It worked."

"Yes, it did. What do you know about our agent's disappearance? I've heard nothing."

"Just call it bad timing," Kaye said. "And you've confirmed the information?"

No answer, but Kaye could hear the DHS man breathing.

"Truthfully," Khalid said at last, "I've not been able to reach Agent Rhoades, which is very unusual, and there's been no word of it through channels."

"We need to meet. Something here doesn't track."

"Explain."

"First, answer a question for me."

"Go ahead."

"What were the test results on the radiation badge?"

Khalid hesitated again before answering carefully. "I've not heard a thing. I don't even know if the testing on the badge was ever completed."

"What? Why?"

"I don't know. That's above my pay grade."

"Look, we need to meet. I know you're in Sun Valley."

Khalid didn't respond immediately, but something about this operation was messed up and he was worried about Rhoades' team.

"The Flippin' Omelet," he said finally. "The patio in twenty minutes."

"How will I recognize you?"

"Kaye, if you're even half the investigator I think you are, in twenty-one minutes you'll realize what a dumb question that is."

Cindy looked at Kaye expectantly. "Well?"

"What's the Flippin' Omelet?"

"It's a locals' breakfast place downtown," explained Cindy. "Why?"

"Can you find it?"

"Of course. Why?"

"I'm meeting Khalid there in twenty minutes."

"You mean," Cindy said sternly, "we're meeting Khalid there in twenty minutes."

"Hmmm?" Kaye focused on Cindy again. "No, not 'we'. I have an assignment for you."

"Really?"

Kaye outlined his plan and what he wanted Cindy to do.

Nineteen minutes later, Kaye dropped Cindy two blocks from the restaurant and then idled the rumbling Road King through the slowly stirring streets. He found a parking place on the same block as the restaurant and backed the Harley against the curb, locked it up, and hung his helmet on the handgrip before strolling toward the small outdoor dining area of The Flippin' Omelet. Even this early, the place was busy with locals fueling up for their day ahead of catering to the tourists.

As he got closer, he scanned faces, focusing on tables with only one occupant. Kaye's gaze settled on a face in the far back corner. The man's eyes met his and the head nodded in acknowledgement.

Mr. Jones.

The hostess approached Kaye, menu in hand and a smile on her face.

"I'm meeting someone, thanks." He brushed by her without taking his eyes off Jones and headed for the man's table.

"Khalid?" Kaye said stonily in greeting. "Or should I call you Mr. Jones?"

"Neither." The man stood and extended his hand. "Don Straithwaite. Nice to finally meet you."

Kaye mechanically shook the DHS agent's hand. "Straithwaite, huh? You sure about that one?"

"I'm sure. Born and raised. I don't make the rules, I just have to follow them."

"My favorite rationalization."

"Point taken. Can we get past that and talk about our current problem?"

"Sure. You go first."

The waiter brought coffee while Straithwaite related in a low voice what he knew, beginning with Kaye's first call to him the previous week. To Kaye's surprise, the DHS agent seemed to know less about what was happening than he did.

As Straithwaite talked, a woman approached the restaurant from across the street, talking loudly into her cell phone. She asked the hostess to seat her outside, ending up at a two-topper not far from Kaye and Straithwaite. She stopped talking long enough to order before immediately resuming her phone conversation, drawing annoyed looks from several other customers.

"Hold on a second," Kaye said to Straithwaite as he stood up and headed toward the woman.

"It's okay," he told her. "Join us."

The two went back to Straithwaite's table and Kaye made the introductions. Straithwaite smiled appreciatively.

"Nice field craft for a street cop." Straithwaite turned to Cindy. "I assume you were taking my picture?"

"Yep." Cindy smiled broadly. "Got some good ones, too."

"Why," Straithwaite asked Kaye.

"In case you were an unfamiliar face. But I saw you get off a marked DHS jet at an American military base. Not much chance you're a ringer."

"Okay, I've told you what I know," Straithwaite steered the conversation back on topic. "Your turn."

Watching for prying eyes and ears and keeping his voice low, Kaye told Straithwaite everything, from the accident until this morning. He saw the DHS agent blanch at the mention of Yousef bin Ali Mahmoud.

"And that brings us to right now," Kaye finished.

"I don't understand this at all," Straithwaite said. "Based on the description of the crate, together with even the remotest hint of anything nuclear, I would have expected a full-scale SWAT entry. Now I can't find Rhoades or his team."

"The woman's in the morgue in Boise. Pancho beat her to a pulp before he killed her," Kaye said. "Who knows, maybe he got all three of them and we just haven't found the bodies yet."

Straithwaite got a stricken look on his face. Clearly, he hadn't considered that possibility. "Jeez," he muttered. "Losing Alison is bad enough. Losing an entire team would be a disaster. But I just can't believe one man, no matter how good he was, could take down an entire team, especially those two. I mean, Rhoades is damn good, but no way Pancho took Kaminski out without a lot of help. No, they're out there somewhere, they have to be."

It sounded like the DHS agent was trying to convince himself.

"We also have to consider the possibility," Kaye pointed out, "that Pancho has help. I don't think he'd have been so quick to waste the other guy in the car if Urrestegui was his only back-up."

"You mean Mahmoud?"

"That's my best guess."

"Okay, I need to call my boss. We clearly have some large gaps in our intel, and we need more troops. What's your next move?"

Kaye, lips pursed, contemplated the question. "I still think we get to Pancho through Urrestegui. But I haven't figured out how. I knocked on the guy's door once and was lucky to get out in one piece."

"You'll figure something out," Cindy said, reaching over to lay her hand on Kaye's.

Before Kaye could answer, his cell phone rang. The caller ID display read 'Idaho State Police'.

"I need to take this," he told Straithwaite as he stood up. "It's Unger."

Kaye stepped over the patio railing and walked casually down the sidewalk before answering.

"Thanks for calling me back, Lieutenant."

"No problem," Unger replied. "Although I'm pissed enough at you that you're lucky I'll even talk to you."

"Excuse me?"

"Tell me why you gave me all that tease information and then had me pulled off the case?"

"For the record, I had nothing to do with that. In fact, I was very opposed to it."

"Big whoop. Same result either way. So, why call me now? Martians poised to invade Idaho?"

"Look, I'm sorry if I put you in a bad spot, but this is not going away. In fact, it's getting worse."

"Really?" asked Unger, his investigator's natural curiosity getting the better of him. "How?"

Kaye told the state cop about Alison Washington, that the rest of her team was unaccounted for, that he was in Sun Valley and why.

"Unfortunately, there's not much I can do for you," Unger said. "The Governor told my boss in no uncertain terms that this was a federal matter and I was to butt out. If you ask me, the Governor probably pissed his Wranglers when the President called him. Tell me something, though. How does an L.A. street cop get to the President of the United States?"

"It's a long story."

"Well, I still got yanked. Now I'm stuck down here working the damndest case I've ever seen."

"Tell me about it."

"Eight people missing. Seven men and the teen-aged son of one of them."

"Any connection?"

"Yeah. They all work together at an RV repair shop. Except the boy, that is. One of the missing guys is the owner, the others are his employees."

"Think they went fishing?" Kaye recalled his conversation with Halberstam.

"I wish. The RV guy's wife said he went to work on Saturday morning to deliver a big overhaul job on one of those megabucks coaches and that's the last time she saw him. The other's wives or significant others all tell the same story. They went to work on Saturday for this big delivery and never came home."

"Everybody?" Kaye was intrigued now.

"Yep, with all their rigs parked out behind the shop," Unger said. "Oh, except one guy. He was too hung over and busy banging some bimbo to make it to work. That's how the locals initially got into this. The guy was pissed because he couldn't find the boss and collect some bonus money he says he was promised, and he drove into the local PD, drunk, to file a theft complaint."

Kaye could only laugh.

"Anyway," Unger went on, "while they were booking bozo for DUI and he's ranting about wanting them to find his boss and get his money for him, the RV guy's wife calls in to report him missing. Things went downhill fast from there. The Sheriff called for help and he got me."

"So," Kaye tried another track, "did they deliver the RV that was overhauled? What did the customer have to say?"

"Well, that's where it gets even weirder. There was no RV in the shop when we went in. No money, no receipts, no plans or specs, no file, no nothing. If it wasn't for Randy, the drunk, insisting there was an RV that had to be done on Saturday for some ignorant prick – his words, not mine – from Sun Valley, we'd have no evidence there even was an RV."

"Did Randy give you the customer's name?" Kaye asked quickly.

"No, says he doesn't remember it. I think the kid's usually pretty toasted, even at work. All he remembers is that the guy was tall, maybe fifty, sort of olive complexion. Some hotshot used car dealer from back east. Always showed up with a posse, and Randy said the guy was obsessed with measuring the reworked spaces in the coach. Every name the kid could come up with sounded Armenian, maybe Russian, but he said the guy didn't have an accent."

"Got anything else? A description of the RV, maybe?"

"The kid remembers that it was silver and a purple color, with some kind of black striping on it. Says it was one of the big ones. There was one thing, though, and it was really weird."

"What's that?"

"This is probably going to sound really strange. Like I said, we found nothing in the office in terms of paper work on the job. But get this. When my crime scene guy first walked into the office, he went down like an eight-point bull during elk season. Had to be hospitalized."

"Why?"

"Chlorine fumes, if you can believe that. Some son of a bitch saturated the entire office with bleach, sprayed the whole place down with it. At first I thought it might be Randy, because he was pissed about his money, but he swears he'd never do that to his boss, even drunk. You ever hear of anything like that?"

Silence.

"Kaye, you still there? Kaye?"

Silence.

"Dammit," cursed Unger. "Damn cell phones."

It wasn't the cell phone.

Kaye sprinted the block and a half back to The Flippin' Omelet.

"Where's Straithwaite?" he demanded of Cindy, who was busy digging in to one of the restaurant's eponymous fare.

"He left," she replied around a bite of eggs. She saw the alarm in Kaye's face. "Why? What's wrong?"

"Pancho has help. Lots of it, too, I think. Let's go. Eat later." He gave Cindy a recap of his conversation with Unger as they hurried to the parked Harley.

"But, how do you know for sure?"

"The bleach. The entire office at the RV shop had been doused with the stuff."

"But, still..." Cindy was skeptical.

"In Halberstam's office, the first time we sat down to compare notes after the shooting, he told me they found Pancho's car abandoned at a body shop. They couldn't recover viable evidence from the interior," Kaye paused, "because the whole car had been sprayed with bleach. It's got to be connected."

"Okay, I'll buy that," Cindy said. "But I guess I still don't see how a missing RV from Twin connects to Pancho."

"Based on some things Unger said, I think the RV is their bomb. That's why Pancho was driving a small car. Somebody else, maybe Mahmoud, brought the big stuff."

"So, it's not a nuke? That's good, right?"

"Maybe, maybe not. Depends on what they're using and if you don't care if Sun Valley is uninhabitable for the next, oh, hundred thousand years or so."

"Oh, Jesus," Cindy whispered, the color draining from her face.

"I need to talk to Straithwaite again, pronto. Did he say where he was going?"

"Only that he was going to call his boss. He wrote down his cell number for you." She fished in a front pocket of her Carhartt's and pulled out a crumpled piece of napkin.

Kaye quickly punched in the number. Straithwaite answered immediately.

"It's an RDD," Kaye said without preamble. "The bomb will be in a large luxury coach coming this way from the Twin Falls area." Kaye recounted his conversation with Unger, including the common link of bleach.

"That's it? Bleach? I don't know…"

"We can't ignore it. We can't afford to."

Straithwaite was silent. "Okay," he said at last. "I'll take it to the boss, and…"

"Rhoades? Aside from the fact the guy's an idiot, you can't even find him."

"Not Rhoades," corrected Straithwaite. "Holdorf. He sent me here, and he's in town for the conference."

"I know."

"How'd you know that? This is supposed to be a secure trip. Officially, the General's in D.C."

Kaye told Straithwaite about Halberstam working security for Senator Chapman, and that Chapman was staying at Holdorf's.

"You trust this Halberstam guy?"

"Absolutely," Kaye said without hesitating. "Good cop. Good guy all around."

"Give me his number, just in case."

Kaye gave Straithwaite the ACSO detective's cell number, then made a decision. "I'm going to the local cops. We need more people looking for that RV."

"I can't endorse that," Straithwaite said cautiously. "My orders are very specific."

"Mine aren't," Kaye said before he hung up. "Where's the police station?" he asked Cindy.

"Um", Cindy hesitated as she looked around. "A couple blocks that way, I think, unless they've moved. I haven't been up here for a while."

"Hop on. We'll find it."

"But Uncle Calvin asked us to wait until he had a chance to talk to the President. Shouldn't we wait?"

Kaye hesitated. Every cop instinct he had told him it was time to blow the whistle on what was going on. Except that local police involvement had thus far been blocked at the highest levels. Did he really stand a chance of walking into a police station and getting them to believe his story? Probably not, he concluded. Best case scenario was they'd let him leave. Worst case scenario was a forty-eight hour mental hold, and that was the last thing he wanted.

"Look," Cindy said, "let's do this. I'll show you Urrestegui's house and then we can ride around a little bit before we go back and check on Dad. Besides, some quality seat time might jog that brain of yours, right?"

Kaye smiled ruefully. "Spoken like a true biker."

41

Don Straithwaite finished his conversation with Kaye and drove like a madman back to his motel room. He needed to talk to the General, and calling him directly was the least of his concerns.

It seemed to take forever for the General to answer the phone. "Holdorf."

From the background conversation it was obvious to Straithwaite that his boss was on the golf course.

"Don Straithwaite, sir. I have a vital operation update."

"Don." There was an edge in the General's voice. "I thought we covered this. You are to report to Dennis Rhoades, not to me. Understand?"

"But that's just it, sir," Straithwaite explained. "I can't reach Rhoades, even on the satellite link. I haven't talked to him since..." he started to say 'Washington was killed' but instead said, "Since Washington went missing, sir."

"Relax, Don," the General said. "I spoke with him yesterday afternoon." There was a hesitation, as though the General was making a decision. "And I'm sorry to tell you, but I've just learned that Alison will not be returning to us."

"I heard that, sir, from Kaye."

"You've spoken to Kaye recently?"

"Yes, sir, just a little while ago. He's in town and told me he was going to the local police."

"Let him," Holdorf said. "He'll get nowhere."

"That's not all, sir. Kaye believes Pancho has help." Straithwaite paused and swallowed hard. "Sir, he thinks it's Mahmoud."

"How does he claim to know this?"

"He says he discovered a commonality between the case in Boise last week and an ongoing investigation in Twin Falls. It's thin, sir, but it's also very unusual."

Straithwaite waited while Holdorf thought.

"Thank you, Don. That information matches and confirms intelligence I'm receiving from the other assets on the case. Kaye has excellent sources."

"I agree. What is my assignment in the meantime, sir?"

"Hang loose," Holdorf said. "Play some golf. Go fishing. Until you hear from Rhoades, that is. He's arriving later today. Once he arrives, coordinate with him and let's see if we can close this whole thing down."

"Yes sir. Thank you." The phone went dead in Straithwaite's hand.

The DHS agent paced, trying to fit the pieces of the puzzle together. If Pancho had killed Washington, the proper DHS response would and should have been to land hard with both boots smack in the middle of the pile belonging to anybody even possibly connected. But, by all accounts, nothing was being done. It made no sense.

Straithwaite gathered his sidearm and two sets of cuffs, a digital camera with long lens capability, binoculars and night vision scope, a blanket and pillow, and all the food and non-alcoholic beverages from the mini-bar.

He'd decided to take his boss's advice and go fishing. As he walked to the Explorer, he hoped they were biting at Robert Urrestegui's Sun Valley mansion.

***

When Robert Urrestegui decided to build his eventual retirement home in Sun Valley, he searched long and hard for the right setting and a design that would do it justice. The result was magnificent, with the home featured in prestigious international design journals on more than one occasion. His only rule was that he not be identified by name as the owner.

The house was a massive structure of logs, stone and glass, situated on five acres with commanding views of the Wood River Valley, Sun Valley, Ketchum and Bald Mountain. The driveway to the house, a hundred yards up the hill, started at the end of the public road.

The dead end would make Don Straithwaite's life easier. With only one way in or out, he would be able to watch Urrestegui's place without getting too close. Now, he just needed a good spot to watch from.

Downhill from Urrestegui's, the houses got closer together, less ostentatious, and progressively smaller. Four houses down, Straithwaite found what he was looking for and turned up the driveway, driving over three days worth of faded newspapers. The house's exterior lights were also on, even though it was midday. Just to make sure, the DHS agent grabbed his fishing creel and went to the front door, where he rang the doorbell several times and waited patiently. He peered through the large windows flanking the ornately carved door. The security system panel was visible, and the system was obviously armed. Straithwaite smiled. It was a brand he knew well.

A quick walk-through turned up a calendar on the kitchen wall with a date the following week circled, and a notation that read 'Return'.

In less than ten minutes the DHS agent had picked up the newspapers, turned off the outside lights, put the Explorer in the garage and set up his gear in the living room, which afforded excellent views of the road and front of Urrestegui's house.

"So much for Neighborhood Watch," he mused aloud as he settled in, soft drink in hand.

42

General Holdorf excused himself as graciously as possible after nine holes. After the call from Straithwaite, he was almost desperate to get back to the house and make a phone call.

"National security," he told the other three with a self-deprecating chuckle. "Robert," he pointed at Urrestegui, "we're still on for dinner. Cocktails at seven. See you then."

Urrestegui nodded. Nothing could keep him from attending the General's dinner party.

"You know, Harry," Halberstam said as they watched Holdorf walk away, "I'm not feeling all that swift myself. Why don't you guys finish the back nine as a twosome."

"Rodge," Chapman protested, "you're my security!"

"Yeah," Halberstam looked at his long-time friend, "but I think we might need to talk about that. In the meantime, I think Mr. Urrestegui here can be trusted to look after you. After all, if something happens to you, how's he going to get his cobalt mine through Congress?" The Captain turned and walked away. He wasn't looking forward to explaining to Leona why they were going home.

"I'm sorry, Harry," Urrestegui apologized.

Senator Harrison Chapman watched his boyhood running buddy walking away, but his greed and political ambition won out.

"He'll get over it. He's naïve and right now he's just mad. Let's just stick with our original plan. We're almost there." Chapman patted Urrestegui on the back.

***

Holdorf went immediately to his library. A monumental painting dominated the wall behind his desk and the room afforded a fabulous view of the Wood River Valley.

He removed the encrypted phone from the drawer and hit the speed dial code.

"Carl, please tell me you have good news." The Vice President's voice was strained. "I just heard that someone is trying to get in to see the President about this operation."

Holdorf was stunned, "Who?"

"A Special Assistant from the Agency. Some retired Marine named Dinsmore. I'm trying to get more."

"Well, sir, I have good news. We've got a fix on Mahmoud."

"Good work, Carl. Do we know yet who has the material?"

"Not one-hundred percent. But high probability it's with Mahmoud."

"Goddamn it, Carl!" the Vice President exploded. "For this to work we must catch Mahmoud red-handed!"

"I understand, Mister Vice President. Please remember that I have as much at stake here as do you."

There was a long silence. Finally, the Vice President spoke, his voice low and murderous.

"Holdorf, I'll see you hang if this operation fails. When you and Chapman brought this to me I thought it was a long shot. Now we're teetering on the brink of disaster because you've mismanaged the operation. Get it right. If you want the job, get it right."

"I've mismanaged nothing, you sanctimonious, bureaucratic desk jockey," Holdorf countered, his voice low. "This will work. We're incredibly close. You keep your end of the bargain, and I'll keep mine."

He hung up.

Holdorf sunk back into his chair, exhausted. He was now fully committed to Operation Bilbao Gambit. He'd either end up in prison awaiting execution, or be Vice President of the United States, perfectly positioned for a run for the Oval Office.

43

The luxury motor coach glided down the highway toward Sun Valley, the inter-cooled twin turbocharged diesel making the speed limit, but not one mile per hour more. Despite the fact that the coach was loaded beyond its recommended gross weight, no bump or imperfection in the road transferred to the occupants.

Less than a quarter-mile ahead, a black Escalade led the way, while a half-mile behind a dark gray Suburban kept pace. Inside the two escort vehicles was enough firepower to overcome any interference that might be encountered. At this stage of the mission, none would be tolerated.

The precautions were unnecessary. Less than two hours after pulling out of the barn outside Carey, Mahmoud slowed the coach as it entered Ketchum.

"We are here, Sayyid," Serenya said. "Praise Allah."

"Indeed, but we have not yet succeeded. Let us hope that Doroteo Arango meets us here."

Pancho and Mahmoud had not spoken since Mahmoud and his cell had penetrated the U.S. border months earlier. They had maintained a total communications blackout, believing that the U.S. government heard everything. Mahmoud realized it was entirely possible that Pancho had been detected and captured, or suffered some other misfortune or delay.

If he arrived to be met by a bewildered homeowner, he would simply claim to be lost and divert to his secondary target, using the explosives aboard the coach to strike a blow at America. If armed adversaries greeted him, he would simply detonate the coach and ascend to Paradise as a martyr to Islam.

The on-board GPS guided them to their destination. The coach had no trouble negotiating the driveway, and Mahmoud saw a familiar figure come out the front door and stride rapidly toward them. Mahmoud breathed a silent prayer of thanks. After shutting down the big diesel he bounded out of the coach and embraced his friend.

"You look well," he said to Pancho. "Your journey was safe?"

"Let's just say it was not without challenges," Pancho answered tactfully. He had already decided not to tell the Arab what he'd learned from Alison Washington.

"And who is this?" Pancho asked politely as he looked at Serenya.

"This is Serenya," Mahmoud replied. "She is the daughter of my cousin and sworn to our cause. I told her father I would train her personally." Then, to Serenya he said, "This is Senor Doroteo Arango Janicot, a leader of his people and a champion of freedom."

"I have heard much about you these past months," Serenya said.

Pancho laughed. "Don't believe everything you hear. Come, let's go inside."

When the coach had turned into the driveway, the Escalade and Suburban had continued past. They would return to the house in Carey. Once there, they would bury their weapons deep under the sagebrush, near Tom Whitworth and his workers, and return to their homelands.

44

Kaye and Cindy returned to the campground in the mid-afternoon. Cindy had pointed out Urrestegui's house, but Kaye had settled for a long-distance look because of the dead-end.

Kaye eased the big bike down the path at Merl and Elaine's, idling to avoid disturbing nearby campers. They arrived just in time to see Mike walk up from the river, fishing pole in one hand and a nice stringer of trout in the other.

"Dinner!" Mike announced triumphantly as Cindy and Kaye climbed off the Road King.

"Good for you, Dad!" Cindy clapped her hands, sharing Mike's obvious delight.

"You probably won't think that while you're cleaning them," Mike teased.

"Dad!"

"I'll do it," Kaye volunteered. "I don't mind."

"No, I'll do it." Merl's voice boomed from behind Kaye and he turned to see the old man standing on the path, grinning broadly. "On one condition. I get to keep the heads."

"Sounds like a deal to me," Kaye said. "I hope you have a good recipe."

"Well," Merl said, "they do make a right fine soup. But Mother's been having some trouble with feral cats getting into the chickens. She won't let me shoot the dang critters, so I need to set a couple traps. 'Bout the only thing them cats like more than chicken is fish, so next time they come around looking for chicken I'll tempt 'em with fish heads and, BAM" he clapped his hands, "I got 'em trapped nice and easy."

"Just like that?" Cindy sounded skeptical.

"Yep, just like that. After all, ain't that why they call it bait?" Merl's eyes crinkled as he turned to Mike. "Now, Michael, just give me them fish and I'll take care of 'em for you lickety-split."

While Merl masterfully cleaned the fish, Kaye sat and listened to the easy banter between the three. He could tell the Grahams loved the old man dearly.

"Well," Merl said with satisfaction as he dropped the last of his prizes into the bag, "that oughta do it. Thanks, Michael."

Cindy hugged the old man. "Thanks, Grandpa Merl. You're the best."

"I agree," Kaye said, standing up. "In fact, right now I think you're a genius."

Merl never missed a beat. "Don't tell me, young fella. Tell Mother. I've been trying to convince her of that for over sixty years." He tipped his invisible hat and strode up the path toward the cabin.

"A genius?" Cindy asked suspiciously. "What brought that on?"

Kaye smiled. "He just explained this whole mess and gave me an idea on how to get to Urrestegui in, what, five or six sentences? Genius, pure and simple."

"Explain," ordered Mike.

"Yeah," Cindy added. "Enlighten us non-geniuses."

Kaye motioned them to sit down.

"We've been wondering why DHS has refused to act on what we think is solid information regarding Pancho, right?"

Two heads nodded in agreement.

"They've stymied us at every turn by hiding information and going to great lengths to keep this quiet, right?"

"Okay," Mike said. "The answer to all your questions is yes. But, why?"

"What Merl said about bait tipped me." Kaye looked back and forth between father and daughter. "They don't want Pancho. They want somebody else. Pancho's just the bait, although he probably doesn't know it."

"That makes no sense," Mike exclaimed.

"How can you say that?" Cindy demanded. "That animal killed my brother and five other people. How can they not want him? That's absurd!"

"No, it's not absurd. But let me rephrase what I said. They want Pancho, but only when the time is right. Not too soon, not too late." He paused, collecting his thoughts and letting the pieces fall into place. "And I'm willing to bet that who they really want is connected to the missing RV from Twin Falls, and that if he isn't here already, he will be soon."

"Mahmoud," Cindy said.

"Exactly."

Mike had been pacing up and down the side of The Mayflower, evaluating what Kaye was saying. "You're right," he said, looking hard at Kaye. "It explains everything we know. Now, the question becomes how we use the intelligence for strategic and tactical advantage."

"I have an idea about that, too," Kaye smiled.

"I'll just bet you do," Mike nodded as he sat back down. "Let's hear it."

"First, does Merl have a truck we can borrow?"

"Consider it done." Mike's voice was confident.

"Okay," Kaye nodded. He spent the next ten minutes outlining his idea. With input from the Grahams, they refined it and allocated their resources.

At four o'clock, Kaye and Mike went to find Merl. Kaye carried a small tarp from The Mayflower's storage bin. When Mike asked to borrow Merl's old green Willys pickup, the old man didn't even ask why. He simply turned around, went inside, and returned to deposit the keys in Mike's hand.

When he went back inside, Elaine asked, "What was that about, Merl? Michael borrowed the Jeep?"

"Don't worry about it, Mother," he reassured the love of his life. "I think there's serious business afoot, though. Serious business, indeed."

"Can we help?"

"I don't think so," he said quietly as he watched Kaye, with Mike in the passenger seat, point the old Willys toward the highway. "But I think we got the right man on the job.

"Now," he added cheerfully as he turned around. "What's for supper, woman?" He saw the look his wife gave him and added hastily, "I'll get it started."

***

316

Kaye drove toward Galena Summit. The old Willys looked rough, but it ran like a top, the only drawback being that it was geared so low it topped out, the engine shrieking in protest, at just over fifty.

It took Kaye less than a half-hour to find what he was looking for.

They'd made about half the return trip when an unmarked police car went by them, headed up the pass. Reflexively, Kaye glanced in the rearview mirror and was surprised to see the unit make a fast u-turn, using every available inch of pavement and shoulder. A blue light on the dash blinked and the emergency lights concealed in the grille were flashing.

"What's the speed limit here, Mike?" Kaye asked, glancing in the mirror again.

Mike saw him check and spun around in his seat. "No way. This old rattletrap can't go the speed limit."

"Maybe not, but he wants us."

After stopping, Kaye kept his hands on the steering wheel and his eyes on the rearview mirror. The late afternoon glare prevented him from seeing into the police car. He was surprised when Captain Roger Halberstam stepped out of the driver's door and settled the white cowboy hat onto his head as he walked toward the Willys.

"Afternoon, Kaye," the Ada County detective said casually. "Thought that was you. Must be my lucky day." Halberstam looked across the front seat and Kaye saw recognition dawn in the Captain's eyes. "Afternoon, Mr. Graham. Wouldn't have expected to find you here."

"Afternoon, Captain," Mike acknowledged.

"What's up?" Kaye asked.

"Step out of the vehicle."

Kaye detected the edge in Halberstam's voice. "What..." he started to ask, but the Captain cut him off.

"I gave you a lawful order, mister. Step out, or go to jail."

Mystified, Kaye opened the door and slid out as Halberstam stepped back out of reach.

"Step to the back of the truck," Halberstam ordered. "Now, put your hands on the tailgate and spread your feet."

Kaye complied. "Can I get an explanation for this?"

"Kaye, I don't like being conned. Especially by another cop during a multiple homicide investigation."

"Conned? What are you talking about?"

"Know what I did this morning?" Halberstam asked. "I played golf with your boss."

"My boss? My Chief is here for the conference?"

Halberstam laughed. "Very good. Real convincing. You know damn well I'm talking about General Holdorf, Regional Director of Homeland Security. I'm sure you recognize the name, right?"

"Sure I recognize the name. I worked some cases with DHS in Los Angeles, but I don't work for Holdorf."

"That's not what he says." Halberstam's stare bored into Kaye's eyes. "He told me you were assigned to follow Pancho."

"Is that true?" Mike had gotten out of the Willys and now stood by the side of the old truck. "Ben, is that true? You could have kept him from killing Aiden?"

"Okay, that's it," Kaye snarled as he pushed himself off the tailgate and spun to face Halberstam. "I've heard enough. I do not work for Holdorf." He turned. "Mike, everything I've told you is the truth. I couldn't have saved Aiden."

"C'mon, Kaye," Halberstam prodded. "You expect us to believe it was a coincidence you were right behind Pancho? Why would Holdorf lie?"

"I do not work for Holdorf. I can only guess why he would lie to you about it."

"Take a stab at it, just to humor an old cop."

"I'd like to hear this, too," Mike said, walking to the back of the truck.

"Captain, did you talk to Holdorf about the case?" asked Kaye. "Did you tell him you were getting information from me?"

"Yeah. Me, him and Harry – Senator Chapman – talked about it some. I didn't tell him we were sharing information, but he figured it out," Halberstam nodded slightly.

"Misdirection," Kaye said.

"What?" Mike asked. "Why?"

"Yeah, why?" Halberstam echoed.

"Think about it. Holdorf doesn't want Pancho stopped, and…."

"Whoa, cowboy," Halberstam interrupted. "Did I just hear you say that Holdorf doesn't want Pancho stopped?"

"Not yet."

"Explain."

The passenger door of Halberstam's car opened and a woman leaned out.

"Roger!" she called, "how much longer will you be? We'll lose our reservation at Redfish if we don't get a move on."

"Not much longer, darlin'," Halberstam answered. "Just another minute."

Mollified, Leona closed the car door.

"You leaving Sun Valley?" Kaye inquired. "What about Senator Chapman?"

Halberstam got a pained look in his eyes. "Harry and I have come to a parting of the ways. Turns out the stereotypes of hard-ass cops and dirty politicians not getting along are accurate."

"Chapman is dirty?" Mike's voice was incredulous.

"Well, he was dusty, at the very least, and it sprinkled this morning," Halberstam said to Mike before turning to Kaye. "Did you tell Holdorf about Urrestegui?"

"I've never spoken directly to Holdorf in my life, but I told my DHS contact. I think we can assume Holdorf got the information. Why?"

"Because Harry Chapman's in bed with Urrestegui on a controversial mining deal. He introduced Urrestegui to Holdorf this morning, we all played golf together, and Urrestegui is having dinner at Holdorf's house tonight."

"That's crazy!" Mike exclaimed. "Why would Holdorf invite Urrestegui to his house, knowing the guy might be connected to Pancho?"

"Sun-tzu," Kaye said quietly.

"Sun who?" Halberstam asked, lost.

"Sun-tzu. Keep your friends close, keep your enemies closer."

Kaye spent the next few minutes briefing Halberstam. When the ACSO cop heard about Yousef bin Ali Mahmoud, he whistled softly and muttered, "Shit, shit and double shit. Makes sense now. Everything fits. Nice work, detective. Oh, and we've tied Pancho to the killing of that young woman. The DHS agent."

"How?"

"A witness came forward this morning with a description of the guy he saw manhandling an unconscious black woman in the parking lot behind Urrestegui's building early Sunday morning. DHS is stonewalling us on a picture of Pancho, but the description fits him right down to a gnat's ass. Unfortunately, we can't tie it to Urrestegui."

"I've got a picture," Kaye told him. "Are you willing to come back to Sun Valley? We could use your help."

Halberstam beamed. "Willing? How about desperate? You just saved my marriage."

Since the suite at the Lodge was paid up for the duration of the conference, and since the Captain was so mad at Chapman he'd left without checking out, it was decided the Lodge would become their base of operations.

The information about Urrestegui dining at Holdorf's that evening filled one blank in Kaye's plan.

When they were ready to head back to town, Halberstam glanced into the Willys' bed again.

"By the way, what's under the tarp?"

Kaye lifted the edge of the tarp to reveal the head of the road kill mule deer buck.

"Bait," he answered with a broad grin.

***

Once the five, including a very pleased Leona, arrived at the Lodge, Kaye called Straithwaite.

"Where are you?" he asked the DHS agent.

"I'm sitting on Urrestegui's place. In direct contravention, I might add, to my superior's direct orders."

"You reached Rhoades?"

"Holdorf. I still can't get Rhoades, which, even if the General doesn't seem concerned, worries the hell out of me."

"Any activity there?"

"None worth mentioning. The guy came home awhile ago, but nobody else in or out."

"No sign of a large motor coach?" Kaye asked.

"Nope, but that doesn't mean it's not already here. The garage area isn't visible from the front of the house."

"I think Mahmoud is Holdorf's real objective. That's why your people haven't moved on Pancho yet. The General's afraid to scare off Mahmoud."

"Kaye, where the hell do you get this stuff?"

"Sorry, I didn't put it together before now. It was the fish heads."

"What? Never mind, I don't want to know. But I've got to admit, it's exactly the kind of thing Holdorf would do. Assuming it's true, what do we do next?"

Kaye explained his plan. As he did, Straithwaite smiled.

45

Robert Urrestegui slid into the Range Rover, cranked up the seat heater, and headed home from Holdorf's dinner party.

It had taken him years to get into that house, and even the long wait had not prepared him.

He saw the first one in the downstairs den after Holdorf graciously acceded to his request for a tour of the house and obviously extensive collection.

"This is very interesting," he said, trying to hide the excitement in his voice.

"Can't remember where we picked that up," Holdorf said too quickly. "It's not even signed. I keep it because it was a gift from my wife."

Urrestegui studied the painting quickly, not wanting to show too much interest. The school, the period, the materials and the technique were all correct.

Holdorf's collection was impressive. Matisse, Chagall, and quite a few other notable artists of the 19th and early 20th centuries were represented.

In the upstairs library he got the shock of his life.

Covering almost the entire wall, the painting was easily ten feet tall and almost twenty feet wide. A mountainous landscape, it was so brilliantly executed that Urrestegui felt he could have stepped into the scene. The artist's mastery was so pure that Urrestegui couldn't discern where the smoke and flames rising from the destroyed buildings became part of the fading rays of a sun setting behind distant peaks shrouded in ethereal mist.

The method was all wrong for the period of Picasso's career, but Urrestegui knew that the man was a master realist before venturing into abstraction and cubism. The theme, though, was perfect, a pure contrast to the cubist horror depicted in *Guernica*.

It had to be the original painting for the Pavilion.

"Oh, my God," Urrestegui whispered reverently.

"Isn't that amazing?" Holdorf asked. "I honestly don't know what it's worth, or even if it's worth a damn cent, but it's the most perfect, beautiful painting I've ever seen, and I've seen a lot of them. Truth be told, my father built this entire house around that painting."

"Hudson River School, right?" Urrestegui asked nonchalantly, leaving Holdorf a way out.

"Very good."

"It's not signed?" Urrestegui said, moving closer.

"It was painted by an Argentine named Montes, who came to America and studied with Bierstadt just after the Civil War. He signed it on the back," Holdorf said glibly. "I don't know if he always did that, or only on works of this scale, because I've scoured the earth looking for his work and the owners of his paintings are just like me; you'd have to kill them to get their Monteses away from them."

Really? Urrestegui thought. *How appropriate.*

Holdorf steered them out of the library. They covered the rest of the house, but Urrestegui's mind stayed on the large landscape.

He was so close, glad now that he hadn't given up.

46

And he had almost given up. When Pancho called and demanded three million dollars a scant month after their first meeting in Bilbao, he feared he'd seriously misjudged the young Basque.

He'd returned to Bilbao to try and salvage the project.

"Three million dollars? Are you crazy?"

"Do you want the paintings or not?"

"Certainly, I want the paintings. But what could possibly cost three million dollars?"

"Strontium-90." A half-smile played on Pancho's lips. "It's how I intend to extract my revenge."

Urrestegui was stunned. He didn't know the particulars, but he knew what Strontium-90 was.

"No way," he said, shaking his head and standing up to leave. "Forget the paintings. I'm not getting involved in anything like that."

"Sit down, Robert. You are already involved. If you choose to end that involvement now, I have no doubt that word of your generous contributions to ETA would soon find its way back to the authorities in your country. They are already investigating you."

"How did you know that?"

"Ah, you Americans," a voice said from behind Urrestegui. "You think you are smart and everyone else is stupid. It will be the end of you."

Urrestegui spun in his chair to see a tall, olive-skinned man with silver hair standing close behind him. The man's eyes glittered and his smile reminded the American of a shark.

"Robert," Pancho said, "allow me to introduce our associate, Sheik Yousef bin Ali Mahmoud. He will be contributing two million toward the purchase of the Strontium."

"Peace be upon you, Robert." Mahmoud intoned unctuously.

Urrestegui turned to look at Pancho, panic in his eyes.

"You son of a bitch. I'll kill you for this, Basque or not."

Pancho and Mahmoud laughed.

"Relax, Robert," Pancho said. "What we are planning is a statement, not a holocaust. And it should also accomplish our other objectives."

Mahmoud sat down and began to outline what they planned, and as it unfolded Urrestegui realized that he could not only end up with the Picassos, he could also use these two to get his mining concession approved.

By the end of the evening, he was on board, promising Pancho and Mahmoud the three million dollars as soon as he could get it out of America without raising suspicion.

Time and distance had blunted his initial horror at what Pancho and Mahmoud planned to do, and he soon saw it as nothing more than a business deal that would profit him immensely.

Pancho and Mahmoud handled the logistics from offshore, which further insulated Urrestegui from what was happening.

Then things got complicated.

Two months after returning from Spain he received an unexpected call from Senator Harrison Chapman. The Senator requested that Urrestegui come to Washington for a meeting concerning the stalled Biscay Basin Group mining concession application. They met at the Watergate for dinner.

Chapman was very smooth. Without saying anything that would make him culpable, he had no trouble communicating that if Urrestegui would help him out, he would help Urrestegui.

Although he felt an instant kinship for the personable Senator from Idaho, whom he recognized as a kindred spirit, Urrestegui graciously declined.

"Thank you, Senator, but I already have a plan in the works that should solve my problem."

"Really?" Chapman said, sipping his brandy. "Would that plan have anything to do with your trips to Basque country and your meetings with Pancho Janicot?"

"Senator," Urrestegui replied smoothly, fighting the panic that rose in his throat, "have you had your nose in my business?"

Chapman sat his brandy glass down and leaned forward, putting his elbows on the table and rubbing his hands together for a moment before looking directly into Urrestegui's eyes.

"As a matter of fact, Robert – you don't mind if I call you Robert – I have. Aside from the fact that I'm the chair of a Senate intelligence subcommittee, I make it my business to put my nose as far into somebody's business as I can so I can get a good whiff of what kind of man I'm about to offer to do business with." The Senator paused, took another sip of brandy, sat the glass back down, and continued. "And I must tell you, Robert, your business ain't got a particularly rosy aroma about it. In fact, I bumped my nose up against the Justice Department a couple times while I was up there.

"Now, I can help you with your mine, and your problem with Justice. Or, I can just as easily make sure you go broke before you go to prison for the rest of your life."

"What do you want?"

"Why, Robert, I'm surprised at you. I don't want anything. I'm simply offering assistance to a valued constituent," Chapman looked at Urrestegui and smiled. "Of course, if and when the time comes, should you choose to express your gratitude in some tangible way, I assure you I would be appropriately grateful."

Urrestegui was hemmed in, and he knew it.

"Senator, I would be most grateful for your assistance."

"Why thank you, Robert. It always gladdens my heart to know that I can do some good for a fellow Idahoan here in Washington, D.C. This town is so tawdry, don't you think?" Chapman leaned back and drained his glass, then signaled the waiter for another.

"There is just one thing," Chapman continued. "The Justice Department won't bother you again, but I really do need to know what you've been doing in Spain. Consider it insurance." The Senator's smile was reptilian. He had Urrestegui, and he knew it.

So did Urrestegui, who quickly decided that it would be in his best interests to have Chapman as an ally. Besides, he reasoned, if Chapman knew of the plan and didn't immediately call the FBI, he'd be just as guilty as Urrestegui. Plus, after the conversation they'd just had, Urrestegui correctly reasoned that Senator Harrison Chapman was not the least bit interested in having a conversation with the FBI.

So, he told him; but only what the Senator needed to know that impacted the mine. He kept knowledge of the paintings to himself.

Chapman never batted an eye. It was as if he already knew.

When Urrestegui was finished, Chapman made it clear that the meeting was over, and the Boisean took his leave.

Now, feeling very close to success, Robert Urrestegui turned the Range Rover up the road toward his house. Ahead, he could just make out what appeared to be an old pickup, stopped in the middle of the road, lights still on.

47

"He's coming," Don Straithwaite said into his cell phone as he watched from his appropriated vacation home. "We see him," Kaye confirmed.

Cindy stood near him, bathed in the glow of the Willys' headlights. On the road between them lay the deer carcass from the back of the truck.

"Are you sure you want to do this?" he asked Cindy.

"A little late to be asking me that, don't you think?" Cindy smiled nervously, watching the approaching headlights. "But, yes, I'm sure. He helped kill Aiden. I'll do whatever I have to do."

"Just do what we talked about. I'll be right over there," Kaye indicated a small copse of young aspens just off the road. "I need him out of his car, here in the light."

Cindy hugged herself, a slight shiver of apprehension coursing through her.

The Range Rover came slowly up the hill. It stopped a car length behind the Willys, its emergency flashers coming on.

Cindy stepped from in front of the Willys to the side, where Urrestegui could see her. Kaye had told her Urrestegui would not feel threatened by a lone woman, and he'd been right. She couldn't see beyond the Range Rover's glaring headlights, but almost immediately she saw a man step in front of them and head toward her.

"Are you all right?" Urrestegui asked with genuine concern, taking in the scene with a cursory glance.

"I'm okay," Cindy replied, thinking the man didn't look like the monster she'd expected. "First I get lost, then this stupid deer jumps out right in front of me and now this old piece of you-know-what won't start."

"Let me see if I can help. First, let's get this deer off the road."

Urrestegui walked back to the Range Rover and returned, donning leather gloves. He walked past Cindy to the back of the dead buck, intending to grab the hind legs and drag it off the road.

Before he bent down, Urrestegui looked around.

"Looks like you got lucky. He didn't even ding your truck."

"I guess I wasn't going very fast."

"Usually takes a pretty good lick to put one down for good." Urrestegui's experienced hunter's eye noticed no blood or fluids on the road, and the blood on the buck's muzzle was dried. He nudged the buck's hind legs with the toe of his boot.

"Okay," he said calmly, approaching Cindy. "Who are you and what do you want from me?"

"She's with me." The low voice came from behind Urrestegui, who spun quickly. Kaye stood ten feet away, his Kimber leveled at Urrestegui.

Cindy walked over and stood slightly behind Kaye, her gaze fixed on Urrestegui.

"What the hell do you want now?" Urrestegui spat vehemently.

"You."

"Me? What could you possibly want with me? I'll see your ass in jail, Kaye, starting with kidnapping and aggravated assault."

"We know who, how and where," Kaye said, ignoring the threat. "What we don't know is when and why."

"Excuse me? Know what?"

"About Pancho. About the bomb and about Mahmoud."

"And how you helped kill my brother," Cindy said.

"I don't know anything about a bomb."

"The dirty bomb," Kaye prompted. "The one Pancho brought the crate of radioactive material for, the crate that was in the back of the van in your garage. The same stuff Pancho and Mahmoud are planning on spreading all over Sun Valley with an RV full of explosives. Ring any bells?"

Urrestegui's face hardened into a mask of denial, but before he had a chance to speak another voice joined the conversation.

"I am impressed by your knowledge of our operation."

Kaye and Cindy whirled quickly in the direction of the voice.

Cindy gasped in terror and clutched Kaye's arm. "It's him!"

Barely discernible in the dim glow of headlights, Pancho stood just off the road. The pulsing amber emergency flashers of the Range

Rover lent an eerily disembodied quality to the Basque. And to the Heckler & Koch MP10 in his hands.

Kaye slowly lowered the Kimber. Even outgunned, he would have risked the first shot had it not been for Cindy's presence.

"They know…" Urrestegui muttered as he moved toward Pancho.

"I heard," Pancho snapped, cutting him off. "Now, take the detective's gun and… No, wait." Pancho's eyes never left Kaye. "Give your weapon to the young lady, and then take three steps backward. I've seen what you can do with those hands."

Kaye complied and watched helplessly as Cindy handed his pistol to Urrestegui, who pushed her backwards to stand next to Kaye.

"Excellent," Pancho said as he walked forward into the light. "Robert told the truth," he said as he appraised Kaye. "You are very formidable looking."

Kaye locked his eyes with Pancho's. "I'd be happy to give you a demonstration."

Pancho laughed mirthlessly. "I think I might enjoy that, but I have other business to complete first."

"Yeah," Cindy said furiously. "Like blowing up Sun Valley, right?"

"Not exactly."

"So, what, *exactly*?" Cindy pressed.

"Unfortunately, you will never know." Pancho's tone was mocking. "Soon, you will join your brother."

"You asshole!" Cindy screamed as she lunged for the Basque.

Pancho reacted swiftly and thrust the H&K's muzzle forward, striking her in the solar plexus and knocking the wind out of her.

Kaye started forward.

"Step back," Pancho said coldly, training the gun on Kaye. "She is not injured."

"Screw you," Cindy managed to say between gasps of breath.

"An interesting invitation," Pancho said. "Perhaps we can discuss it later, but right now we need to get off of this road."

"How do we do this?" Urrestegui asked.

The Basque thought for a moment. "The woman will drive the Range Rover. You follow in the truck with Kaye. Let him drive." Pancho looked at Kaye and Cindy. "If he tries to escape, I will execute the young lady. Understood?"

Kaye nodded.

"Excellent." Pancho nodded back. "Now, throw your cell phones into the trees."

Kaye and Cindy complied. Pancho and Urrestegui then escorted them to the vehicles. Pancho kept his gun trained on Cindy as she pulled the Range Rover around the Willys and headed up the hill.

Kaye followed in the old Willys, pulling around the deer carcass. Urrestegui sat as far away as he could, keeping the Kimber pointed at Kaye's head. As Kaye drove, he used his left foot to surreptitiously pump the brake pedal, praying that the old truck's bulbs worked and that Straithwaite was paying attention.

Dot-dot-dot. Dash-dash-dash. Dot-dot-dot. Pause. Repeat.

Don Straithwaite was paying attention, watching as closely as he could from that distance. As near as he could tell, things had gone according to plan until a fourth person came into view. Straithwaite debated whether to call Kaye and decided against it. As he understood it from the Graham woman, Kaye had gotten the best of Stan Kaminski. If he could do that, he probably didn't need whatever meager help Straithwaite could offer from a quarter-mile away.

When the headlights of started up the hill toward Urrestegui's, the DHS agent was caught flat-footed.

"Dammit!" he exclaimed, grabbing the binoculars. As he watched the two vehicles climb the hill he saw the single rear light of the Willys flash weakly against the night and grabbed his cell phone in panic.

S.O.S., the light had blinked. S.O.S.

"What?" Halberstam asked through the phone.

"We've got trouble. Pancho has Kaye and Cindy."

"Shit, shit and double shit."

48

I t had been a very productive evening for General Carl Holdorf.
Several people had approached him and made it clear that when
– not if, they had all stressed, but when – he was ready to mount
a campaign for the Oval Office, he could count on them for
organizational and financial support.

Holdorf had been careful to react with surprise and humility,
thank them profusely for their expression of confidence in his
abilities, and make light of such a thing ever happening. But he also
tucked the mental chits into the back of his mind for future
withdrawal.

Most of all, though, the General was pleased with the time he'd
spent with Robert Urrestegui. The man didn't know nearly as much
about art as Holdorf would have expected of someone claiming to
have a large collection. Urrestegui had asked generally inane
questions and hadn't challenged the General's sometimes purposely
more inane answers. At least, Holdorf mused, the unsophisticated
Idahoan had recognized the pure genius of the painting in the library.

Holdorf had also cautiously probed Urrestegui about his guest's
investments abroad. Urrestegui had talked quite candidly about his
investments in Spain, claiming he was losing his ass and bemoaning
the ventures as the worst business decisions of his career.

Later, as the General drifted off to sleep, his mind wandered into
the future and was pleased by what it saw. He was still a young man,
really, in terms of national leadership. There was still plenty of time
to serve as Vice-President, possibly even Secretary of State, before
becoming the first soldier since Ike to assume the Presidency.

***

Normally a light sleeper, Holdorf always slept well in Sun Valley. This was his refuge, his respite from pressure and the limelight.

He hadn't been asleep long, though, when something woke him. He lay quietly, listening for a repeat of whatever had disturbed him, but heard nothing. He rose and headed for the bathroom, deciding it had been his bladder that had sounded the alarm.

When he came out, the soft voice nearly frightened him to death. "Good evening, General."

Holdorf regained his composure and stared intently at the barely discernible features of the man in the chair next to the antique Chippendale highboy.

"Agent Kaminski? What are you doing here? Where's Dennis Rhoades?"

"One question at a time, General. First, why don't you climb back in bed and get comfortable. We need to talk."

"I'm up. Let me get a robe..."

"In bed, General." Kaminski's voice stayed low, but the menacing tone rattled Holdorf. He climbed back into the bed.

"What do you want?"

"The whole thing's gone to hell, General. Totally gone to hell."

"Explain."

"Alison and Dennis are dead."

"Both of them?" Holdorf was shocked. "Pancho?"

Kaminski ignored the question. "We never even got a visual on the son of a bitch, and we've lost him and the material. It's all gone to hell."

"No it hasn't. Pancho's here, in Sun Valley. The operation is still in motion."

"What about Mahmoud?"

"I have reason to believe he's here, too."

"Reason to believe?" mocked Kaminski. "Are you kidding me, General? Pancho got in without us knowing it, even though we knew he was coming!" Kaminski stopped, getting his voice under control. "We knew they were coming and the bastards still got in undetected. If it hadn't been for that traffic accident and that L.A. cop, we still wouldn't know they were here."

"Relax. Who cares how they got in? We knew where they were going. Wasn't that the point in the first place? We have to show the American people they are not safe, that it takes a firm hand to protect their freedoms. The American people need a demonstration of what will happen to them if they continue to insist on being…"

"Being what, General? Free? You're going to poison and kill how many people to convince them they should put their freedom in your hands?"

"Save the lecture. Freedom brings responsibility. We both know that. In fact, as I recall, you were fully informed regarding the nature of this operation before you signed on."

"True enough. But that was before."

"Before what?"

"Before we lost control of the operation. Before Pancho killed Alison Washington."

"Is that what this is really about? Because if it is, I can only remind you that losses happen. We're soldiers. Washington died a hero, protecting her country."

"Bullshit! She died promoting your political ambitions. No more, no less, so don't shovel that patriotic bullshit at me."

"Don't lose sight of the prize, soldier. I just spoke to The Man a little while ago. The operation is still ongoing. You still have your duty."

"Duty?" Kaminski laughed softly. "General, you're just chock full of platitudes for the middle of the night. Freedom. Duty. But you left out honor. What happened to honor?"

"Listen to me…."

"No, you listen to me. This was supposed to be a controlled operation. Track, intercept, intervene and capture. Nobody on our side was supposed to die." Kaminski paused. "Alison died, and Pancho and Mahmoud are going to detonate whatever bomb they came up with. We can't find them in time to stop them and we both know it."

"So what? Let them. Parameters have changed. Capturing the Muslim is essential. That's worth the short-term cost. This operation is far from beyond salvage."

"Salvage? Is that what you call thousands of people dying of radiation poisoning? Salvage?"

"It's low yield material with a short half-life. Remember?"

"Remember?" Kaminski hissed as he rose to his feet. "How could I forget? We sold it to him, you son of a bitch!"

"The threat had to be credible. You agreed."

"Yes, I did. And now we have ourselves one genuine, credible threat, don't we?" Kaminski stood still, his shoulders slumping and his arms hanging limp at his sides in the posture of a defeated man.

"So," Holdorf said, "the question now becomes how to deal with that threat without compromising the operation."

"You can get out of bed, General."

"Good man," Holdorf said with a smile as he bolted out of bed and stepped toward Kaminski.

In all his combat experience, in all his exhibition or competitive fights, Stan Kaminski had never thrown a punch backed by as much raw fury and loathing as the one he launched at Carl Holdorf. Only a last second hesitation kept him from killing his boss. The heel of his hand struck the General flush on the point of the chin with the force of a freight train, instantly rendering Holdorf unconscious and collapsing him in a heap against the bed.

Kaminski leaned down to check the General's pulse. It was strong, and when Kaminski lifted an eyelid, the pupil contracted.

"You'll live. Temporarily, anyway."

It took the DHS agent five minutes to dress the General. Then he quickly made the bed. He stripped one pillowcase and put it over Holdorf's head, tying it in place with the belt from the man's robe.

He let himself out the same way he'd gotten in, being careful with his burden lest he disturb anyone else in the house. When he reached the blue Mustang he unceremoniously dumped Holdorf into the none-too-spacious trunk before handcuffing the man's hands behind his back.

"Congratulations, General," Kaminski muttered. "You've just been promoted to field asset." Then he slammed the trunk.

Two down, two to go, Kaminski told himself as he slid behind the wheel, *and I bet I know where you are.*

49

"What do we do?" asked a frantic Mike Graham.

He, Don Straithwaite and Roger Halberstam had gathered at the Sun Valley Lodge suite. It was almost two in the morning.

"We have to go get them," Mike continued, desperation in his voice. "They have Cindy. We need to storm the place, now."

"With what?" Straithwaite looked at Mike sympathetically. "We have two pistols between us. We'd never make it up the driveway."

Mike knew the DHS agent was right, but Pancho had his daughter and he'd be damned if he was going to just sit there and do nothing.

"We need to call the cavalry," Halberstam said. "Everybody, and I mean from the Pope on down."

"Start with the locals?" Straithwaite asked.

"Nah," Halberstam replied. "Waste of time. This is a big county. They probably have one guy on graveyard and he's probably parked someplace, asleep. I've got a few people I can call, and I'm going to start calling in favors. Don, call that General of yours. He's an ass, but tonight we need him. Mike, call that Marine friend of yours, pronto."

Mike called the number he had for Dinsmore, only to get the Langley operator. She noted his name on The List, told him Dinsmore was in the air and promised to have the Sergeant Major call as soon as possible. He paced nervously while the two cops continued working the phones. Periodically, he heard Roger Halberstam mutter 'shit, shit and double shit' after slamming down the phone.

Thirty minutes later, the frustrated trio sat down to regroup.

"Well," Straithwaite said, "that was a waste of time. The night operations officer at the office refused to put me through to the General."

"I convinced some of my guys to come on my say-so," Halberstam reported. "But between gearing up and transit time, it'll be hours before they get here."

"Calvin will call as soon as he can." Mike added. "What about the State Police?"

"Called the Colonel at home," Halberstam said. "Soon as I said Sun Valley he hung up on me. The fix is in on this one."

"Well, fuck this," Mike said darkly, grabbing his jacket and hobbling for the door. "Me and my boy gave three legs for this country and now I can't even get a cop when I need one. I'm done being nice."

"Where you going?" Halberstam asked carefully.

"I'm going," answered Mike defiantly, "to wake up a damn General."

Halberstam and Straithwaite looked at each other.

"Hold on, Mike!" Straithwaite called after the ex-Marine, who was already out the door and headed down the hall. "We're coming with you!"

***

Holdorf's house was dark. As soon as Straithwaite stopped the Explorer, Mike piled out and headed for the front door as fast as his prostheses allowed, Halberstam and Straithwaite close behind.

Ignoring the doorbell, Mike began pounding on the door with his fist, at the same time yelling, "Holdorf! General Holdorf, wake up! Answer the door, damn it!"

Lights came on inside and a woman's voice came from the intercom speaker next to the door.

"Go away immediately, or I will call the police."

"You do that," Mike replied. "Their number is 9-1-1. In the meantime I want to see General Holdorf."

"The General has retired for the evening. Come back in the morning."

"I'm not waiting until morning, damn it!" Mike exploded. "They killed my boy and now they've got my daughter! Open this door or I'm coming through it!"

"Mike," Don Straithwaite stepped between the distraught father and the intercom. "calm down. Let me talk to her, okay?"

"Calm down? My daughter could be dead already!"

"Roger," Straithwaite said, steering Mike toward Halberstam, "help me out here, please."

Halberstam put his arm around Mike's shoulder and steered him away from Straithwaite, who looked up at the smoked plastic cover in the corner of the porch.

"Who am I speaking to?" He kept his voice calm.

"Ilsa Schmidt. I am the General's household assistant."

"Ms. Schmidt, my name is Donald Straithwaite." He reached into his pocket and held his open ID wallet up toward the camera. "I'm an agent with the Department of Homeland Security in Los Angeles. I work for your boss, too, and it's very, very important that we speak with him immediately. Would you please open the door?"

"As I told the other gentleman," the woman's voice was patient, "the General has retired for the evening. I'm certain that if you just come back in," there was a pause, "five hours, the General would be happy…"

"Listen to me," Straithwaite said. "I don't have five hours. You don't have five hours. I have three agents missing and presumed dead. This man," he pointed at Halberstam, "is a detective investigating the murders of six people in Boise over the past week. Two people, including a police officer, have been kidnapped by the people we believe are responsible, and we believe those people have a bomb."

There was a brief moment before the door opened slightly and Ilsa Schmidt peered out.

"A bomb?" she asked nervously.

"Yes, ma'am," Straithwaite replied. "We really need to talk to the General."

Schmidt opened the door and waved them inside.

"Wait here, please. I will wake the General.

A moment later, clearly agitated, she returned.

"The General is not in his room, or his library."

"Shit, shit and double shit," Halberstam swore softly. "This just keeps getting better and better."

"Does the General have any weapons in the house?" Straithwaite asked.

"Yes," Schmidt replied. "There is a cabinet of sporting firearms in the downstairs den. Why?"

"Because it's time for us to make a house call," Mike said.

While Mike and Straithwaite were retrieving the guns, Chapman came down the steps, tying his robe as he descended

"What's going on here?" he asked, looking at Schmidt and Halberstam.

"These gentlemen are looking for the General," Schmidt answered. "They say there is a bomb."

"That's nonsense," Chapman said dismissively. "I've spoken to the General about this, and we believe it's all a big hoax." He looked at Halberstam. "Rodge, I would ask you and your...posse...to leave this house immediately."

"Sorry, but this ain't your house to order me out of," Halberstam said pointedly. "Something here stinks, Harry, and it ain't me. I swear to God, if I find out you're mixed up in this I'll skin you alive and fly your hide from the flag pole on top of the State Capitol. You won't be able to get elected dog catcher when I'm done."

"Rodge, I..." the Senator sputtered, clamping his mouth shut when he saw the look in Halberstam's eyes.

Minutes later, carrying several guns and a bag of ammunition from Holdorf's gun cabinet, the three climbed into the Explorer and headed for Robert Urrestegui's house.

They made no pretense of stealth or strategy. Straithwaite simply barreled the Explorer up the driveway and around the house into the motor court. Guns ready, all three piled out.

Except for several small outside lights the house was dark and their unannounced arrival provoked no response. With a Browning automatic twelve gauge at port arms, Mike headed for the back door. The long day was starting to tell and he had slowed noticeably. Tired as he was, he still mustered the energy and adrenaline to break in the back door before Straithwaite or Halberstam could stop him.

The house was large and took some time to search. It was empty. Mike was visibly deflated after finding no sign of Cindy.

The group reassembled in the motor court.

"They left quick, I think," Halberstam offered. "Lucky for us they didn't even bother to arm the security system." He glared at Mike.

"We should check the garages," Straithwaite said, his eyes on the large overhead door of the RV bay. "Especially that one." He wanted to find Cindy and Kaye, but he was also desperate to find the potential bomb vehicle.

To Straithwaite's chagrin, there was no coach inside. But the garage wasn't empty. Inside, looking lost in the cavernous space, sat Merl Bates' old Willys pickup.

Mike was exhausted physically and emotionally. He leaned heavily against the fender of the Explorer.

"We'll find them." Halberstam tried to comfort him.

"We have to," Mike muttered, almost sobbing. "I just buried my son. I can't lose my daughter, too. I can't."

Don Straithwaite overheard. "Mike, don't give up. If there's one person who can save your daughter, it's Ben Kaye. He's as smart and tough as they come. Don't give up," he repeated, trying to hide his own misgivings.

"I need some sleep," was all Mike could say.

"We all do," Halberstam said. "Let's go back to the Lodge and catch some shut-eye. At first light we start looking for that RV. We find it and we find what we're looking for. We don't, well..." he left the thought unfinished.

50

K aye's mind raced as he followed the silver Range Rover carrying Cindy and Pancho into the motor court of Urrestegui's house. He knew Pancho intended to kill them, and he hoped Straithwaite had seen his distress call and was rallying the troops to get them here in time. He carefully surveyed his surroundings, looking for any possible avenue of escape. The first thing he noticed was a black Kawasaki Ninja parked beside a garage door sized to accommodate a large RV.

Pancho exited the Range Rover and walked around to the driver's side. He opened the door and extended his hand to Cindy, but she ignored it and slid out. Kaye had no trouble reading her lips and the epithet she hurled at her captor.

"Okay," Urrestegui said from the passenger seat of the Willys. "Get out slowly and walk over to the woman."

Kaye complied, urged by the unwavering machine gun in Pancho's hands.

Urrestegui joined Pancho. "What do we do with them?"

"We kill them, of course."

"You can't kill us!" Cindy protested.

"Oh, but I can." Pancho smiled.

"Not at my house," Urrestegui said.

"Too little, too late, Urrestegui," Kaye remarked. "You're already in this so deep, what're a couple more murders?" He was trying to buy time. If Pancho took them elsewhere, Kaye's team would lose their trail. "Besides, now that we're here, I'd like to take the tour. Heck of a place you've got here." He looked across the motor court at the large overhead door. "Is that where the bomb's parked?"

"Silence!" Pancho ordered. "On your knees, policeman."

"No thanks."

Pancho kept his eyes on Kaye, but swung the muzzle of the MP10 until it pointed directly at Cindy. "On your knees or she dies."

Kaye saw the terrified look in Cindy's eyes. He gauged the distance between himself and Pancho and knew it would be suicide to try and close the gap.

"On...your...knees," Pancho hissed.

Cindy started to sob quietly, covering her mouth with her hands as Kaye slowly lowered himself to a kneeling position on the cobblestones.

Pancho smiled viciously as he started to walk behind Kaye.

"No," Cindy sobbed. "Please, no."

"Don't get too close," Urrestegui said. "He's as dangerous as a lion or leopard."

While he lowered himself to his knees, Kaye kept his ankles flexed, his toes curled under his feet. Like a catapult strains against its tether, his legs were tensed and poised to explode. He waited, like the lion Urrestegui compared him to, for exactly the right moment to spring, knowing, just as a lion does, that timing would be the difference between living and dying.

Pancho had intended to step behind Kaye, press the muzzle of the MP10 against his skull, and shoot him. But he saw Kaye's posture and changed tactics. As he passed just beyond Kaye's peripheral vision he stepped in quickly next to the kneeling man and swung the metal butt of the machine gun downward.

The piercing scream that burst from Cindy's lips was the last thing Kaye heard before slumping unconscious to the cobblestones.

Pancho smiled at Cindy and Urrestegui. "Now, let us hope we can lift him."

"You bastard!" Cindy screamed at Pancho, who stepped close and slapped her hard across the face.

"Silence! Sit down."

Cindy collapsed to the ground next to Kaye and cradled his head in her lap.

"What do we do with him now?" Urrestegui asked.

"If you don't want me to kill them here, we'll take them elsewhere. First, we need something to tie them with. Have you some rope, or, better yet," the Basque looked down at Kaye, "some chain? And," Pancho added as an afterthought, "bring a pillow case, too."

Urrestegui went off to find what they needed while Pancho stood guard over his captives.

"Where are you taking us?" Cindy demanded.

"Does it matter?"

"You're going to kill us, aren't you? Like you killed my brother and those other people."

Pancho stared at her. "I admit that was unfortunate. Believe me, that old man pulling in front of me was not part of my plan. I had to kill a friend."

"So, what is your plan?"

"I am striking a blow against fascism and collecting a debt of honor."

"You're a lunatic," Cindy said, shaking her head. "You have no idea what you're talking about."

"Really? And you are a typical American, with your head in the sand."

"We've got rope," Urrestegui interrupted, returning with a second man. "No chain, but nobody can break this." He held up a length of half-inch nylon rope.

Cindy looked up and gasped when she recognized the second man. "You! What are you doing here?"

"You remember me?" The man grinned. "I didn't think you would."

They bound Cindy first, securing her wrists behind her back and then pulling her ankles up to meet them. She fought unsuccessfully to keep them from putting the pillowcase over her head before unceremoniously dumping her into the back of the Range Rover.

A moment later the three captors dumped the unconscious Kaye next to her.

"So," Cindy overheard Urrestegui say. "You still haven't answered my question. Where are we going?"

"Mahmoud rented another house here for the week," Pancho said. "We'll take them there."

"You didn't tell me about another house."

"There are things you did not need to know. Believe me, it was better that way."

The silver Range Rover headed down the driveway, melting into the darkness.

***

Stan Kaminski had scouted Robert Urrestegui's house earlier in the day. In fact, Don Straithwaite had missed spotting his fellow DHS agent by less than fifteen minutes. None of that mattered now, as Kaminski drove from Holdorf's toward Urrestegui's.

The General had regained consciousness and Kaminski soon grew tired of the muffled shouts that filtered to his ears from the trunk. Finally, he pulled over, walked to the back of the car and opened the trunk.

Holdorf felt the fresh night air and started to shout, "Kaminski, you let…"

"Shut up, General," Kaminski cut him off by prodding his captive with the muzzle of the .44 magnum. "The next time you make noise, I'm going to put a round through the back seat into the trunk. We'll call it Mustang roulette."

"Where are you taking me?" Holdorf asked evenly, knowing Kaminski was unbalanced enough to kill him for the slimmest of reasons.

"I'm taking you to a little sit down with Robert Urrestegui. You can explain to him why he's going to hang for treason just so you can move up the ladder."

"You can't do that!"

"Really? Gee, let's see. You're tied up. I have the car and the gun. You know what? I think I can."

"You're insane, Kaminski."

"You're wrong, General. For the first time since I got sucked into this operation I am one hundred percent sane. You need to be quiet now. Even with all my expensive government training, I'm still a lousy shot when I'm driving." He slammed the trunk and got back in the car.

About a quarter-mile from the turn-off to Urrestegui's house, Kaminski saw headlights turn onto the road and head his way.

When the two vehicles met, Kaminski recognized the silver Range Rover from the 'vehicles registered to' list Alison had pulled up on Urrestegui. He also glanced quickly sideways as the Range Rover went by, careful not to turn his head too obviously, and kept up his speed.

"Shit!" he muttered. "Pancho."

Kaminski waited until the Range Rover's taillights disappeared from his rearview mirror before dousing the Mustang's lights. Using the hand brake lever to slow the car without the telltale glare of brake lights, he made a sliding u-turn and sped back in pursuit of the Range Rover.

51

Kaye regained consciousness slowly. His head felt like it was trapped inside a cylinder bore of his Road King, the pain slamming him like a giant piston as he tried to force his eyes open.

"Ben," he heard a faint voice. "Can you hear me? Ben?"

"It's okay. I'm okay," he muttered, barely coherent. The piston slammed him again and his eyes fluttered.

"Ben, wake up," the voice prodded again.

Kaye forced his eyes open against the pain. There wasn't much light. He lay curled on his side, but when he tried to extend his legs, he couldn't, and realized he was restrained.

Focusing with intense effort on his breath, Kaye closed his eyes and brought his mind together. The voice still called his name, but he willed it out of his consciousness as he gathered his faculties. He embraced the slamming piston, welcoming it until it simply dropped away as he returned to full consciousness. He saw Cindy lying next to him, also tied securely.

"I'm okay," he said quietly.

"Thank God. I thought he was going to shoot you."

"I'd have killed him first."

The confidence in Kaye's voice comforted Cindy. "I believe you."

"Believe it. Where are we? Urrestegui's?"

"No, Pancho said Mahmoud had another house, but I don't know where. He blindfolded me."

"How long were we in the car?" Kaye hoped it would give him some idea of their whereabouts.

"Ten or fifteen minutes, I think, and it never felt like we were going fast. Lots of stop and go, if that helps."

"Probably means we're still in Sun Valley, or at least close. How long have we been here?"

"Gosh," Cindy said, bewildered. "I don't know. Maybe an hour, maybe longer, but...."

"That's okay."

"I heard them talking in the car. I don't think they knew I could hear, because they kept their voices pretty quiet."

"What did they say?"

"They talked about some painting Urrestegui saw at Holdorf's house tonight. Urrestegui told Pancho he might decide to keep it, and that pissed Pancho off. It turned into an argument when the deputy guy started asking questions, too."

"Hold it. The deputy guy? Who's the deputy guy?"

"One of the cops who came after the shooting. He's in on the whole thing."

"The younger one or the older one?"

"Younger. I don't think I knew his name, even."

"McMurray," Kaye said softly, thinking about the events of that day. "That explains a lot. What else."

"Pancho said they'd decide about the painting after everything was over, but I don't think he was happy about it. He wants to return it to the Basque people. Called them the rightful owners."

The conversation stopped, each lost in their thoughts.

McMurray and Urrestegui had tied Kaye's hands behind him, taking turns around his wrists before pulling his ankles up and using the same length of rope to bind them together. Kaye tested the ropes. They gave some, but even his strength wouldn't overcome them.

One of the very first lessons his Roshi had ever imparted flashed across his memory. A quick test left him satisfied.

"I'm scared," Cindy whispered. "They're going to kill us."

"No, they're not. We're getting out of here."

Cindy watched as Kaye shimmied away from her until there was room for him to roll onto his back. He then pulled his knees to his chest, leaving his bound feet just above his buttocks. With incredible effort, he pushed his hands downward and pulled his knees toward his head. The nylon rope creaked as it began to stretch, and Kaye could feel it tightening around his wrists and ankles, shutting off blood flow as effectively as a tourniquet. His hands began to throb, but still he pushed. The muscles on his arms and shoulders knotted as he gave one supreme effort. The rope gave just enough that he at last was able to swing his hands forward under his feet.

Urrestegui, underestimating Kaye's unusual proportions, had left a little too much slack between ankles and wrists. Kaye rolled over and sat up, flexing his hands rapidly before going to work on the knots securing the rope around his ankles.

"How'd you do that?"

"Practice. Now, roll onto your stomach so I can untie you. Wizard though I am, I still can't untie these," he held out his arms, "but I can untie you."

Moments later, they stood free, massaging their wrists and flexing their ankles to restore circulation.

Kaye looked around. Except for a few boxes stacked in one corner, the room was empty. He went to the window and peered out. They were on the third floor, above a stone patio. Alone, he could easily handle the height, but he knew Cindy couldn't, and he wasn't about to leave her alone. He might be able to carry her down, but the drop was considerable and he wasn't willing to risk it.

Cindy saw the look of concern on his face. "What's wrong?" she asked.

"We're too high to get you out that way. We'll have to try going through the house."

"Then you go. Get some help and come back."

"Not a chance. I'm not leaving you here alone."

At that instant, the door to the room flew open and light flooded in, the shadow of a man stretching across the floor. It was Pancho, and he still carried the H&K MP10. McMurray, pistol in hand, stood close behind.

"Kaye," the Basque said darkly as he centered the machine gun on Kaye's broad chest. "Your capabilities continue to impress me."

"Thank you. Wish I could say the same." He looked beyond Pancho to McMurray. "I really hate dirty cops."

Anger flashed in Pancho's eyes as he backed away from the door. "Come with me. I have someone who wants to meet you."

52

Stan Kaminski knew about sleep deprivation. He'd often gone for thirty-six or forty-eight hours outside the wire without sleeping, functioning on a combination of adrenaline and amphetamines. But, even with the drugs, he knew that there came a time when performance decreased in an inverse square for each additional hour of wakefulness. It was now early Tuesday morning and Kaminski had slept less than ten hours since Saturday. He was tired. He was becoming ineffective, and he knew it.

With the Mustang's lights off, and using only the transmission and emergency brake to control his speed, he carefully trailed the silver Range Rover.

His quarry made a right turn, and the visible glare of brake lights told Kaminski the Range Rover had stopped. He pulled over quickly, careful to stay blacked out.

The Range Rover's brakes released and Kaminski followed the headlights bouncing off the trees to trace the vehicle's path away from the road. After what he estimated to be a couple hundred feet the headlights stopped moving forward and went out.

"Gotcha," Kaminski muttered, a smile playing on his lips.

He turned on the Mustang's lights and drove as slowly as he dared past where the Range Rover had turned. He purposely drifted all over the road, looking to anyone watching like just another early morning drunk trying to make it home.

The house had a wall around it, but to the DHS agent it didn't look too tall to get over, nor did it appear to be topped with wire or glass. As he went by the driveway he glanced quickly to the right. An iron gate bridged the gap between two substantial stone pillars. No problem, but the guard behind the gate, weapon cradled casually in

349

his elbow as he stared at the passing blue Mustang, looked like he might be.

Kaminski kept driving for a half-mile before pulling over and going dark.

He needed a plan. He could easily go over the wall, but there could be more guards. The one he'd seen had been alert and Kaminski knew he couldn't make another pass without raising suspicions.

He'd need to go back on foot, and for that he needed some rest. Besides, he reasoned, the guard had probably been alert because the Range Rover had just shown up. With an hour of down time the guard would be almost as tired as he was right now.

Kaminski checked his watch. He got out, went around and opened the trunk, then yanked the pillowcase off the General's head.

"Comfy?"

Holdorf glared at him. "I'll have your ass for this, Kaminski."

"General." Kaminski sighed. "I don't think you understand the gravity of your situation. Your life as you knew it has ended."

"You stopped here to kill me?"

Kaminski had to give the man credit. Even now there was no fear in the voice, only defiance. He understood how the man had become a General, but it was too bad he'd also become a piece of shit in the process.

"No. I stopped here to take a nap."

"A nap? You're crazy."

"No, I'm just tired. I'll need some energy and my wits about me when I go into that house down the road to kill Pancho Janicot and anybody else unfortunate enough to be home."

Holdorf's eyes widened. "You found them? Damn it! I knew I could count on you! Do you know if Mahmoud is there?" The General once again was commanding the operation, oblivious to the fact he was trussed up in the trunk of a car.

"Yeah, I got them. And I'm going to kill every stinking one of them. But first I'm going to sleep for a while. If you yell, or wake me, I'll kill you." He started to close the trunk.

"Wait, damn it! Let me out of here. I can help you. We'll take them down together, you and me, and I'll forget about all this."

"Really? You'd forget about all this?"

"Yes, I swear. It never happened. We planned everything together. We get them together. Nobody has to know otherwise."

"I'll have to get back to you on that, Carl. I need to check with Alison first." He slammed the trunk.

His wristwatch woke him ninety minutes later. It took only a few minutes to get ready. He wolfed down two energy bars and drank a twenty ounce orange juice while he prepped his armament. He moved the .44 mag to the middle of his back. Its cycle time was far too slow to be his primary weapon. Instead, he'd use the silenced Glock he'd taken from Rhoades. He had four full magazines, and knew that if he got into a firefight requiring more rounds than that, it wouldn't matter anyway. He strapped an eight-inch combat knife to his lower right leg, outside his pants.

The last thing he did was stuff the end of the pillowcase into Holdorf's protesting mouth. It was a sign of Stan Kaminski's self-confidence level that he never even considered the possibility that he wouldn't be back to finish that job later.

The DHS agent moved quickly until he spotted the wall ahead. There was enough vegetation that he wasn't concerned about video surveillance. From a position of concealment he scanned the area with the night vision scope. The top of the wall still looked clean and he saw no signs of guards outside the wall.

The next stop was a tree not far from the wall, a convenient limb providing a view inside.

He saw only the one guard manning the gate and, as he'd hoped, the period of inactivity had lulled the man's senses. He now sat in a folding chair, his weapon across his lap, and the movements of his head told Kaminski he was barely staying awake.

Using the night scope, Kaminski carefully studied what he could see of the house. No cameras or motion lights were visible.

Two minutes later he was over the wall, using the landscaping for cover as he cautiously made his way to a position behind the dozing guard.

Fifteen feet of open ground separated Kaminski and the sleepy man. The DHS agent covered it like a panther, swiftly and noiselessly, the knife in his right hand held in an overhand grip.

Just as Kaminski reached him, the guard's head dropped backward in the relaxation of sleep. Fighting to stay awake, his eyes snapped open to see the intruder's face above him. Before he could cry out a hand slapped over his mouth and nose, and a slashing blade cut him deeply from ear to ear until only his spinal column kept him from being decapitated. The move was so swift that the dying guard's grunt of surprise escaped from his severed trachea rather than his mouth.

Kaminski wiped blood on the dead man's pants and sheathed the blade. A quick search turned up a small radio on the guard's belt. He took it, then checked the man's weapon and smiled. H&K MP10. He knew the weapon well. It had a full magazine inserted with another full one taped, upside down, to that one. He dragged the body to a nearby clump of bushes before heading for the house.

***

McMurray led the way, with Cindy following. Kaye was between Cindy and Pancho, the latter staying a discreet ten feet behind, his weapon pointed at his captive's spine.

The group filed down a flight of wide, curving stairs into a large foyer area. McMurray stepped aside and motioned Cindy into an adjoining room.

When Kaye and Cindy entered, Urrestegui and a tall, deeply-tanned, gray-haired man rose from the large leather sofa. A strikingly beautiful woman pushed away from the stone fireplace that covered the entire opposite wall and sauntered lazily toward them, anticipation dancing in her eyes.

"Excellent timing," Yousef bin Ali Mahmoud said. "Robert and I have just finished catching up." He looked briefly and dismissively at Cindy before settling his gaze on Kaye. "Detective, or should I say Mr., Kaye, I presume. I was certain my friends were exaggerating, but now I see they were not."

"You won't get away with this," Cindy said.

Mahmoud's gaze shifted from Kaye to Cindy. He smiled thinly.

"Unfortunately for you, I have already gotten away with it."

"No, you haven't…" Cindy started to insist.

"Enough!" snapped Mahmoud. "Sit down, both of you, and hold your tongue, woman, or I will cut it out. Now," he looked at Kaye, "I would be most interested in knowing how you learned so much about our operation."

"Why should I tell you?" Kaye asked casually.

"Why not? If you refuse, I will simply kill the woman, and then ask again."

Kaye stared intently at Mahmoud, whose eyes left no doubt he would do exactly as he said. He decided to try and buy them all the time he could.

"Your boy," Kaye turned to look at Pancho, "made a mistake. A big one."

"Liar," sneered Pancho, who looked confidently at Mahmoud. "I made no mistake."

"Really?" Kaye baited the Basque. "You don't call leaving evidence you were transporting radioactive material at the accident scene a mistake? I would, since it had your fingerprints all over it."

"I did not leave…" Pancho started to protest, then stopped and looked at Kaye through half-closed eyes. "You found it?"

"What can I say," Kaye said drolly. "I'm good at what I do."

"Found what?" Mahmoud asked, turning to Pancho.

"Ramon's radiation exposure badge," Pancho explained. "I disposed of it after the accident. That he found it was a sheer stroke of luck."

"He's right, Mr. Mahmoud," McMurray said. "Our people searched the entire area twice and they didn't find it."

"Then your people," Mahmoud said, "are incompetent. Serenya," he turned to the young woman, "have you learned anything from this?"

"Yes, Sayyid. Do not trust to luck. Trust to planning."

"Excellent," Mahmoud said before turning back to Pancho. "You would do well to remember that in the future, Doroteo Arango."

Pancho stared coldly at his friend and ally, then nodded curtly.

"It doesn't matter," Urrestegui said. "If he knows, then others know, too. We have to move quickly."

"Well said, Robert," nodded Mahmoud. "I have already taken action." He turned to Pancho. "Is the device activated?"

"Yes, it's ready."

"Excellent." The Arab paused to think for a moment. "Mr. McMurray, you will drive the coach. Serenya, go outside with him and check the wind direction. Select the location option that will yield maximum dispersion. Then return and we will deal with these two." He eyed Kaye and Cindy as McMurray and Serenya left the room.

"Do not forget the final connector," Pancho said quickly to McMurray, who nodded before turning to follow Serenya from the room.

"Doroteo Arango," Mahmoud continued. "Take Robert with you and proceed as planned." He nodded to Urrestegui. "I hope you retrieve everything you seek."

The two left by the front door.

"So, it is just the three of us," Mahmoud said. Now holding a small pistol, he stood ten feet from Kaye and Cindy.

"Looks that way," Kaye said. Next to him, he could feel Cindy trembling in fear. He needed to get to his feet somehow. If he could, he knew he could get his hands on Mahmoud before the Arab's small-caliber pistol could kill him, giving Cindy a chance of escape.

They heard a big diesel fire up and then settle into a barely audible idle. Mahmoud turned his head at the sound. Kaye knew he had to move before Serenya returned or the odds of success would tip too heavily against him. He scooted forward slightly while Mahmoud was distracted.

He put a hand on Cindy's knee and squeezed gently to reassure her. She turned to look at him and he met her eyes.

"Be ready to run," he barely whispered. "Don't stop, don't look around, just run."

"Ben, no," she whispered back desperately, gleaning from his look what he was planning.

"Be ready."

"Silence!" barked Mahmoud. "You," he pointed at Cindy, "move to the end of the couch, now!"

Kaye saw the fear in her eyes. "It's okay. Scoot down." When she moved he'd move.

Before Cindy could change positions Serenya reentered the room. She, too, now carried a pistol, and it wasn't small-caliber.

"He's leaving," she said simply to Mahmoud. In the background they all heard the explosives-laden coach heading down the driveway. "Shall we kill them now?" Her voice was excited.

Before Mahmoud could answer, Pancho rushed back into the room.

"I can't find Mohammed," he blurted. "He was not at the gate and doesn't answer the radio."

"Where is Robert?" Mahmoud asked.

"I sent him ahead," replied Pancho. "He must be in position before the explosion."

An enraged Mahmoud turned to Kaye and Cindy. "If this is your doing, you will die horribly, begging for Allah's mercy."

"Sorry," Kaye said. "Don't know any Mohammed."

"Stand up!" ordered Pancho, his intent unmistakable as he raised his pistol.

Kaye rose and helped Cindy up, keeping an arm around her waist.

"May I?" Serenya stepped next to Pancho, smiling in anticipation.

Pancho hesitated, reluctant to surrender the pleasure of killing Kaye.

"Yes," he said finally, stepping aside. "Kill them, but not too quickly."

Serenya stepped forward and looked at the two captives. She would first disable the huge American and then make him watch while she took her time with the woman. Smiling sadistically, she raised her pistol toward Kaye.

The shot made everyone in the room except Kaye flinch. Cindy screamed involuntarily.

An expression of disbelief flashed on Serenya's face as the perforation in her chest began to seep red. She managed a half-turn toward Mahmoud before her eyes went blank and she fell to the floor, dead.

"Serenya!" Mahmoud screamed.

"Nobody move! Lower your weapons!"

Kaye turned in the direction of the shouted commands. Taking short, sliding steps across the floor while he swept Mahmoud and Pancho with the muzzle of the MP10 was Stan Kaminski.

"Kaye, you all right?" Kaminski asked, glancing quickly sideways.

"We'll make it. How'd you know where to find us?"

"Don't you get it?" Kaminski's voice was exasperated. "This has all been a setup to catch our friend Mahmoud over there. That's why we never moved on Janicot."

"A trap?" Mahmoud uttered incredulously.

"That's right, you son of a bitch," snarled Kaminski, glaring at the Arab. "The Mossad handed you to us on a platter. You don't really think that was a Russian Colonel selling Strontium on the breakwater in Syria, do you? We knew you'd never be able to resist. Except Holdorf and Chapman screwed it up."

"Holdorf and Chapman are in on this?" Kaye asked.

"Along with the Vice-President," Kaminski nodded. "The original mission was Holdorf's idea, sanctioned by Chapman's committee. Lure Mahmoud out and take him down. But when Pancho showed up in Beirut with Mahmoud, it put a whole new spin on things. They knew Pancho is ETA, and Chapman knew Urrestegui was being investigated by Justice and had links to Pancho."

"Oh, God," Cindy murmured.

"My sentiments exactly," Kaminski nodded. "And when Chapman put the arm on Urrestegui, personal ambition took over." He spun toward Pancho and hissed, "Isn't that right, Pancho? She told you, didn't she, before you killed her?"

"Yes, she did," Pancho said, smirking. "That, and much more."

"You knew this was a trap!" Mahmoud shrieked. "And you did not warn me!"

"There was no need. Was there, Agent Kaminski? You were actually helping us."

"Until you killed her, you bastard," Kaminski snarled at the Basque.

"You intended to allow the bomb to detonate?" Mahmoud was incredulous.

"Not if we could catch you red-handed with it," Kaminski replied. "But when Pancho showed up, and you weren't with him, Holdorf got worried. He needed you to whip up America's Christian outrage against Islam."

"Brilliant," the Arab said. "A plan I, myself, would be proud to conceive."

Kaminski laughed. "Conception wasn't the problem. Delivery turned out to be the bitch. Turns out Chapman's been screwing us all along."

"What?" Kaye asked.

"He's playing both sides," Kaminski spat. "Benefits politically and financially if the bomb goes off. He's been manipulating this from the beginning."

"Do you have proof?" Kaye asked.

"Not that will stand up in court. But when Pancho came into the picture, we discovered – quite illegally, I might add – that Chapman had put a Congressional secrecy seal on Pancho's file and quashed a Justice Department investigation of Urrestegui."

"We got Pancho's file," Kaye said. "Don Straithwaite had it."

"Yeah," Kaminski said. "Thank Alison Washington for the file." He glared at Pancho before continuing, "And we didn't know anything about Urrestegui until you tipped Straithwaite. If Holdorf knew, he never told us, and if he didn't, it's because of Chapman."

"What about the paintings?" Cindy asked.

"That painting belongs to The People," Pancho exclaimed angrily.

Kaminski looked at the Basque. "What paintings? I don't know anything about paintings."

"Urrestegui believes that Holdorf is sitting on a treasure of Picasso paintings stolen by the Nazis before World War Two," Pancho said, shrugging. "I think he's crazy, but he claims to have seen them."

"So," Mahmoud spoke up, "Agent Kaminski, please, lower your weapon. It sounds as though we share a common objective. Let us negotiate a win-win outcome to this situation."

"Don't do it, Kaminski," Kaye muttered.

"Stay out of this, Kaye," Kaminski shot back. "In fact, you and the girl get out of here right now. Get going!"

"Not if you're going to let these two go."

Kaminski's eyes never left Pancho and Mahmoud, but Kaye saw a sneer on the DHS agent's lips.

"Don't worry about that. Now, you and the lady get the hell out of here. Stop the bomb."

"Ben, please," Cindy whispered, pulling on the arm she clutched.

"Go on," Kaminski urged. "If you want, you can wait for me outside. This shouldn't take long. Oh, and Kaye?"

"Yeah?"

"For the record, this came out different than what I signed on for. I got in too deep," Kaminski said and then smiled. "And you are the hardest hitting son of a bitch I ever met. Now get going."

Kaye grabbed Cindy's arm and led her outside.

They quickly headed for the gate, barely visible in the first hint of daylight.

Just as they passed through the gate gunfire erupted inside the house. Kaye's trained ear easily differentiated between the bursts from the MP10 and the rapid-fire pops of the pistols. After a few seconds the gunfire ceased. Seconds later, a single shot punctuated the end of the battle.

"Which way to town?" Kaye asked.

"Uh," Cindy looked around before pointing. "This way."

"Good," Kaye said, seeing there was cover closer in that direction. "Now, run, and I mean run. Use those legs!"

"Ben, what…?"

"That last shot was a pistol. I think Kaminski lost."

"Oh, God," Cindy said, a crestfallen look on her face. Then she gathered herself and took off at a full run toward town.

They made a strange pair. The tall, leggy woman running like a deer down the road looked like she should easily outdistance the huge man running with her, but he kept up effortlessly, helping her when her pace flagged.

A half-mile from the gate Kaye spied a car parked on the side of the road. To his great relief, the keys were on the front seat and the window was down.

"Looks like we found a ride," he said. "Get in."

"Can we…?"

"Yes. Under the circumstances, definitely yes. We need to get to the Lodge. If it makes you feel better, I'll fill it with gas before I return it."

She cocked her head. "You hear something?"

Kaye listened and heard muffled sounds coming from the trunk. He quickly opened it.

Inside, handcuffed and gagged, General Carl Holdorf's eyes flooded with relief when he saw someone, anyone, other than Stan Kaminski looking down at him.

But the General's relief was short-lived.

"Well, well, well." Kaye looked at Cindy with a broad grin. "A traitorous art collector all trussed up and ready to go. Must be my lucky day."

53

Fifteen minutes later they stood in Halberstam's Sun Valley Lodge suite.

Kaye had taken pity on Holdorf, deciding not to leave him in the trunk. Instead, he plucked the General out and, with one hand, carried him by the belt into the Lodge. The stunned desk clerk, preparing for the early morning rush, saw the tall, disheveled redhead first, then the bloodied giant carrying a handcuffed man, as they headed for the elevators.

"Excuse me! Excuse me!" the clerk called after them. "If you're not registered guests I will call the police!"

A weary Kaye stopped and turned, fixing the young man with a stare that would have melted glass.

"Kid, I am the police."

The commotion of their arrival awoke the exhausted Mike Graham, who sobbed uncontrollably as he wrapped his daughter in his arms. Straithwaite was wide-eyed at the sight of his boss, bound up like the fatted calf.

Kaye handcuffed Holdorf to the bed just vacated by Mike and quickly briefed everyone. Straithwaite kept glancing at the General in disbelief and Halberstam was first stunned, then enraged, to hear of McMurray's involvement. Leona overheard everything, her expression one of shock and horror. The Captain saw and turned to her.

"Leona," he said, grabbing her shoulders forcefully. "I want you to get out of here. Go home. You hear me?"

Leona gathered herself and stared back at her husband. "Roger Halberstam, after all these years, if you don't know me better than that, you must be one sorry detective." Then she hugged him. "I'm helping. I'll fix everyone something to eat and – oh, wait! I don't have to do that. I can call room service!"

While everyone ate, Leona tended to the cut on Kaye's head. They tried to come up with a plan, knowing the local authorities would refuse to help.

"We have to find it," Cindy said, voicing what everyone else knew. "Then hope there's enough time to get the right people here to disarm it."

"How much time do we have?" Straithwaite asked Kaye.

"I don't know. They never said."

"We need to split up," Halberstam said. "With five sets of eyes we should be able to cover this town pretty quick. It ain't a very big place."

"Assuming it's parked outside," Mike said.

"It will be," Kaye assured. "Mahmoud wants maximum dispersion of the radiation. Detonating inside a structure would hinder that."

Straithwaite leaned forward. "Kaye, did they mention what radioactive substance they're using?"

"Strontium," Cindy spoke up first. "Kaminski said that the Mossad agent sold them Strontium."

"Did he mention a number?" Straithwaite probed. "There are multiple Strontium isotopes."

"No, I don't think so." Cindy shook her head and looked at Kaye.

"He didn't say," Kaye added.

"Well, that's still a good thing, relatively speaking," Straithwaite said. "Strontium is nasty if you breathe it or it gets onto your skin, but even a thick piece of glass shields it. And it has a pretty short half-life."

"How short?" Mike asked.

"About thirty years," Kaye answered for the DHS agent, a theory forming in his head.

"Did Kaminski say how much?" Straithwaite followed up.

"No," Kaye and Cindy said in unison before Kaye added, "But Holdorf knows."

Straithwaite stood up. "Leave this to me," he said grimly as he headed for the bedroom.

"Look," Kaye said, "I have an idea. It might sound crazy, but I think we should concentrate our initial search as far as possible from where you played golf yesterday, Captain."

"Why?" Halberstam asked.

"Because I think I finally figured out Urrestegui's real objective."

"Yeah," Cindy volunteered, "the paintings."

"I don't think so," Kaye said. "Maybe it started with the paintings, but I think it's the cobalt mine. Think about it. The mine's long term profit would be many times the value of any paintings, which he'd have to sell in order to make any money."

"But how does a bomb get him his mine?" Cindy asked.

Roger Halberstam slapped both knees. "Shit, shit and double shit!" he exclaimed. "I got it! I think. Go ahead, Kaye."

"Why can't Urrestegui get his mine?" Kaye asked, looking around the group.

"Easy," Mike answered. "The people around here don't want it and they have a lot of clout."

"Right," Kaye agreed. "Go on."

"But the bomb isn't going to kill all the people," Leona said anxiously. "Roger? Is it?"

"No, Leona, not all of them."

"You don't have to kill the people," Kaye said. "You just have to kill Sun Valley."

"Huh?" Cindy asked. "I'm lost."

"Cindy," Kaye asked her, "why is Sun Valley famous?"

"Well, let's see. Skiing, fishing, the mountains, the celebrities. Oh, yeah, and the money."

"Same as Aspen," Kaye nodded. "Do you think Sun Valley would be famous or expensive if all the celebrities and famous people – the very same people who have the clout your dad mentioned – didn't live here?"

"Probably not. But they're not going to just…" She stopped, and Kaye saw the light of understanding kindle in her eyes.

"Exactly." Kaye slapped the arm of the couch as he stood up. "For Pancho and Mahmoud this is about the bomb, the radiation, the casualties and shaking American security." He paused. "But for Urrestegui it's purely economic. The wealth will flee this town instantly if even one square foot of it is uninhabitable because of radiation. Once the wealthy flee, this is just another lazy sheep town in the mountains."

"And," Halberstam said, "once that happens, the politicians won't give a rat's ass about big trucks rumbling through the middle of town all hours of the day and night. In fact, they'll call it economic development and grab hold of it like a prize thoroughbred."

Kaye nodded. "That's how Urrestegui gets his mine, and that's why I think you should start searching away from the golf course. Urrestegui said his cobalt mine was almost under it, correct? If he contaminates that area, he'll have to wait years to get started."

Don Straithwaite came back into the room, a pained look on his face. "Sixty kilos, in five kilo increments, but he says there's no way to know if they're using it all on this operation."

"I'd bet they are," Kaye said. "Sixty kilos is, what, just over a hundred thirty pounds? With packaging and containers, maybe two hundred pounds. The old sheepherder I talked to said it took both Pancho and his partner to lift the crate out of the trunk. So, yeah, I'd say all of it."

"I agree," Straithwaite said. "Makes strategic sense, too. What I'd like to know is how they got enough conventional explosives together to do this. The General claims not to know, but at this point, who knows?"

"Urrestegui?" Mike suggested. "He owns mines."

"I don't think so, Dad," Cindy said. "I bet Mahmoud got it somehow. Now," she turned to Kaye, "I have a question for you."

"That would be?"

"You said 'you' should search a minute ago, not 'we' should search," she said pointedly. "Aren't you searching for the RV with us?"

"No, I'm not," replied Kaye. He looked across at Mike Graham. "I made a promise to a fellow Marine that the man who killed his son wouldn't get away. I intend to honor that promise."

Mike's eyes met Kaye's and the gratitude in them was evident.

"What do we do with the General?" Cindy asked as she rubbed her dad's back.

"Leave him here," Kaye said. "He's not going anywhere."

"I agree," Straithwaite said. "For what it's worth, I officially placed him under arrest. That felt really good."

They decided to split up and search in the way that would maximize available vehicles. Halberstam would use his cruiser, Straithwaite his rental Explorer, Mike the blue Mustang and Cindy the old Willys, which Halberstam had driven back from Urrestegui's. Leona would stay at the Lodge, just in case, and watch Holdorf.

They would investigate every large luxury coach they found. No one, though, was to make contact until another member of the search team arrived to back them up.

Kaye's Kimber was long gone. Between Halberstam's and Straithwaite's service pistols and the guns they'd taken from Holdorf's house they came up one short when Cindy insisted on being armed, too.

"If I see Pancho, I'm going to kill the son of a bitch," she said.

Kaye talked to Halberstam for a minute before the Captain lifted his pant leg, reached into his boot, pulled out a small .38 Special with a shrouded hammer and handed it to Kaye. "Hope your finger'll go through the trigger guard," he said.

"It'll work. Thanks," Kaye said. "I knew you'd have a back-up piece. The best cops always do."

Leona heard the compliment and beamed proudly at her husband.

***

On the way out of the Lodge, Mike detoured to the concierge desk and scooped up a handful of local Chamber of Commerce maps. In the parking lot he spread them on the hood of Halberstam's Crown Vic and the group quickly lined out and assigned search areas.

"Remember," Straithwaite told them, "if you see a possible, do not approach alone. Call somebody else, keep watch and wait for backup. If you determine it's the wrong RV, let everybody know, and note the license number so we can keep a list and not duplicate efforts. It may have been painted, too, so check every one you see. And, remember, we're looking for one of the big, expensive diesel pushers, so don't waste time on anything else."

Cindy walked to Kaye and stood close, wrapping her arms around his waist.

"Please be careful," she said.

"I'll be fine." He put his hands on her shoulders. "Just find that bomb."

She leaned in and kissed him lightly on the lips.

Kaye waited as the odd caravan of vehicles left the village parking lot and headed toward Ketchum. After he watched the old

Willys grind out of sight, Kaye opened a saddlebag and pulled out the Big Boar Motorcycle Club vest. He donned it, snapping closed the chains with their silver boar's head ends.

No helmet today. Instead, he donned a black leather skullcap and tied it behind his head. The top of the cap bore the same fierce visage of a wild boar that adorned his vest, and the long tail that hung partway down his back displayed the iconic profile, barbed wire and guard tower graphic encircled with the words 'POW-MIA Never Forget'.

Kaye swung over the big bike, pulled it up effortlessly, settled into the saddle, and raised the kickstand. When he thumbed the starter switch, the big v-twin rumbled instantly to life, roaring like a tethered beast, straining, waiting to be loosed to do its master's bidding.

Not yet, Kaye willed himself. Not yet. Warm up first. Then we'll go. A minute later he felt the first heat begin to ripple from beneath him and kicked the shift lever into first.

"Okay," he muttered. "Let's go. We've got business."

With a thunderous roar, Kaye flew from the parking lot. He could see the road in both directions and blew the red light at forty-five, leaning hard as he cut the corner and headed for General Carl Holdorf's house.

54

A fter an hour of searching, during which the group checked five possible matches, Mike Graham rolled slowly into the Warm Springs Village RV parking area at the base of Bald Mountain's north face.

The park was over half full. Mike cruised through and quickly identified three coaches that fit their search criteria.

One had a passenger vehicle on a tow bar behind it, both bore Alberta Canada license plates, and both were coated with enough road grime to convince Mike it wasn't the one. He parked and watched the other two while he called Don Straithwaite, who was working the adjacent search grid.

"Hey, Don, I've got two maybes in the Warm Springs lot. Can you head this way?"

"On the way." The DHS agent hadn't turned up a single possible match yet.

Before Straithwaite arrived, Mike crossed the coach with Florida plates off the list after seeing an elderly couple open the windshield curtains and then disembark, hand in hand, to head into the Village.

"So, that leaves one," Straithwaite looked at the last coach after Mike told him about the lovebird seniors. "Right color scheme."

"Idaho plates, too," Mike observed. The coach sat quietly with no signs of activity. All glass except the windshield was heavily tinted, obstructing any views of the interior, and the privacy curtains effectively covered the windshield.

"Stay here. I'll mosey through and see what I can find out."

"Okay," Mike assented. "Be careful, and don't be too obvious."

Straithwaite smiled. "I'll try."

The DHS agent casually meandered through the lot, choosing the route that left him mostly obscured in case someone inside the target coach was watching. Eventually, he came out along the right side of the big coach and quickly tried to get a glimpse inside. No luck.

When he rounded the back of the coach, Straithwaite held his hand near the shield covering the big diesel's exhaust stack. He could feel the warmth still seeping through.

"The engine's still warm," he reported back to Mike. "I've got a strong feeling about this one. We need to get a look inside."

"Well," Mike said, "the best way to get inside is to be neighborly and knock on the front door." Then he was off, hobbling gamely on his sore legs directly toward the coach while Straithwaite moved to a closer vantage point.

Mike didn't make it to the door.

"Hey!" The voice called from his right. He looked and saw a short, heavy woman in hot pink sweats headed toward him at a fast walk. "You gotta sign in, you know," she said when she got closer. "It ain't free to park here."

"Excuse me?"

"Ain't this your rig?" She looked at him suspiciously. "Never stops amazing me how you guys that can afford to buy and run these monsters try to stiff us for a day's parking. Ought to be ashamed of yourself, I say."

"Oh, no," Mike raised his hands in surrender. "This isn't my coach. I can't afford anything like this."

"Then what're you and your buddy doing hanging around it?"

"Well," Mike thought quickly. Over the woman's shoulder he saw Straithwaite hurrying toward them. "We thought this might be some friends of ours that we expected yesterday over at the Lodge, and...."

"We got better facilities here than they got over to the Lodge," the woman interrupted. "You oughta move over here."

"I'm sure you do. Anyway, I was just about to knock on the door and see if it was them."

"Is it them?" Straithwaite asked, startling the woman. He'd heard just enough of the conversation to pick it up in stride.

"Don't know yet." Mike shrugged. "This nice lady says they haven't registered yet."

"Really?" Straithwaite feigned concern. "That doesn't sound at all like George and Gracie."

"I agree," Mike said. "Should we wake them and make sure everything's okay?"

"You're wasting your time, boys," the woman sniffed. "Ain't nobody home."

Straithwaite asked, "And you know this because...?"

"I seen 'em leave," she said with a knowing nod. "George, or whatever his name is, anyway. Didn't see no woman. Heard the rig pull in real early, right before sun-up. I sleep real light." She nodded conspiratorially. "So, when I hear that big diesel roll in and shut down, I get up real quick like, throw on a robe and head for the door." She stopped, glancing back and forth at Mike and Straithwaite.

"And...?" Mike prompted her.

"Well, no sooner do I get proper covered up and open the door, I see this fancy silver SUV zoom in and pull up next to that there coach. A man piles out like it's on fire, jumps into that SUV, and they hightail it outta here like a scalded jackass. Hey," she looked at them suspiciously, "either of you drive a silver SUV?"

"No, ma'am," Mike answered, looking at Straithwaite, who nodded back. This had to be it. Mike walked away to call Halberstam and Cindy.

"How many people were in the SUV?" Straithwaite asked the woman.

She thought for a second, closing her eyes. "Your friend George got in the front seat," she said confidently. "So I think it was just them two."

"Ma'am, do you have a crowbar I could use?"

"A crowbar? Why would you be needing...?" She quickly figured it out. "Oh, no, you don't. Registered or not, you can't be breaking..."

Straithwaite reached into his back pocket and interrupted the woman by dangling his open badge wallet in front of her face.

"Yes, ma'am, I most certainly can. A crowbar?"

"Holy crap!" Her eyes widened at the sight of the badge. She cackled gleefully, "I knew it! It's stolen, ain't it? I told Marvin something wasn't right!"

"Crowbar," Straithwaite reminded her.

"Coming right up!" She turned and hurried toward the office, still congratulating herself on sniffing out a lawbreaker.

"Roger and Cindy are on the way," Mike announced as he returned. "Now, I've got a question."

"Go ahead and ask, but I don't know, either. Let's get inside first and see what we're up against."

"Fair enough."

The RV lady returned with a crowbar.

"Ma'am, I'm sorry," Straithwaite told her, "but you need to leave the area. This is official government business."

"Mister, this is my property!"

"Enough! Either you go back inside and stay there, or I promise you, you'll be in Cuba before lunch."

"I'd do what he says, ma'am," Mike said to the indignant woman. "Here, let me walk you." He took her elbow and steered her toward the office.

Straithwaite hefted the crowbar as he studied the coach. The main door was too obvious, too likely to be rigged. The driver's position had a large sliding window, but that, too, could easily be rigged. He studied the coach closely as he walked around it. There had to be a way in. The DHS agent knew there might not be any booby-traps at all, but he wasn't willing to bet his life, and lots of others, on it just yet.

The screech of skidding tires interrupted his concentration. Halberstam had arrived, and was halfway out of his car before it came to a full stop.

"What've we got?" Halberstam asked.

"This is it," Mike, who had walked up behind them, answered. "Lady who owns the place saw Urrestegui's Range Rover pick up the driver right before sunrise."

"Okay, good," Halberstam nodded. "I called my boss on the way over. Told him we found the bomb and threatened to crucify him and the Governor in the press if he didn't get off his ass and take action, pronto."

"And?" inquired Mike.

"The FBI has a team airborne out of Hill in Ogden, but they'll be awhile. Our arson and explosives guy is en route on a medical chopper. There's also some Fed named Dinsmore on board, with orders from the President to arrest Holdorf. Told 'em we already took care of that." Halberstam smiled. "Should be here within the hour. If a human built this bomb, Rudy Moore can disarm it."

"Given time," Straithwaite qualified. "We've got to get inside first." He set aside the crowbar and eyed the roof access ladder as he spoke.

"The roof?" Halberstam read Straithwaite's mind. "A skylight, maybe? These rigs usually have 'em."

Straithwaite reached the top of the ladder and looked out over the roof. Two AC units, a satellite dish, a smoked glass skylight and two translucent, square white plastic covers dotted the top of the coach. One of the plastic covers looked slightly askew.

"Hey," he called down. "It looks like one of the skylights is open." He clambered onto the roof and carefully walked forward about fifteen feet. Indeed, one of the plastic vents was open about two inches. Straithwaite sprawled out on the roof and carefully examined what he could see of the hatch's underside. He saw no wires or indications of any sensors or transmitters. No time like the present, he thought as he stood up.

Bending over, the DHS agent hooked the fingers of both hands under the edge of the skylight hatch, took a deep breath, thought of his wife, and heaved with all his might.

At first, the skylight held. Then, with a rapid series of small pops, it gave way and Straithwaite found himself flat on his butt, sliding toward the edge of the roof with the skylight in his hands. He quickly found purchase on the other skylight and stopped.

"Okay up there?" Mike's voice called out.

Halberstam's cowboy hat appeared above the top of the ladder. "What in hell was that?"

"I made us a way in," Straithwaite smiled and held up the skylight.

"You'll never fit through there," the Captain said as he climbed onto the roof. "Looks like a job for a skinny old man."

As Straithwaite scooted back to the opening, he knew Halberstam was right. He was too big.

The scream of the old Willys making top speed reached them and they looked up to see the battered old truck coming fast into the parking lot.

"Hey, Mike," Straithwaite called down. "Cindy's here."

"I hear her," Mike called back.

From their elevated vantage point, the two disparate peace officers watched the old Willys skid to a stop. Cindy jumped out and ran to embrace her father.

"Got kids?" Halberstam asked out of the blue.

"Not yet. You?"

"Four times blessed, Leona and me, and six grandkids. Best thing that can happen to a man." He chuckled, adding, "Short of marrying the right woman, that is."

"Did that already." Straithwaite absently reached up with his left thumb and rubbed his wedding ring.

"Good for you, young fella." Halberstam slapped the DHS agent on the back as he handed over his cowboy hat with the other hand. "Guess I'd better get to it. And if you bend my hat, fed or no fed, I'll have your ass."

The Captain sat down and swung his lower legs into the opening. Even for him, it was going to be tight. He studied the opening for a moment, then leaned across and locked the fingers of both hands over the opposite edge. Then he slid slowly forward until his backside was barely on the roof, nearly all of his weight now over the hole.

He looked at Straithwaite.

"Don't look so worried, cowboy," Halberstam said. "I've gone down the chute onto nastier bulls than this."

Then, with a slight shift, he slid off the edge and disappeared into the maw of the RV. His chin cleared his knuckles by less than an inch and he caught himself before his feet hit the floor. Silently praying the floor below was clear, he dropped to solid footing.

As his eyes adjusted and he began to make out details of the coach's interior, cold fear gripped him and he muttered, "Shit, shit and double shit."

On the roof, an impatient Straithwaite chafed at the silence. "Captain, what do you see? Is this the right coach?"

Finally, he saw Halberstam's stricken, ghostly white face staring up at him from below and heard the man's strained answer.

"Oh, yeah, this is the one. Sweet lord of mercy Jesus, help us."

***

Cindy sped into the Warm Springs RV lot and saw her father hobbling toward her. Her heart almost broke at the sight, knowing he'd spent more time on his prosthetics and walked farther in the last week than in the past six months. They'd put his wheelchair in The Mayflower, but he'd refused to use it.

As she got out of the Willys she saw Straithwaite and Halberstam standing on the coach's roof.

"Dad!" She cried and ran to embrace her father. "Are you all right?"

"I'm fine. I'm pretty sure we found it. Roger's about to go inside."

"Through the roof?"

"Booby traps. Can't be too careful."

"Oh, God," Cindy groaned. "I didn't think of that."

Arm in arm, they watched as Halberstam handed Straithwaite his hat, then sit down and disappear into the coach. After what seemed to Cindy like a long time the DHS agent stood up, looked down at them grimly, and nodded. Then he turned and headed for the ladder.

"What now?" Cindy shivered.

"I have no idea. I'm leaving that to the pros."

Straithwaite reached the front of the coach just as Halberstam opened the front door. The two conferred quietly before Halberstam hurried to his car and picked up the radio. Straithwaite disappeared into the coach.

Cindy and Mike walked to the open door and looked inside.

"Don," Mike called out. "Is it safe? Can we come inside?"

Straithwaite walked into view. "Don't touch anything."

Cindy led the way, then turned and helped her father up the steps. When she turned into the coach, her first impression was how beautiful it was.

That impression changed as her eyes adjusted to the darkness. Atop the polished burl table rested a laptop computer, multiple cables issuing from its various ports. Those cables went to connectors that joined other cables, which spread through the coach like a giant black spider web.

A digital timer shone on the laptop's screen. As Cindy watched it counted down under forty-eight minutes. "Oh, God," she gasped softly.

"My sentiments exactly," echoed Straithwaite grimly.

"Cynthia, do you think you can figure out how to shut it down?" Mike asked. He turned to Straithwaite. "She's a computer programmer."

"Oh, Dad, I wouldn't know where to start. I mean, maybe, with enough time. But not in less than an hour."

"Let's go outside." Straithwaite herded them toward the door.

As the trio stepped off the steps, an ashen-faced Halberstam met them.

"It's not good," the Captain said. "Rudy's still twenty minutes out. When I described the setup and told him all the wires were black, and what the timer read, he only had one suggestion."

"What?" Straithwaite asked urgently.

Halberstam looked them each in the eye, then took a handkerchief from his pocket and tilted back his hat to mop his brow.

"He said, and I quote, 'get the goddamn thing started and drive it as far away from town as you can, because it's probably gonna go off.'"

Mike broke the ensuing silence.

"Cynthia, listen to me close, girl." He grabbed his daughter by the shoulders and stared into her eyes. "You get back in that truck and get to Merl's. Go as fast as you can. When you get there, get him and Elaine in that truck. I don't care how you do it, just do it. Then you drive like hell toward Galena. Go as fast and get as high as you can, and don't stop until you get to Stanley."

Cindy's face went pale with shock and she said nothing.

"Cynthia Elizabeth!" Mike shouted. "Look at me! Do you understand me?"

"But, Dad, I..."

"Don't argue with me! Just do it, damn it!"

Cindy started to cry as she realized what her father was planning to do. "No, Daddy, please. Come with me. Please, come with me."

"No, not this time." Mike's voice was soft now and he tenderly wiped a tear from his daughter's cheek. "You're right about me. What you said."

"No, Daddy, I didn't mean..."

"Hush, baby girl, and listen. This is my time to step up and swing that hammer you were talking about. And you know what else?"

"What?" Cindy's voice was barely audible.

"I think this might be why your Uncle Calvin saved my ass that day in the boonies. To be right here, right now."

Cindy fell into her father's arms, hugging him with all her might as she sobbed into his shoulder.

"I can do this," he whispered in her ear. "I need to do this. Besides, I have no intention of being in that thing when it blows."

Cindy leaned back. "You promise?" she asked through tears.

"I promise. Now, get going. Time's wasting. And don't take any guff from Merl, you hear me? Tell him whatever you have to, but get him and Elaine over the pass. If you hurry you can make it."

"I love you, Daddy."

"I love you, too, Stretch."

Cindy let go of her father and looked into his eyes. "See you later, Dad."

"Count on it." He smiled broadly for her sake. "I love you."

Mike watched her drive away, returning her wave out the driver's window before she disappeared. He turned back to Straithwaite and Halberstam.

"Okay. How do we do this?"

"Mike, look," Straithwaite's voice cracked, "you should go. I'll do this. It's my job."

"And mine," Halberstam added. "You're a civilian, Mike. Let us do this."

"No chance. And may I remind you that time keeps running while we stand here arguing. Besides, I have a plan."

"Let's hear it," Straithwaite said.

"First, I hope one of you can start this thing." Mike looked at them. "Because, in case you didn't notice, there are no keys."

Halberstam shook his head. "Don't look at me."

"I can do it," Straithwaite said shakily. "I think."

"Okay, you're elected. Get started." Mike turned to Halberstam. "Roger, get the hell out of here. Your services are no longer required and that lovely wife of yours needs you. Beat it."

Halberstam started to argue, then looked down at his boots before looking up. "Mike, I…" His voice broke.

"Just get. I'll call you later."

Halberstam headed for his cruiser, pulling out his cell phone on the way. They heard him trying to convince Leona to get into a cab and head for Hailey. "Tell the driver to go around through Elkhorn… No, don't go through town… Leave him there. Somebody'll find him… Yes, darlin', I'll catch up… I promise… I have one thing to do first… Now, skedaddle!"

Don Straithwaite worked feverishly under the raised engine cover at the back of coach as Mike watched. The DHS agent reached up and closed the cover, wiping his hands together.

"Okay, let's go inside."

Inside, Straithwaite threw himself onto the floor and snaked a hand up under the glittering console. He pulled it out, grasping a bundle of wires. Quickly, he found the two colors he sought. Then he pulled a small pocketknife and cut them, stripping one end of each color. He touched them together and the big diesel spun, but didn't catch. He repeated the process and this time the engine rattled noisily to life.

"Okay," he looked at Mike. "What now? You want me to ride with you and try to disarm this mess?"

"Hell, no! You're my escape capsule. At the end of the pavement that way," Mike pointed west, "are two fairly decent Forest Service roads. I'm going to drive this sucker as far into the hills as I can in the time we have."

"Gotcha!" Straithwaite anticipated the rest of the plan. "I'll follow. When you stop, we'll haul ass out of there. Good idea."

"If we accept that this thing's going to explode, all we can do is try and minimize the damage. Plus," he looked at the surrounding trees, "those people know nothing about mountain weather. The wind almost always changes soon after the sun comes up. If we go that way, it'll blow the radiation away from town."

"How much time do you think we need to get away? We have," Straithwaite looked at his watch, "thirty-five minutes."

"Five minutes to spare, I think. That should get us away from the blast, especially if I can bury this sucker in a ditch someplace and we get around a ridge. That gives us a good half hour to stop anybody heading up the road and get out of town. That's more than enough. I hope."

"Five minutes it is, then. I'll honk and flash my lights at ten minutes. You start looking for a place to ditch."

"Okay. Let's roll."

At the end of the pavement, Mike didn't even slow down, barreling onto the Forest Service road and stirring up a cloud of dust that forced Straithwaite to back off a bit.

"Please let this work," the DHS agent repeated over and over again as he followed the speeding coach deep into the heart of the Sawtooths. He checked his watch. According to the timer, they still had twenty-five minutes.

Unfortunately for him and Michael Graham, he was mistaken.

On board the coach, one of the tiny black wires had relayed a signal to the laptop when Straithwaite sparked the ignition wires, alerting the software that the coach was being tampered with. The software immediately adjusted the internal timer without altering the timer displayed on the laptop's screen.

Zero was no longer zero.

55

Kaye knew that his last, best chance to catch up with Pancho Janicot was at Holdorf's house, and that all rested on the Basque going there to help Robert Urrestegui retrieve the paintings Cindy had heard them discussing.

The black Harley blasted through the cool Sun Valley morning as Kaye concentrated on putting together a plan. Outgunned and likely outnumbered, a frontal assault was out of the question. He needed surprise to have any chance of success.

On the road leading to Holdorf's house Kaye slowed and started tracking house numbers. Approaching the spot where the road crossed a small saddle between two hills, he knew he still had several houses to go. Shutting down the big bike, he coasted to a quiet stop on the side of the road. Holdorf's house would be over the crest, down on the left. Halberstam had given him directions and a description of the house. He was confident he would recognize it.

Kaye walked to a point where he could see down the other side of the hill and carefully surveyed the surrounding terrain. Less than two hundred yards away, and slightly lower than where he stood, the house was easy to pick out. No vehicles were visible, but trees limited his view of the house and grounds.

The slope behind the house grew steeper as the hill climbed away. The ridge at the top curled around, losing elevation, to become the saddle where Kaye stood. Satisfied with his plan, he walked back to the Harley, locked it, then crossed the road and headed into the pines and scattered aspen groves, careful to stay below the crest of the ridge on the side away from the house.

Following the terrain, with an occasional careful check over the top of the ridge, it took him fifteen minutes to reach a safe vantage point atop the hill behind the house.

Kaye smiled. Parked close alongside the house, on the side he hadn't been able to see before, were Robert Urrestegui's silver Range Rover and a white van similar to the one he'd seen in the Biscay Basin Group garage. The cargo doors of the van were open.

As he watched, Urrestegui came out through the open garage doors. He carried a long cylindrical object and carefully placed it into the van's cargo area before going back inside. Kaye checked his watch. Two minutes later, Urrestegui reappeared, carrying another canvas, this one still in stretchers. Urrestegui made two more round trips, with the elapsed interval never varying by more than several seconds.

Kaye calculated a route to the house using the best available concealment. He should be able to make it safely to a clump of trees near the house on the first hop. The big unknown was whether someone was keeping watch and would see him coming, but Kaye reasoned that if there were any lookouts they would probably focus on watching the road in front of the house.

Kaye watched Urrestegui carry another painting out and lay it in the van. As soon as the man headed inside, Kaye leapt to his feet and headed down the hill. He reached the aspens and knelt behind a large rock just in time to hear voices. Peering out, he saw Urrestegui, this time accompanied by McMurray, head again for the van. Each carried a rolled canvas.

"How many more, Uncle Robert?" McMurray's voice drifted to Kaye.

"I'm not sure. I had no idea there were so many. You hear stories, but this is like finding the lost city of gold."

"Yeah, well, don't forget who owns a couple suburbs of your lost city."

Urrestegui laughed. "Don't worry about that. Your mother would kill me. Just be patient. It'll take some time, and a lot of lawyers, to figure out. When I make some money, you make some money."

"For that kind of money, I can wait," McMurray said seriously. He looked at the growing pile in the back of the van and asked, "Are we going to take them all?"

"Why not? He can't report them stolen. Hell, his family stole them in the first place."

"What do you think happened to Holdorf?"

"I have no idea, but I'm glad Chapman called me. Saved us a lot of trouble to be able to do this now instead of having to wait. Pancho's sure pissed, though. He wanted Holdorf for himself."

Kaye continued to watch, listen and consider his options as the two continued to load the back of the van. He hadn't expected McMurray to be here. The little .38 Special only held five and Halberstam had given him only one full speed loader.

His other consideration was that it was Pancho he really wanted. He'd deal with Urrestegui and McMurray if forced to, but only to get to Pancho.

Urrestegui and McMurray returned, carrying more paintings.

"How much time do we have, Uncle Robert?"

Urrestegui looked at his watch. "Enough. This is the last of these. The only one left is the big one upstairs."

"Will we make it?" McMurray sounded worried. "I don't want to be anywhere near here when the bomb goes off."

"Pancho's almost done upstairs. We'll make it."

"He should have just cut it out of the frame. Would've been a lot faster."

"No, that would have meant the possibility of damaging the painting or losing the signature. Without it, nobody will ever believe the painting is authentic."

"What if it's not signed? What if it was stolen first?"

"It'll be signed," Urrestegui assured his nephew. "I'll go check on Pancho. You stay here, and keep your eyes open."

"Will do."

Kaye smiled thinly. Pancho was here. He also now understood Urrestegui's willingness to get involved with Janicot and, by association, Mahmoud. Not only was the man after his cobalt mine, if the paintings were genuine, their value was almost incalculable.

It also sounded like they were almost ready to leave, which meant he'd have to go through McMurray and Urrestegui to get to Pancho.

McMurray stood near the front corner of the house, smoking a cigarette as he kept watch on the street.

"Like I said before, I really hate crooked cops."

The voice from directly behind so startled McMurray that the cigarette fell from his mouth as he spun around.

"You!" McMurray exclaimed, his eyes growing wide.

"Yeah, and you have a big problem, deputy," Kaye said as he grabbed McMurray by the throat.

McMurray tried to shout a warning, but as he opened his mouth the pain of Kaye's steel grip paralyzed his vocal cords.

At the same time, Kaye reached up and grabbed McMurray's right shoulder, his thumb out and pointing at the man's throat. With a quick downward yank, he snapped McMurray's collarbone and the man gasped in agony. Kaye used his left hand to keep the semi-conscious man from collapsing, pulled his right fist back and dealt a crushing blow to the side of McMurray's lolling head. Without a sound, the deputy's eyes rolled back in his head and he became dead weight.

Kaye carried McMurray around the corner of the house and dumped him into the bushes. He didn't know, or care, if he'd killed the man. Pancho was the objective. The crooked deputy had simply been an obstacle to remove.

"Patrick!" It was Urrestegui's voice. "Damn it, Patrick, where are you?"

Kaye flattened himself against the front of the house and waited.

"I swear to God, kid, if you're out here getting high again, I'll kick your ass." Urrestegui spoke loudly and Kaye could tell the man was heading directly toward his hiding place.

Urrestegui stepped around the corner, fully expecting to find his nephew. Before he realized it wasn't McMurray standing there, a huge hand clamped over his face, lifted him to his tiptoes and dragged him around the corner.

"Quiet," growled Kaye, "or I'll kill you. Understand?"

Urrestegui tried to speak, but couldn't. He tried to nod his head, but it was locked in a crushing grip. All he could do as he danced on his tiptoes was raise his hands in surrender, so he did. Another hand closed on his throat as the first one released from his face. He gasped for breath.

"Remember me?" Kaye asked.

Too paralyzed with fear to speak, Urrestegui managed a nod.

"I've got some bad news for you, Uncle Robert. The deal's off. No paintings. No cobalt mine and, with any kind of luck, no bomb, either. I'd say you're seriously screwed here. What would you say to that?"

The hand on Urrestegui's throat was too tight for him to speak, or even nod again, but Kaye could see the answer in the man's eyes.

"Good," Kaye said. "We're on the same page, right?"

He let Urrestegui nod.

"Good. Pancho's inside, right?"

Another nod.

"Is Mahmoud here?"

A single shake told him no.

"You sure?"

Nod.

"Do you know where he is?"

Shake.

"Excellent. You're doing well. Now, you're going to take me to Pancho. I'll be behind you, and if you even wiggle wrong, I'll break your neck before you take another step. Got it?"

Another weak nod.

Kaye backed the dancing Urrestegui toward the driveway. Once on solid footing he grabbed the man by the belt, lifted him off the ground and spun him around. As Urrestegui turned, Kaye relaxed his grip on the man's throat enough that his hand ended up wrapped tightly around the back of Urrestegui's neck. In his other hand he carried the little .38 Special, its muzzle pressed against Urrestegui's head.

"Okay, lead the way."

Urrestegui led him through the garage into the house. When they entered the kitchen Kaye saw a woman's body, the front of her blouse soaked with blood, lying on the kitchen floor. From the kitchen Urrestegui continued through the dining room, eventually coming to the main foyer.

Sprawled on the floor, dressed in a smoking jacket and slippers, Senator Harrison Chapman lay in a pool of blood, half his head missing.

"Was that necessary?" Kaye asked.

"Pancho…" Urrestegui croaked.

"Right. Can't say the man didn't deserve it. Upstairs?"

Nod.

At the top of the stairs Urrestegui turned left and led Kaye down a hallway overlooking the foyer. Several rooms opened off the hallway to the right, and Kaye stopped to check each one before continuing. Kaye stopped Urrestegui just as his captive stepped through the door of the room at the end of the hall. Large and sunlit, the room was clearly Holdorf's study. Bookcases covered the far wall.

To the left, the wall consisted mostly of French doors leading to a terrace overlooking the valley. The wall to the right was empty, a symmetrical pattern of gaping holes in the plaster.

The room's furniture was pushed against the walls, and a large painting lay face down on the Aubusson carpet. Pancho Janicot knelt on the far side, absorbed in the task of removing the painting from its frame and complex stretchers.

Kaye pushed quickly against Urrestegui's neck, but kept him from moving forward.

Urrestegui got the message and noisily cleared his throat.

Pancho glanced up and then looked back down to focus on the task at hand. "Where have you been? Where is your nephew? These damn tacks…"

Kaye prodded Urrestegui again and this time the man spoke. "Pancho."

"What!" Pancho snapped, looking up in irritation.

Kaye realized that Pancho, his eyes adjusted to the bright sunlight of the room, couldn't see him behind Urrestegui in the relative darkness of the hallway.

"Stand up, Janicot," Kaye ordered loudly. "Put your hands over your head."

Pancho betrayed no emotion as he stared past Urrestegui. "Officer Kaye," he said smoothly as he got to his feet, making no move to raise his hands. "I must say, I admire your determination. You don't give up, do you?"

"Not when I'm after someone like you." Kaye could see the butt of a Beretta 9MM in Pancho's waistband.

"Like me? And how would you describe me?" As he spoke, Pancho opened his hands questioningly and took several small, casual steps to his right.

"Murderer and terrorist."

"I disagree. I'm a soldier in the fight for economic and political freedom, just as you are. The only difference is that we fight on opposite sides, with different goals." Pancho continued to sidle to his right, as if not wanting to step on the painting.

"Have it your way. Just know that I am way past being a cop here. If I decide to take you out of here by your feet instead of on them, I'll be more than happy to do that."

The Basque's eyes narrowed. This was not how American policemen were trained to act. "You'd just shoot me down?"

"Oh, yeah." Kaye's tone left no doubt. "By the way, where's Mahmoud? Did he check out already? I found his friend in the bushes outside the house."

"Mahmoud departed slightly ahead of schedule. Unfortunately, he was wounded before I killed Agent Kaminski."

"He's not dead?"

"No."

"Too bad. And why shoot Chapman? I thought he was on your side."

"So did I, but Agents Washington and Kaminski proved otherwise. My only regret now is that the thief Holdorf was not here so I could kill him, too."

"I've got Holdorf," Kaye said. "We'll catch Mahmoud, and you'll spend the rest of your life in prison."

"I don't think so. I've already enjoyed American hospitality once. I have no intention of surrendering."

The sudden smile that played on Pancho's lips told Kaye that he'd let himself be lulled into a tactical disadvantage. He held Urrestegui's neck in his left hand and the gun in his right. Pancho had moved to a position nearly forty-five degrees to Kaye's left and less than fifteen feet separated them. If Pancho moved any farther left Kaye would have to contend with Urrestegui and the edge of the doorway in order to get off a shot. Kaye quickly pushed Urrestegui into the room, stepping just inside. He saw more furniture pushed against the wall. A small credenza stood just to his left, inside the door.

"Last chance, Janicot."

"What is to prevent me from simply shooting you?"

Kaye heightened his guard. "Well, considering I already have a gun pointed at you, you'd have to be incredibly stupid, or incredibly fast."

"I assure you I am not stupid." Pancho's voice took on a brittle edge. "Sorry, Robert. This is for The Cause."

Kaye had milliseconds to react, at the same time realizing that Pancho was, indeed, incredibly fast. By the time he squeezed the trigger of the unfamiliar little .38, Pancho had slid sideways another full step and freed the Beretta from his waistband.

The Basque's first two shots seemed to come before he'd even leveled the pistol, drowning out the sharp report of the .38 Special. The 9MM slugs hit Urrestegui in the chest, killing him instantly. The sudden dead weight off-balanced Kaye and he reacted barely in time, swinging Urrestegui's body around to catch Pancho's next two shots. Firing blind, he squeezed off two more shots as he hurled Urrestegui's corpse in Pancho's direction.

Pancho dove to the floor and fired again, low under the credenza.

The slug shattered Kaye's left ankle and he crumpled backwards to the hallway floor. As he fell, he saw splinters peel from the edge of the credenza as Pancho tried for the kill shot.

Landing awkwardly on his back, Kaye used his good foot to push farther backwards into the hallway, out of the doorway. His instinct was to stand, but he resisted, and it saved his life. Pancho quickly sent three rounds through the wall where Kaye torso would have been had he stood up.

"Policeman," Pancho called out, "I'm coming for you."

Kaye stayed quiet. He knew where Pancho was and knew the Basque was trying to goad him into revealing his position.

Instead, he waited silently, the .38 trained on the doorway. He risked a quick look backwards and saw an open door about ten feet behind him.

Keeping his eyes and gun trained on the study, Kaye used his good leg to push himself toward the open door. As he got close, he caught sight of an object on the polished hardwood floor. The full speed loader, jarred from his vest pocket by the fall, lay just outside the study.

Just as Kaye drew even with the open door, Pancho swung quickly into view down the hall, his 9MM up and ready.

Kaye had no choice but to fire twice, very quickly, as he scrambled through the door out of the hallway. He didn't wait to see if either of his rounds hit home.

One of Pancho's shots hit Kaye in the left hip as he rolled.

Once inside, Kaye kicked the heavy wooden door closed.

"Policeman," Pancho spoke loudly enough for Kaye to hear through the door. "I've got your reload out here. Too bad."

Kaye forced himself up, all his weight on his right foot, locked the door and looked around desperately for anything he could use as a weapon. The General's bedroom walls were covered with citations and photographs of him with various Presidents and dignitaries. Kaye hopped around the room, checking the nightstands and dresser drawers for a gun. Nothing.

He leaned against the wall, feeling the blood from his hip running down his leg. There had to be something. His eyes scanned the room again. From his vantage point he could now see the walk-through to Holdorf's closet and en suite bathroom. Rolling across the bed to save steps, Kaye headed for the closet. Inside, he found a rack of uniforms in dry cleaner's plastic, and started searching furiously.

"C'mon, c'mon," he muttered, steeling himself against the pain in his left hip and leg. "You're a General. You've got to have one."

He redoubled his efforts as Pancho fired twice through the heavy bedroom door.

Finally, behind the tie rack, on a single peg on the back wall, he found it.

The long, polished scabbard was intricately detailed with gold filigree and the belt chain was made of gold. A single blue gemstone was inlaid into the butt end of the hilt. It was a work of art, but the well-worn grip, tightly wrapped with sweat-stained leather, betrayed the true purpose of the Army saber.

Kaye snatched the scabbard from the peg. He grasped the hilt and withdrew the gleaming yard of elegantly curved, engraved steel. He dropped the scabbard and hopped to a spot against the bedroom wall that would put him behind the door when it opened. He crouched on his good leg and waited silently.

Although his left ankle was shattered, the heavy lace-up boot was doing a decent job as a makeshift splint. Kaye could feel blood soaking his sock and filling the boot around his toes, but very little oozed from the perforation in the leather. His hip was a different story. The entry wound bled steadily. He couldn't feel an exit wound, and held the saber in his right hand as he applied pressure to the wound with his left.

He waited.

After the shots through the door, everything had gone deathly quiet. Kaye had no way of knowing if Pancho was down, had left the house, or waited for him on the other side of the door. But he wasn't about to open it to find out. If this was going to be a game of cat and mouse, he'd do his best to be the cat, although he needed help and he needed it fast.

He reached for his cell phone. He'd rolled on it to get into the bedroom, and it came out of the carrier in pieces. Tossing it aside, he scanned the nightstands for a telephone. Nothing.

A slight noise caught Kaye's attention. He looked and saw the doorknob turn very slowly until the lock stopped it.

What'll he do? Kaye asked himself over and over. *If it was me, I'd shoot the lock, shoot through the wall behind the door, kick the door, then come in low and fast to the open side of the door. That's the best one-man entry technique into an unknown room. He's good. That's what he'll do. Be ready.*

The first two shots came in rapid succession, disintegrating the cover plate on the inside of the door, leaving the knob hanging precariously in the hole. The next two followed almost instantly, coming through the wall above Kaye's head and raining plaster chunks and dust onto his head.

Kaye counted aloud softly, "One, two...."

The door burst open as Pancho kicked it, swinging it hard toward Kaye.

One, two, he counted silently this time as he caught the door with his left hand. On three, he leaned his left shoulder into the door, pushed hard off his right foot and exerted all his strength to send the door back the other way.

It worked. When the door closed halfway, Kaye felt it hit and heard Pancho's grunt of surprise. Kaye continued pushing, hoping Pancho had been knocked off balance enough for him to get to the Basque with the saber.

Suddenly, the resistance was gone and the door swung out of Kaye's path. Pancho had gone down, but, quick as a cat, was regaining his feet. Blood soaked the left shoulder of his shirt and a deadly smirk played on his lips when he saw Kaye.

What the terrorist didn't see was the gleaming saber in Kaye's right hand.

Pancho pushed to his feet and raised the Beretta toward Kaye in one smooth movement.

Kaye brought up the point of the saber and lunged forward. Pancho saw it and tried to twist out of the way, but he was a breath too slow. The saber slid in just below the ribcage, going deep.

Transfixed, the Basque looked down at the steel piercing his body and then looked at Kaye with wide, hate-filled eyes.

Kaye leaned onto the saber again and it slid home to the hilt, the two men close together. Still, Pancho was silent, staring at Kaye.

"Die, you son of a bitch," Kaye rasped.

"I die for The Cause," Pancho said softly as a smile twisted his lips. "But you die, too. And for nothing."

Kaye knew he was going to die. He thought of his father, all the gentle taunts about his size cutting him to the quick. Alzheimer's had turned his father into a mere shell, but he spoke to Kaye now.

"C'mon, Ben," the voice chided gently, "don't give up. Remember, you're a gorilla. Don't let this punk get you."

Ben Kaye heard and went berserk. His huge body tensed, and he reached for Doroteo Arango Janicot.

Pancho screamed in agony as Kaye grabbed him, and for the first time Kaye saw fear in the Basque's dark eyes. The saber was forgotten as a crazed Kaye set about destroying his enemy with his bare hands.

Pancho mustered his last ounce of strength and raised his pistol. Pressing it against Kaye's side, he pulled the trigger. Then, torn and broken, he died in Kaye's hands.

Kaye grunted from the pain of the bullet tearing into him. He dropped Pancho's lifeless body. Then, slowly, he crumpled to the floor and rolled onto his back. He vaguely heard a siren in the distance, getting louder and closer with each wailing rise and fall.

Suddenly, the floor pitched violently under him, rocking the house up and down, back and forth. Objects from the dresser and the walls crashed to the floor. The motion stopped as suddenly as it had begun, but bare seconds later the airborne shock wave hit the house, rattling the windows hard just before the sound of the approaching siren was drowned out by the long, low rumbling sound of an explosion.

Kaye knew it was the bomb detonating.

They'd lost after all.

The last thing he heard was the sound of wings beating the air. He closed his eyes, waiting for the Angel of Death come to collect his spoils.

56

He woke slowly, aware of someone holding his hand before he could get his eyes to focus.

"Welcome back," a familiar voice said softly.

As consciousness returned, Kaye turned his head and saw Cindy seated next to the hospital bed.

"Glad to be…" he croaked, unable to say more.

Cindy held up a glass of water and he took a long pull on the straw.

"Glad to be back," he managed to say. "Where am I? What happened?"

"You're in the hospital in Los Angeles."

"How long have I been here?" He could barely whisper.

"Two weeks. The doctors put you in an induced coma after they flew you here from Boise. They didn't think you would make it." Her voice cracked and she took a drink before continuing. "They didn't know how strong you are."

"You been here the whole time?"

"Pretty much. I can prove it, too. Want to see my bedpan?"

Kaye smiled weakly. *She's just like Amy.*

"Pancho?"

"You got him."

"I thought he got me, too."

"He would have, if it weren't for Roger. Instead of getting Leona and getting out of Sun Valley once we knew we wouldn't be able to disarm the bomb, he went to Holdorf's house looking for you. And if he hadn't diverted the medical chopper carrying Rudy Moore, you wouldn't be here. It was that close."

"Your Dad? Please tell me Mike's okay."

A tear spilled from Cindy's eye and rolled down her cheek.

"He, uh," her voice broke again, and he felt her grip tighten on his hand. "He and Don Straithwaite died in the blast. He was a hero, Ben. Both of them. They got the RV started and out of town before it exploded. Don was supposed to help them escape, but something obviously went wrong."

"I'm so sorry," Kaye said. After a pause, he asked, "And Mahmoud?"

"No sign of him. But Lieutenant Unger wanted me to tell you that it was Mahmoud who was responsible for killing all those men from Twin Falls. That kid, Randy, identified Mahmoud's picture. The FBI found their bodies."

Kaye was silent, pondering what had happened.

"The paintings?"

"That has all turned into an international sensation. Seems there was a vault in the house that contained hundreds of artworks, all apparently looted by the Nazis. They're worth so much money that it'll take an army of lawyers years and years to figure it out. The General may even get to keep them."

"Holdorf's not in jail?"

"Free as a bird. The Vice President, too. They both claim that the whole thing was a covert intelligence operation approved by Senator Chapman's committee, and that it all just went horribly wrong. The other committee members lined up to protect Chapman's reputation, and there's nobody left to say different. So...."

"Business as usual."

"Looks that way. Uncle Calvin is still digging, but even he doubts anything will ever come of it."

"Is he okay?"

Cindy hesitated. "Yeah, I guess. He doesn't say much, but I know losing Dad hurt him badly. He aged ten years overnight." Another tear rolled down her cheek. "No remains were found, but they dedicated a special monument to Dad next to Aiden. Uncle Calvin put his Medal of Honor inside so it wouldn't be empty." She started to sob. "Said...Dad deserved it...more than he...did."

Kaye let her cry.

"Sorry, I thought I was past that."

Kaye didn't know what to say, so he kept his mouth shut.

"I'm glad you woke up," Cindy said.

Kaye gently squeezed her hand. "Thanks for being here when I did."

Cindy shifted in the chair and Kaye saw her visibly stiffen.

"What are you going to do now?" she asked. "I mean, are you going to go back to work? When you can, I mean. Roger told me you were thinking about quitting."

"Yeah, I don't know how that's going to turn out, but I need to find out."

They sat together in silence for a few minutes

"Well, now that I know you're going to be okay..." She looked at him plaintively. "I think I just need to get away and try and get over all this. Does that make sense?"

"Makes sense to me," he said. "Look, Cindy, I..."

She shrugged her shoulders and Kaye could see the tears in her eyes.

"On that note," she went on, standing up and sliding her hand out of Kaye's, "I'll take my leave. I'm glad you're going to be okay, and I truly, truly appreciate everything you did for me and my family. I'll never forget you, Ben."

"And I'll never forget you. I'll be back to pay my respects to Mike as soon as I can."

"You don't need to do that."

"Yeah, I do."

Cindy leaned over and kissed him lightly on the forehead.

EPILOGUE

The hissing pop of air brakes got Kaye's attention. He looked down the driveway to see a semi parked at the end of the cul de sac in front of the house. The driver hopped down, sheaf of papers in hand, and headed toward his house.

"Hey, I'm back here!" Kaye called out.

"You, uh," the driver looked at the papers, "Ben Kaye?"

"That's me."

"Where do you want it?"

"What is 'it'?"

"C'mon, I'll show you."

"Don't know why we need an inspection report," the driver grumbled once they'd reached the back of the trailer and he started to raise the door. "Thing looks like a piece of crap, if you ask me. Too bad, too."

Inside the trailer, its flat tires chocked firmly upright and straps holding it tightly to an aluminum motorcycle pallet, rested a faded red 1941 Harley-Davidson FL. A plastic bag was zip-tied to the left front handlebar and Kaye could see a large envelope inside.

"Where'd this come from?"

"I got no clue. I'm local. They don't send the long haul paperwork out with me."

The driver used a motorized hydraulic pallet jack to maneuver the bike onto the lift gate and lower it to street level. Once down, he looked at Kaye again.

"So, where do you want it?"

Kaye had him roll it to the garage behind the house. The driver looked at the other motorcycles parked inside.

"So, you restore Harleys?" he asked, a gleam of envy in his eyes.

"Once in a while," Kaye admitted. He signed the necessary paperwork. "Thanks, I'll take it from here."

Kaye pulled the envelope from the plastic bag. Inside he found two smaller envelopes, one marked 'bike paperwork' and the other with 'Ben' on the outside. He opened the latter first.

'Dear Ben,
I hope your recovery is going well. I can't think of anyone more deserving of this. Please enjoy and treasure it. I know that Dad and Aiden will be watching over you when you ride.

Cindy Graham'

Kaye looked at the old Harley, the bike Mike Graham's father had given him all those years ago. To Kaye, it was beautiful, and he now had a project to occupy his time during his recuperation.

Most of the bike was there. The only things missing completely were the front fender light housing, speedometer, saddlebags and kick start lever. The seat was in tatters, having long ago surrendered to the mice. All the tin was in good shape.

He found the fender light on, of all places, a website hosted in Switzerland. A working, original aircraft style speedometer, a hallmark of the '41, was located in upstate New York. He had a seat and new saddlebags made that copied the originals exactly.

The engine was the 74 cubic inch Knucklehead, so named because the four huge bolt heads atop the cylinders looked like the knuckles of a clenched fist. It was the Motor of the Future back then, serving with distinction until being supplanted by the Panhead.

Kaye wanted to ride the bike, so decided not to do a faithful restoration. Instead, he went with new parts in critical places, crafted to maintain the spirit of the original. He managed to keep the engine about fifty-fifty, new versus old. He badly wanted to use the original cylinder jugs and was pleased to find them in good enough shape without the necessity of sleeving. He opted for new pistons. The heads were a write-off, though, and were replaced with modern reproductions for better airflow and combustion using modern gasoline. He used a new camshaft grind and carburetor to better match the new heads and pistons. The '41 had been the first model to come with an extended brass intake manifold. Since it would handle the improved airflow, it stayed.

He tore down and rebuilt the original four-speed transmission. In '41 the rider clutched with his foot and shifted using a lever mounted on the left side of the gas tank. Kaye considered changing the setup to the current hand-clutch, foot-shift configuration, but decided it would change the character of the bike too much. He'd just have to learn to do it suicide-style.

It was the kick-start lever that gave him fits. The '41 came with a new, larger diameter muffler, and needed a longer lever for clearance. After buying several guaranteed-to-fit 'originals' from self-proclaimed experts on the Internet, only to find they were too short, Kaye was about to give up and have a new one fabricated when he struck gold. Walking through a swap meet in Pacoima, he found an original, long shaft kick-start lever, complete with the original pedal. It was like finding a diamond in your front yard.

Once the mechanicals were nailed down, Kaye turned his attention to the tin. The paint had to be perfect, in the original Flight Red.

While he worked on the '41, Kaye was also following up on an investigation of his own. He made good progress, finding what he was looking for just before the old Harley was completed.

He decided to kill the proverbial two birds with one stone.

It was a sunny, crisp day in early March when Kaye fired up the '41 and headed north from Los Angeles on Pacific Coast Highway, following the coast until he cut 101 at Oxnard. He'd ridden enough shakedown miles to have confidence in the old Knucklehead's performance, and with the new heads and carburetor it ran like a trooper.

He rode north on 101, old-style aviator goggles shielding his eyes, reveling in the musical sound of the old v-twin's exhaust. Older drivers honked and waved, giving him the thumbs-up. Little boys pointed and waved excitedly, and every stop for fuel threatened to become an extended question, answer and bullshit session.

Without a doubt, everywhere the Flight Red FL went, she was an unqualified hit.

Kaye spent the first night in Lompoc.

Next morning he rode Pacific Coast Highway to Pismo Beach, picked up the one-oh-one to Atascadero and then went northeast on Highway 41 to Lemoore and night number two.

It's about fifty miles from Lemoore to Madera. Kaye spent the morning stopping in the local *tienditas* and *panaderias* making inquiries, finally finding an old-timer who wasn't too suspicious of the huge gringo to answer his questions and point him in the right direction.

"If you get to the Chowchilla road," the old man told him, "turn around. You missed it."

Armed with the old man's directions, Kaye rode west from Madera. About five miles from town Kaye spotted the side road that cut north. He slowed the old red FL and turned in. Once upon a time the road had been gravel, maybe even asphalt, but hard use and heavy vehicles had run most of the stone into the compacted soil, creating a hardpan where nothing would grow.

Kaye didn't have an address, or even know for certain on which road he'd find the house he'd come looking for.

Luckily, in front of the second house in an old woman sat in a lawn chair, enjoying the spring sunshine. Suspicious at first, she finally pointed and told him to go down two streets, turn right, and look for the spotless green house.

She had accurately described it. The green paint was fresh and the yard, filled with flowers and surrounded by a four-foot chain link fence, was immaculate.

Kaye shut down and retrieved two packages and an envelope from the saddlebags, noticing the curtains in a front window move as someone peered out.

He let himself through the latched gate and walked to the front door. He knocked and waited, hoping the door would open. It did, but not very far. Kaye saw a woman peeking through the small gap that the still-attached chain permitted. She looked him up and down before speaking.

"May I help you?"

"I hope so. I am searching for Guadalupe de la Rosa."

"Are you a friend of Senora de la Rosa?" Kaye could hear suspicion in the woman's voice.

"No," Kaye admitted. "I've never met her. My name is Ben Kaye. I have something for her, and I hoped this might be the right house."

"I'm sorry," the woman apologized softly. "I think you are in the wrong place."

As the door started to close, Kaye had a sudden hunch.

"It's from Maria," he blurted.

The door stopped and Kaye heard a sharp gasp, followed by a small, choked sob. The chain fell away and the door swung fully open.

The woman was, Kaye guessed, in her sixties, barely five feet tall, slim and dignified. An apron covered her housedress. Behind her, the TV was on, but turned down.

She held tightly onto the door, just in case, and looked at the giant stranger on her front porch. Kaye could see hope mixed with fear as she fought back tears.

"I am Guadalupe de la Rosa. Please come in."

"Thank you, Senora," Kaye said, mustering all the courtesy and respect he could. The living room was replete with religious icons. A large crucifix hung on one wall. Two pictures of Christ flanked the TV, and a small replica of Michelangelo's La Pieta rested on the coffee table.

Senora de la Rosa offered him a seat and refreshments. Only then did she perch on the edge of an overstuffed chair next to Kaye, her back straight and her eyes anxious.

"Now, Senor Kaye, please tell me about my Maria." She reached into her apron pocket, withdrew a worn Rosary and began fingering it nervously.

Kaye took a deep breath and dove in. He told her about Maria's life in Boise as he had been able to piece it together over the past months. That her daughter had graduated from college with honors pleased the old woman immensely.

Senora de la Rosa nodded quietly while Kaye spoke, as if he only affirmed what she already knew.

He expected her to break down when he told her that Maria had died.

She didn't.

"I knew."

"Ma'am?"

"A mother knows. God tells us. Months ago God told me my beautiful Maria had finally come home safely." The faith in her words was total and complete. "How did she die? Did she suffer?"

"No, she did not suffer. A bad man, a very bad man, killed Maria by accident when he was trying to kill me."

Kaye looked down at his feet, his voice betraying the guilt he carried over Maria de la Rosa's death.

"It was not your fault. It was God's plan. You caught this man." It wasn't a question.

"Yes."

"That is good. That is good. Now, tell me why you have really come. What other news do you bring?"

Kaye reached into the envelope he'd brought and pulled out the photograph of Maria and her two sons. Only when he handed it to her did she begin to cry.

"Madre de Dios." She crossed herself. "She is so beautiful. And such handsome sons, with their mother's smile." She clutched the photograph to her breast.

"They have their grandmother's smile. I can see where Maria got her beauty."

Guadalupe blushed at the compliment. The love in her eyes was plain to see as she studied the photograph.

Kaye reached into the envelope again and withdrew a single piece of paper, which he handed to Maria's mother.

"Your grandsons now live with their father near San Francisco. Here is his name, address and telephone number." He could see the questioning look in the old woman's eyes as he spoke. "Don't worry. I've already spoken to him and he agrees it would be a good thing for his sons to get to know their grandparents."

"How can we ever repay you?"

"You don't need to repay me. It is my privilege and honor to help you and your family. There is one more thing."

Kaye handed her the packages he'd laid at his feet.

"Please don't open them until I'm gone. Inside is something for you, your husband and your grandsons. It's a small token of appreciation from me and the United States of America for your daughter's sacrifice." Kaye paused for a moment, remembering how he and Calvin Dinsmore had threatened the Secretary of Homeland Security with public exposure of the role her agency had played in the events in Sun Valley before she agreed to the payment. "Use it to help those boys."

"If that is what you wish."

"Good, then I'll be going," Kaye said, standing up. "Thank you very much for your hospitality, Senora de la Rosa. I'm sorry we had to meet under these circumstances."

"We must accept the things we cannot change. It is God's will."

The '41 Knucklehead started on the first kick, and Kaye turned a tight half-circle before rolling on the throttle and heading toward the highway.

Highway Ninety-nine north to Sacramento and I-80, then east to Winnemucca to US 93 north. Boise by tomorrow night.

ACKNOWLEDGEMENTS

In my life I've doubtlessly written millions upon millions of words of every variety and description possible, from a daily cartoon strip to assisting in the drafting or statutes and regulations. Before I sat down to write The Bilbao Gambit, I always thought that the toughest part of 'writing a novel' would be putting together an intriguing story and telling it well. Boy, was I naïve. Actually getting the story on paper the first time around was the easiest part of the process. To paraphrase someone much more talented and inspirational than I'll ever be; I got by with a lot of help from my friends. To those people goes much of the credit for this book.

First, to my wife Julie, thank you for your constant support and encouragement, and for believing in me even when I doubted myself.

To Caitlin Barnett, my editor: Thank you, thank you. I think this young woman has an incredible talent and understanding for language and what makes a story 'tick'. Any errors in this book belong to me, not to her, because I either tweaked it afterward without telling her, or foolishly ignored her counsel.

I also discovered that 'self-publishing' is the biggest misnomer in history. Many thanks to Brandi Doane-McCann for her inspired cover design, and to Sarah Billington at Billington Media for her help in navigating the treacherous waters of modern publishing formats.

To my test readers, especially Joshua Bates, Deborah Benner and Leslie Davis; I appreciate your time and suggestions.

And if you're reading these acknowledgements, that means you're at the end of The Bilbao Gambit. To you, the reader, my biggest thanks of all.

COMING SOON...

...Watch for the next Ben Kaye case

THE KUNDUZ PAYBACK

A needless slaughter in the northeastern mountains of Afghanistan sends ripples across the globe to Los Angeles as Detective Ben Kaye and his new partner catch the case after a prominent plastic surgeon takes a flier from his 17th floor office window.

What first looks like a drug robbery gone bad turns out to be anything but. With help from the FBI, Kaye determines that the doctor was murdered because he refused to violate doctor-patient confidentiality and reveal the whereabouts of a mystery patient.

With Kaye chasing the murderer, the intelligence community chasing the mystery patient, and the American and British governments pulling strings behind the scenes, Kaye has to put it all together before the killer comes for him.